Also by Christian Jacq:

The Ramses Series
Volume 1: The Son of the Light
Volume 2: The Temple of a Million Years
Volume 3: The Battle of Kadesh
Volume 4: The Lady of Abu Simbel
Volume 5: Under the Western Acacia

The Stone of Light Series
Volume 1: Nefer the Silent
Volume 2: The Wise Woman
Volume 3: Paneb the Ardent
Volume 4: The Place of Truth

The Queen of Freedom Trilogy
Volume 1: The Empire of Darkness
Volume 2: The War of the Crowns
Volume 3: The Flaming Sword

The Judge of Egypt Trilogy
Volume 1: Beneath the Pyramid
Volume 2: Secrets of the Desert
Volume 3: Shadow of the Sphinx

The Mysteries of Osiris Series
Volume 1: The Tree of Life
Volume 2: The Conspiracy of Evil
Volume 3: The Path of Fire
Volume 4: The Great Secret

The Black Pharaoh
The Tutankhamun Affair
For the Love of Philae
Champollion the Egyptian
Master Hiram & King Solomon
The Living Wisdom of Ancient Egypt

About the translator

Sue Dyson is a prolific author of both fiction and non-fiction,
including over thirty novels, both contemporary and historical. She
has also translated a wide variety of French fiction.

The Mysteries of Osiris

The Tree of Life

Christian Jacq

Translated by Sue Dyson

SIMON &
SCHUSTER

LONDON • SYDNEY • NEW YORK • TORONTO

First published in France by XO Editions under the title
L'Arbre de Vie, 2003
First published in Great Britain by Simon & Schuster UK Ltd, 2005
A Viacom company

1 3 5 7 9 10 8 6 4 2

Simon & Schuster UK Ltd
Africa House
64-78 Kingsway
London WC2B 6AH

www.simonsays.co.uk

Simon & Schuster Australia
Sydney

A CIP catalogue record for this book is available
from the British Library

HB ISBN 0-7432-5956-4
TPB ISBN 0-7432-5957-2

Typeset in Times by SX Composing DTP, Rayleigh, Essex
Printed and bound in Great Britain by
Mackays of Chatham plc, Chatham, Kent

If all remains stable and in a perpetual state of renewal, it is because the sun's course has never been interrupted. If all things remain perfect and whole, it is because the Mysteries of Abydos are never unveiled.

Iamblicus, *The Mysteries of Egypt*, VI, 7

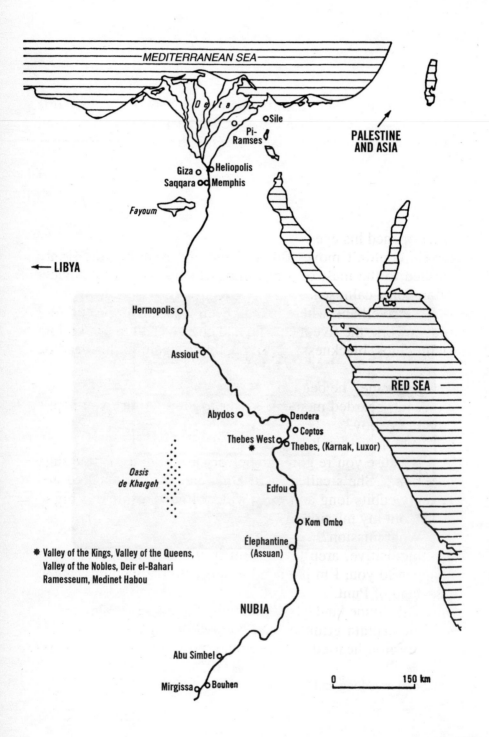

MEDITERRANEAN SEA

Delta

○ Sile

Pi-
Ramses

PALESTINE
AND ASIA

Giza ○   ○ Heliopolis
Saqqara ○○ Memphis

Fayoum

← LIBYA

Hermopolis ○

Assiout ○

RED SEA

Abydos ○   ○ Dendera
                ○ Coptos
Thebes West ○
❋   ○ Thebes, (Karnak, Luxor)

Oasis
de Khargeh

Edfou ○

Kom Ombo ○

Éléphantine ○
(Assuan)

❋ Valley of the Kings, Valley of the Queens,
Valley of the Nobles, Deir el-Bahari
Ramesseum, Medinet Habou

NUBIA

Abu Simbel ○

Mirgissa ○○ Bouhen

0   150 km

Iker opened his eyes.

He couldn't move. Bound hand and foot, he was firmly lashed to the mast of a big ship, which was sailing quickly along on a calm sea.

The riverbank where he had been walking at the end of a day's work, the five men who had charged at him and hit him with clubs, blackness . . . His body was painful, his head on fire.

'Untie me,' he begged.

A fat, bearded man came over to him. 'Aren't you happy there, my boy?'

'Why have you kidnapped me?'

'Because you're going to be very useful to us. A fine ship, isn't she? She's called *Swift One*, and she's a hundred and twenty cubits long and forty wide.* I need a ship this big to carry out my mission.

'What mission?'

'Inquisitive, aren't you? But in view of what's going to happen to you, I'm prepared to tell you that we're sailing to the land of Punt.'

'The divine land? That's nothing but a tale for children.'

The captain grinned. 'Do you really think a hundred and twenty lion-hearted sailors would have set sail to conquer a

*62.4 metres long and 20.8 metres wide.

children's tale? My crew aren't dreamers; they're down-to-earth fellows who are going to get rich – very rich.'

'I don't care about riches. I just want to become a scribe.'

'You can forget about your palettes and brushes and papyrus. You see, the sea is a god every bit as dangerous and powerful as Set, but I know how to placate it when it attacks us with its storms. We'll have to make a very special offering if we're to reach Punt, so when the next storm hits we shall throw you overboard alive. By drowning, you'll win us protection.'

'But . . . why me?'

The captain put a finger to his lips. 'State secret,' he whispered. 'I can't tell anyone, not even someone who has only hours left to live.'

As the captain walked away, Iker almost burst into tears. To die at only fifteen, and not even to know why, was the height of injustice. Furiously, he tried to free himself from his bonds, but it was no use.

'Don't waste your time, boy. Those knots were tied by a professional,' observed a forty-year-old with a deeply lined face, who was sitting nearby eating an onion. 'I'm the one who tied you up, and what Turtle-Eye does is done well.'

'Don't become a murderer! If you do, the gods will punish you.'

'Listening to you is spoiling my appetite,' and Turtle-Eye went and sat near the bow.

Iker was an orphan, brought up by an old scribe who had taken a liking to him, and he had displayed a very keen taste for learning. By dint of perseverance, he would undoubtedly have been taken on by the administration of a temple, where he would have lived out his days happily.

But now there was nothing left but this immense stretch of water which was going to engulf him.

A young sailor passed close by the prisoner, an oar balanced on his shoulder.

'Hey, you!' called Iker. 'Help me!'

The man stopped. 'What do you want?'

'Untie me, I beg you!'

'And then where would you go, you fool? It would be stupid to drown yourself before the right moment. At least by dying when it's necessary, you'll make yourself useful. Now, shut up and keep quiet, otherwise Sharp-Knife swears he'll cut your tongue out.'

Iker stopped struggling. His fate was sealed.

But why him? Before dying, he would at least have liked to get an answer to that question. A state secret? How could a penniless apprentice scribe possibly threaten Egypt's powerful pharaoh, Senusret, the third of that name, who governed the country with an iron hand? The captain must have been lying. His band of pirates had probably just grabbed the first person who happened along.

Turtle-Eye gave him a little water to drink. 'It's better that you don't eat anything. You're not the sort to have sea legs.'

'Does the captain really know how to predict a storm?'

'He certainly does.'

'Supposing there isn't one? Then you could let me go.'

The captain nudged Turtle-Eye aside and said, 'Don't even think about it, my boy. Your destiny is to be a sacrifice. Accept it, and enjoy the magnificent view: is there anything in the world more beautiful than the sea?'

'My parents will organize a search for me, and you'll all be arrested.'

'You haven't got any parents, and no one will even notice you've disappeared. You're already dead.'

2

There was not a breath of wind, and the heat was becoming unbearable. Most of the sailors had flopped down on the deck and were dozing. Even the captain was drowsy.

Iker had gone beyond the limits of despair. This crew of cut-throats was determined to do away with him, whatever happened, and he had no chance at all of escape.

He was terrified at the thought of being swallowed up by the sea, far from Egypt, without any funeral rites, without a tomb. It wouldn't just be physical death, it would be annihilation, the punishment reserved for criminals.

What crime had he ever committed to deserve such a fate? He wasn't a murderer or a thief, nor was he dishonest or lazy. Nevertheless, here he was, condemned to the worst of punishments.

Far in the distance, the surface of the water sparkled. Iker thought it was just a simple interplay of reflections, but the affected area grew and grew. A sandbar emerged and began to get larger and larger, as fast as a wild beast leaping on its prey. At the same moment, hundreds of little clouds arrived from nowhere, invading the sky to form a dark, compact mass.

Jolted out of his stupor, the captain stared in disbelief.

'There was no warning of this storm,' he muttered, astounded.

'Wake up and give the crew their orders,' demanded Turtle-Eye.

'The sails – haul in the sails! Every man to his post!'

The thunder rumbled so fiercely that most of the sailors were frozen to the spot.

'We must sacrifice the lad,' Sharp-Knife reminded the captain.

'Deal with it,' the captain ordered.

As soon as he was untied, Iker decided, he'd fight. True, he had no chance of overcoming his adversary, but at least he'd die with dignity.

'I prefer to cut your throat first,' said the sailor. 'You won't be quite dead when I throw you overboard, and the sea-god will be satisfied.'

Iker could not take his eyes off the flint blade that was about to take his life.

Just as its tip was entering his flesh, a bolt of lightning pierced the clouds and was transformed into a tongue of flame, which set fire to Sharp-Knife. He collapsed, howling.

'Look out!' roared Turtle-Eye. 'There's a monster wave coming!'

A huge wall of water was charging towards the ship. None of the sailors, although they were all experienced, had ever seen such a horror. Rooted to the spot, conscious that there was nothing they could do, they stood motionless, their arms hanging by their sides, their eyes fixed on the wave, which thundered down on *Swift One* with a terrifying roar.

The fingers of Iker's right hand scratched at something soft and damp.

Sand . . . Yes, it must be sand.

So the otherworld was a desert flooded by the insatiable sea, no doubt populated by frightful creatures which devoured the condemned.

5

If he still had a hand, perhaps he also had a foot – even two. They moved, and so did his left hand.

The young man dared to open his eyes, then lift his head. He was lying on a beach, a magnificent beach of white sand. Not far off, many trees were growing.

But why did his body feel so heavy?

Iker found that he was still tied, by the waist, to a fragment of the mast. He freed himself with difficulty and got slowly to his feet, still wondering if he was dead or alive.

Out to sea floated the shattered wreck of *Swift One*. The giant wave had ripped out her mast, and Iker with it, carrying them to this sun-drenched island, with its luxuriant vegetation.

He had suffered only scratches and bruises.

Unsteadily, he explored the immediate area. A few sailors might have had the same good luck as he had, in which case he must be ready to fight. But the beach was deserted. The ship and her crew had been swallowed up by the furious sea, and the only survivor was Iker, the offering promised to the ravening sea-god.

Iker realized that he was hungry. Venturing into the centre of the island, he found date palms, fig trees, vines and even a garden where cucumbers were growing, close to a crystalline spring. Iker gorged himself on fruit before it occurred to him that he could not, after all, be the only inhabitant of this fragment of land, lost amid the waves.

Why was the other person – or persons – hiding and how would he behave towards the intruder?

Apprehensively, he explored further. He found no one, and not even the slightest trace of an inhabitant. His only companion was his own mind. But a boy of fifteen would soon have exhausted his supply of memories.

Worn out by so many strong emotions, he fell asleep in the shadow of a sycamore tree.

As soon as he awoke, he inspected his realm a second time,

with the same results. He saw that large fish were not afraid to swim close to the beach, so they would be easy to catch. With a branch and some strands from the rope that had bound him, he made a fishing-rod and he found an earthworm to use as bait. Scarcely had his rudimentary hook entered the water when a sort of perch speared itself on it. The castaway ran no risk of dying from hunger here.

Now he had to light a fire, and he lacked the materials usually used in Egypt, principally a bow or a drill with a bow. However, as luck would have it, he found a piece of soft wood and another piece, long and pointed, which he thrust into the first one, held between his knees. By rotating the second piece as swiftly as possible, he managed to create enough heat to produce a spark and then a small flame. He immediately fed it with well-dried palm-frond ribs and grilled his fish.

But before Iker could eat, he had a vital duty to perform: he must give thanks to the gods for saving his life. He raised his hands above the flame in a gesture of prayer, but even as he did so thunder began to roll, the trees swayed and the earth shook.

Terrified, the young man tried to run away. He stumbled, and hit his head hard on the trunk of a fig tree.

3

Bolts of lightning, a fiery sky, a gigantic snake with golden skin and eyebrows of lapis-lazuli! This time, Iker was well and truly dead, and a monstrous spirit from the other world was bearing down, intent on crushing him.

But the snake stopped and merely observed him. 'Why did you light this fire, little man?'

'To . . . to pay homage to you.'

'Who brought you here?'

'No one. It was a wave . . . The boat, the sailors . . . And then . . .'

'Tell me the whole truth, and do so at once, otherwise I shall reduce you to ashes.'

'Pirates kidnapped me in Egypt, and they were planning to throw me alive into the sea to appease it. But the captain did not foresee a violent storm. The ship was destroyed, and I am the only survivor.'

'It is God who saved you from death,' said the snake. 'This island is the Island of the *Ka*, the creative power, the sap of the universe. Nothing exists without it. But this realm was struck by a star fallen from the summit of the sky, and all was set aflame. I, the lord of the divine land, the wondrous land of Punt, could not prevent the end of this world. And what of you – will you save yours?'

A burning sensation awoke Iker. The fire had spread to a

bush and the flames were licking the young man's calves. Leaping away, he checked that in reality there was no giant serpent on the prowl. Then he busied himself putting out the spreading fire.

What a strange dream . . . Iker could have sworn that the snake was no illusion and that it really had spoken to him, with a voice which resembled nothing known and which he would remember for ever.

Once the last flames were extinguished, the young man headed for the stream.

Two chests lay on the ground beside it. Iker rubbed his eyes. When he looked again, the chests were still there. He approached slowly, as if they were a threat. Someone was playing with his mind. Someone who was hiding in the undergrowth and had just brought out this loot from the *Swift One* or some other ship. Someone who wouldn't hesitate to kill the intruder so as not to have to share his treasure.

'You have nothing to fear from me!' yelled Iker. 'I'm not interested in your wealth. Instead of fighting each other, let's cooperate in order to survive!'

There was no answer.

Iker explored the little island again, changing direction constantly, retracing his steps, suddenly speeding up or slowing down. All his senses on the alert, he watched for the smallest sign of the presence of an adversary. But there was none.

So he had to face facts: he really was the only inhabitant of the island. But these chests . . . It was probably just that he hadn't noticed them before. They must have come from a previous shipwreck, and a wave had carried them here.

All that remained was to open them. They contained linen bags and porcelain flasks from which a pleasant smell wafted, probably precious perfumes worth a small fortune.

Had Iker really escaped death? The island might be less brutal than the pirates' ship, but fate seemed no kinder. True, he could survive for several months, perhaps several years, but solitude would eventually drive him mad. And what if the spring dried up, or he failed to catch any fish? To build a raft, he'd need tools. And yet . . . wouldn't it be suicide to sail off on this unknown sea on board a frail craft?

The young man thought constantly of the revelations of the golden snake, lord of the wondrous land of Punt. How could this tiny island be the divine land bursting with fabulous, coveted wealth? It was ridiculous.

The snake existed only in Iker's imagination. But why had it spoken of the need to save his world? A pharaoh reigned over Egypt, so the country wasn't in danger.

Egypt, so far-off, so inaccessible! Iker thought of his little village, near the shrine of Madu, a mysterious place to the north of Thebes. Thanks to the old scribe who had brought him up, he had seldom had to work in the fields and instead had devoted himself to reading and writing. This privilege had attracted much jealousy, but he had scorned his enemies, for learning nourished his soul.

In the sand of the beach Iker traced the hieroglyphs he was mastering. They made up a phrase praising the scribe's profession. Then he watched the sunset, gazed for a long time at the starry sky and fell asleep in the hope, mixed with fear, of seeing the gigantic snake again.

Iker was hungry again, and decided to catch and grill another fish. Taking his fishing-rod, he went down to the beach.

To his amazement, it had been covered up by the sea. A passing phenomenon, he hoped. He cast his line several times, but no fish took the bait. Puzzled, he dived in and swam about for a long time, but did not spot a single one.

Finding his footing again, Iker noticed that the sea was continuing to rise. Or was it that the island was sinking? He stood still on the beach, and the tide reached his calves, then his knees, then the tops of his thighs. At this speed, the Island of the *Ka* would soon disappear.

Gripped by panic, Iker climbed to the top of the tallest palm tree, skinning his hands and feet. Panting and breathless, he thought he was having another dream when he saw a white sail appear in the blue vastness.

4

Iker shouted for help at the top of his voice, and waved his arms frantically. He knew it was a waste of time, a pathetic gesture – the ship was a long way out, much too far away to see him – but he persisted. If the lookout was keen-eyed, he might spot him. And surely the crew would be curious when they saw that the island was being submerged?

For a moment, Iker thought the ship was changing direction and coming nearer, but then he had to give up hope. He closed his eyes. This time there would be no storm and no monster wave to save him. The water would reach his chest, then his head, and he would let himself sink into his warm, blue coffin.

Yet his desire to live was so strong that he opened his eyes again. This time there was no doubt: the ship really was heading for the island! Iker started waving and shouting again.

As the sea was by now licking round the trunk of the palm tree, Iker quickly climbed down and swam as fast as he could towards his saviours. Strong arms hoisted him aboard, and he found himself facing a stocky man with a hostile expression.

'There are two chests floating over there,' the man ordered his crew. 'Get them aboard.' Then, to Iker, 'You, who are you?'

'My name is Iker and I'm the only survivor of a shipwreck.'

'What was the ship's name?'

'*Swift One*. She was a hundred and twenty cubits long, forty wide, and had a crew of a hundred and twenty.'

'Never heard of her. How did it happen?'

'An enormous wave overwhelmed us. And I found myself alone on the island over there, which is now disappearing.'

The astounded sailors watched the sea rise and rise until it covered the treetops.

'If I hadn't seen that with my own eyes, I'd never have believed it,' said the captain. 'Which port did you sail from?'

'I don't know.'

'Are you fooling with me, boy?'

'No, Captain. I was kidnapped and knocked out, and when I woke up I was tied to the mast. The captain said I was to be thrown overboard to appease the sea-god if there was a storm.'

'Why didn't he do it?'

'Because the storm arose so quickly that it took him unawares. A sailor did try to sacrifice me, but the wave was faster than he was.'

Seeing the captain's sceptical face, Iker decided not to tell him about the golden snake and its revelations.

'Your story's decidedly odd. You're sure there are no other survivors?'

'Not one.'

'And what about these chests? What's in them?'

'I don't know,' Iker replied cautiously, seeing that they were closed again.

'We'll see later. I saved your life, don't forget that. And your story doesn't hold water. No one's ever heard of a ship called *Swift One*. You spotted those chests a long time ago, didn't you? And you got rid of their owner. But things went badly, the ship sank and you were clever enough to escape with your loot.'

'No!' protested Iker. 'I told you the truth. I was kidnapped and—'

'That's enough, boy. I'm not stupid, and you won't pull the wool over my eyes. Whatever else you do, don't try to resist.'

At a sign from their captain, two sailors seized Iker, bound his hands behind his back and tied his feet to the rail.

The port was bustling with ships coming and going. Manoeuvring skilfully, the captain brought his vessel gently to her moorings.

Iker did not yet dare believe that he was safe and sound. No doubt the fate in store for him was an unattractive one.

The captain came over to him. 'In your place, boy, I'd be discreet, very discreet. Ship-wrecker, thief, perhaps even murderer: that's a lot for one man, don't you think?'

'But I'm innocent. I'm the victim.'

'Of course, of course, but the facts are obstinate, and the judge won't take long to reach his verdict. If you play the devil, you won't escape the death penalty.'

'But I haven't done anything wrong.'

'That won't wash with me, boy. Here's what I propose, and you can take it or leave it: either I keep the chests and we never saw each other, or else I take you to the authorities and all my crew will testify against you. Choose – and be quick about it.'

Choose? What a joke!

'Keep the chests.'

'Good, my friend, you're being reasonable. You've lost your loot, but you've saved your life. Next time you try something like that, organize yourself a bit better. Above all, don't forget: we've never met.'

The captain blindfolded Iker, and two sailors untied his feet and led him ashore. Then he was forced to walk fast and for a long time, a very long time.

'Where are you taking me?' he asked.

'Be quiet or we'll knock you out.'

Soaked with sweat, Iker found it more and more difficult

to keep up the pace. Were his torturers taking him away from the port to kill him in some deserted place?

'Give me some water, please.'

No one even replied.

Never would Iker have thought he could bear it. But an unknown force inside him refused to give in to exhaustion.

Suddenly, he received a violent push in the back. He rolled down a slope, and thorns tore into his flesh. At last, his fall ended in soft sand. Worn out, his mouth dry, Iker knew he was going to die of thirst.

5

Something was eating his hair. The pain was so sharp that Iker jerked into consciousness. The goat backed away in alarm.

'You're taking the food out of his mouth,' lamented a hairy goatherd. 'A fine animal like that – you might have waited till he'd had his fill.'

'Untie me, please, I beg you, and give me something to drink.'

'Give you something to drink perhaps, but untie you . . . Where have you come from? I've never seen you around here before.'

'Pirates kidnapped me.'

'Pirates, here, in the middle of the desert?'

'It was on a boat, and then they forced me to disembark and walk a long way.'

The goatherd scratched his head. 'I've heard more believable stories in my time. You're an escaped prisoner, aren't you?'

The young man almost broke down in tears. Would no one ever believe him?

'Well,' went on the goatherd, 'you don't look very dangerous. But with all the pillagers around these parts, it's better to be cautious. Here, drink a little.'

The water in the gourd was tepid, but Iker drank it greedily.

'Gently, gently! I'll give you some more soon. I'm going to take you to the headman of my village. He'll know what to do with you.'

Iker obediently followed the man and his goats. What was the good of running away? It would only prove his guilt. It was up to him to convince the headman that he was sincere.

As soon as they spotted the stranger, the village children came running up.

'He must be a bandit!' exclaimed one of them. 'Look, the goatherd caught him, and he's going to ask for a big reward.'

The goatherd raised his staff to frighten the children away, but they stood their ground. And the procession arrived at the headman's house amid much laughter and childish babbling.

'What is going on here?' demanded the headman.

'I found this boy in the desert,' explained the goatherd. 'His hands were tied behind his back, so I was suspicious.'

'We'll see about that later. You, boy, come inside.'

Iker obeyed.

The headman pushed him unceremoniously into a small room where a thin man armed with a club was sitting.

'You're lucky, lad. I was in the middle of discussions with a soldier from the desert-guard patrol. What's your name?'

'Iker.'

'Who tied your hands?'

'Some sailors. They rescued me from a desert island, but then they abandoned me not far from here so that I'd die of thirst.'

'Don't tell lies,' said the headman. 'You're probably just a petty thief who thought he could escape punishment. What crime did you commit?'

'None, I promise you!'

'A good beating will soon bring your memory back.'

'Let's hear his story,' advised the desert guard.

'If you've got time to waste, fine, you sort this affair out. I'm going to attend to my grain-stores. But if you take this little thief away, leave me some official documentation, for form's sake.'

'Of course.'

Iker prepared himself for blows from the guard's club, but what could he say other than the truth?

'Give me more details,' said the guard.

'What's the point? You won't believe me.'

'How do you know? I'm used to identifying liars. If you're telling the truth, you have nothing to fear.'

His voice uncertain, Iker recounted his misadventures, omitting only the dream in which he had seen the great golden snake.

The guard listened attentively. 'So you were the only survivor, and this island disappeared beneath the waves?'

'That's right.'

'And your rescuers kept the chests?'

'Yes.'

'What was their ship called?'

'I don't know.'

'And their captain?'

'I don't know that, either.' Even as he answered, Iker realized that his tale did not stand up. No one with any sense would believe it for a moment.

'Where do you come from?' asked the guard.

'From Madu.'

'Have you got family there?'

'No. An old scribe took me in and taught me the rudiments of his profession.'

'You say you can read and write. Prove it.'

The guard presented Iker with a wooden tablet and a brush dipped in black ink.

'My hands are tied,' Iker reminded him.

'I shall untie you, but don't forget that I know how to handle my club.'

With careful strokes, the young man wrote: *'My name is*

Iker and I have not committed any crimes.'

'Perfect,' commented the guard. 'So you aren't a liar.'

'You mean . . . you believe me?'

'Why shouldn't I? I told you, I'm used to telling the difference between honest folk and liars.'

'Then am I free?'

'Go home and consider yourself lucky to have come through your adventures alive.'

'Will you arrest the pirates who wanted me dead?'

'They'll be dealt with, you can rely on that.'

The guard took back his writing-materials and began to write the document the headman wanted. Iker dared not leave the room.

'Well, boy, what are you waiting for?'

'I'm a bit scared of the villagers.'

The guard called out to one of the onlookers who had gathered in front of the headman's house. 'You there, give this lad a mat and some water.'

Thus equipped for the journey, Iker felt just as lost as he'd been on the Island of the *Ka*. Was he really free? Could he really go back to his village?

The guard watched him leave. Without waiting for the headman to return, he hurried away to rejoin his comrades, who were combing the area in quest of information about the crew of *Swift One*.

They were no more members of the desert guards than he was.

6

At noon, the burning summer sun transformed the eastern desert into a furnace. The few creatures that could survive in this hell, such as snakes and scorpions, had burrowed beneath the sand.

However, the five men continued on their way. Their leader was a lanky, bearded man, a good head taller than his men, dressed in an ankle-length woollen tunic and a turban. His eyes were deeply sunken in their sockets and his lips were sunburnt, but otherwise he seemed impervious to the heat, and he kept up a steady pace.

'We can't go any further,' grumbled one of the other men. Like his companions, he had been sentenced for theft. Under the bearded man's influence, he had fled the farm where he was doing compulsory labour to work out the end of his punishment.

'We aren't yet at the heart of the desert,' said the leader.

'What more do you want?'

'Just obey me and your future will be bright.'

The grumbler shook his head. 'I'm going back.'

'You'll be arrested and sent back to prison,' warned a red-haired fellow called Shab, 'the Twisted One'.

'That would be better than this hell! At least in my cell I'd be given food and water, and I wouldn't have to go on walking for ever and getting nowhere.'

The bearded man gave him an icy look. 'Are you forgetting who I am?'

'A madman who thinks he has a sacred mission!'

'All the gods have spoken to me, it is true, and their voices today are only one, for I alone am the bearer of the truth. All those who oppose me shall die.'

'We followed you because you promised us we'd get rich. And we surely aren't going to get rich here.'

'I am the Herald. Those who have faith in me will become rich and powerful; the others will die.'

'I'm tired of hearing you say that. You've lied to us and you won't admit it – that's the real truth.'

'How dare you insult the Herald! Ask my pardon at once!'

'Goodbye, you poor madman.' The grumbler set off back the way they'd come.

'Shab, kill him,' the Herald ordered calmly.

Shab looked unhappy. 'But he escaped with us, and he—'

'Strangle him, and let his miserable carcass serve as food for the wild beasts. When you have done it, I shall take you to the place where you will have the revelation. Then you will understand who I truly am.'

This was not Shab the Twisted's first murder. He always attacked from behind and stabbed his victim in the neck with a sharp flint blade. He had been under the Herald's spell right from their first meeting, and was convinced his leader, whose words cut like a razor, would take him a long way.

Without hurrying, the red-haired man caught the fugitive, executed him cleanly and rejoined the little group.

'Have we much further to go?' he asked.

'Don't worry,' replied the Herald. 'Just follow me.'

Frightened by the murder, the two other thieves dared not utter a word of protest. They, too, were under the spell of their guide.

Not a single drop of sweat appeared on the Herald's brow,

not the least sign of fatigue affected his walking. And he gave the impression that he knew exactly where he was going.

In the middle of the afternoon, when his companions were on the point of collapse, he halted. 'It is here,' he said. 'Look carefully at the ground.'

The desert had changed. Here and there were whitish patches.

'Scratch some up and and taste it, Shab.'

The red-haired man obeyed. 'It's salt,' he said in surprise.

'No, it's the foam of the god Set, which springs up from the depths of the ground. It is destined for me so that I may become stronger and more merciless than Set himself. This flame will destroy temples and fields, and will annihilate the pharaoh's power so that the true faith shall reign, the faith I shall spread throughout all the world.'

'We're thirsty,' one of the thieves pointed out, 'and this won't help.'

'Shab, give me a lot of it.'

Watched in amazement by his three followers, the Herald ate so much salt that his tongue and his mouth ought to have been on fire.

'There is no better drink,' he said.

The youngest thief picked up a piece of the crust and ate it. At once, he gave a terrible cry and began to roll about on the ground – he felt as if his whole body was on fire.

'No one but myself can decree the will of God,' said the Herald, 'and whoever tries to rival me shall meet the same fate. It is right that this impious man should die.'

The unfortunate man convulsed a little more, then stiffened.

The two surviving disciples prostrated themselves before their master.

'Lord,' implored Shab the Twisted, 'we do not have your powers and we recognize your greatness. But we are dying of thirst. Can you relieve our suffering?'

'God has appointed me to favour true believers. Dig, and you shall be satisfied.'

They dug frenziedly. Soon they uncovered the edges of a well. Encouraged by the discovery, they dug even faster, and reached a layer of dry stones which they removed in record time. And water appeared.

With the belts of their tunics, they made a rope to which they attached a flask.

Shab the Twisted dipped it in the well and brought it up full. He offered it to the Herald. 'You first, my lord.'

'The fire of Set is enough for me.'

Shab and his companion moistened their lips, then drank in small mouthfuls before wetting their hair and necks.

'As soon as you have regained your strength,' decreed the Herald, 'we shall begin our conquest. The great war has just begun.'

7

Sobek-Khu, 'Sobek the Protector', commander of Pharaoh Senusret's personal bodyguard, was even more vigilant than usual. To ensure the king's safety, he was using only six guards. He considered them far more effective than a whole battalion of soldiers, not all of whom would be vigilant all the time, for these six men were like wild animals, constantly on the alert and ready to pounce at the slightest sign of danger. And Sobek was not content merely to command: more agile, faster and stronger than all his men, he took full part in their daily training sessions, during which no man held back.

At Memphis, the capital, protecting the monarch already presented a thousand and one problems. Here at Abydos,* in unknown territory, he had to prepare for unexpected dangers.

During the voyage, there had been no untoward incidents. At the landing-stage, only a few unarmed priests had welcomed the pharaoh, who had gone immediately to the Temple of Osiris.

The king was a stern-faced giant of fifty, four cubits, three palms and two fingers tall.† The third pharaoh to be named Senusret, he bore the ritual names of 'Divine by

*Abydos lies 485km south of Cairo (close to ancient Memphis) and 160km to the north of Luxor (ancient Thebes).
†According to Manethon; this height is equivalent to over 2 metres.

24

Transformations', 'Divine by Birth', 'He Who Is Transformed', 'The Power of the Divine Light Appears in Glory' and 'The Powerful Goddess's Man'.*

During the first five years of his reign, although there had been no open challenges to his authority, a few of the provincial governors had not given Senusret their support. They were rich enough to maintain their own armed soldiers, and to behave, on their own ground, like rulers themselves.

Sobek the Protector feared that they and their soldiers might move against the pharaoh, for they saw him as an obstacle which, sooner or later, would threaten their independence. The visit to Abydos, sacred territory which played no part in the country's economy, had been kept secret. But could one really keep a secret in the palace at Memphis? Convinced that one could not, the commander had tried, but in vain, to persuade the king to give up this journey.

'Anything to report?' he asked his men.

'Nothing, sir,' they replied one after another.

'The place is deserted and quiet,' added one of them.

'That's normal for the domain of Osiris,' said Sobek. 'Station yourselves in the appropriate places, and intercept anyone who tries to approach the temple.'

'Even a priest?'

'Anyone – no exceptions.'

'The Great Earth' was the traditional name of the territory reserved for Osiris, the god who held the secret of resurrection. It was he, the first ruler of Egypt, who had laid the foundations of the country's civilization. He had been murdered but had vanquished death, and he now ruled over those 'of just voice'. Only the celebration of his mysteries

*S-n-Useret, from which comes the transcription Senusret. Other interpretation: 'Brother of Osiris', Senusret III came to the throne around 1878 BC

could confer upon Pharaoh, who was his heir, his super-natural dimension and his ability to maintain links with the creative powers. If the rites of Osiris were not carried out, Egypt would not survive.

A few fertile fields where the best onions in the land grew, a few modest houses arranged along a canal, the desert bounded by a long cliff, a large lake surrounded by trees, an acacia wood, a small temple, some shrines, some stelae, the tombs of the first pharaohs and that of Osiris: this was Abydos, outside time, outside history. Here stood the Island of the Just and the gate of heaven, guarded by the stars.

Senusret entered the small hall in which the priests were awaiting him. All stood up and bowed.

'Thank you for coming so quickly, Majesty,' said the High Priest, an old man with a slow voice.

'Your letter spoke of a great misfortune.'

'You shall see it for yourself.'

When the priest and the pharaoh emerged from the temple, Sobek and one of his men made to fall in as an escort.

'You cannot accompany us,' objected the old man. 'The place we are going to is forbidden to everyone but priests.'

'That is most unwise. If ever—'

'No one may violate the law of Abydos,' cut in Senusret.

The king removed the gold bracelets he wore on his wrists and entrusted them to Sobek. On the sacred territory of Osiris, all metal must be removed.

Racked with anxiety, the commander watched the two men move away. They walked round the tree-rimmed Lake of Life, then along a path bordered by stelae and shrines to reach the sacred wood of Peker, the vital and secret centre of the country.

At its heart was an acacia tree, the tree that, as it grew on Osiris's tomb, showed his worshippers that the ruler of the righteous had come back to life. Through his presence in this tree, Osiris united heaven, earth and the spaces underground.

In him, death was joined to life, and another, radiant life enclosed them.

Senusret immediately saw the extent of the disaster: the acacia was withering away.

'When Osiris is reborn,' the High Priest reminded him, 'the acacia is covered with leaves and the country is prosperous. But Set, the murderer and disruptor, always tries to kill it. Then life leaves the living. If the acacia dies, violence, hatred and destruction will reign upon this earth.'

'Have you watered it each day with water and milk?'

'I have not neglected my duties, Majesty.'

'Then a malevolent being knows how to manipulate the power of Set and use it against Osiris and against Egypt.'

'The texts state that this acacia's roots go down into the primordial ocean, drawing up the energy that gives it life. Only a particular kind of gold could cure the tree.'

'Do we know where it comes from?'

'No, Majesty.'

'I shall find out. And I know how to slow down, if not stop, the degeneration of the acacia: I shall build a temple and a house of eternity at Abydos. They will produce effective magic, which will slow down the process and give us time, let us hope, in which to find a remedy.'

'Majesty, there are not enough priests here to—'

'I shall bring priests and builders who will devote themselves exclusively to this task. All will be sworn to absolute secrecy.'

Suddenly, a far-fetched idea came into the king's mind. 'Could someone have stolen the sacred vase?'

The priest paled. 'Majesty, you know very well that would be impossible.'

'Let us check, all the same.'

Senusret verified that the door of Osiris's tomb was tightly shut and the royal seal intact. Only he could give the order to break the seal and enter the shrine.

'Even if a madman forced this door,' said the High Priest, 'he still would not be able to reach the vase, let alone steal it.'

'Abydos needs better protection,' declared the king. 'From now on, it will be guarded by soldiers.'

'But, Majesty, no outsider may–'

'I know the law of Abydos, since I am its holder and guarantor. No outsider shall sully the domain of Osiris, but all the ways leading to it shall be watched.'

From the top of the sacred mound, Senusret gazed upon the sacred space where the fate of his country, his people and, even more, a certain vision of the ultimate reality was being played out. When he acceded to the throne, he had known his task would be no easy one, because of the extent of the reforms that were necessary. But he had not imagined that his principal adversary would be the new death of Osiris.

Senusret strode determinedly into the desert, towards a virgin area between sand-dunes where the farmed area ended. Indifferent to the sun's bite, he had a vision of the building of his temple and his house of eternity, which would put back the fatal day by acting as a bulwark against the forces of darkness.

Who could be responsible for this attack, which was as unforeseeable as it was terrifying? The king would need all the strength a man could have, in order not to give in to despair, and to do battle with his invisible enemy.

8

After a taxing two-day march, Iker had had the good luck to be picked up by a trading-caravan on its way to Thebes. Its leader had at first been reluctant to accept a useless mouth to feed but his attitude had changed when the young man revealed that he could read and write.

'I've got some tablets bearing promises to purchase,' he said. 'Could you check them?'

'Show them to me.'

The caravan leader was impatient and immediately asked, 'Do they really say that palace officials undertake to pay me?'

'Indeed they do, and you've got good prices.'

'Experience, my boy, experience. Now, about you. Where do you live?'

'At Madu.'

'That little village in the back of beyond? What on earth were you doing in the desert?'

'Do you by any chance know two sailors called Turtle-Eye and Sharp-Knife?'

The merchant rubbed his chin. 'The names don't mean anything. What's the name of their ship?'

'*Swift One*. A hundred and twenty cubits long and forty wide.'

'Never heard of her. You aren't making this up, are you?'

'I must have got it wrong.'

'Yes, you must. *Swift One* . . . You can be sure that if such a boat existed people would know about her. Anyway, what do you say to putting a little order into my tablets and papyri? One can never be too careful with the tax authorities.'

Iker did so, much to the merchant's satisfaction. And the journey continued to the rhythm of the donkeys' pace, and the necessary regular halts, during which the young man ate the dried fish and onions he was given in exchange for his work.

Despite the questions that preoccupied him, Iker savoured the moment when the caravan finally left the arid track and entered lush green countryside enlivened by palm groves. The dangerous sea and menacing mountains were far behind him now. Peasants were harvesting vegetables in well-irrigated fields.

'Tell me, lad,' said the caravan-leader, 'how would you like to work for me?'

'No, I want to get back to my teacher so that I can continue to learn the trade of scribe.'

'Ah, I can understand that. One doesn't necessarily earn much, but one is well-respected. Well, good luck, my boy.'

Iker breathed in the scented air and the gentle warmth of spring. Eager to reach his village, he hurried along the paths he had walked so often during his childhood, in order to isolate himself and immerse himself in the serenity of the landscape. Although he had not disliked playing with his friends, he had always preferred to meditate on the mysteries of the world and the invisible powers.

The village of Madu was made up of small white houses, built on a promontory and sheltered from the sun by acacias, palm trees and tamarisks. At the entrance was a well, watched over by a guard.

He thought he was seeing a ghost. 'You aren't . . . You can't be Iker!'

'Yes I am. It really is me.'

'But what happened to you?'

'Nothing important.' Knowing the guard's fondness for gossip, Iker preferred to save his confidences for his teacher.

'You might do better to go away again.'

'Go away?' said Iker indignantly. 'I've only just got back. I want to go home and continue my studies.'

The guard shrugged and said no more.

Iker hurried to the home of the old scribe who housed and educated him. As he passed, little girls stopped playing with their dolls, and women carrying provisions halted, with suspicious looks on their faces.

When he reached the house, he found the door closed and the windows boarded up. Anxiously, he knocked and knocked again.

A woman came out of the house next door and said brusquely, 'It's no use knocking. The old man's dead.'

The sky fell on the young man's head. 'Dead! When?'

'A week ago. When you left, you broke his heart.'

Iker sat down on the doorstep and wept. By kidnapping him, the pirates had killed his adoptive father.

'Go and see the headman,' advised the neighbour. 'He'll tell you more.'

Despite his grief, Iker could tell that the villagers were hostile to him. Everybody considered him responsible for his master's death. For the first time, he felt the unbearable pain of injustice. But he would explain everything, and the wound would heal.

His head and heart heavy, Iker walked slowly to the house of the headman, who was giving instructions to the workmen charged with the upkeep of the canals.

'It can't be our apprentice scribe! Is it really you? What a surprise! I was sure I'd never see you again.' The headman, a plump man of fifty, spoke in a tone that was both sarcastic and biting. He dismissed the workmen with a contemptuous wave of his hand.

'You made your protector die of grief, Iker, and you must

31

answer for your crime before the gods. If I could, I'd send you to prison.'

'You are wrong – I'm innocent! Pirates kidnapped me, and I only escaped from them by a miracle.'

The headman burst out laughing. 'Invent something more believable! Or shut up and leave.'

'But . . . but I want to go home.'

'Are you talking about the house? The old scribe didn't write a will in your favour, so I've requisitioned it. The villagers all despise you – you no longer have a place among us.'

'But you must believe me! I really was kidnapped, and I—'

'That's enough. I hope remorse will rot your soul. If you don't leave at once, I shall order my servants to drive you out with clubs. Oh, there's one more thing. Your guardian wanted me to give you this box if ever you came back. Another act of foolish generosity on his part, but I am obliged to carry out his last wishes. Now leave Madu, Iker, and don't ever come back – for any reason whatsoever.'

Clutching the box to his chest, Iker went miserably back the way he'd come. He waited until he was a long way from the village, then found a quiet place in the shade of a tamarisk, and opened the box: he found that its wooden catch was broken. Inside lay a small, sealed roll of papyrus. Its seal had also been broken and then clumsily mended.

The few lines it held purported to be by the old scribe, cursing his pupil and promising him a thousand punishments. But Iker knew his teacher's writing well enough to see at once that this was a crude imitation.

At the bottom of the box lay a thin layer of plaster. Iker scratched it gently with a piece of wood. A message appeared, and his heart leapt.

I know that you did not run away like a thief. I pray that you are safe and well. My life is ending and my last wish *is that you become a good scribe. If you come back to Madu, I hope that villain of a headman will give you the will by which I leave my house to you, along with this box containing my most beautiful writing-implements. But a stranger has come here. The headman gets on wonderfully well with him. I sense dark forces on the prowl, which is why I have chosen to hide this message, using the method I taught you. Do not linger in this region, but leave at once for the province of Dju-ka, 'the High Mountain'.* This will be the first stage of your journey. May the gods lead you to the end of your quest. Whatever ordeals may face you, do not give in to despair. I shall always be by your side, my son, to help you to accomplish a destiny of which you are as yet unaware.*

*Present-day Qau el-Kebir.

9

When Medes entered his luxurious house in the centre of Memphis, two servants hurried to wash his feet and hands, put on his indoor sandals, perfume him and serve him cool white wine from the oases.

He was an imposing man, dressed as always in the finest-quality linen, as befitted the head of Egypt's Treasury, one of the most senior officials in the country. He was often invited to dine at the palace, and had even eaten at the king's own table.

As part of his duties, he checked the inventories of the temples that redistributed riches after sanctifying them. On the very day of his appointment, Medes had seen that he could use his privileged position for his own advantage. By cunning use of the secretariats of accounting-scribes, stewards and archivists, he stole little but often. Acting with extreme caution, he left no trace of his misappropriations and falsified the relevant documents with such skill that even a practised eye could detect nothing.

But today Medes was neither satisfied nor happy. For one thing, he was stagnating. Pharaoh Senusret might have granted him an important post, but he wanted more. No one was more skilful than he. He was the best and wanted to be recognized as such. If the king stubbornly persisted in failing to do so, Medes would have to take action, perhaps of a violent kind.

Senusret had many enemies, beginning with the extremely rich provincial governors – with whom Medes had a good understanding. If the pharaoh made the mistake of attacking their prerogatives, his reign would be brief. As it was, people were whispering that one of his predecessors had been murdered.

Medes was also wondering about the true nature of power and the best way to appropriate it. In order to facilitate his thefts of supplies destined for the temples, he had become a temporary priest. As he participated in the rituals, he had come into contact with the sacred. Flaunting his enthusiasm for spiritual practices, flattering his superiors, presenting himself as a generous donor, Medes was fascinated by the mysteries to which he did not have access. Only the pharaoh and certain permanent priests were admitted to gaze upon them. And it was from them that the king derived the essential part of his power.

The doors of the covered temple remained closed to the Treasurer. In this realm, which Medes assumed to be as vital as trade and agriculture, he did not yet have any influence. And he was certainly not ready to abandon his offices and live the life of a recluse.

The situation seemed impossible to resolve. But recently the loose tongue of a dignitary from the Temple of Hathor, at Memphis, had supplied him with first-class information regarding the Land of the God, the land of Punt. Like everyone who knew this legend, Medes was amused by it. The common folk and children had a taste for the miraculous, and they had to be distracted with such tales.

But, according to his informant, Punt was not a legend. The Land of the God did indeed exist, and it contained extraordinary things, including a matchless kind of gold, formerly used in great secrecy by certain shrines. In exchange for some expensive furniture, and before dying of a heart attack, the gossip had given vague indications of where Punt lay. It wasn't much, but enough to undertake a search.

'Master,' announced Medes's steward, 'your visitor has arrived.'

'Tell him to wait. I need to rest for a few minutes.'

For a while now, Medes had been getting fatter. Although endowed with great energy, still undiminished at forty-two, he had a tendency to eat and drink too much in order to calm his dissatisfactions. As replete as himself, his wife had to prove inventive and perverse when they attempted to attain the heights of pleasure.

Medes was a compact, stocky man, with black hair plastered to his round head. His face was moon-shaped, his chest broad, his legs short and his feet plump.

Sometimes he had the feeling that he was suffocating, especially when he did not get what he wanted quickly enough. But his greed was such that he overcame it to continue his forward march. And this meeting with one of his emissaries would probably be a decisive stage.

On the street side, his house was well-protected: windows with wooden openwork, a heavy main door made of beams and held shut by a large bolt, a permanently guarded servants' entrance. Two floors, fifteen rooms, a terrace, and an open-sided room opening on to the garden, where a lake had been created.

Medes received his visitor in the shade of a pavilion. He was the 'desert guard' who had questioned Iker.

'I hope you've brought me good news,' said Medes.

'More or less, my lord.'

'You have the gold?'

'Yes and no. Or rather, perhaps . . .'

Medes felt his anger mounting. 'I do not care for imprecision in business matters. So let us go through the points one by one. When did *Swift One* return to port?'

'She didn't, my lord. She went down with all hands.'

'Went down? Are you certain of that?'

'I have only one witness statement, but it seems accurate.'

'The captain's?'

'No, that of the young man you had kidnapped – you remember, my lord, the boy who had no family and who liked solitude and study so much. I found him in a small town near Kebet.'

'I know, I know! The ideal sacrifice to calm a storm. The headman of Madu pointed him out to us – and hasn't regretted it. But how can he be the only surviving witness?'

'I don't know, but it's a fact. He told me that an enormous wave destroyed *Swift One,* that by some miracle he was washed up on a deserted island, and that he was rescued by another ship. The captain didn't believe a word of his story, but did seize two chests found floating off the island before he freed his passenger – who everyone thinks is mad.'

'Can it be that the boy reached Punt?' wondered Medes. 'Could he find the island again?'

'According to him, my lord, it sank beneath the waters and disappeared.'

'What did the chests contain?'

'Something aromatic – probably ointments.'

'Nothing else?'

'He didn't mention anything else.'

'And you let him go?'

'What else could I do, my lord? In my role as a desert guard, I pretended to register his statement. The headman of the town detected nothing wrong, and we had no reason to hold this sick-minded storyteller.'

'Did it not occur to you that he was lying?'

'I believe he was telling the truth.'

'I am not so sure. Did he give you the name of the ship that rescued him?'

'He doesn't know it.'

'That boy was making a fool of you!' thundered Medes. 'He deceived you with tales for children, so as to hide the truth.'

'I assure you—'

'He must be found again – and quickly! He probably went back to Madu. The headman will have driven him away, but may know in which direction he was heading. When you catch him, make him talk, then get rid of him.'

'You mean . . .?'

'Precisely.'

'But, my lord—'

'That urchin has no family, and no one will take any notice of this new and final disappearance. Hide his body, and the vultures and rats will deal with it. And you will be handsomely paid. Now go.'

Medes could not hide his rage. To equip a boat and assemble a band of pirates capable of sailing as far as Punt, he had had to spend without counting the cost, while avoiding attracting the attention of the authorities. It would be some time before he could pursue this adventure further.

As soon as the visitor had left, it occurred to Medes that the crew who had picked up the survivor would certainly not have held their tongues. They had probably talked about the survivor from the sinking island in the port taverns, and the captain would be trying to trade the contents of the two chests. Even if they were only ointments, he would get a small fortune for them. If this strange cargo was still more valuable, he would have to find a skilful, rich person to deal with.

It was clear that the captain, if he really existed, would not go unnoticed. So Medes summoned his fellow criminal Gergu, an inveterate pleasure-seeker and a formidable collector of taxes. Gergu would know a legal way of handling matters and bring him back his due.

10

On the voyage back to Memphis, Senusret came to a full realization of the terrifying challenge that had been issued to him, just when he was planning to attack the provincial governors who had refused to give up even a fraction of their prerogatives.

Ever since Osiris had created Egypt, formed from the Nile Delta and Valley, a pharaoh had ruled the Two Lands after firmly binding them together. As 'the Man of the Bee', he governed the North; as 'the Man of the Reed', the South. The bee produced honey, flower-gold, vital for healing; the reed had a hundred uses and, in the form of papyrus, became a base for hieroglyphs, 'the Words of God'. Thus, in the person of Pharaoh, protected by Horus, master of the heavens and son of Osiris, whose task was to watch over his father, all the forces of creation were reunited. And it was up to him to unite the disparate parts of the country.

Senusret had no fewer than six formidable adversaries, six provincial governors who considered themselves autonomous and paid little heed to the king based in Memphis. Fortunately, they had not yet thought of forming an alliance, for each of them clung fiercely to his independence. Because of this situation, Egypt was growing poorer. Leaving things as they were certainly avoided serious conflicts, but was leading the kingdom into decline.

Strange to tell, five of the six ruled provinces near Abydos. Was it one of them who had succeeded in using Set's capacity for destruction against the Tree of Osiris? If so, Senusret would fight a merciless battle, both to bring the tree back to health and to save Egypt.

He must begin by obtaining as much information as possible about these six potentates, in order to identify the guilty party. Next, he must strike effectively, not allowing the enemy the chance to recover. But to whom could he entrust such a delicate mission? The Memphis court was full of flatterers, intriguers, ambitious men, cowards and liars. Only Sobek the Protector was devoted body and soul to his duty, without a thought for his own personal benefit.

Senusret would have to use the meagre forces at his disposal and, above all, to trust his intuition. As for the quest for the gold with the power to heal the acacia, it would be even more arduous. Legend had it that the green gold of Punt possessed exceptional qualities, but no one knew where the Land of the God was. And did it still produce the precious gold? There remained the mines in the eastern desert, under the control of the local governors, and those of Nubia, which lay out of reach.

Here again, the task seemed impossible. Senusret did not have the means to undertake such a search. The solution was self-evident: he would have to create them.

But his first priority was to give the Tree of Life new energy. So the pharaoh at once began to draw up plans for a temple and a house of eternity, to be built at Abydos.

People were working hard in the fields. The spring harvest was a good one, and nothing must be wasted.

A day's march from Madu, Iker reached a large estate, and presented himself to the steward to offer his services as an apprentice scribe.

'You're in luck, my boy,' said the steward. 'I've a lot of

sacks to count and mark. When you've done that, you can draw up an inventory of them.'

That was a week's work at a fitting rate of pay: food, a mat, a flask and a pair of sandals. As he worked, Iker fulminated against the headman of Madu, that criminal who'd destroyed the old scribe's will and stolen the house intended for his pupil. He'd also trampled on the dead man's last wishes by opening the box, stealing the writing-brushes and forging a set of accusations against Iker. How could anyone be so vile? The young man was discovering a cruel, pitiless world, where falsehood and betrayal triumphed.

But an immense joy wiped away these discoveries: his teacher knew that he had not run away, and had not lost faith in him. Yet what a strange message he had left! What quest, what destiny, did it mean? Suddenly, his old master seemed as mysterious as the golden snake on the Island of the *Ka*.

Iker would have liked to lodge a complaint against the headman of Madu and have him sentenced. But who would believe him? Unless the will could be found, the young man could not prove he should inherit his teacher's home. He'd find no help at Madu, only accusers who would reproach him for leaving the village without a word.

When all the sacks were listed in the inventory, Iker prepared to continue on his way.

The steward was sorry to see him go. 'You seem a good, conscientious scribe. Wouldn't you like a permanent job?'

'Not for the moment.'

'You're still young, of course, but don't be a wanderer all your life. Here's something to keep you going for a few days.' He handed Iker a bag generously filled with bread, dried meat, onions, garlic and figs. 'Where are you planning to go?'

'To the region of the High Mountain.'

'I warn you, the chief of that territory is not an easy man to deal with.'

*

Low walls separated the fields and held in the water for as long as necessary. With great skill, the peasants ensured that their land was irrigated well. Prosperity was on the increase, but there was no feast day for the lazy man.

As he entered the province of the snake-goddess Wadjet, 'the Verdant', Iker realized something: the name Dju-ka, 'the High Mountain', contained the same word, *ka,* as the name of the Island of the *Ka,* the realm of the serpent lost for ever in a dream. Was this mere chance, or was it a sign of the destiny the old scribe had written of?

Ka, 'high', 'raised' . . . Towards what mysterious goal must Iker climb? And what was this *ka,* this secret energy which was written in hieroglyphics as two raised arms?

Lost in thought, he bumped into a man armed with a staff.

'Hey, boy! Look where you're going!'

'Forgive me, but . . . aren't you the officer who questioned me?'

'I am indeed. I had a little difficulty finding you.'

'What do you want?'

'Your statement was very vague. I want more specific information.'

'I've told you everything I can. The one you should arrest is the headman of Madu.'

'Why?'

'He's a thief. He destroyed a will of which I was the beneficiary.'

'Can you prove it?'

'Unfortunately, no.'

'Then let's go back to your statement and those two chests containing valuable items. You must have inspected the contents. Give me the details.'

'Something aromatic – I thought probably ointments.'

'Come on, boy, that isn't enough. You know more than that.'

'I assure you I don't.'

'If you aren't reasonable, you'll find yourself facing serious problems.' The man hit Iker hard across the legs with his staff. The young man fell, and his attacker pinned him to the ground. 'Now, tell me the truth.'

'I've told you!'

'What's the name of the ship that rescued you?'

'I don't know.'

A dozen blows from the staff rained down on Iker's shoulders, making him cry out in pain.

'What are the names of the ship and her captain?'

'I don't know!'

'You really aren't being reasonable, boy. I want this information and I'll get it – otherwise I'll kill you.'

'I swear to you, I don't know anything!'

The man beat his victim again, but got nothing more from him. Reluctantly, he had to accept that Iker was telling the truth and really could tell him no more.

Iker's whole back, from neck to buttocks, was covered in blood. After another flurry of blows, he fainted. He was scarcely breathing.

His attacker dragged the body towards a papyrus thicket bordering a canal. Iker was in his death throes, he reckoned, and wouldn't last long. Since it would be his wounds that actually killed him, the false officer would not be completely responsible for his death. With a view to future judges, here below as well as in the afterlife, that was just as well.

11

At first there was unbearable pain. Then it eased, with a sensation of coolness the like of which Iker had never felt before. Suddenly, his back stopped hurting, and he half-opened his eyes to find out which world his attacker had sent him into.

'He's awake!' exclaimed a young girl's voice.

'Are you certain?' asked another voice, a man's this time.

'He's looking at us, Father.'

'In the state he was in, it's a miracle he survived.'

Iker tried to sit up, but a searing, burning sensation kept him lying on his mat.

'Whatever you do, don't move,' ordered the girl. 'You're very lucky, you know. I found you in a papyrus thicket consecrated to the goddess Hathor. Usually I just lay an offering there, but dozens of birds were flying about and screeching, so I dared to go in – their behaviour was so strange that I wanted to make sure there was nothing wrong. I told my father I'd found you, and peasants brought you here. For three days I've been covering you with the most effective balm, made of natron, white oil, the fat of hippopotamus, crocodile, lizard and grey mullet, olibanum and honey. The province's head doctor even gave me pills of myrrh extract to soothe your pain. I was the only one who believed your wounds weren't fatal.'

She was brown-skinned, pretty, and very vivacious.

Her father, a sturdy peasant, seemed hostile. 'What happened to you, boy?'

'A man attacked me to rob me.'

'What had you got that was so valuable?'

'A mat, a flask, some sandals, my writing-materials . . .'

'That's all? And where did you come from?'

'I'm an orphan and I hire myself out as a junior scribe.'

'You're costing me a lot, boy – a lot, I tell you.' The peasant walked away.

'Don't worry,' said the girl. 'Although he's bad-tempered and rude, my father's a good man. My name's Little Flower. What's yours?'

'Iker.'

'You aren't a very handsome sight at the moment. But when your wounds are healed, you might not be too ugly.'

'Do you think I'll be able to walk again?

'In less than a week, we'll go for a walk in the countryside together.'

Little Flower had not exaggerated. Thanks to the combined effects of the balm, remedies for pain and numerous massages, Iker was soon able to stand up. By a miracle, none of his bones had been broken, and the marks of the blows were already beginning to fade.

And yet there were no walks in the country, for the farmer had other plans. 'You're stronger than you look,' he said, 'and you owe me a lot of money, because your treatment has cost a fortune.'

'How can I repay you?'

'On my farm I don't need scribblers. On the other hand, I do need a farmhand.'

'I fear I may not be much use.'

'It's your choice: either you pay me by working, or you'll spend several years in prison – the ruler of our province doesn't like crooks. I can enlist you in a team of peasants under the direction of an overseer. You'll live in a small house and will have a piece of land where you can grow your own vegetables. But before I give you anything, I want the truth. Who are you really, and why were you attacked?'

Iker wondered if he had fallen into yet another trap and if this farmer was cut from the same cloth as the headman of Madu. He decided to be cautious. 'I tell you again, I'm a junior scribe and I come from the Theban region. My ambition is to become a public writer and to go from village to village writing letters of protest from victims of the government. The man who attacked me stole my writing-materials.'

The farmer seemed to believe him. 'First, pay off your debts. If you like the work, you can stay. If not, you can leave.'

The overseer was reasonably friendly, but he did not do the new arrival any favours. Iker had first to clean the farmyard, then keep the poultry-yard clean. This was a walled porch, its roof supported by wooden pillars shaped like lotus-stalks. Grey geese with white heads were raised here, along with quail, ducks and chickens. The youth in charge of feeding them brought big baskets of grain, which he poured into troughs, and the birds had the use of a pond fed by channels.

On the third day, Iker had to intervene. 'I think there's been a slight mistake,' he told the feed-bringer, a gangling, unshaven fellow.

'What sort of mistake?'

'On the first day, all six baskets were full. Yesterday only five were, and today they are much less full.'

'What's that to you?'

'I'm in charge of this poultry-yard. The birds must be fed properly.'

'A little more, a little less,' and he shrugged. 'Do you want to share the difference?'

'I want you to bring six full baskets.'

The youth realized that Iker was serious, and that it was no use trying to bargain with him. 'You won't tell the farmer, will you?'

'Of course not, if you correct your mistake.'

Iker had not made a friend, but the poultry-yard showed its noisy appreciation.

He constantly asked the same questions over and over again, even though he knew he wouldn't find any answers here. Before he could continue on his way, he must pay his debt, so he worked unstintingly in order to be free again as soon as possible.

'How are you getting on with your new work?' asked Little Flower one morning, watching Iker stroke a fine goose which had become almost tame.

'I am doing it as best as I can.'

'You aren't in pain?'

'No. Thanks to your care, I'm better now. You saved my life, and I shall always be grateful to you.'

'Hathor would have stopped you dying. I just helped you recover more quickly.' Little Flower frowned with vexation. 'My father's told me I mustn't spend time with you.'

'Is he angry with me?'

'Oh no, but you intrigue him because you aren't like the farmhands. He's ordered me to marry a real peasant so that I can give him fine children and my husband and I can take good care of the farm.'

'When you're lucky enough to have an honest, courageous father, you must listen to him.'

'You talk like an old man! Tell me, Iker, you don't want to become a real peasant, do you?'

'I still have a big debt to repay, but my true profession is that of scribe.'

'I must go now. If my father caught us, he'd beat me.'

*

'Never seen such a fine poultry-yard, my boy!' said the farmer. 'I like people who put their heart into their work. But you don't seem to mix much with your fellow workers.'

'I prefer to be alone with the birds.'

'Well, that's going to change. There's a lot of barley to be cut, and you're going to learn to use a sickle.'

Iker did not even think of protesting.

He was put into a team of strong, experienced reapers, who stared in amusement at the novice.

'Don't be afraid to wear yourself out, my lad,' said one of them. 'The fields are big, it's a good year, this land's rich, we aren't short of anything, and the lambs' meat is better than ever. But you have to deserve it. So make a firm cut and don't hold us up. I don't know anyone who's died from working too hard.'

Iker soon had a suntanned face. The thing that kept him going was the music: the flute-player varied the rhythm, but ended all his melodies with gravity.

'Your face is swollen,' remarked one of the reapers, 'because you've had your head down for too long. Go and see the flute-player – he'll cool you down.'

Feeling ill, Iker willingly obeyed. Some cool water on his neck and temples, then a few mouthfuls to drink, soon set him to rights.

'Reaping is harsh work,' said the musician, 'which is why I'm playing for your *ka*s. In this way, you and your comrades will have the energy you need.'

'What is the *ka*?' asked Iker.

'That which enables us to live, to exist and to survive. Osiris invented music so that harmony might make our hearts swell. It celebrates the moment when we cut the barley and the wheat, that sacred act which reveals their spirit, Osiris himself.

Iker drank in the words. 'Where did you learn all this?'

'In the principal temple of the province. The master of

music taught me the flute, and I shall teach it to my successor. Without it, without the magic it passes on, the harvests would be nothing but exhausting toil, and the spirit of Osiris would leave the ripe ear.'

'Osiris . . . Is he the secret of life?'

'Back to work, Iker!' ordered the team-leader.

The flute-player picked up his instrument again.

Iker continued to wield his sickle, but he had the feeling that each movement was now giving him strength instead of exhausting him. Was that what the *ka* was, the nascent energy of work well done?

12

The other harvesters did not have to pick up the ears of grain, but this new task had been imposed on Iker. He tied up the sheaves and put them into sacks, which were brought to him by a peasant boy.

'How much longer are we going to have to toil like this?' complained the boy. 'We've already got enough for our village.'

'There are other villages,' Iker reminded him, 'and the harvest won't be this good everywhere. We mustn't think only of ourselves.'

The boy looked at him suspiciously. 'You're on the farmer's side, aren't you?'

'I'm on the side of doing one's work well.'

The peasant shrugged and held out a new sack.

'Break for the midday meal,' announced the overseer.

In the shade of a reed hut, appetising food had been laid out on a mat: hotcakes filled with vegetables, crusty golden loaves, garlic roasted in oil, salted curds made from goats' milk mixed with fine herbs, skimmed milk, dried fish, marinated beef, figs, pomegranates and cool beer.

Iker was starving, but the feed-bringer stopped him sitting down and said, 'There's no room here. Go and sit somewhere else.'

'But this is my team. I don't know the others.'

'We don't want anything to do with you. We hate tell-tales.'

'Me, a tell-tale?'

'I told the lads you'd reported me to the farmer for not bringing enough grain to the poultry-yard.'

'That's a lie!'

'You always keep yourself to yourself, so just go on doing it. Don't disturb us while we're eating. If you do, we'll give you a good thrashing.'

Iker had no wish for a fight.

'Here's some bread and water,' sneered the youth triumphantly. 'Try not to slow us up after your feast. If you do, we'll report you to the farmer.'

The exile walked away and slowly ate a few mouthfuls – this would not be anything like enough to give him the energy needed for his work.

As he was lost in thought, frightened shouts made him turn his head. A royal cobra had emerged from its hiding-place, right in the middle of the revellers. They had all leapt up as one man.

'Chase it towards Iker!' roared the feed-bringer.

By drumming their feet on the ground and throwing earth, the farmhands did so. Iker had not moved.

This cobra had much larger eyes than normal, its scales were golden, and it moved with hypnotic grace. Spellbound, the young man thought of the serpent of the Island of the *Ka*.

'It's the goddess of the harvests!' exclaimed a peasant. 'Let it do as it wishes and whatever you do don't harm it – if you do, the harvest will be spoilt.'

Iker knelt and laid before the cobra the remains of his piece of bread. Then he raised his hands in a sign of veneration. A profound silence fell.

The distance between him and the snake was less than three paces. The pair were as motionless as statues, but the cobra would surely not wait much longer to strike.

The passage of time was interrupted. And a miracle occurred, as in the time of Osiris when the thorn did not sting, when savage beasts did not bite. Satisfied with the gesture of offering, the snake disappeared into the next field. There was no better omen for the quality and size of the harvest.

'The lads and I want to apologize,' said the feed-bringer awkwardly. 'We couldn't know you were protected by the goddess. We hope you aren't too angry and that you'll agree to share our meal. And naturally you should be the leader of our team. That way, we'll feel protected, too.'

Starving hungry, Iker did not need to be asked twice.

'As team-leader,' the overseer told Iker, 'you're authorized to lead the donkeys to the threshing-floor. Unload the sacks in silence, leave the priests to do their work and don't ask questions.'

'Is there a ceremony, then?'

'I told you, don't ask questions.'

At the head of five donkeys, which knew the way better than he did, Iker headed for the threshing-floor, which was near a temporary grinding-wheel. The animals halted of their own accord, without any need for him to use his staff.

There were two scribes there, who noted down the number of sacks. Half the grain was destined for the peasants and their families, the other half for the provincial bakery. Their work done, they withdrew.

Now there remained only the nine team-leaders, seven winnowing-girls and three priests, one of whom was the flute-player.

'The threshing-floor looks rectangular,' he said, 'but in fact it's round. Within it is hidden the hieroglyph *Sep tepy*, which means "the First Time", the instant when creation appeared. May the goddess of harvests be honoured.'

His two colleagues brought forward a small wooden

offering-table, on which they laid a vase of milk, some bread and some cakes.

'We mourned when the good shepherd Osiris was buried,' went on the flute-player. 'The grain was put into the earth, and we thought that it was dead for ever. How abundant the harvest has been – we can rejoice! The wheat and barley grow on the back of Osiris: he bears the riches of nature, never tires and never utters any complaint. Let the team-leaders lay the contents of the sacks upon the threshing-floor.'

Iker was so happy to be taking part in the ritual that he did not even feel the weight of his burden.

'Bring the donkeys forward,' chanted the flute-player, 'and make them walk in a circle.'

'Drive them back,' chanted another priest. 'Let them not strike my father! The donkeys of Set must not bruise the grain of Osiris.'

'The mystery must be accomplished to its end,' intoned the flute-player.

The donkeys walked round and round, as reflective as the humans who were watching the scene.

Without fully understanding its significance, Iker sensed that he was present at a vital act. He would gladly have asked a hundred questions, but he respected the silence.

'Let the grain be purified,' sang the flute-player.

The two other priests took the donkeys away from the threshing-floor and it was the winnowing-girls' turn to begin work. Their task accomplished, they filled the sacks and placed them on the donkeys' backs.

'Let the followers of Set take Osiris to the heavens, from where he will spread his benefits over this earth,' said the flute-player.

A procession formed, and moved off towards the grain-stores.

'Let the team-leaders unload the donkeys, climb to the top of the grain-stores and empty in their contents.'

Thus, thought Iker, the grain-store is assimilated into the heavens, dwelling-place of the spirit of Osiris, contained in the grain.

Deeply affected by the rite he had just seen, he walked slowly down the steps cut into the side of the grain-store, so as to engrave each second of this adventure in his memory. The contact of his bare feet with the limestone steps added to the intensity of this ritual, which was offering him a new reality.

The priests, the team-leaders and the winnowing-girls prostrated themselves before a giant of a man with deep-set eyes, heavy eyelids and prominent cheekbones. His gaze was so piercing that it froze Iker with fear. This stern man had a straight, thin nose, a curving mouth, a broad chest and large ears, capable of hearing the softest sound in the universe.

He wore a linen shirt with one strap, which passed over his left shoulder, and a rectangular apron on which was depicted a griffon crushing the enemies of Egypt.

The flute-player's hand forced Iker to flatten himself to the ground.

'Worshipful Pharaoh, the one who gives us life.'

13

Senusret raised to the heavens the offering of wheat and barley, which was returning to the gods. Then he climbed the steps to the top of the tallest grain-store and, with an ember, lit a brazier in which little balls of incense had been placed.

As he carried out this rite, the king thought of the young man whose gaze he had met. He knew no gaze like it.

As attentive as ever, Iker listened to the pharaoh's words.

'Osiris dies and lives again: he offers himself to feed his people. Father and mother of humanity, he produces grain with the secret energy that is within him in order to enable human beings to survive. All live by his breath and his flesh, he who came from the Island of the Flame to become incarnate in the grain. We eat the body of Osiris; we continue to exist thanks to flower-gold.'

Little Flower presented the king with a doll made of ears of grain. Copies of this betrothed of the wheat would be made, and one would be displayed on the front of each house until the next harvest.

Then the flute-player brought a large and beautiful basket made of supple reeds coloured yellow, blue and red. The bottom was reinforced by two wooden crosspieces.

'Here is the basket of mysteries, Majesty. Within it, that which was scattered has been brought back together.'

'Let it be returned to the temple,' ordered Senusret.

Trembling with emotion, the owner of the farm appeared and prostrated himself. 'Majesty, my most beautiful cow is calving. The miracle is taking place again.'

All the participants in the ceremony went to the stable. The flute-player spoke magical words to aid the delivery, while the head cowman helped the animal, which licked his hand. Fighting the pain, the cow stretched her neck and pushed down. The cowherd stroked her flanks to calm her.

'The Word is found among bulls,' said the pharaoh, 'knowledgeable intuition among cows. They must be treated with the greatest respect.'

His reassuring voice calmed the cow. And out came the head of a little calf, which the cowherd pulled gently, at the same time as its front feet. It was speckled, with dark brown eyes, and was magnificent.

The cowherd laid it before its mother, who licked it for a long time.

Everyone awaited her decision. She turned a deep, determined gaze upon Iker.

'Go to her and pick up the calf,' ordered the flute-player.

A little clumsily but with great tenderness, Iker took the little creature in his arms, and it showed not the slightest anxiety.

'The new sun has appeared,' concluded the pharaoh. 'May the festival of the harvest's end bring us all together in joy.'

For Sobek-Khu and his men, there was no question of relaxing and taking part, even for a little while, in the rejoicing. Because of his poor health, Wakha, governor of the Cobra province, had not been able to attend the ritual with the king. But was that merely a clever ploy enabling him to decline all responsibility in the event of an assassination?

Venturing into hostile territory like this seemed mad, but that was Senusret's decision, and the commander of his bodyguard must adapt to it. Fortunately, the court at Memphis knew nothing of the king's true plans.

56

'What have you found out about Wakha?' asked Senusret.

'He seems to be a good administrator, Majesty. He's loved by the humble folk, and he's never spoken openly against you. His major concern, like his predecessors', is to finish his house of eternity.'

'Does he keep any men under arms?'

'Not many, only those he needs to keep order – not counting the desert guards who watch the routes to the Dakhla and Kharga oases. This province ensures the safety of the caravans.'

'Did you make inquiries about the boy I pointed out to you?'

'His name is Iker. He's a farmworker whom the farmer took on recently.'

'We must not lose sight of him.'

Sobek jibbed at this. 'If you think he's dangerous, Majesty, why not arrest him?'

'He isn't a threat.'

'But then . . .'

'Simply have him watched without him knowing it.'

Wakha, governor of the Cobra province, was an old man, racked by pain in his joints. He greeted the pharaoh on the threshold of his incredible house of eternity, which recalled the creations of the time of the great pyramids. The gigantic tomb climbed up towards the summit of the cliff, soaking in the power of the High Mountain. Its successive sections were linked by staircases.

From the temple of welcome a long roadway led to a first courtyard; the ramp ended at a pillared porch opening on to a second courtyard enclosed by high walls. Next came a shrine housing the chamber of resurrection. At the end of the journey, in the main passageway, was a niche for the *ka*, the point of contact between the earthly world and the afterlife.

'A splendid monument – almost worthy of a king,' commented Senusret.

'I realize that, Majesty, and I beg you not to see any provocation in it. Such has always been the local tradition, but it will die with me.'

'Why?'

'Because your reign will be a great reign and you have decided to put an end to the independence of the provincial governors.'

'Why do you say that?'

'Because you are here.'

'And if it were true, how would you react?'

'By agreeing with you unreservedly, for this disorder has gone on too long. At the moment, the damage is minimal, but it is time to re-establish the law of Ma'at firmly. By reuniting the provinces and maintaining their union with an iron fist you will make Egypt prosperous. Will you permit me to sit down on this stone bench?'

Senusret nodded.

'I am happy to have lived long enough to know this moment,' said old Wakha. 'A weak king would have scattered power and destroyed the country.'

'Not all the provincial governors share your opinion.'

'I am not unaware of that, Majesty. With five of them, the confrontation is liable to be harsh, even violent. But, whatever happens, do not draw back. The great families were wrong to attach themselves to the hereditary nature of offices, forgetting that the quality of a man and his skills should take precedence over birth. The system has become so rigid that it must be shattered. It is you who reign, no one else.'

The king's expression was unreadable. He showed no sign of satisfaction.

'Your opponents are rich, arrogant and determined,' Wakha went on. 'You can rely on me, my men and the people of my province to support you in your enterprise.'

'Another war has been declared,' revealed Senusret.

'Who is attacking us?'

'Someone who is capable of wielding the power of Set, and who is determined to make Osiris die again.'

Wakha's face darkened. 'And you assume, Majesty, that it is one of the provincial governors who are hostile to you.'

'The possibility cannot be ignored.'

'How can our land have engendered such a monster? By doing that, he would ruin everything achieved since the time of the gods, and plunge us into darkness.'

'That is why I must identify him, while making Egypt united and strong.'

'I have no information on such a demon,' said Wakha.

'Then have you any about Punt?'

'It is a beautiful legend, Majesty. A long time ago, sailors apparently discovered the location of this miraculous country and brought back gold from it.'

'Are there any seams of gold in the territory you control?'

'No, none.'

Senusret looked again at the resplendent tomb. 'Are you satisfied with your stone-cutters, Wakha?'

'Their works speak for themselves, Majesty.'

'I am going to need these craftsmen for a long time, and they will be sworn to secrecy.' Senusret was about to find out if Wakha really was an ally.

'They are at your disposal, Majesty.'

14

Gergu the tax-collector was a thickset man, a constant drinker who was rarely drunk, and a lover of women, whom he considered objects whose purpose was to give pleasure. Divorced three times, he had enjoyed mistreating his wives, who were so terrified by his violence that none of them had dared to lodge a complaint against him. As for his only daughter, she had taken refuge with her mother and had sworn never to see her brute of a father again.

Linking up with Medes had given Gergu the opportunity for a new destiny. Becoming the Treasurer's right-hand man, under cover of his official offices, gave him impetus. He could now, with impunity, exercise his natural cruelty both on the victims who were pointed out to him and on those he chose.

Not only was the work well paid, but it also promised notable promotion. Medes was bound to climb higher in the government of Egypt, and Gergu would follow him.

A sailor by training, he himself took the helm when he travelled by boat, but he was less at ease when travelling on land – when he did, he sweated a good deal and, being a superstitious man, always carried at least ten amulets.

Gergu was therefore relieved to reach Kebet. He found the desert oppressive, and like his superior he found the heat unbearable. But it was here, in this town, that he would begin to track down the two chests Medes wanted. His hunter's instinct rarely deceived him, and he had ferreted out enough wild animals to sense that the gang of pirates could not be far away.

With his team of men armed with clubs, Gergu wasted no time. He went into every tavern and questioned every innkeeper. In the sixth one he got the answers he wanted.

'That's right,' said the owner, 'a few drinkers were boasting that they'd got their hands on an unexpected treasure and they caroused until morning.'

'Did they say what the treasure was?' asked Gergu.

'Valuable perfumes and ointments, judging by what I heard.'

'Where from?'

'They didn't say.'

'And where did these carousers go?'

'The most excited one, the one they called Captain, mentioned that his parents have a farm south of the town. They said they'd be undisturbed there while they awaited the result of the negotiations. I really don't know any more.'

'You've done well, innkeeper. So long, that is, as you haven't lied.'

'Of course not! This isn't going to cause me any problems, is it?'

'On the contrary,' replied Gergu with a greedy smile. 'If you agree to join my network of informants, you will even earn a nice fat fee from it.'

'I'll show you where the farm is.'

The pirate captain was staring at the two chests, from which a delicious fragrance still emanated. Every time he tried to open them, they became so burning hot that he had to give up. His men were getting impatient, but none of them wanted to take the risk of falling victim to a curse. They certainly possessed something worth a fortune, but how could they best trade it? It would be best if they made the trade in a large town where they could pass unnoticed. They must leave Kebet, and perhaps go as far as Memphis.

The most annoying thing was having to share. For the moment, the captain needed bearers. Later, things would be different.

The sound of a struggle broke into his thoughts. Outside, people were fighting. He ought to have gone outside, but he could not abandon the chests. Fierce shouts rang out, then there was silence for a few seconds.

Gergu burst into the room. 'Aha! No doubt this is the famous captain and pirate chief! And not alone . . . With the two chests the tax authorities are searching for.'

'The tax authorities? But—'

'Have you declared these valuables to the government?'

'Not yet, but—'

'One of your men is dead, and the others have been arrested. By attacking and wounding my guards, they have committed a very serious crime and will be punished severely. Neither they nor you will ever see the sea again.'

'But I didn't fight!'

'Only cowards try to avoid their responsibilities,' replied Gergu.

'These chests don't belong to me. Take them and let me go.'

'How did you come by them?'

'Purely by chance. I rescued the survivor of a shipwreck from a deserted island.'

'Where is it?'

'It isn't anywhere any more. I saw it sink into the sea.'

Gergu slapped him. 'I dislike people who lie to me. You're going to tell me truth – now.' He thoroughly enjoyed beating the captain.

His nose and several ribs broken, his face covered in blood, the captain gave in and described everything that had happened.

Reluctantly, Gergu became convinced that the man was telling the truth. 'What is in these chests?' he demanded.

'I haven't been able to open them. When I try, they burn my fingers.'

Gergu did not try it himself. Boldness was not in character, and he was not paid to take risks. This affair seemed more and more bizarre, and he was returning to Medes to unravel the threads of the skein.

A servant brought cool beer for Medes and his visitor.

'Did the boy talk?' Medes asked impatiently.

'He really didn't know anything, my lord,' said the false officer, 'and all he did was repeat his ridiculous story. I think he was so terrified when the ship sank that he lost his mind.'

'Did you get rid of him?'

'Your orders were carried out.'

'It is best that you keep well away from this region for a while. I've found you an excellent post in Faiyum – not much work, a nice house, and good pay. Your passage is reserved on a boat.'

The man bowed and withdrew.

Frustrated, Medes rapidly gulped down two cups of beer. He did not doubt that the interrogation had been carried out well and that the little scribe had indeed lost his mind. All that remained was the two chests – if they existed.

The answer was not long in coming.

The following evening, a red-faced, happy-looking Gergu presented himself at the entrance of Medes's home, and he was received immediately.

'I've got the chests, sir!'

'Where are they?'

'In a disused storehouse, closely guarded by some of my men. I thought they might be seen if they were brought here.'

'That's good thinking. What about the crew?'

'We shan't hear any more of them. They'll rot in the prison camp.'

'What did the captain tell you?'

'I didn't treat him gently, believe me! But the poor fellow's gone mad. All I could get from him was some tale about a lad and those chests being picked up from a deserted island, a ship going down in a storm, the island sinking into the sea, and the lad being the only survivor.'

Medes did not hide his disappointment. 'It seems that may be the truth. We've lost *Swift One* and her crew – the sea didn't want the little scribe as an offering. That expedition, to which I devoted so much hard work and patience, has ended in failure.'

'You are forgetting the chests. No one's opened them yet.'

'How can you be sure of that?'

'They're protected by a curse.'

'Then we shall break it.'

The two men went straight to the storehouse.

Medes remained convinced that Punt really did exist, and these surprising events only strengthened his belief. As for the wave that had destroyed his ship and killed her crew, it proved that the Land of the Gods knew how to defend itself and protect its riches.

Given their size, the two chests must contain a veritable fortune.

'That's strange,' said Gergu. 'They don't smell of anything any more. Up to now, they've given off an incredibly sweet fragrance.'

'Open them.'

Geru recoiled. 'It's said that they burn your hands if you try.'

'Give me your knife,' said Medes angrily. He succeeded in forcing the blade into the join between two planks. 'You see? Nothing's happening.'

Slightly reassured, Gergu continued the work.

In the chests there was nothing but mud, which gave off a fetid stink.

15

After a gruelling day, the mildness of the evening was heavenly. With the end of the harvests, the pace of the peasants' work slowed down, afternoon naps got longer, and everyone congratulated themselves on the exceptionally rich harvest, which they firmly believed was due to the pharaoh's presence. Like their governor, the inhabitants of the Cobra province had become fervent supporters of Senusret.

The last glimmers of daylight faded quickly, giving way to a sweet-scented night. Both animals and humans were hungry, and dinners were eaten with much enjoyment round open-air fires.

But Iker, who was sitting alone on a boundary stone marking the edge of a field, had no appetite. No one here knew Turtle-Eye and Sharp-Knife. He'd hoped that someone would recognize his description of the false officer who'd tried to kill him, but no one had. The would-be murderer evidently did not come from this region and, having carried out his crime, had fled.

Asking questions was getting Iker nowhere, so he shut himself away in silence. He must leave this area if he was to continue his investigation, but where was he to go? And paying off his debt would take a long time yet.

There was only one bright point in his desolation: the ritual celebrated in the pharaoh's presence. Never had Iker dreamt that he would see the monarch. Like the others, he had scarcely dared look at him.

'If you don't eat anything,' whispered Little Flower, 'you'll die.'

'That wouldn't matter much.'

'You're very young, and full of talent. Why not accept your situation, win my father over, and succeed him?'

'Because there are still too many unanswered questions.'

'Forget them.'

'I can't.'

'You're complicating your life for nothing, I assure you.'

'The ritual celebrated on the threshing-floor wasn't simple.'

'Those are just old peasant customs. Don't fret about them.'

'Why did Pharaoh honour that mystery with his presence?'

'Because he wants to ensure the support of the governor and people of our province. As you saw, the king's by no means a weakling willing to share power. Soon he'll confront the local despots who are determined to disobey him. We at least shall be left in peace. Forget about the past, and think of the future. I exist: so do this farm, these fields, these grain-stores. If you want, all this can belong to you.'

'Don't forget your father forbade you to have anything to do with me.'

Little Flower smiled. 'Since you were chosen to hold the calf, the symbol of the reborn sun, things have changed. No one here would dare say a word against you now. We could spend tonight together.'

She had put on rather too much face-paint, but her charms had never been so tempting.

'I must think,' he said.

'And when you've thought, what then?'

'You'd despise me, Little Flower, and you'd be right. Your words have touched me, I admit, and I really must think.'

*

As bad-tempered as ever, the farmer hailed Iker. 'The oxherd's ill. Take the oxen to the canal so they can drink and swim.'

At the farm, a feast was being prepared to mark the end of the harvest. Everywhere in the countryside, there would be a great celebration followed by several rest days. This quiet happiness was surely the work of Senusret, who had just left the province after celebrating the rites in the main temple.

The oxen did not have to be persuaded to go and cool themselves down. They set off for the canal of their own accord, the young man simply accompanying them. Their favourite place was bordered by old willows, which shed an agreeable shade. They placidly descended the slope and sampled the canal water with obvious pleasure.

Iker sat down on the bank. He'd lain awake all night imagining spending a peaceful life with Little Flower. But the scenes he had imagined – of himself as a good father and model farmer, her as a perfect wife and attentive mother, fine harvests, fine herds, well-filled grain-stores – gave him no joy.

He could not lie to himself: the trials he had undergone could never be erased from his mind. Understanding their significance remained his most important goal.

A strange wind began to blow; it seeming to come from every direction at once. The oxen stopped drinking.

And then Iker saw her: a woman of sublime beauty, with golden hair and the smoothest skin, emerged from the foliage. A dazzling light shone out from her long white gown. For a moment, just one moment, their eyes met.

It was she. No one else could equal her.

'You look strange, Iker,' said the feed-bringer. 'Where have you been with the oxen?'

'By the canal, where the willows grow.'

'Ah, now I understand. You thought you saw the goddess,

too. You're not the first, don't worry. The play of light and shade creates the image of a magnificent woman, whose praises the oxherds sing. Unfortunately, she's only an illusion. Little Flower, on the other hand, is very real,' he said with a smirk. 'Rumour has it that she's taken a fancy to you. It's serious, isn't it?'

'Rumour is a poison upon which no one should feed.'

'More pointless words! You're on the right path, Iker. We all dream about Little Flower – you do realize she's the farmer's daughter, don't you? Let's go and help get the feast ready. This year it should be tremendous.'

Several reed shelters had been erected to protect the revellers from the sun. Around them ran the children, constantly getting in the way of the cooks, who ended up giving in and handing them pieces of cake.

Indifferent to all this bustle, Iker took the oxen back to the stable.

When he emerged, he bumped into Little Flower.

'Have you thought?' she asked.

'I don't think I'm capable of making you happy.'

'You're wrong.'

'You accord me much too much importance, Little Flower.'

'You're not like the others, and it's you I want.'

Angrily, she turned her back on him and went back to her father, who was overseeing the preparation of the food.

Before the men could satisfy their hunger, the gods must be honoured. Twenty women bearing offerings decked an offering-table with food which had been consecrated by the temple and reserved for the Invisible Power that presided at the banquet. Each priestess – and each was more ravishingly beautiful than the last – wore a black wig, a clinging dress covered with a mesh of blue beads, and bracelets at wrist and ankle.

The last one outshone them all. She was so exquisite that she captivated even the most jaded onlookers. With her noble bearing, features of unequalled refinement, and slender figure, she seemed to have come from a world where perfection reigned. The divine goldsmith had fashioned her beauty, drawn the curve of her eyebrows and made her eyes as bright as the morning star.

Calmly and slowly, as if she were alone in a temple, the young priestess laid an open lotus-flower on the offering-table, so that the perfume of the afterlife would preside over the human celebrations. Then she withdrew with a grace that enchanted everyone.

When she passed close by him, Iker realized who she was: the woman who had appeared to him among the willows.

16

'How are you feeling?' Little Flower asked Iker, who was lying on his mat with a damp cloth over his brow.

'Please close the door – even a glimmer of light's unbearable.'

She changed the cloth. 'Do you want me to massage you?'

'No, thank you, there's no need.'

'This attack of indigestion seems very severe.'

'Yes, it is.'

'You're a bad liar, Iker. Anyway, I was watching you and you hardly ate a thing. It isn't indigestion that's keeping you in bed.'

'It doesn't matter.'

'Yes it does, it matters a lot. Why are you in this state?'

'I don't know.'

'Well I do. Do you think I didn't see how you looked at her, with your heart in your eyes?'

'Who are you talking about?'

'That priestess all the men were staring at – especially you. You're quite capable of falling ill and falling in love at the same time.'

'You don't understand, Little Flower.'

'You're wrong there. I understand only too well. And don't go and lose yourself in a dream that'll never come true. That girl's a priestess who lives in the temple and only comes out to celebrate rituals. You'll never see her again.'

Iker sat up. 'Which temple?'

'That isn't your concern. Anyway, no one knows – and it's better that way. Why don't you wake up at last and see that I'm real, not a dream?'

'Please, Little Flower, leave me alone.'

Iker wanted to engrave deeply in his memory the moment when the young priestess had noticed him. He ought to have spoken to her, asked her name, made some move, however small, to hold her back.

'Is it the first time she's come here?' he asked.

'Yes – and the last.'

'You must know her name.'

'Sorry to disappoint you.'

'Well, someone must have invited her, someone who could tell me about her.'

'Don't be too sure of that. Now, get up and go to work. This story of indigestion won't work any more. You've got a debt to repay, remember.'

Life would be meaningless if he never saw the beautiful priestess again. Unfortunately, as Little Flower had said, no one knew her name or anything about her. She had been merely a sublime apparition during a ritual, and the only solution was to forget her.

But Iker loved her, and no other woman held any attraction for him. Whatever the difficulties, he must find her again. And in the meantime, he would work and pay off his debt.

'This is the most difficult time of year,' the grain-bringer told him. 'The accounting-scribes come to check the number of animals in each herd. No question of trickery, or you get a beating and a big fine. What's more, you have to be nice to the ugly devils.'

The scribes sat down in the shade of a canopy, the most

senior with the benefit of a cushion. Iker took an instant dislike to the man's arrogant and self-satisfied expression.

Oxen, cows, donkeys, sheep and pigs began to file past in reasonable order, all noted down by the scribes. Iker found a discreet position from where he could see how they worked. Several times the senior scribe, who took no notes and was content merely to observe, demanded cool beer.

Once the count was done, he summoned the farmer. 'I have re-examined my colleagues' estimates,' he said coldly. 'Out of seven hundred pitchers of honey, you owe seventy to the tax authorities; and out of seventy thousand sacks of grain, you owe seven thousand.'

'That's a big increase in the tax, and nobody told me,' protested the farmer.

'I have just done so.'

'I shall lodge a complaint with the provincial court.'

'That is your right – but remember that I sit on it as an adviser. The health of your animals seems unsatisfactory. If you refuse to pay, the authorities concerned with animal health will fine you heavily.'

'Don't listen to him – he's a thief,' cut in Iker, and he snatched a papyrus from the scribe's hand and brandished it. 'Just look at this document. On his orders, the scribes have written down false figures – they've increased the number of animals so that the tax will be higher.'

The senior scribe was caught unawares, and a muscle began to twitch in his cheek.

There was a rumble of anger among the peasants.

'Arrest that insolent youth,' ordered the scribe. 'Can't you see that he's lying so as to set you against the authorities? If you dare attack me, you will all go to prison.'

For a few moments, the situation was a stalemate.

'Don't do anything stupid, lads,' advised the feed-bringer. 'The tax-collector's right. Anyway, it's between him and the farmer – it's nothing to do with us.'

The scribe beckoned forwards four guards armed with staves. 'Arrest that scoundrel,' he ordered.

Iker ran for his life. He knew the area better than the scribe's guards did, so he had a fair chance of escape.

With the help of the feed-bringer, who was glad to be rid of an inconvenient rival, the guards searched the huts, the reed shelters, the stables, the fields and the thickets. The wanted man had disappeared.

'He won't go far,' declared the tax-collector.

'Unless he leaves the province,' the farmer corrected him.

'I'll get you, just you wait!'

'And what will you do about this?' replied the farmer sarcastically, brandishing the papyrus.

'You can hardly read!'

'I can read well enough to see it's true that you're a thief. And my men won't stand by and see me robbed.'

'Well, well . . . let's forget the whole matter. It is a mere writing error, which I shall correct immediately.'

'Let's forget the unjustified rise in my taxes as well.'

'You are very lucky: I'm an understanding man. But do not ask any more of me.'

The guards decided to search the area around the farm for two more days, in the hope of gathering clues or statements from witnesses. They set off to begin their search, and the crowd slowly dispersed.

As she walked home, Little Flower thought of the handsome young man with the broad brow and intense green eyes, who'd escaped from her. In his soul burnt a fire whose intensity annoyed her, but she'd eventually have calmed it. Iker was so different from the other boys who courted her – he had the bearing and the determination of a true leader. As his wife she'd have pushed him to acquire more land, to enlarge their estate and take on new workers. Their success would have been dazzling.

But her favourite was now no more than a runaway criminal.

Little Flower closed the door of her bedroom, which no one, not even her father, was allowed to enter. She carefully put away her her gowns, wigs and mantles in large baskets. A good part of the profits from the farm went to make her elegant, and in her washroom she had two alabaster boxes containing her face-paints, lotions and so on.

As she turned, a man appeared from behind a curtain.

She stifled a scream. 'Iker! What are you doing here?'

'It's the best hiding-place I could think of.'

'The guards are searching for you, they—'

'I haven't done anything wrong – quite the contrary, in fact.'

'You can't fight that tax-collector.'

'Of course we can! We can prove that he's committing fraud, and he will be convicted.'

'It's not as simple as that.'

'Call your father, and let's plan what to do. I shall be the main witness.'

'I tell you again, it isn't that simple.'

'What do you mean?'

'Everything's possible, on one condition: that you marry me.'

'I can't lie – you know that. And . . . Little Flower, I'm not in love with you.'

'What does that matter? The important thing is that we'd make a good couple and get very rich.'

Iker shook his head. 'We'd have nothing but bad fortune, you can be sure of that.'

'Is your refusal final?'

'Yes.'

'You don't know what you're losing.'

'Forgive me, but I have other demands on me.'

'That priestess you're so stupidly besotted with,' sneered Little Flower.

'I want to have that tax collector convicted. Without justice, this world would be unbearable to live in. Will you go and fetch your father?'

Little Flower thought for a moment. 'Very well.'

Iker kissed her gently on the forehead. 'No corrupt scribe will ever try to cheat you again – you'll see.'

She went out of the bedroom, and he waited for her summons. He did not have to wait long.

'You can come out now, Iker,' Little Flower called.

When he emerged, three guards threw themselves on him and bound his hands behind his back.

Huddled in her father's arms, Little Flower averted her eyes.

'Things have turned out well in the end,' said the farmer. 'My daughter did well to warn the guards that you were hiding here and threatening her. You've turned out to be just an insolent petty thief in debt. You deserve to be made an example of, and no one will miss you.'

'Goodbye, Little Flower,' said Iker. 'I don't owe you anything any more.'

17

The sentence could not be appealed: a year's forced labour for insulting a government scribe in the exercise of his duties, violence towards the guards, and trying to run away.

The judge, presiding over a court made up of provincial headmen, had little interest in Iker's explanations. The overwhelming testimonies of the tax-collector, the scribes, the farmer, his daughter and the feed-bringer had convinced the jury.

During the long journey to the copper mines of Sinai, Iker was not ill-treated. He was given plenty of food and water, and was even shown some sympathy by the desert guards, who warned him about the ordeal awaiting him.

'Fortunately for you,' said their commander, 'you're young and healthy. Anyone with a worn-out constitution would not last a year.'

'I'm not guilty of anything. All I did was unmask a corrupt tax-collector.'

'We know that, lad, but we obey our orders. Letting you run off into this desert would cause major problems for us – and in any case you'd stand no chance of getting out alive. Better to take your punishment, even if it is unjust.'

The caravan was under the protection of Soped, 'the Pointed One', a falcon with a sharp beak who ruled over the burning, lonely wastes of the Eastern Desert. Hidden in a triangular sacred stone, in the image of a ray of light descending from the heavens, the god protected his faithful from raids by the sand-travellers, lawless looters who attacked caravans and killed merchants.

Fascinated by the desert, Iker soon forgot the farm and its despicable inhabitants, and he forgot his resentment, too. He often saw before him the face of the beautiful priestess. When she opened her eyes and looked at him, he felt strong enough to lift mountains and ignore his weariness. As soon as she disappeared, he felt empty, defeated, almost incapable of taking another step. The desire to see her again was so strong that he regained his confidence. Yes, he would surmount this new obstacle and would set off in search of her.

Eventually, they reached Timna in the heart of the desert.* A circular depression surrounded by steep hills housed the copper mines, which had been worked since the days of the earliest pharaohs. Donkey caravans regularly brought the miners supplies of food, clothes and tools. Because of the harsh conditions, the specialist miners were often relieved. As for the convicts, they had to adapt or die. They were watched constantly by vigilant guards, so could never be idle. They had to dig and strengthen wells and galleries to make the miners' work easier.

The buildings – houses, storehouses and prison – were of dry stone. The only place made of cut stone was the shrine to Min, lord of life, protector of quarrymen and miners, he who unleashed the thunder and the storms that filled the water-pools. Thanks to him, the workmen charged with bringing the copper out of the mountain's belly never went short of water.

When the caravan arrived, the mine overseer, a stocky man with a swarthy face and a gruff voice, looked astonished. 'Where are the convicts?' he asked.

'There's only one,' replied the officer. 'This boy.'

*30km north of Eilat (Edom).

'Is this a joke?'

'Not for him.'

'What crime has he committed?'

'He showed that a tax-collector in the Cobra province was dishonest.'

'But . . . that's not a crime!'

'A farmer, his daughter and those close to him testified against him. Verdict: a year here.'

'That's a bit much! Why didn't he appeal?'

'He didn't have time. It seems everybody was in a hurry to get rid of him.'

The overseer scratched his head. 'I don't like that . . . I don't like it at all. Have you got the official documents?'

'Here they are. We'll leave the lad with you and when we're rested we'll be off. Next time, we'll try and bring you a better workforce.' He let his men fall out and go and get some rest.

The overseer stared at Iker. 'What's your name?'

'Iker.'

'Age?'

'Sixteen.'

'Peasant?'

'No, apprentice scribe. I was attacked and robbed, then—'

'Your story doesn't interest me. You shouldn't be here, but that's how it is and nobody can change anything.' The stocky man walked round Iker. 'Let's see . . . You're too tall to slide into a tunnel and you aren't strong enough to be a miner. I'll put you in the team that tends the furnaces. I can't do any better than that, my boy.'

'Thank you.'

'Try to hold out, and don't tread on anyone's toes.'

Two guards took Iker into a little dry-stone hut. On the ground were two mats.

'Wait here.'

The place wasn't exactly cheerful, and the mountains were

openly hostile. It felt so far from Egypt as to be in another world. But Iker refused to despair. He would get out of this prison and find the priestess again.

A man of around twenty, with a square face, thick eyebrows and a round belly, came into the hut. 'Are you the new lad?'

'Yes. My name's Iker.'

'I'm Sekari. We're in the same team. They say you're innocent.'

'Yes, I am.'

'So am I. Now listen. It's better not to talk about the past, just live in the present. Our chief is Crooked-Face, a bad man and aggressive with it – be very careful not to annoy him. He's a habitual criminal and he's already been here ten years. He survived the mine and now he rules over the furnaces – the guards don't dare discipline him. As regards rations, I warn you they're not very generous and not very good. But you've fallen on your feet. The cook likes me, and I get extra. As I rather like the look of you, I'll gladly let you into our group, but on two conditions: first, you hold your tongue; second, you take on a share of my work.'

'Agreed.'

Sekari knelt down and dug in the ground in the darkest corner of the room. He pulled out a small alabaster vase and removed its cloth stopper. He emptied some pellets into the palm of his hand and held them out to Iker.

'Swallow these.'

'What are they?'

'A mixture of carob seeds and dill. It'll help you avoid diarrhoea and other digestive problems – people have died of them before now.'

Iker swallowed them, and Sekari dug up another treasure.

'Protecting the body isn't enough. You must also take care of your soul, otherwise you'll give up and lose your life-force. To be at peace, wear this around your neck.'

Sekari handed Iker a little cord from which hung a series of minuscule cornelian amulets, depicting a falcon, the bird of Horus, or a baboon, the animal of Thoth, patron god of scribes.

The young man rubbed them between his fingers for a long time.

'Right,' said Sekari, 'we'd better go to work now or we'll be punished.'

Crooked-Face was a monstrously hairy man, who was afraid of no one and nothing, not even the searing heat from the copper-smelting furnaces.* As soon as he set eyes on the new arrival, he took a dislike to him.

'In this place, boy,' he growled, 'no one's innocent. Toe the line or I'll squash you like a bug, and no one would say a word about it. One mouth less to feed – that would be good news.'

Iker met Crooked-Face's gaze squarely. 'You may be stronger than I am, but you don't frighten me.'

'You can start by sorting out the ingots for storage. Afterwards we'll see.'

While the dross remained on the surface, the melted copper was deposited at the bottom of the furnace and ran into channels from which the raw metal was extracted. After that it was melted again in a crucible, then poured into moulds before being hardened by hammering. The metal was next transformed into ingots, which were listed and numbered in preparation for their transport to Egypt.

A month later, Iker was still sorting and storing the ingots. Crooked-Face had not told him off once.

'It's very odd,' commented Sekari. 'He's not usually so easy-going.'

'I obey him and keep my mouth shut: that's probably why. Besides, you gave me very effective amulets.'

*Temperatures ranged from 700 to 1,000 degrees.

'So much the better for you. But stay on your guard.'

'I don't suppose you've ever heard of two sailors called Turtle-Eye and Sharp-Knife, have you?'

Sekari thought for a while. 'No, those names don't mean anything to me.'

'Could you ask the other prisoners?'

'If you like. Are they friends of yours?'

'I lost sight of them and I'd like to know where they came from. And I'd also like another look at the false desert guard who tried to kill me.'

'A false guard? You're sure of that?'

Iker described his attacker.

'Fine, I'll ask around. But I can't promise anything.'

Sekari's efforts proved fruitless: none of the convicts knew anything. Iker mastered his disappointment and conscientiously got on with his work, which in truth was not very difficult.

'Good work, little lad,' said Crooked-Face, almost pleasantly. 'You've earned a better job than that. Your time here should at least be profitable. You must learn everything about copper, beginning with the furnaces. Tomorrow, we'll clean them together. It's a sacred privilege, you know. I'm granting it to you because you know how to keep your place. That's rare, and deserves to be rewarded.'

Crooked-Face lumbered away. He could no longer stand this boy, who was clearly an informer sent to find out how the convicts organized themselves. The main object was himself, Crooked-Face! Iker was going to denounce him, and he'd be sent back to work in the mine galleries.

There was only one solution: to roast his head in a furnace and make everyone think it was an accident.

The sun was rising. Sekari stretched and yawned. 'I'm helping the cook today. How about you?'

82

'I'm cleaning the furnaces with Crooked-Face,' said Iker.

'He really has got a soft spot for you! Anyone would think he wants to train you so you can succeed him.'

As they emerged from their hut, Iker and Sekari were stopped by the mine overseer and a squadron of desert guards.

'You two, Crooked-Face and three other convicts are being transferred,' said the overseer.

'Where to?' asked Iker.

'To the turquoise mines of Hathor.'

'Why?'

'Orders from above.'

'But we've behaved well, we haven't done anything—'

'The turquoise mines need men urgently. Be disciplined and work hard, or you'll be brought back here. And if that happens, I can promise you special treatment.'

18

All the land routes to Abydos were guarded by soldiers, who let no one pass. The only way to enter the sacred territory of Osiris was from the river, and the landing-stage was under close guard. A whole flotilla, led by the pharaoh's boat, docked there.

Under Senusret's eye, the sailors unloaded blocks of stone, bases of columns and paving-slabs. Then the team of craftsmen from the Cobra province disembarked, among them a master-builder, sculptors and carpenters. All had taken an oath to keep silent about their work. They knew that they would not see their loved ones again until it was finished.

The High Priest bowed before the king, who asked, 'How is the acacia?'

'Its condition has not changed, Majesty.'

'I have come to create a temple, a house of eternity and a town,' announced Senusret. 'South of the site I shall build Wah-sut, 'City of Everlasting Sites'. The men working there will receive daily supplies of meat, fish and vegetables. Butchers and cooks will live there, and the priests and craftsmen will have everything they need.'

'What is our role to be, Majesty?'

'According to my latest decree, no priest from Abydos can be transferred elsewhere. None of them will be subject to compulsory agricultural work, no institution will have the right to take any portion of the territory of Osiris. Two sorts of priests will be admitted: permanent and temporary. When a team of temporary priests withdraws to be replaced by another, it must have carried out its task to perfection, on pain of punishment. The permanent priests will be led by the Shaven-headed One, responsible for the rites of the House of Life; the Servant of the *Ka*, who will venerate and maintain the spiritual energy; he who pours libations upon the offertory tables; he who watches over the wholeness of the great body of Osiris; he whose action is secret and who sees secrets; the seven female musicians who enchant the divine soul; and, finally, he who carries the Golden Palette on which are written the words of knowledge, which I entrust to you.'

The king handed the old man the precious palette.

'I shall strive to be worthy of your trust, Majesty. When will you appoint the holders of the other offices?'

'Choose the ones who are most skilled in the rituals. But before proceeding further, I must know if the spirit of the place is favourable to us.'

Senusret went off alone into the desert; despite repeated expressions of concern, the Protector was forbidden to follow.

Since the dawn of time Abydos had been watched over by a mysterious deity, Khentimentiu, 'He Who Leads the Beings of the West'. Though he had passed to the other side of darkness, he nevertheless walked the realm of the living when the gates of the Invisible were opened. Without his sanction, the pharaoh's plan was doomed to failure.

Sensusret halted at the spot where the shrine of his temple would be built. Here, the earth entered into a particular kind of resonance with the sky.

All of nature fell silent.

Then came the song of a bird, a breath of wind . . . Suddenly, it appeared from nowhere. A black jackal, long-legged, with a very long tail and large, erect ears. It was wary, and kept at a good distance from the intruder. Senusret quickly understood what it wanted. The incarnation of the Leader of the Western Beings was ordering him to reveal his intentions.

'I must stop the acacia's decline,' said the king. 'To do so, I shall build a temple where each day a ritual will be celebrated maintaining the life-force of this place. But it would be ineffective without the presence of a house of eternity, where the mysteries of death and resurrection will be accomplished. It is not for my own glory that the craftsmen will bring these structures to birth, but so that Osiris may remain the keystone of Egyptian civilization. Read the plans for the work in my heart, and mark them with the seal of your power. Without it, they will not come into existence.'

The jackal sat down on its haunches, raised its head to the sun and sang a chant so intense and so profound that it vibrated through the souls of every creature dwelling upon the Great Land of Abydos.

The Herald and his followers had crossed a limestone plateau, following a series of rocky hills interspersed with peaks. Here and there, there was a small island of unexpected greenery where they rested for a few hours before setting off again into the desert.

Under the spell of their leader, who was impervious to fatigue and doubt, the men were still managing to set one foot in front of the other. They had even stopped wondering how long they would survive in this furnace.

'We won't find them,' said Shab the Twisted. 'We'd better give up, my lord.'

'Have I ever failed you?'

'No, never, but how can we believe in this legend?'

'Have you ever seen corpses torn to pieces by the monsters of the desert?'

'No.'

'I have. And that day I understood that these creatures have the power we need. When we have it, we shall be invincible.'

'Wouldn't a good, well-trained army be better?'

'An army can be defeated, but the one I shall put together will be different.'

'With respect, my lord,' said Shab, 'at the moment it's just a gang of ragged bandits.'

'Do you think mere bandits would still be alive if they had not heard my words?

'Well, I must say . . . The fact they're still on their feet is incredible.'

There were only about twenty of them, but they had agreed to follow the Herald when he promised them riches after harsh battles. Convicted criminals who were sought by the law, they were glad to have escaped their due punishment.

Each time one of them was preparing to give up or rebel, the Herald comforted him with his eyes and voice. A few words, spoken in an even, spellbinding tone, set the wanderer back on the right path. A path which, however, had led them into the depths of an endless desert.

At nightfall the lead marcher thought he spotted the *sedja*, a monster with a snake's head and a lion's body.

'Lads, I'm having a hallucination! And if it isn't one, just see what I'm going to do to this horror!' He ran towards the creature, intending to smash its head with his club. But the serpent's neck dodged aside, and the lion's claws sank into the attacker's chest.

'So it really does exist,' whispered a terrified Shab.

Up loomed the *seref*, with a falcon's head and lion's body, and the *abu*, an enormous ram with a rhinoceros's horn on its snout. Two of the gang tried to run away, but the monsters caught them and slaughtered them.

In a reddish glow that set the desert on fire, there then appeared the *sha*, the animal of Set, a quadruped with a head similar to the okapi's. At first it looked less fearsome than the other three, but its reddish eyes froze the survivors to the spot.

'What are we going to do?' asked Shab, his teeth chattering.

The Herald raised his arms. 'All the gods inspire me, those of evil as well as good,' he declaimed. 'The light of day and the force of the darkness dwell within my spirit. They speak only to me, and I alone am their interpreter. Whoever disobeys me shall be annihilated, but whoever obeys me shall be rewarded. I shall make these many powers into only one, and I shall be its only propagator. The whole world will submit. There will be but one faith and but one master.'

Only Shab the Twisted had not flattened himself in the sand to avoid being seen by the monsters. He could not believe what he saw.

The Herald walked boldly up to the three murderous creatures, passed his hands slowly over the claws, the beak and the horn, and soaked himself in the blood of their victims. Then he tore out the *sha*'s ember-like eyes and laid them on his own.

A sudden, vicious sandstorm blew up, knocking Shab to the ground. As brief as it was violent, it gave way to an icy wind.

When Shab looked again, he saw the Herald seated on a rock. There was no trace of the monsters.

'My lord, was it only a nightmare?'

'Of course, my friend. Such creatures exist only in the minds of the fearful.'

'And yet there are dead men, torn to pieces.'

'They were killed by a wild beast maddened by our presence. I know now what I wanted to know, and we are going to have our first brilliant success.'

Shab realized he must have seen one of those mirages that were so common in the desert. But why had the Herald's eyes become blood-red?

19

Before leaving for the turquoise mines of Sinai, which were south-west of the copper mines, Sekari prepared a potion made by crushing and filtering cumin, honey, sweet beer, limestone and a plant he called 'baboon's hair'. The potion would both help the men remain strong and repel the many snakes that roamed the desert. In addition, he advised everyone to cover their entire bodies with onion paste, to drive away snakes and scorpions. The paste would also bestow on them the advantage of developing the five senses, no mean advantage in a hostile environment.

Only Crooked-Face refused to take these precautions, but he smelt so bad that even a horned viper would hardly risk biting him.

'How do you know all these things about plants, Sekari?' asked Iker in surprise.

'Before doing some very stupid things, I was a gardener and bird-catcher. Look, see this scar on my neck? That's from an abscess I got from the heavy yoke I carried, with water-pots on the ends. How many thousands of times I carried them! My speciality was hunting birds in gardens. I love them, those little creatures, but some of them are very destructive – if we didn't deal with them, we'd have no fruit left to eat. So, with my spring-loaded trap and my net, I captured them to make them understand that they must go and feed elsewhere. Except for the quail, which ended up on the grill or in a stew, I let the others go. I even learnt to speak to them. With some, all I had to do was imitate their song and they avoided the orchard.'

'What were they, those "very silly things"?'

Sekari hesitated. 'You know, in our professions, you can't declare everything to the tax authorities, otherwise there'd be no end to it. There was a taxation scribe who took an interest in me, a tall, very ugly fellow with spots on his nose. A two-faced swine who pretended to be honest, when really he lied as easily as he breathed. In short, when he invaded my territory, I set a small trap. The fool was stupid enough to get tangled up in the trap and he suffocated a little bit. Nobody regretted it, but all the same the law said I was guilty. As there was an accidental aspect, I wasn't sentenced to death, but I shan't get out of the mines for a long time.'

'Neither of us has had much luck with tax-collectors. Are you hoping your sentence will be reduced for good behaviour?'

'Yes. That's why I'm keeping my head down. Discreet and useful: that's my motto. In that way, the guards will notice me.'

'Do you know the turquoise mines?'

'No, but apparently the work isn't as hard as in the copper mines.'

'Why do you think we're being sent there?'

'No idea. If you want a piece of advice, beware of Crooked-Face.'

'He's been quite friendly with me,' objected Iker.

'That's just what's bothering me. He may have only been convicted of theft, battery and wounding, but that man's a natural killer. I'm convinced he hates you and is just putting on a show.'

Iker did not take the warning lightly. He rubbed his amulets, realizing that, despite his first impressions of Crooked-Face, he had lowered his guard.

On the journey, he, the apprentice scribe, would carry the triangular stone of Soped, covered with a cloth. No sand-travellers had been reported in the area, but it was better to ensure the god's protection.

'We're almost there,' announced an officer.

The site was impressive.* A succession of mountains led off into infinity, and dry riverbeds surrounded a plateau set slightly apart from the hollows over which it loomed. A few thorn trees, a mass of broken rock, yellow and black sandstone, red hills and a fierce wind gave life to this landscape, which was both forbidding and beautiful.

The caravan of guards, prisoners, and donkeys carrying water and food set off up the sloping track that gave access to the plateau.

At the entrance to a processional road bordered by stelae and leading to a temple, a sturdy fifty-year-old man was waiting for them.

'My name is Horure,' he said, 'and I'm in charge of the men sent by Pharaoh Senusret. Mining is particularly arduous here because of the heat, and I need more miners, which is why you were transferred. We're in the fourth month of the hot season, which is utterly unsuitable for mining turquoise, which cannot tolerate these temperatures – it loses its intense blue-green colour. Nevertheless, the pharaoh has ordered me to bring him back the most beautiful stone ever discovered, and we must succeed in doing so. Every day we shall make offerings to Hathor, the queen of this place, and ask her to guide our work. Today you may rest. Tomorrow at dawn you will start work.'

The living quarters were to the east of the temple. The free men, who were paid well for their work, looked uncertainly at

*Its modern name is Serabit el-Khadim; the plateau is about 20 square kilometres.

the criminals who were being imposed on them. And the look of Crooked-Face did not exactly reassure them.

Several dry-stone huts had been turned into cells, whose doors were locked and guarded. Sekari and Iker went into theirs and found food laid out on mats: pancakes stuffed with chickpeas, dates and water.

'I've known worse,' said Sekari, and he threw himself on the food.

Surrounded by guards, the team of convicts was drawn up in front of Horure. Without a word, they followed him into a temple made up of a succession of pillared courtyards, whose offering-tables were covered with offerings. Iker had the impression of changing worlds as he entered this sacred realm where silence and the scent of incense reigned.

Horure led them to a large courtyard flanked with water-tanks and pools of purification. He raised his eyes to the mountain and said, 'You stand before the shrine of Hathor, our protector. May she guide our search and offer us the perfect stone.'

On an offering-table, he placed an alabaster cup containing wine, a necklace, two sistra and a statuette of a she-cat. Then he raised his hands in prayer. 'When the goddess is angry and wants to punish humans, she takes the form of a lion. In the desert, she slaughters wanderers, but when the Distant One returns to the land loved by the gods, she is transformed into a she-cat, gentle and affectionate. She possesses turquoise, the symbol of joy and renewal, capable of triumphing over misfortune and decrepitude. This stone transmits its energy to the children of the Light and causes joy to be born in their hearts. Hathor, it is you who permit the sun to rise and bring our world back to life each morning. May your radiant light enter our hearts.'

Iker experienced each phrase as a revelation. He felt so good in this shrine that the face of the beautiful priestess reappeared. She was there, very close to him, sharing his emotion. But the brief ceremony ended all too quickly, and everyone left the temple.

Horure led the convicts to the foot of a forbidding cliff. 'This place is dangerous,' he said, 'which is why it is reserved for you. When we presented the statue of Min to the mountain, the statue drew back. In other words, the mountain is pregnant but she refuses to give us her fruit. Trying to dig a gallery would offend her, and she would take revenge by killing the miners. Caution suggests we wait until the mountain grants us permission to explore her, but as I told you we're in a hurry.'

'Why can't we dig somewhere else?' asked Sekari.

'Because I am convinced that a unique, unchanging turquoise is hidden here. It is up to you to choose: either you accept the risk, or you'll be sent back to the copper mines. If you succeed, you'll be given your freedom.'

Freedom! The word echoed in Iker's head.

'I refuse,' said Crooked-Face. 'I'd rather go back to my furnaces. If experienced miners won't touch it, the thing is bad.'

The other prisoners agreed.

'I will do it,' said Iker. 'I will try, anyway.'

'You're mad!' protested Sekari. 'Didn't you hear the overseer? The god Min himself drew back.'

'Just give me the necessary tools.'

'Iker, be reasonable. You're heading for your death. You'd never survive on your own.'

'Won't you come with me? Can you really not choose between crouching in a copper mine where your chances of survival are slim, and regaining your freedom quickly?'

Torn, Sekari gazed at the rock face. 'If you look at it like that . . . But you can go first.'

'Very well.'

'Any more volunteers?' asked Horure.

'No,' replied Crooked-Face, who was delighted to be rid of the informer.

Horure went down on one knee and raised his hands to the mountain in a sign of worship. 'The gallery you dig will bear the name of "She who makes the miners prosperous and permits the perfection of Hathor to be seen". May the living stone give a kindly welcome to the shock of the tools. May she know that we are toiling for the Light and not for ourselves.'

He handed the two volunteers picks and hammers made from flint and dolerite.

'Where do we begin?' asked Sekari.

Horure pointed. And the song of the tools shattered the mountain's silence.

20

Sniffer was thoroughly pleased with himself. After scouring the trails of the isthmus of el-Suweis for ten years and robbing countless caravans, he had defeated his main rival without a fight: the man had died stupidly by falling into a ravine. Unable to agree on a successor, his men had chosen to join Sniffer's band, which was now the most fearsome group of sand-travellers in the region. Their attacks would be all the more devastating now, and not a single merchant would escape them.

Sometimes they took everything, sometimes they were content to take part of the goods and make their victims swear not to lodge a complaint, on pain of reprisal. They never failed to rape the women, who also had to submit to the law of silence.

'Caravan in sight,' announced a lookout.

'A rich one?' asked Sniffer greedily.

'It doesn't look like it.'

'Then what is it?

'Twenty or so men.'

'Desert guards?'

'Doesn't look like it. They must have got lost. They're just a rag-tag band of no use to us.'

'We could recruit a few and kill the rest.'

'Let's see.'

The sand-travellers were unwillingly impressed by the

bearing of the tall man walking a few steps ahead of the band. His eyes were as fierce as a wild animal's.

Ashamed of his feelings, Sniffer hailed the tall fellow. 'Who are you, friend?'

'The Herald.'

'And what are you heralding?'

'The fact that Pharaoh's enemies must submit to my will if the tyrant is to be crushed.'

Sniffer stood with his hands on his hips. 'What? And why should anybody help you?'

'Because I am the sole interpreter of the powers. And only I can overcome him.'

'You've lost your mind, friend, but you amuse me.'

'In that case, why is your voice shaking?'

'Your insolence doesn't impress me!'

'If you want to live, submit to the Herald at once.'

Sniffer burst out laughing. 'Enough of this nonsense! I am going to examine you one by one. I'll take on the strongest fellows, and the rest can die in the desert.'

The Herald stretched out his arm. 'One last time, will you submit?'

As Sniffer prepared to strike, the Herald's hand was transformed into a claw and his nose into the beak of a bird of prey.

'It's the falcon-man!' exclaimed one of the sand-travellers. 'He'll slaughter us all!'

He and his fellows flattened themselves in the sand, hands on their heads. By staying absolutely still, they might escape the monster's rage. An icy wind made them shiver.

Eventually, one of them dared to raise his head and look. He saw Sniffer's corpse, its throat cut.

'Does anyone else refuse to obey me?' asked the Herald in a gentle voice.

The sand-travellers prostrated themselves before their new master.

*

'That's it,' said a sweat-covered Sekari, 'the supporting props are in place. Now we stand a slight chance of getting out alive.'

When Iker first went down into the gallery he'd discovered, he hadn't realized that its ceiling was in danger of collapsing. Had it not been for Sekari, the two explorers would have been buried alive.

'We've not done badly so far,' said Sekari. 'We've only been digging for a few days, and we've already found this tunnel at the heart of the rock. It's almost as if it was waiting for us.'

'I think it could do with a few more props.'

'You're right. We'll shore it up better before we go any further.'

Horure was astonished to see the two madmen emerge alive once again.

'A splendid find, sir!' shouted Sekari.

'Turquoises?'

'Not yet, but we've found a gallery which undoubtedly leads to them.'

The news spread rapidly round the domain of Hathor. Crooked-Face and the others had been given menial work to do while they waited to return to the copper mines. Jealousy had been added to their bitterness, because since beginning their dangerous adventure Iker and Sekari no longer mixed with the other convicts, and they had much better food, too.

As the sun was going down, Horure came over to Iker and Sekari and sat down. 'You've both shown great courage,' he said.

'Well, I've almost run out of it,' retorted Sekari. 'Don't you think we've done enough?'

'I must have the most beautiful turquoise in the world. Your work won't be over until you've found it.'

'May I ask you a question?' said Iker.

'Yes.'

'Have you by any chance heard of two sailors called Turtle-Eye and Sharp-Knife, or their ship, *Swift One*?'

'I'm a man of the desert, not the sea. Try to rest now. The day after tomorrow, you go back into the belly of the mountain.'

The caravan halted beside the one river that still contained a little water. Watched by the desert guards, the merchants unloaded their donkeys, which hurried off to drink.

'Another three days,' said the guide, 'and we'll reach the edge of the Delta, where there'll be canals, trees and grass. I'm more than happy to be leaving the desert at last. The journey's seemed very long this time.'

'Count yourself lucky to have come out of it alive,' said the guards' commander. 'The place is getting more and more dangerous.'

'Attacks by sand-travellers, you mean?'

'The last one was a real massacre.'

'Why doesn't Pharaoh take stronger action?'

'It seems he has other concerns. Still, I'm here with ten experienced men.'

'Let's go and fetch the reserve jars. We deserve a good meal.'

Each guide knew the places where, under the magical protection of small stelae and amulets, provisions were hidden and regularly replenished. They served to refresh tired travellers who had underestimated how much food they'd need for their journey.

To their horror, they found the stele broken and the amulets torn apart.

'Who would dare do this?' demanded the officer angrily. 'These barbarians no longer respect anything!'

'And all the food's gone,' said the guide.

'I shall write a report immediately, and it'll cause quite a stir,' promised the officer. 'This time the army will comb the whole region.'

Suddenly they heard a shout of alarm: 'The caravan's being attacked!'

The guide tried to run away, but two sand-travellers caught him and shattered his skull with their clubs. The officer squared up to the enemy, but was soon overwhelmed by weight of numbers.

Surprised not to be killed, he was led before a tall, thin man with red eyes.

'How many years have you been patrolling the desert?' asked the Herald.

'More than ten.'

'Then you know the region very well. If you want to avoid being tortured, tell me which sites Pharaoh thinks are the most important, and describe them in detail.'

'Why?'

'Just answer. Above all, be accurate.'

The officer described the forts, the obligatory caravan halts, the copper and turquoise mines.

'Turquoise,' repeated the Herald in a strange voice. 'Does a god protect it?'

'Yes, Hathor does.'

'Is she always benevolent?'

'Not when she takes the form of a ferocious lioness who roams Nubia and devours rebels. But with turquoise one can appease her.'

'Is the mining area guarded?'

'Always.'

'I don't need you any more, soldier, since you aren't the sort of man who'd betray his country.'

The Herald turned away from the officer, who was immediately executed by Shab the Twisted.

21

Iker felt as though he was suffocating. He coughed and coughed, but doggedly continued to dig out the gallery leading towards the heart of the mountain.

Sekari was exhausted after strengthening the supporting props, so was resting and watching his companion in misfortune. 'It's not leading anywhere, Iker. By playing with chance, we'll end up being crushed by it.'

'The rock's very solid here. I can hardly make any progress at all.'

'And we still haven't found a single turquoise.' Sekari heaved himself up and struck the rock furiously with his pick.

'There, look!' exclaimed Iker. 'You've broken through!'

They saw a glimmer of blue-green.

Sekari carefully trimmed the wick of his lamp so that it wouldn't smoke, and brought it closer. 'Turquoises – they're turquoises!'

Horure's scowl did not bode well. 'These are second-rate stones,' he pronounced. 'Their colour's dull, lifeless. I couldn't possibly take them back to the court.'

'You said yourself that it's the wrong season for mining them,' Iker reminded him.

'You can have one day's rest, and then you'll continue. I know that the queen of turquoises is hiding in this mountain

– I *know* it is – and I want it. And your freedom depends on finding it, don't forget.'

Overcoming their disappointment, after their day's rest Iker and Sekari set to work again.

Iker had enough willpower for two. 'I've got an idea,' he said.

'Oh yes? It's not something mad, by any chance?'

'Suppose we were to dig at night? If you let moonlight into the gallery, the rock-face comes to life, and I'm sure it doesn't breathe in the same way as it does in the daytime.'

'And when are we going to sleep?' asked Sekari.

'Let's try.'

Sekari shrugged.

The moment they entered the mine the atmosphere was indeed very different. The two men had the feeling that they were entering a shrine where mysterious forces were at work. They went slowly and cautiously along the gallery until they reached the far end.

Sekari's lamp went out. 'That was all I needed! I'm going to fetch another one.'

'Wait a minute.'

'But it's pitch dark in here.'

'Not quite.'

'Ah . . . you're right.'

From the rock there emanated a blue glow, intense and yet gentle.

'Perhaps we should get out as fast as possible,' suggested Sekari.

'Give me the small pick.'

With great care, Iker cut away the rock around the glow. A magnificent turquoise appeared, its brilliance dazzling its discoverers.

Iker gazed at it. At the centre of the stone was the face of the beautiful priestess, and she was smiling at him.

*

'Excellent,' acknowledged Horure, 'really excellent. I've never seen a turquoise of such quality.'

'Then . . . are we free?' asked Iker.

'When I give my word, I keep it. You can leave for the Nile Valley with the next caravan.'

'We'll need documents for the authorities.'

'Here they are.'

Iker took the wooden tablet and clutched it to him: it had given him back a future.

'Doesn't finding a stone like that merit some wine?' suggested Sekari.

Horure pretended to think. 'You're asking a lot . . . but the thought did cross my mind.'

Sekari emptied three cups in rapid succession, then drank more slowly, taking enough time to taste his wine at the same time as eating enough for four. 'If only there were some women around here, my happiness would be complete,' he said. 'But I'll soon be spending some happy evenings . . . Have you got a special girl, Iker?'

'I am in search of a woman.'

'Only one? Where did you meet her?'

'First of all beside a canal, under a willow.'

'Ah yes, the goddess who appears to oxherds. That's a charming old legend, but I'm talking about a real woman.'

'She is real.'

'How do you mean, she is real?'

'I met her again.'

'Still under a willow?'

'No, at a festival in the country. And I've just seen her for the third time, at the heart of the turquoise.'

Sekari emptied another cup of wine. 'You've worked very hard, Iker, and you haven't had much sleep. All these emotions have disturbed your mind. A few hours' sleep will set you right again.'

'I don't know her name, but I know she's a priestess.'

'Ah. And is she rather pretty or rather plain?'

'She's the most beautiful woman in the whole world.'

'You sound as if you're really in love! I hope your priestess doesn't belong to the Golden Circle of Abydos.'

'What do you mean?'

'It's an expression we gardeners used of initiates who've withdrawn into a temple.'

'She can't have done, because she was taking part in the festival as a bearer of offerings.'

'That's a hopeful sign. But I hope it wasn't her last appearance before rejoining her colleagues.'

'Why the "Golden Circle", and why Abydos?'

'Now you're asking more than I know. Abydos is the most mysterious place in Egypt, where Osiris comes back to life so that the country may continue to live in harmony, as everyone knows. The rest doesn't concern people like us.'

'Do you think it's possible to enter this Circle?'

'To be frank, I couldn't care less about it. And neither can you, at heart.'

'How can you say that?'

'Because you've got urgent things to do. Aren't you searching for the two sailors who caused all your troubles?'

'Two sailors, a ship, and a false desert guard who tried to murder me,' murmured Iker. 'And then there's the land of Punt.'

'Oh no, don't dive back into legend! Don't you realize that you've become the greatest discoverer of turquoise ever, and that this important fact may perhaps be told to the pharaoh himself?'

'You're forgetting that Horure's the commander here, and he's the one who'll be considered to have found it.'

'Yes, you're probably right there,' conceded Sekari. 'But we're free!'

'Will you help me in my search?'

The gardener looked uncomfortable. 'You know, I'm a

peaceful lad and all I want is a peaceful life, with no problems. Trouble isn't my strong point.'

'I understand. So our paths will separate here.'

After all the wine he'd drunk, Sekari fell into a deep sleep as soon as he stretched out on his mat.

Iker, though, couldn't sleep. He went out of the hut and gazed up at the stars. Why was destiny manipulating him like this? Where was it taking him?

Thinking of the priestess both calmed him and yet caused him pain. If she really was inaccessible, he'd never be happy again. But he mustn't give up hope, because he could now resume his profession and his quest. The discovery of the turquoise was an encouraging sign. By facing danger, by detecting the mountain's secret, Iker had arrived at his goal. If he carried on acting like that, he'd pick up his attackers' trail and would eventually find out why they had chosen him as their victim. And he was convinced that Hathor would guide him towards the woman he loved.

Iker thought he heard a muffled cry, coming from the head of the main access track to the plateau. A guard was always posted there.

He went towards the track, but his instinct told him to keep hidden. As he got nearer, he made out the shapes of several men crouching behind the rocks. They had appeared so quickly and silently that everything appeared normal.

But Iker knew he was right: intruders had killed the guard and were violating the territory of the goddess. His brow suddenly dripping sweat, he tried to make for Horure's house.

Other shapes barred his way. Then a shout shattered the quiet of the night.

'Attack,' roared Shab the Twisted, 'and kill them all!'

22

After killing the plateau's sentries, the attackers poured in like a wave.

Watched calmly by the Herald, who did not even need to raise a hand, Shab the Twisted and the sand-travellers began to massacre both guards and miners. Horure tried to organize some semblance of resistance, but Crooked-Face broke his neck with a rock and yelled to the attackers, 'Strike hard, my friends! I'm with you!'

Distraught, Iker was about to hurl himself into the battle when he was flattened to the ground.

'Play dead,' a voice hissed in his ear. 'They're coming this way.'

Bloody clubs in hand, several sand-travellers passed by, fortunately without paying them any attention.

'We must get away from here as fast as we can,' whispered the voice when they had gone.

Iker wiped the sand out of his eyes. 'Is that you, Sekari?'

'Have I changed that much? Shake yourself!'

'We must fight, we must—'

'Don't be crazy – we'd have no chance.'

Reeling like a drunkard, Iker let Sekari drag him away.

'What's your name?' asked the Herald.

'Crooked-Face.'

'Why did you help us?'

'I was sentenced to life in the copper mines, but then I was transferred here to find the queen of turquoises.'

'Did you succeed?'

'I didn't. But an informant called Iker extracted it from the belly of the mountain.'

'Where is this marvel?'

'Probably in Horure's house. I killed him with my own hands. I enjoyed getting rid of my jailers, and I'm going to inflict the worst of all punishments on them, the one reserved for the most evil criminals: I'm going to burn their bodies.'

The Herald nodded.

While Crooked-Face and Shab the Twisted were lighting pyres, their leader searched Horure's house. It did not take him long to find an alabaster box containing the exquisite turquoise.

While his band were feasting, proud of their first great victory, the Herald held the precious stone up to the moonlight, to charge it with energy. It would thus become a decisive weapon on his road to conquest.

'Who are you really?' Crooked-Face asked him, rather tipsily.

'The man who will enable you to kill as many Egyptians as you like.'

'Then you're a general.'

'I'm much more than that. I am the Herald, who will extend his cult and his new religion over the entire land.'

'And what's in it for me?'

'My disciples shall have glory and wealth.'

'I don't care about glory, but wealth . . . yes, that interests me.'

'Half of the turquoises in the treasury of this mine are yours.'

Crooked-Face almost drooled at the prospect. 'You're a truly fine commander! I haven't the brains for leadership, but for pay like that I'll certainly follow you. But try not to get soft.'

'Have no fear.'

'The only thing that annoys me is not having identified the body of that lad Iker. But the corpses are burning so well that you can't recognize any of them.' Crooked-Face took a deep swallow of wine, and asked, 'Aren't you drinking with us?'

'Someone must keep a clear head.'

Staggering, Crooked-Face found his way by the light of the braziers where the bodies were being burnt and joined the noisy horde of victors.

Neither Sekari nor Iker would have believed they could run for so long. Completely out of breath, they sat down on some flat stones.

'We mustn't stop for long,' warned Sekari. 'Those bandits will try to catch us.'

'Who do you think they are?'

'Probably sand-travellers. Usually they attack caravans.'

'Crooked-Face helped them.'

'That's hardly surprising. He has an evil heart.'

They set off again and walked until they were exhausted. Thirst scorched their throats.

'How can we find water?' asked Iker.

'I've no idea.'

'Let's face the truth: surviving is going to be difficult.'

'I don't like your truth at all.'

'We'd probably be better off if we'd been killed in the fighting.'

'No, we wouldn't – at least we're alive. Rub your amulets together and press them against your throat.'

Iker did so, and his thirst eased.

'My turn now.'

Suffering less, they continued to put distance between themselves and the place of slaughter.

By noon the sand was so hot that it burnt their feet. They dug a deep hole and took shelter in it, their kilts over their heads as protection from the sun. When the temperature dropped, they set off again. By now their thirst was so intense that even the amulets could no longer ease it.

In front of them stood a mountain glimmering gold.

'We won't have the strength to get over it,' said Sekari.

'It's moving.'

'What did you say?'

'The mountain's moving,' said Iker.

'It's a mirage, just a mirage.'

'No it isn't. It's moving towards us.'

Watching closely, Sekari had to admit that his companion was right. 'We're going mad, my poor friend, that's what it is.'

Rocks were coming away from the summit, rolling down the face and falling on to the ground with a crash.

'It's an earthquake!' cried Sekari, not knowing which way to run.

'Look at the colour of the mountain,' urged Iker calmly.

As the rocks shattered, a blue-green tint appeared.

'It's Hathor,' breathed Iker. 'She's protecting us. We must stay here and worship her.'

Although unconvinced, Sekari nevertheless knelt down and called upon the sky-goddess. Inches from his left foot, a fissure opened. 'This place really isn't safe,' he said.

'Gaze upon the work of the goddess.'

The entire mountain had become turquoise, and the worrying noises were quietening down. As the earth stopped moaning, Sekari glanced into the fissure. And what he saw there stunned him.

'It looks like . . . water!' He plunged in his arm and it came out wet. 'It is, Iker, it's water! We're saved!'

'We must drink slowly.'

For the first time in his life, Sekari found that water tasted as delicious as wine.

The two sprinkled themselves with it, washed and slaked their thirst.

'But we haven't got a water-skin,' lamented Sekari. 'If we leave this source, we'll be finished. What's more, I'm getting really hungry.'

'Hathor is protecting us,' Iker reminded him. 'Let's spend the night here and wait for another sign.'

'If you benefit from the favours of any more goddesses, let me know straight away, won't you?'

'Like you, I'm just a starving man lost in the desert. But this world is much more mysterious than it seems. If we can read certain messages, we may find a way out.'

'Well, then, let's go to sleep.'

Sekari was dreaming of an enormous joint of beef grilled with fine herbs, and of a jar of cool beer, when Iker shook him awake.

'Wha . . . ? What's happening? Has the mountain moved again?'

'The sun's just risen. Let's get started. We must walk until it gets too hot.'

'Walk? I'm not leaving this water.'

'We mustn't keep our guide waiting.'

The gardener leapt up and looked around. 'I can't see anyone.'

'Up there, in the sky.'

A falcon was flying in broad circles above their heads.

'Are you poking fun at me, Iker?'

'My old master taught me that the name Hathor means "Dwelling of Horus",* and the incarnation of Horus is precisely this falcon, which the goddess has sent to guide us.'

*Hathor is a transcription of the Egyptian *Hut-Hor*. *Hut* means 'dwelling', 'domain' or 'temple'.

Sekari shook his head sadly. 'The desert has addled your mind.'

'Come on, let's follow it.'

'But what about the water?'

'It'll show us other sources.'

'I'd rather stay here.'

'Would you also rather see the sand-travellers arrive?'

That argument won the day. Still protesting, Sekari followed Iker.

'Your falcon isn't bothering with us any more,' he pointed out, 'just with its prey. Look, it's flying off and abandoning us.'

But the falcon came back. Sometimes it flew ahead, sometimes it wheeled above the men it was protecting.

After several hours of walking, they felt the burning of thirst again.

'The falcon's landing,' cried Sekari. He turned his head to watch it and bumped into something hard.

'And you have just found a little stele. Shall we dig?'

At the foot of the modest monument were two jars containing dried fruit. A little further off was a spring of clear water.

'It's not what you'd call a feast,' commented Sekari, 'but it'll certainly do.'

23

The two travellers had ceased to count the days. They followed the falcon, which, after guiding them towards the east, headed in a southerly direction. Each time the bird landed, Iker and Sekari found water or food or both. And they had not encountered a single sand-traveller.

Gradually the desert became less barren, its aridity relieved by thorn bushes and dwarf tamarisks.

With a powerful flap of its wings, the falcon rose towards the sun and disappeared in the dazzling light of noon.

'Our guide's leaving us,' said Sekari in alarm.

'Look over there: another one's taking its place.'

At the top of a hill stood a beautiful white gazelle with lyre-shaped horns.

Sekari smiled. 'A storyteller told me that the gazelle's the animal of Isis and that it enables lost travellers to find their way again,' he said. The gazelle bounded off. 'But unfortunately it was only a story.'

'Don't be so sure,' objected Iker.

'Didn't you see it run off?'

'Let's follow its tracks. It may be waiting for us further on.'

Iker was right. The beautiful creature amused itself by disappearing and reappearing, executing prodigious leaps and mad runs, without making the two humans it was protecting worry for too long.

The landscape was changing, the desert receding, vegetation becoming more abundant.

'If my instinct's right,' said Sekari, 'we're approaching the plateaux that overlook the Nile Valley. How delightful these humps and hollows are – the plants here spring up at the first drop of rain. Soon we'll see balanites and acacias. Do you realize what we've done? We've survived the desert!'

'Thanks to Hathor, the falcon and the gazelle,' Iker reminded him.

'I'm going back to my gardens. What about you? Why don't you forget the past?'

'Not only will I not forget it, but I have a new task: tracking down the queen of turquoises. That stone enabled me to see the woman I love. I'm certain it will help me see her again.'

'The sand-travellers will have stolen it. And if, by bad luck, you do track them down they'll kill you. Come on, Iker! There are thousands of pretty women!'

The scribe halted in his tracks, crouched down and made Sekari do the same. 'There are men coming,' he said, 'about twenty of them, with bows and dogs . . . They're coming towards us.'

'They're probably just hunters.'

Still unaware of the danger, the gazelle was grazing nearby. Iker stood up and waved his arms wildly. 'Run! Run away – quickly!'

Scarcely had the animal bounded away when barking rang out. An arrow whistled past Iker's ear, and a man shouted, 'Don't move or I'll kill you.'

The archer had taken aim; he was not joking. He was soon joined by his colleagues and a rather edgy pack of hounds.

Sekari had not even tried to run. 'We're honest men,' he declared.

'More likely sand-travellers hunting our game,' snapped

an unshaven officer whose chest was covered with scars, reminders of an uncooperative animal. 'In the province of the Oryx,* that offence carries a severe punishment. You attacked us so we were obliged to shoot – it was self-defence. But I'll allow you one small chance: run as fast as you can. We might miss.'

'We won't run,' said Iker. 'We've recently escaped from murderers who destroyed the domain of the turquoise, and we did not think we were going to be struck down by even crueller barbarians.'

Some of the hunters looked embarrassed.

'We aren't barbarians,' protested one of them. 'We're soldiers of the desert guard in the service of the province's governor, Khnum-Hotep. Our job is to protect the caravans and bring him back game. Who are you?'

'I am, Iker, an apprentice scribe, and my companion is Sekari, a gardener.'

'Rubbish!' cut in the officer. 'You're spies and thieves. If you don't run for it, I'll cut your throats here and now.'

'Your men would denounce your crime.'

The officer unsheathed his dagger, but a soldier blocked his arm and said, 'Sir, you shouldn't do that – it's for the governor to decide. We should simply take these two suspects to him.'

When the four bearers set down Khnum-Hotep's travelling-chair with its high, sloping back, they sighed with relief. Fat, strong and a big eater, the governor of the wealthy province of the Oryx was a considerable weight. As he had three richly decorated travelling-chairs, and travelled around a great deal, being one of his bearers was no sinecure.

As soon as he set foot on the ground, his three hunting-

*The sixteenth province of Upper Egypt; its best-known archaeological site is Beni Hasan.

dogs, a very lively male and two plump females, rushed towards him.

'It's more than a whole morning since we saw each other, my loves!' said Khnum-Hotep.

The male stood up and put his forepaws on his master's shoulders. The bitches yapped jealously. Long caresses reassured them.

'Have they been fed properly?' Khnum-Hotep asked his steward.

'Oh yes, my lord.'

'You aren't lying, I hope?'

'Oh no, my lord. What's more, they didn't leave a scrap.'

'This evening they shall have hare in sauce, like me. Not to spoil one's dogs is to insult the gods.'

At the prospect of this feast, the three dogs licked their lips; they knew the words 'hare in sauce' very well indeed. Then they followed their master into the luxurious palace of his capital, Menat-Khufu, 'the Wet-nurse of Khufu', so named because it was the birthplace of Pharaoh Khufu, builder of the largest pyramid on the Giza plateau.

After inspecting one of the rich agricultural estates where the peasants worked hard but benefited from excellent returns, Khnum-Hotep liked to sit down in his favourite high-backed chair. It was made up of two large wooden boards joined at the top and fixed into the seat, and could support his weight without creaking. Thanks to his managerial abilities, his subjects had a remarkably comfortable life. And there was no question of a pharaoh, even one called Senusret, meddling in his affairs. If the king should ever try a forcible takeover, he would encounter fierce opposition.

A servant brought a wide-mouthed basin, another a copper jug with an elongated spout. The second servant poured water over Khnum-Hotep's hands; his master washed them at length three times a day, using a vegetable soap.

Then he was handed his favourite ointment, based on

purified fat cooked in flavoured wine. It gave off a sweet odour which repelled insects.

Without waiting for the order, his cup-bearer presented him with a splendid cup clad in gold leaf, its decoration depicting lotus-petals. It contained the master's favourite brew, a clever mixture of three mature wines, which revived his energy.

'I am sorry to trouble you, my lord, but the commander of one of the desert patrols would like to see you as soon as possible.'

'Send him in.'

The officer bowed very low. 'I have arrested two dangerous men, sir. They were hunting on your lands and attacked us. If I hadn't intervened, my men would have killed them. How would you like me to get rid of them?'

'Are they sand-travellers?'

'Difficult to say, I—'

'For a soldier of your experience, that's a very vague judgment. Bring them to me.'

'That's not necessary. They—'

'I decide what is or isn't necessary.'

Hands tied behind their backs, Iker and Sekari were brought before the governor.

'I give bread to the hungry,' said that imposing man, 'water to the thirsty, clothing to the naked, a boat to him who has none, but I punish criminals severely.'

'My lord,' said Iker earnestly, 'we aren't criminals, we're victims.'

'That is not the opinion of the officer who questioned you.'

'I chased away a gazelle because it was the messenger of the goddess who saved our lives.'

'This scoundrel's either a madman or a liar!' exclaimed the commander.

'Untie the prisoners and withdraw,' ordered Khnum-Hotep.

'My lord, your safety—'

'I shall attend to it myself.'

Sekari was frightened almost out of his wits, but Iker stayed calm.

'Now, my lads, the truth. You are on my territory and I want to know everything.'

'We were employed in the turquoise mines of the goddess Hathor,' said Iker.

'As miners or prisoners?'

'As prisoners transferred from the copper mines.'

'Then you are indeed criminals!'

'I was sentenced to a year's hard labour because I exposed a dishonest tax-collector.'

'And what about you?' Khnum-Hotep asked Sekari.

'Me . . . me too, my lord,' stammered the gardener.

'You'd be foolish to take me lightly.'

'My friend and I were ordered to explore the mountain and to discover the queen of turquoises,' Iker went on calmly. 'As we did indeed find it, we were freed.'

'And you have proof of what you are saying, of course?'

'Here it is, my lord.'

Iker took from his kilt the wooden tablets, signed by Horure, which made him and Sekari free men, washed clean of their offences.

Khnum-Hotep read it carefully, bit it, tried to scratch it. 'It seems authentic.' He had heard of Horure, who was loyal to Senusret and a renowned desert miner. Evidently this proud, determined young man was telling the truth.

'What happened to the queen of turquoises?'

'The domain of the goddess was attacked by a gang of armed men, who were helped by a prisoner called Crooked-Face – he murdered Horure. All the guards and miners were slaughtered, and their corpses burnt. We're the only survivors.'

'Iker wanted to fight, my lord,' put in Sekari, 'but it would have been suicidal, so we ran away.'

'And you crossed the desert without food or water?'

Iker described the successive miracles that had enabled them to survive. His honesty was so evident that Khnum-Hotep did not doubt his tale in the least, especially since the gods often intervened in the desert.

For the first time the sand-travellers had actually dared to attack the turquoise mines, even though they were under Pharaoh's protection. But it was not up to Khnum-Hotep to alert Senusret. Others would eventually warn him that his authority had been severely dented, and he would be busy with more pressing tasks than confronting the dignitaries who were resisting the extension of his power.

'What can the two of you do?'

'I'm a gardener,' replied Sekari.

'And I'm an apprentice scribe.'

'My province is rich because people here work hard,' said Khnum-Hotep. 'An extra gardener might be useful, but I don't need any more scribes.'

24

'On the other hand,' Khnum-Hotep went on, 'I do need more soldiers so that my little army can resist any attacks. As you're young and healthy, that's the perfect answer for you.'

'But I want to be a scribe, my lord, not a soldier,' protested Iker.

'Listen to me carefully, young man. The gods have entrusted me with a great undertaking: to make this province the most prosperous in the land. Here, widows lack nothing, young girls are respected, everyone has enough to eat, no one begs. The weak are shown no less favour than the strong, and there are no conflicts between the rich and the poor. Why? Because I am the pillar of this land, whatever the difficulties may be. When the annual floods were inadequate, I myself compensated the farmers and cancelled tax arrears. The higher taxes are, the less initiative people show. Neither fraudsters nor corrupt officials have any right of citizenship in my territory. But nothing is more fragile than this happiness. A danger is arising and its name is Senusret: sooner or later, he will try to seize my province. You are either with me or against me. If you want to benefit from my welcome, become one of my soldiers. You won't regret what you learn.'

Khnum-Hotep had surprised himself by deploying so many arguments to persuade the young stranger. Usually he confined himself to giving orders, and he brooked no contradiction.

'I shall trust you, my lord.'

Once again, Medes had shown himself to be a generous donor. The High Priest of the Temple of Ptah had thanked him warmly, not suspecting that the offering came from stolen food supplies. But Medes still came up against the sealed gateway to the covered temple, and he had to accept that he would never succeed in bribing those who held the key. How could he discover the secret of the shrines?

He put off this concern until later, for the capital was seething with interesting rumours. Senusret had apparently decided to undertake a virtual reconquest of the provinces, beginning with the Cobra province, over which old Wakha ruled. Naturally he had no chance of succeeding, but nevertheless his decision must not be taken lightly, for Senusret had a strong character and would not be daunted by the obstacles he would face.

Medes's wealth depended to a large extent on his excellent relations with the provincial governors, whom he informed, via intermediaries, about what was happening at court. With the exception of his fellow criminal, Gergu, no one knew the real Medes or realized that, deep in the shadows, he was constantly stirring up trouble.

But many of the rumours were contradictory, and Medes had for some time been having the greatest difficulty finding which ones were true. It seemed clear that Senusret had re-established his sway over a good many of the courtiers and was maintaining this confusion himself, so as to move more easily along his chosen path.

If the king succeeded in unleashing a real whirlwind, Medes would be borne away by it. There was only one way to prevent that disaster: kill its initiator.

But the murder of a king could not be accomplished on the

spur of the moment, especially when he was protected by an officer as efficient as Sobek-Khu, who distrusted everybody, even and especially those close to the king. Medes could not afford even the smallest lapse in caution.

Relying on chance was stupid. He would have to draw up a plan which would enable him to strike with speed and absolute accuracy.

The instructor struck Iker's legs, and he fell heavily on to his back.

'You're not paying attention, lad. Get back up and try to hit me in the belly.'

The attempt ended in utter failure, and the young man found himself on the ground again – with more bruises.

'I'm going to have my work cut out here,' said the instructor. 'But with goodwill, you'll eventually be able to fight.'

Iker gritted his teeth and launched himself into the attack again, knowing that it would take weeks, even months, before he could equal the other young recruits, who all laughed at him.

First, he must not complain about the destiny that had brought him here, and he must learn as much as possible from his situation. Next, he must constantly watch the most battle-hardened soldiers and imitate them.

Instead of weakening him, the fact that he had neither friend nor ally increased his energy tenfold. Unable to rely on anyone but himself, Iker drew from his solitude the strength to concentrate on this new apprenticeship and on it alone. In unarmed combat, he learnt many holds and seldom made the same mistake twice. He soon realized that speed was more important than strength, and that it was possible to turn an attacker's own violence against him.

The instructor was no more talkative than Iker. Sparing in his explanations and comments, he made him repeat a movement a hundred times, even when he was tired or in pain. And, as his pupil never uttered the smallest protest, he treated him even more harshly than the others.

'Tomorrow,' he announced, 'some of you will be eliminated from the basic course. To find out who will go and who will stay, you will now fight unarmed. Only those with two victories will be kept on.'

Iker's opponent was much the taller and stronger of the pair. 'Come on, little lad,' he jeered. 'Let me give you a crushing hug!'

Iker went down on one knee.

'So you're giving up without even fighting, are you? It doesn't surprise me. Only the lads from our province make good warriors.'

'You must be the exception that proves the rule.'

'What did you dare say?'

The fellow rushed forward, fists clenched. Iker shifted position, stuck out a leg to bring him down, knocked him over backwards and jammed his right arm across his throat. When the loser struck the ground with his left hand, the instructor ordered Iker to loosen his grip.

The second opponent was less stupid. He attacked unexpectedly and succeeded in getting his arm under Iker's thigh in an attempt to throw him. But the young man held firm, freed himself, slipped behind the fighter with unexpected speed and seized him by the ankles. The loser collapsed on to his face, while the victor flattened him to the ground and half strangled him.

The instructor nodded approvingly. 'Two victories. Good. Go and get something to eat and drink.'

Some fifty young soldiers started. Although the instructor had said it was an endurance race, some set off too fast, wanting to outshine their comrades. Iker began at the back, but he had learnt from the experience acquired during his march through the desert. Without forcing the pace, he overtook his competitors one by one, surprising himself with his own stamina.

The next day, the ordeal began again – and was still more demanding.

'The best of you must cover, in eight hours, a distance only a little less than that from here to Asyut,' announced the instructor.* 'Most messages are carried by boat, but military messengers sometimes have to travel by land, so I want well-prepared men.'

As he ran, Iker thought constantly of the beautiful face he had seen in the queen of turquoises. He drew confidence from that remarkable sign. He would find her again; and those who had condemned him to death.

Suddenly he spotted fragments of razor-sharp flint on the track, and instinctively threw himself to one side, rolling down a slope and slamming into the trunk of a tamarisk. Although dazed from his fall, he had avoided the worst, for deep cuts in his feet would have put him out of action for a long time.

After his head had cleared, Iker gradually made up the distance that separated him from the leader, a soldier's son who loathed him and was always jeering at him in front of the other recruits.

As Iker was overtaking, the other man tried to unbalance him with a jab of the elbow.

Iker dodged it and called back over his shoulder, 'I won't tell the instructor about the flints. We'll settle this between us at the barracks.'

*

* The race distance was about 100km. On modern tracks, designed for competition, athletes can cover this distance in a little more than six hours. The calculation made for ancient times takes account of the difficulties of the terrain and observations made in Kenya, for example.

'The Nubians are the best at fighting with staffs,' the instructor told the recruits. 'One of them taught me the methods I'm passing on to you. You're going to put them into practice in a fight, and you will not hold back. I need two volunteers.'

'Me, sir,' said Iker, certain the soldier's son would also volunteer.

He was right: his rival jumped at the opportunity.

The two were about the same size and strength but, as usual, Iker was banking on his speed. He allowed his furious opponent to think he was scared of attacks, and made him wear himself out in a series of ineffective lunges and blows that missed.

With his light, rigid staff, Iker struck only once, right in the middle of the man's forehead. The soldier's son fell in a heap.

The instructor examined him. 'When he wakes up, he'll have a terrible headache.'

'I could have hit harder,' said Iker.

'You've changed, lad – I hardly recognize you any more.'

'I hate cowards.'

The instructor gave him a sidelong look. 'Anything to add to that?'

'The matter has been settled.'

'Good. I'm not interested in what goes on between soldiers, provided they're disciplined, skilful and brave. As for you, you've yet to to learn how to jump.'

At first, the rope stretched between two poles was not very high. But it was raised so much that it seemed impossible to get over. And it required as much skill as willpower to tame it and not balk at the obstacle. Iker proved the best at this game, too.

While he was jumping, a pretty brown-haired woman, aged around forty, appeared on the training-ground and went over to the instructor.

'Lady Techat,' he said, bowing. 'What good things have you brought us?'

'Some cheese and vegetables. Tell me, what is that young man's name?'

'Iker.'

'Is he from our region?'

'No, but he's an excellent recruit. I'm certain I shall make an officer of him.'

The lady Techat, who was a businesswoman and treasurer of the province, smiled enigmatically. As she saw it, Iker deserved better than that.

25

When the first stone of Senusret's shrine was laid, after the foundation ritual, which was conducted by the king himself, one branch of the acacia tree grew green again.

Unfortunately, no other branches followed suit but hope was nevertheless reborn. The path had been set out: to build a new temple and a new house of eternity, in order to fight the darkness that threatened to invade the domain of Osiris.

Senusret had checked the quality of the materials and had spoken with each of the craftsmen. The temple and tomb must be completed as quickly as possible, it was true, but not to the detriment of the work's power.

And as soon as the site was established, the new team of priests appointed by the Bearer of the Golden Palette also set to work.

The Shaven-headed One kept the sacred archives of the House of Life, which no one could enter without his agreement. The one charged with watching over the one-ness of the great body of Osiris was equally vigilant and several times a day checked the seals placed on the door of the divine tomb. As for the priest who saw the secrets, he celebrated the daily rites in the name of Pharaoh, together with the Bearer of the Golden Palette. Thanks to the magic of the Word, the link with the Invisible was maintained. By venerating the ancestors and the beings of Light, the Servant of the *Ka* contributed effectively to strengthening it; and the priest who each day poured the libation of fresh water onto the offering-tables activated the subtle substances hidden in matter, so that the divinities might feed upon them and protect Abydos.

All were fully aware of the importance of their tasks. They, the permanent priests, organized the work of the temporary ones, who had been questioned at length by the forces of order, and whose answers had been meticulously checked. For even the smallest fault, a temporary priest would be expelled from the domain of Osiris: the gravity of the situation left no room for laxity.

The same thoroughness was applied to the seven priestess-musicians, who were of very diverse origins and included both a senior figure from the court and a peasant's daughter. One of them was so beautiful and so serene that even the old Bearer of the Golden Palette was not impervious to her charm. Any man would wish to be the father of a young woman like her, radiantly lovely and with eyes full of joy and hope. There could be no doubt that she would one day be initiated into the great Mysteries and would no longer have to carry out the office of bearer of offerings at festivals celebrated in the outside world. But to attain the status of a permanent priest or priestess, especially at Abydos, one must know all the steps of the ascent and go through all the stages leading to the covered temple. Such had been the rule since the beginning, and so it would remain.

Entirely devoted to his office, cheered by the work the pharaoh had entrusted to him, and determined to fight against the darkness to his last breath, the old priest failed to detect an unexpected danger.

One of the permanent priests, a tall, thin beanpole of a man with an ugly face and a prominent nose, was dissatisfied with his life. To all outward appearances he was devoted to spirituality, an illusion which had deceived even him until he discovered his true nature, which was as ice-cold as a winter wind. He had a taste for power: not the power of a king, which was constrained by outside events and a thousand and one other things, but secret power, exercised in the shadows.

As the years passed, he had realized the full importance of Abydos and the Mysteries of Osiris. The very survival of the pharaohs depended on them. This was the realm over which he must rule, for it housed the secrets of life and death.

Educated at a school for mathematicians, he had expected to become High Priest when the present incumbent died or retired. However, the arrival of Senusret and the reorganization of the priests had brought his plans to nothing. The crowning disappointment was that the Bearer of the Golden Palette had appointed him to an office he considered beneath him, far below the one he had hoped for. True, he belonged to the upper ranks of the priesthood, but he wanted more.

He blamed that accursed Senusret for his disappointment, and his resentment grew more bitter by the day. But how could he get rid of the king and obtain what was rightfully due to him?

For the Herald's band, which had grown to more than two hundred men, crossing the marshes had been particularly taxing, because of the humid heat and the incessant attacks by insects. Two men had died of snake-bite, and another had been killed by a crocodile. But nothing lessened the determination of their leader, who never hesitated over which direction to take.

They had to enter a half-flooded forest of reeds and wade through mud. It was hard going, but it meant they ran no risk of encountering Senusret's soldiers, and every evening they ate their fill of grilled fresh fish.

Shab the Twisted and Crooked-Face wanted to loot the few fishing-villages they passed, but the Herald forbade it.

'It wouldn't take long,' protested Crooked-Face.

'The pickings would be worthless, and we must leave no trace of our march. The attack on Hathor's domain was only a way of finding our feet. Soon we shall strike harder.'

'May we know where we're going?'

'Beyond the King's Walls. That's why we must be so careful and venture into areas reputed to be virtually impassable.'

'Surely you aren't planning to attack the Egyptian forts, my lord?'

Everyone had heard about the long line of defences built by the first Senusret to strengthen the north-eastern border of the country and block any attempt at invasion. Linked to each other by visual signals, the numerous forts, guard-posts and checkpoints housed archers authorized to fire on anyone who tried to force a way through.

'It's still too soon,' agreed the Herald, 'but our time will come. The King's Walls make Egypt feel secure, but we shall prove that that feeling is illusory.'

'All the same,' objected Shab, 'they're manned by trained soldiers and—'

'Just go on trusting me, and all will be well. Our first objective is to get across the border without being spotted. The next is to make contact with our new allies.'

'Who are they, my lord?'

'The Asians and sand-travellers who live in squalid conditions in Canaan and are constantly persecuted and humiliated by the Egyptian government. They dream of rebellion but fear it would end in bloody repression. All they need is a leader – that is to say, myself, the Herald.'

Shab was fascinated. And Crooked-Face, though he thought his leader was crazy, believed he could organize a series of raids which would yield enough loot to make his followers rich. It remained, however, for them to get past the King's Walls without being captured, and that was something Crooked-Face believed impossible.

He was wrong.

Showing no sign of impatience, the Herald sent out scouts to find the way through that was least well guarded. That done, he spent several days observing the behaviour of the Egyptian soldiers and trade-post officials.

In the middle of a moonless night, he awoke his men and ordered them to follow him. In absolute silence, they slipped through behind one of the forts, unseen by the soldiers on guard.

'The Herald really is a great man,' admitted Crooked-Face.

'When you have the good luck to find someone like him,' agreed Shab, 'you should stay with him.'

'And he isn't too greedy when it comes to looting.'

'He isn't interested in that. But I am. Do you agree that the two of us should take the lion's share, as we're the Herald's main assistants, and the rest of the men can divide up what's left?'

'That suits me,' said Crooked-Face. 'If anyone complains, I'll break his back – nothing like it for setting an example. But tell me, what is it that our leader wants?'

'His obsession is the rule of absolute and definitive truth, whose sole repository he is and which must be imposed on all of humanity. As he's often told us, either you submit or you die. His main enemy is the pharaoh, who utterly rejects this teaching.'

'You're strangely learned, Twisted One.'

'I'm just repeating what I've heard the Herald say.'

'Well, I don't give a curse for it! The important thing is that he's a good warlord and that he imposes his new faith by blood and the sword. The more Egyptians we kill, the richer we'll be.'

When the Herald encountered the first Asian herdsmen, he introduced himself as a fierce opponent of Senusret and soon gained the attention of the tribal chiefs. He accepted the obligatory game of long debates that came to nothing, but got what he wanted: to talk with their secret leader. He was a blind, white-bearded old sand-traveller who hated Egypt. He orgainzed attacks against poorly protected caravans, and had executed any Canaanite suspected of being an enemy informant.

As soon as the Herald entered the austere room where the old man stayed, confined to his armchair, the sand-traveller smiled ecstatically.

'So you're here at last! I've hoped for you for so long. I can inflict no more than a bee-sting, but you, you will unleash thunder and carnage! You must put an end to the Rule of Ma'at and to the reign of her son, the pharaoh.'

'What do you advise?'

'A head-to-head battle would be lost before it began. Take with you a few of my most loyal men who are ready to give their lives for our cause, and sow terror on Egyptian soil. Attack in such a way as to kill as many people as possible and spread panic among the population. Senusret will be held responsible, and his throne will crumble.'

'I am the Herald and I demand the absolute obedience of the fighters you place at my disposal.'

'You have it. But you will have to train many more. Let me touch your hands.'

The Herald held them out.

'It is strange . . . I could swear they were a falcon's talons. You are just as I dreamt you would be: fierce, merciless, indestructible.'

'If you had had the means, where would you have begun your conquest?'

'At Sichem* – no question about it – because the garrison there is only small. The population will be easy to inflame and the victory will be spectacular.'

*Present-day Napluse.

'Then Sichem it shall be.'

'Call my servants and tell them to carry me to the threshold of my house. Have all the supporters of armed struggle gather there at once.'

With astonishing energy and vehemence for a man of his age, the sand-traveller preached total war against Egypt. He presented the Herald to the people both as his successor and as the only leader capable of leading his supporters to victory. Then, in a final paroxysm of hatred, he collapsed and died.

26

The little town of Sichem was dozing in the sunshine, and the soldiers were going unhurriedly about their daily routine, of which training exercises were only a tiny part. After ten years in this remote corner of the kingdom, the garrison commander no longer tried to stop the local people's incessant smuggling. As to other matters, the heads of the leading local families reached agreement on most issues among themselves. People stole from each other, murdered each other now and then, settled scores by stabbing each other in the back, but without disturbing public order. On this point, the commander was adamant: agreeing not to know anything, he did not want to see anything, either.

He had also given up trying to levy the correct taxes. The Canaanites told such ingenious lies that he could not distinguish truth from falsehood, and he did not have enough men to check. So he contented himself with taking a minimum tax on the harvests people were willing to show him. Each year it was the same charade: his subjects complained of the heat, the cold, the insects, the wind, the drought, the rain and a hundred other calamities that had reduced them to poverty. The commander did not even listen to all this any more, because it was so boring that it would have sent the most hardened insomniac to sleep.

Every single day, he prayed to Min, to whom a shrine had

been built north of the barracks, begging the god to let him return to Egypt as soon as possible. He longed to see his native village in the Delta again, to have an afternoon snooze in the palm-grove that grew beside the canal where people bathed in the hot season, and to be able to take care of his old mother, whom he had not seen for far too long.

He had written many times to Memphis asking for a transfer, but the military authorities seemed to have forgotten him. Resignedly accepting his misfortune, the commander had made for himself a peaceful life in which strong beer, often of less than the best quality, played a major part.

He was sitting idly in his office, enjoying a cup of cool beer, when his second-in-command came in.

'Sir, a caravan has arrived from the North.'

'Anything of interest?'

'I haven't carried out the inspection yet.'

'Forget it.'

'But the settlement—'

'The Canaanites will do the work for us. They have a good understanding with the Syrian caravan-owners.'

'But, sir, they'll falsify the delivery documents, lie about the quantity of produce and—'

'As usual,' the commander said wearily. 'But never mind that. What's this I hear about you being infatuated with a local girl?'

'We're seeing each other, it's true.'

'Is she pretty?'

'Yes, and very gifted.'

'Well, don't marry her. The girls here obey their tribes rather than their husbands, and always end up wrecking even good men.'

'There's something else, sir. One of our lookouts tells me some trouble has started at the southern entrance to the town.'

The commander was suddenly wide awake. 'Are you serious?'

'I haven't checked that yet, either.'

'Then do it immediately. A contract is a contract. If the Canaanites have forgotten that, I shall remind them.'

The officer saluted and went out.

Two hours later, he had still not returned, and the commander was having bad premonitions. He ordered the garrison to take up arms and follow him. From time to time, a show of force had its uses, and if the natives had caused his officer any trouble they were going to find out who really wielded authority in Sichem.

More than three hundred men were gathered in a compact mass at the southern entrance. The commander was surprised to see that most of them were unknown to him.

He could certainly not confront so many men with his small detachment, particularly as the soldiers, wholly unprepared for a fight, were already quaking with fear.

'Sir,' suggested one of them, 'we might do better to turn back.'

'We embody law and order in Sichem, and no gang of strangers is going to endanger that.'

A young woman came forward out of the crowd. 'Would you like to know where your second-in-command is, Commander?'

'Who are you?'

'The woman he dishonoured and sullied. He thought I'd have to stay silent for ever, but neither he nor you foresaw the arrival of the Herald. Thanks to him, the Canaanites will destroy Egypt.'

'Free my officer immediately!'

The young woman smiled fiercely. 'As you wish, Commander.'

Crooked-Face threw three sacks at the Egyptian officer's feet. 'This is what's left of that torturer.'

With unsteady hands, the commander opened the sacks.

The first contained his officer's head, the second his hands, the third his penis.

The crowd parted to make way for a tall man with a neat beard and strange red eyes. 'Lay down your arms and order your men to obey me,' he said in a clear voice.

'Who the devil do you think you are?'

'I am the Herald, and you, like all the other inhabitants of Sichem, must submit to me.'

'On the contrary, you must obey the legal representative of Egypt's authority. If you instigated this crime, you'll be executed along with its perpetrators.'

'You are being unreasonable, Commander. If I tell my men to attack, your puny force won't hold out for long.'

'Follow me this instant. Otherwise—'

'I am offering you one last chance, Egyptian. Either you obey me, or you die.'

'Seize this rebel,' the commander ordered his men.

The Herald's followers rushed to the attack. Crooked-Face stabbed the commander in the chest, then he was finished off by Shab the Twisted, who in a frenzy trampled on his face. Not one of the Egyptian soldiers outran their pursuers.

The people of Sichem cheered their new master, who at once began converting them to his new religion. As he advocated overthrowing the pharaoh and extending the Canaanites' territory, they enthusiastically adopted the new beliefs.

With shouts of joy, the barracks and the Temple of Min were razed to the ground. In future, no temple would be erected to the glory of a deity, and no deity would be depicted in any form or material whatsoever. Only the words of the Herald would be engraved everywhere, so that they would enter everyone's mind by constant repetition.

The victor and his men took possession of the mayor's house, the mayor having been stoned to death for collaborating with the Egyptians.

'I want half the land,' said Crooked-Face.

'Agreed, but that isn't very much,' said the Herald, leaving Crooked-Face flabbergasted. 'After all your suffering in the copper mines, don't you think you deserve more?'

'If you look at it like that . . . What do you suggest?'

'We must train young fighters who are ready to die for our cause while inflicting deep wounds on Egypt. Would you like to take charge of the training?'

'As my name is Crooked-Face, I'd like it very much indeed. But there'll be no play-acting – even in training, I shan't hold back.'

'That's exactly how I intend it to be. Only the most battle-hardened few will be sent off on missions. Together with Shab, we shall prepare the men who are to be sent out, and every morning I shall explain to all my followers the reasons for our struggle.'

Shab the Twisted was more and more proud of being so closely associated with such a conquest. The Herald's simple words overwhelmed him and made him even more committed to his leader than before.

Here, at Sichem, the great adventure was taking shape.

27

The court at Memphis was in turmoil. There were persistent rumours that Senusret, who had returned to the capital, was soon to summon the senior dignitaries who made up the King's House, the pharaoh's symbolic body, sometimes compared to rays of sunlight; its members were sworn to secrecy regarding the deliberations of this inner council, in which the country's future was worked out. Their office could not be reduced to that of ordinary ministers; their role consisted of passing on and bringing to life Pharaoh's decrees, as an earthly expression of the creative Light.

In this realm as in many others, Senusret was introducing profound reform. He was about to reduce the numbers belonging to the King's House, and everyone was wondering, with mingled worry and hope, if he would be one of the fortunate ones chosen. A few old courtiers had sharpened the ambitions of younger men by stressing the enormous responsibility that those selected must bear.

Medes stamped about in impatience as he awaited word of who had been chosen. Would he keep his position? Would he be transferred or, worse still, exiled to some provincial town? He was sure he had made no mistakes and so had given the king no grounds for excluding him. But did Senusret fully appreciate his talents?

When he was told that two of Sobek the Protector's men

were asking to see him, Medes felt faint. What clue could possibly have set that accursed guard-dog on the trail? Gergu . . . Gergu must have said too much. But that miserable rat would not survive his mistake, for Medes would accuse him of a thousand crimes.

'We are to escort you to the palace,' said one of the soldiers.

'Why?'

'Commander Sobek-Khu will explain.'

There was no point in resisting.

Medes thought furiously as they went. He must not let his fears show, for he might be able to plead innocence and succeed in convincing the monarch. He began considering what he should say.

But face to face with Sobek his courage failed him and the fine words he had prepared died on his lips.

'His Majesty,' said the commander, 'has ordered me to inform you that you are no longer in charge of the Treasury.'

Medes could hear his cell door clanging shut.

'You are now in charge of the secretariat of the King's House. In this capacity, you will register royal decrees and see that they are carried out throughout the land.'

Medes thought he was dreaming. He would be close to the very heart of power! True, he would not be one of the innermost circle whose centre was Pharaoh, but he would touch it. Situated just below the highest men of the kingdom, he would be the first to know their true intentions.

It was up to him to make the best possible use of this new situation.

There were only four people in the audience chamber at the royal palace in Memphis: Sobek the Protector, Sehotep-ib-Ra (which meant 'He Who Gives Fullness to the Heart of the Divine Light'), Senankh and General Nesmontu.

They sat in silence, not daring to look at each other or think about the fact that they really had been chosen by the king to form his inner council. None was thinking of the honours; all dwelt on the difficulties that awaited them, knowing that Senusret would accept neither failure nor prevarication.

When Pharaoh appeared, symbol of the One that united the many in harmony, they stood up and bowed. By means of his *nemes* headdress, the king's thoughts crossed the heavens in the manner of the divine falcon, gathered in the sun's energy and celebrated the most mysterious of communions, that of Ra and Osiris. By means of his kilt, whose name, *shendjyt*, was analogous to that of the acacia, *shendjet*, the king bore witness to his knowledge of the great Mysteries; by his solid gold bracelets, to his symbolic belonging to the divine sphere.

The king sat down slowly on his throne. 'Our most important function,' he began, 'is to make Ma'at reign over this earth. Without righteousness and without justice, man becomes a wild beast and our society becomes uninhabitable. Our hearts must prove vigilant, our tongues trenchant, our lips must speak the truth. It falls to us to pursue the work of God and the gods, each day to begin creation again, to found this land once more as a temple. Great is the Great, of whom the great are great. None of you is capable of behaving less than honourably, none of you must weaken the royal art.'

The king's gaze alighted on Sehotep, an elegant, high-born man of thirty with a narrow face enlivened by eyes which sparkled with intelligence. The heir to a rich family, an experienced scribe, with a mind so quick that at times he was edgy, he was not well liked by the courtiers.

'Sehotep, I appoint you sole Companion, Bearer of the Royal Seal and overseer of all Pharaoh's works. You shall see that the secrecy of the temples is respected and the livestock is prosperous. Be upright and true like Thoth. Do you swear to fulfil your duties unfailingly?'

'I do,' said Sehotep, his voice full of emotion.

The next man Senusret turned to was a forty-year-old with

plump cheeks and a round belly. He looked like a high liver and lover of good food, but behind this deceptive appearance was a meticulous specialist in public finances, coupled with a leader of men who was as uncompromising as he was feared. He had only a very limited supply of tact, and was therefore often at loggerheads with people he considered flatterers or idlers.

'You, Senankh, I name minister for Egypt's trade and resources, High Treasurer and head of the Double White House. You shall see that wealth is justly shared out so that no one goes hungry.'

'I swear to do so, Majesty.'

That left only old General Nesmontu. Although he was now widely regarded as too austere and too authoritarian, he had distinguished himself during the reign of Pharaoh Amenemhat. An austere man, he was indifferent to honours, and lived as simply as an ordinary soldier in Memphis barracks. His only ideal was to defend and protect Egyptian territory, whatever the cost.

'You, Nesmontu, I appoint to lead our armed forces.'

The old soldier was known – and often criticized – for his blunt speech, and he lived up to his reputation. 'It goes without saying, Majesty, that I shall obey your orders scrupulously, but I must remind you that the provincial governors' forces, if brought together, would form an army larger than ours. There is also the serious matter of the inadequacy of our weapons and equipment and the dilapidation of our buildings.'

'On the last two points, draw up a report immediately, so that we may correct these deficiencies. As to the rest, I am aware of the gravity of the situation and I shall not fail to act.'

'You may count upon my absolute dedication, Majesty,' promised the general.

Sobek the Protector would gladly have withdrawn from this assembly, in which he felt he had no place, but the sovereign gazed gravely at him.

'You, Sobek-Khu, I appoint commander of all the guard

141

forces in the kingdom. It is your duty to maintain security without either weakness or excess harshness, to guarantee the free circulation of people and goods, to see that the rules of navigation are respected, and to arrest troublemakers.'

'I swear to do so,' declared Sobek. 'But may I ask Your Majesty to grant me the favour of not confining me to an office? I would like to continue to ensure your close protection with my select team.'

'You must find your own way of reconciling all your various duties.'

'You may rely on me, Majesty.'

'The pharaoh embodies a vital function,' Senusret went on. 'Although that function has neither son nor brother to carry it on, he who exercises it must restore the constructions of his predecessor and accomplish his own ruling name. Only a weak man has no enemies, and the struggle of Ma'at against *isefet* – violence, falsehood and iniquity – never ceases. But it has taken a new turn, for certain of our adversaries, above all those determined to destroy the monarchy and Egypt itself, are invisible.'

'Do you fear for your life, Majesty?' asked Sehotep, frowning.

'That is not the most important thing. If I die, the gods will designate my successor. It is Abydos that is in danger. Assailed by dark forces, the Tree of Osiris is close to death. Thanks to new buildings which will give out a regenerative energy, I hope at least to stay the process. But I do not know who is behind it, and until he is identified we must fear the worst. Who is it who dares to wield the power of Set and thus endanger the resurrection of Osiris?'

'There's no doubt in my mind,' said General Nesmontu. 'It must be one of the provincial governors who have refused to recognize your full and absolute authority. Rather than submit and lose his privileges, one of those villains has decided to adopt the most destructive kind of policy.'

'Could any Egyptian really be mad enough to want to destroy his own country?' wondered Senankh.

'A potentate like Khnum-Hotep,' said Nesmontu grimly, 'will draw the line at nothing to preserve his hereditary power. And he is not the only one.'

'I can vouch for Wakha, governor of the Cobra province,' declared Senusret, to the general's great surprise.

'With utmost respect, Majesty, are you sure he has not deceived you?'

'His sincerity is not in doubt. Wakha wishes to be my loyal servant.'

'There are still five other rebels, and they are much more formidable than he is.'

'Sobek is charged with investigating them. I shall try to persuade them.'

'Not wishing to be pessimistic, Majesty, but what are your plans in the event of failure?'

'Willingly or by force, Egypt must be reunified.'

The general nodded. 'I'll prepare my men for battle – their training will begin this very day.'

'Majesty, there is nothing more destructive and disastrous than civil war,' protested Sehotep.

'I shall resort to it only in absolute extremity,' the king assured him. 'Now, there is one other vital thing to be done: we must find the gold that can heal the acacia.'

'Seek for it among the provincial governors,' said General Nesmontu. 'They control the desert tracks that lead to the mines, and they have all amassed huge fortunes. With such wealth, they can pay their own and hired soldiers generously.'

'You are probably right,' said the king heavily, 'but nevertheless I shall charge Senankh with the task of exploring the treasury of every temple in the land. Perhaps he will find what we need.'

The pharaoh stood up, to indicate that the audience was at

an end.

Now every man knew the vastness of his task.

Sobek opened the door of the audience chamber for the pharaoh and almost fell over one of his men who was waiting outside, visibly nervous.

'Bad news, sir. The desert guard who has just passed me this report is a man to be taken seriously.'

After reading the brief but alarming text, Sobek decided he must ask the pharaoh to prolong the meeting of the inner council.

28

'According to this report, Majesty,' said a shocked Sobek, 'the turquoise mines of Hathor have been attacked and the miners murdered. The desert guards who patrol that region found only burnt corpses.'

All the members of the King's House were devastated. Senusret looked even sterner than usual.

'Who could have committed such an appalling crime?' asked Sehotep.

'The sand-travellers,' said General Nesmontu. 'Each provincial governor is concerned only with his own security, so between them they are allowing the sand-travellers to prosper.'

'But they usually only attack caravans,' Sobek pointed out, 'and they are well aware that laying waste a royal domain would bring them the worst kind of troubles.'

'Only if we could catch them, and you know how difficult that is. This tragedy is extremely serious. It shows that the rival tribes have united in order to mount a general rebellion.'

'In that case,' said Senusret, 'they will not leave it here. Bring me immediately the latest reports on the King's Walls and the Canaan garrisons.'

Senankh entrusted the task to Medes, who brought them with commendable speed. On examining them, the king saw that only one place had failed to respond: Sichem.

'It's manned by a small, low-grade garrison,' said Nesmontu, 'and the commander takes little interest in his duties – he constantly asks to be transferred. If the town was attacked by a large band of determined sand-travellers, it may not have held out. We can probably expect an uprising in the region and attacks on our border forts.'

'Place them on full alert,' ordered Senusret. 'General, mobilize all our regiments immediately. As soon as they are ready to march, we shall leave for Sichem.'

Crooked-Face was in his element. His new job, teaching men to become terrorists, pleased him so much that he lost count of the hours of increasingly demanding and brutal training to which the men were subjected. None of the fighting was simulated, and each day several men died. Crooked-Face did not care – he dismissed them as incompetent rubbish. The leader wanted attack troops who could face any danger without flinching.

The Herald's daily sermon, which was compulsory for everyone in Sichem except the women, who were confined to their homes, put fire in people's hearts. He did not conceal from them the necessity for a fierce struggle, but that was the price of total victory. As for the brave men who would succumb in battle, they would go directly to heaven, where beautiful women would satisfy their whims while wine flowed freely.

Shab the Twisted watched the listeners, seized any who were less than enthusiastic and handed them over them to Crooked-Face, who used them as targets for his archers and his knife-throwers.

However, although revelling in this unexpected life, Crooked-Face was uneasy. 'My lord, I'm worried that our current success may be short-lived. Don't you think the pharaoh will eventually respond?'

'Of course.'

'Shouldn't we be . . . less visible?'

'Not yet, because it is the nature and extent of his response that interest me. They will enable me to know Senusret's true character, and then I shall decide my strategy. The Egyptians are so respectful of the lives of others that they behave like men who are afraid. But my people know that the impious must be wiped out and that the true God will impose himself by force of arms.'

The Herald visited the poorest families in Sichem, and explained to them that the sole cause of their poverty was the pharaoh. For that reason they must entrust even their youngest children to the Herald, so that they might be transformed into soldiers of the true faith.

During a final trial of unarmed combat, Iker had, thanks to his speed and agility, knocked down two opponents who were bigger and stronger than he. With ten of his comrades, he had become a soldier of the province of the Oryx, in the service of Khnum-Hotep.

'Iker,' said the instructor, 'your orders are to guard the warship docks, and you'll have the lady Techat as your superior. Don't for one moment think she'll be lenient or kindly just because she's a woman. Governor Khnum-Hotep appointed her treasurer and overseer of storehouses precisely because she's extremely strict. He's even entrusted the management of his personal affairs to her, against the wishes of his advisers. To be frank, my boy, you couldn't have a tougher officer. Be very wary of her. She's like a lioness who enjoys killing and eating men.'

The instructor led his pupil to the docks, where they were greeted by a surly overseer.

'Do you mean this young boy's going to ensure our safety?' he said sarcastically.

'Don't be fooled by appearances, and above all don't rub him up the wrong way.'

The foreman looked at Iker more closely. 'If that warning hadn't come from the instructor of our soldiers, it would have made me laugh. Follow me, boy, and I'll show you your position. There's only one order: don't let anyone into the docks without telling me.'

Iker discovered an entirely new world. The craftsmen were making the different parts of a warship. As he watched a pine mast, a tiller, a stem, a hull, a ship's rail and benches for oarsmen took shape. With great skill, some of the shipwrights assembled a veritable mosaic of small planks, while their colleagues made strong ropes and linen sails.

Fascinated, the young man followed each movement with extreme attention and carried it out in his mind. He was brought abruptly back to reality when a sturdy fellow bumped into him, trying to push past.

'Who are you?' Iker asked, holding him back by the arm.

'I'm going to see my brother – he's one of the carpenters.'

'I must inform the overseer.'

'Who do you think you are? I don't need permission.'

'I have my orders.'

'Do you want a fight?'

'If I have to.'

'I'll fetch the whole team, and we'll soon teach you a lesson.'

The fellow lifted his arm, summoning the craftsmen to his aid, but he lowered it almost instantly and took a step back as if he'd seen a monster. Iker turned round and saw the lady Techat, looking very elegant in a pale-green dress.

'Go away,' she ordered the troublemaker, and he ran off without further ado.

Techat walked right round the young soldier, who stood as still as a statue.

'I like those who put their duties before their own interest, even their own safety. You conducted yourself well during your training, I am told. Do you come from a family of officers?'

'No, my lady, I'm an orphan.'

'And you wanted to become a soldier?'

'I want to become a scribe.'

'Can you read, write and count?'

'Indeed yes, my lady.'

'If you wish me to help you, you must tell me more.'

'My life was stolen from me and I want to know why.'

Techat seemed interested. 'Who is trying to harm you?'

Iker tried his luck. 'Two sailors, Turtle-Eye and Sharp-Knife. Their ship is called *Swift One*.'

A long silence ensued. Then Techat said, 'Describe Turtle-Eye.'

The young man did so.

'I have a feeling he is not unknown to me, but I cannot be certain. I must make inquiries, which will probably take some time.'

Iker began to dream that at last there might be hope. But then suspicion gripped him. 'My lady, why should you want to help me?'

'Because I like you. Oh, don't misunderstand me, my boy! I only like men of my own age – so long as they don't hinder me in my work by claiming to be more skilful than I am. You, Iker, are not like anyone else. A strange fire burns in you, a fire so powerful that all the envious can think of is stealing it. That is probably the cause of your problems.'

Still on his guard, Iker was reluctant to tell her anything more.

'I shall see to arranging your transfer,' said Techat. 'First thing tomorrow, you shall become assistant to the keeper of the province's archives. There are many documents waiting to be filed, and perhaps you will be happy there.'

29

Medes's household was in uproar. Alarming rumours had been heard: he had been dismissed from all his offices and transferred to a small town in the South where he would end his career amid general indifference. The beautiful Memphis house would be sold, the servants dispersed.

Since early morning, Medes's wife, in a state of high anxiety, had been calling constantly upon the services of her hairdresser and her face-painter.

'Have you found that pot with the five-fats pomade yet?'

'Not yet,' replied the hairdresser.

'This carelessness is intolerable!'

'Could you have put it away in your ivory box?'

The distraught mistress of the house looked in the ivory box, and there was the pot of pomade. Without offering any apology, she had the servant anoint her hair with this miraculous pomade, made of the fat of lion, crocodile, snake, ibex and hippopotamus.

'Make sure it soaks well into my scalp,' she ordered, 'and then you are to rub my head with castor oil. That way, I shall never have grey hair.'

After Medes's fall his wife would no longer be able to buy expensive but vital aids to beauty. Divorce was out of the question, because it was he who had all the wealth. If she accused him of adultery, she would receive half of it. All the same, she would need solid proof, on pain of being sentenced to receive no food pension at all.

'Paint my face better than that!' she raged. 'You can still see red patches on my cheeks and neck.'

The face-painter applied a layer of powder compounded from the pods and seeds of fenugreek, honey and alabaster, a special mixture which removed the signs of aging.

When Medes entered his wife's bedchamber, he stood for a moment, looking at her. 'How are you feeling, my darling?

She leapt up, pushing away the serving-women. 'You . . . we . . . are we ruined?

'Ruined? Quite the opposite: I've received a big promotion. In his wisdom, the pharaoh has recognized my talents.'

Medes had difficulty in calming her as she covered him with kisses.

'I knew it,' she panted, 'I knew it. You are the best, the greatest, the most—'

'My new position carries heavy responsibilities, darling.'

'Will we be even richer?'

'Certainly.'

'What position has the king awarded you?'

'I am to head the secretariat of the King's House.'

'Then you'll know lots of secrets, won't you?'

'Indeed, but I've sworn not to repeat them to anyone.'

'Not even to me?'

'Not even to you.'

Affairs of state held no great appeal for her. His wealth enabled her to satisfy all her whims, and to her that was the main thing.

While the excellent news spread from floor to floor in the house and then throughout the whole district, Medes withdrew into his office where, a few minutes later, he received Gergu.

Gergu was chewing two pastilles made from aromatic

reeds and terebinth resin. They cleansed the mouth and sweetened the breath.

'Congratulations on your appointment,' he said. 'We shall have our hands a little freer, shan't we?'

Medes unrolled a papyrus. 'This is a complaint against you.'

'A complaint? By whom?'

'One of your former wives, whom you hit while you were drunk.'

'Hmm, it's possible . . .'

'It's certain – there was a witness. You forced her door, threatened her and slapped her.'

'That's not too serious.'

'It is in Egypt.'

'This witness, who is it?'

'Her personal maid, a young provincial girl.'

'We might be able to—'

'I've already taken care of it,' said Medes. 'She has gone back to her godforsaken hole with substantial compensation, and your wife has received several brand-new pieces of furniture, accompanied by apologies from you which I wrote myself. The complaint has been withdrawn.'

Gergu collapsed on to a low chair. 'I owe you at least a jar of highest-quality beer, sir.'

'Forget your old conquests and control your hatred of women, Gergu. A principal inspector of granaries owes it to himself to be respectable.'

'Me? Principal inspector . . .'

'Senankh, my superior, has signed your promotion.'

'First thing tomorrow, I shall go hunting! I'll bring you back a fortune by bleeding my dear citizens white.'

'You'll do nothing of the sort.'

Gergu gaped. 'But I have the official power, I—'

'You and I are entering a new dimension. For several years we have worked well but modestly. Our new status allows us to hope for better. Nevertheless, we shall be much more exposed and must therefore be more careful than ever.'

'I don't quite follow you,' confessed Gergu, feeling for his amulets, both to reassure himself and to clear his mind.

Medes strode tensely up and down the room. 'I am now the first person informed of the decisions taken at the highest level of the state. It falls to me to transcribe the decrees made by Pharaoh and to disseminate them. Any false move, any obvious betrayal, would immediately point to me as the culprit. Manoeuvring for my own benefit is therefore likely to be particularly difficult, for the king and his counsellors will examine my acts and deeds closely.'

'Then your promotion is a disaster.'

'Not if I know how to use it in the right way. You still have freedom of movement, and through you I shall continue to maintain our networks of friendships and influence. At the heart of the senior level of administration, I shall create others.'

'And what about our new ship, which will be vital for reaching Punt and bringing back the gold?'

'Let's not think about that for the moment. Senusret has given a curious order: to draw up an inventory of all the treasures of the temples, in order to know their true riches.'

'Why is that curious?'

'Because the king already knows. I believe he's searching for something else, but what? You will be linked to this mission, so try to find out more; at the same time, you must identify the most interesting shrines. And that isn't all. Pharaoh has decreed general mobilization of the army.'

'So he's made up his mind to attack the provincial governors.'

'You don't understand, Gergu. Something has just happened in Canaan, but its extent and seriousness I don't yet know.'

'To cause such a reaction, it can't be nothing.'

'I agree. Another thing I don't yet know is whether General Nesmontu will be in overall command of the troops or if the pharaoh himself will.'

'In other words, Senusret might die in battle and the government in Memphis might be overthrown.'

'Let's prepare for any kind of upheaval of that order,' agreed Medes. 'The four men who make up the King's House are incorruptible and their faith unshakeable. But they are only men. By spending time with them, I shall identify their weak points and work out how to use them. As for Senusret himself, he benefits from personal protection arising from his knowledge of the secrets of the covered temple. Without it, any attempt to take power would be futile. And I still do not know how to breach that insurmountable wall.'

'We'll succeed, you can be sure of that!'

'In the meantime, Gergu, don't put a foot wrong. You must become a respectable man and an example to your subordinates.'

Gergu gave a mocking smile. 'If any of them tries to imitate me, I'll break his head.'

The two allies guffawed. Then Gergu suddenly became serious again.

'What if we were to content ourselves with what we've already achieved? Our profits are far from negligible. The risk has its enjoyable side, but it's still a risk, and Punt is very, very far away.'

'Not as far as you think,' said Medes. 'You're an excellent sailor, and you really only enjoy yourself in a storm. How could you give up when we're only at the start of the voyage? Besides, you're like me: you love power for power's sake, strength for the sake of strength.'

Gergu conceded that this was true.

'The sages of Egypt condemn greed and ambition,' went on Medes, 'but they're wrong. Those are incomparable stimulants, which enable us to go beyond our normal limits.

154

And the events I foresee strengthen me in that belief.'

'One question bothers me,' said Gergu. 'But before I ask you, give me something strong to drink.' He gulped down two cups of date wine. 'Why do we do evil things?'

'Because evil fascinates us. And what do you call evil?'

'Opposing Ma'at, righteousness and the Light.'

'You're just repeating the old sages' nonsense. Do you think they'd ever make you wealthy and offer you the place you want so badly?'

'I'm still thirsty.'

Medes mused that from time to time it was necessary to shore up his henchman's shaky morale. Gergu was wrong: they were not yet doing evil, for they still had no supporters or intermediaries inside a temple.

30

In a single day, Iker had got through more work than two scribes usually did in a week, and this had made many of the others jealous. Had it not been for the lady Techat's protection, he would have had much trouble. His superior decided to make things as complicated as possible for him, but Iker was undaunted. Meticulous and persevering, he checked all the documents as he filed them, in the hope of finding the names of Turtle-Eye, Sharp-Knife and *Swift One*. But all his toil produced no results.

When he was summoned by Techat, however, he was not discouraged.

'Have you found anything?' she asked.

'No, my lady. Have you had better luck?'

'No, I've found nothing, either.'

'I didn't invent those men and that ship.'

'I don't doubt your word, but remember what I told you: the search may be a long one.'

'You haven't remembered anything more specific?'

'Unfortunately, no, but I'm almost certain that fellow Turtle-Eye passed through our province. You must change your ideas, my boy. We are going to celebrate the festival of the goddess Pakhet,* and you shall be my shade-bearer.'

*Pakhet, 'She Who Claws', was a female cheetah and dwelt in a cave venerated by priestesses, for the most part the wives of provincial nobles. Her cult was based at Speos Artemidos, near Beni Hasan.

The Tree of Life

On Techat's boat, which in company with the boats of other noble ladies, was heading for the sacred site of the goddess, Iker relished the purity of the air and the gentleness of the steady wind. Sailing on the Nile was still a delight. For a few moments, he thought he might stop travelling, settle in this province and spend the rest of his days in tranquillity. But the unanswered questions assailed him again, leaving him in the state of a man dying of thirst, for whom a drink of water is a matter of life or death. No, the events that had brought him down were not meaningless. It was up to him to find out how to interpret them and decipher the enigma of his destiny.

The boat moored, and they disembarked. Iker protected the lady Techat from the sun with a shade-giver composed of a long handle and a rectangular linen sheet.

She pointed to a magnificent ebony tree a little way away, whose branches hid the entrance to the sacred cave.

'Whatever you do, Iker, don't touch that tree,' she warned him. 'The goddess often hides there in her incarnation as a cheetah, and she leaps on any outsider who doesn't know the words of pacification.'

'How can one learn them?'

'You're very inquisitive.'

'At least tell me what part Pakhet plays.'

This boy, thought Techat, is definitely not cut from the same cloth as most men.

She said, 'She masters the destructive fires and can transform herself into a snake, which throws itself upon the enemies of the sun to prevent them doing harm. When they see her, it is too late. But her function is not only to win battles for the Light. By her magic, she assists the return of the annual flood, which brings prosperity to the whole country.'

'How does she do that?'

'Don't you think you're going too far?'

'I shall go as far as you let me.'

'Let's just say that she is an ally of Osiris. Don't ask me anything more – just watch and keep silent.'

Either Techat knew but would not tell him, or she did not know and was acting out a part. For Iker, the result was the same either way: she would provide no more explanations.

As they reached the cave, an aged priestess emerged from it.

'May the gates of the heavens be unlocked,' she said, 'so that the divine presence may appear in its glory.'

Four other, younger priestesses emerged, and bowed before the first. Their hair was drawn back in a strange style reminiscent of the king's White Crown. They wore a short kilt held up by straps which covered their breasts.

'Thus come the four winds of heaven,' said the old priestess. 'May they be mastered so that the wealth of the land is ensured. Here is the north wind, cool and refreshing.'

The first young girl began a slow and solemn dance; the beauty of her movements entranced Iker.

'Here is the east wind, the opener of the heavenly gates, that which creates a perfect path for the Divine Light and gives access to the paradises of the otherworld.'

The second dancer was no less graceful than the first, moving fluently to an enchanting rhythm.

'Here is the west wind, which comes from the bosom of the One, before the creation of the Two. It comes from beyond death.'

The third dancer surpassed her colleagues. As if imbued with the spiritual message she symbolized, she developed more dramatic and more demanding movements, some of which evoked the struggle between death and the will to overcome it.

'Lastly, here is the south wind, which brings the regenerative water and makes life grow.'

At first, Iker thought he was mistaken, taken in by an

uncanny resemblance. Then he concentrated all his attention on the face of the young priestess, whose dancing was of supreme grace. From her there emanated a light which translated the intensity of the reborn life offered by the south wind.

It was she.

Yes, it really was she. He recognized her despite her unfamiliar costume and headdress.

'Hold the shade properly,' complained Techat. 'I'm in the sun.'

Iker corrected its position, without taking his eyes off the beloved woman, whose dance seemed appallingly short.

The four winds were motionless. The old priestess placed a lotus-flower on each one's brow.

'Thus are revealed the divine words hidden in nature. May these flowers, whose sweet scent gives life to the Light, be the guarantors of the miracle of resurrection.'

From each lotus sprang forth a dazzling brightness.

Then the five priestesses climbed into a boat and drew away from the sacred territory of Pakhet. When they had gone, a banquet was to be held there in honour of the noble ladies. Iker and the other servants would eat apart.

'You look overwhelmed,' observed Techat.

'No – that is, yes. That ritual is very disturbing.'

'Were you by any chance moved by the dancers' beauty?'

'Who wouldn't be? The one who embodied the south wind reached absolute perfection. Do you know who she is or what her name is?'

'No, I don't. The priestesses come from Abydos to celebrate the rites of Pakhet, then they return to their temple.'

'Have you seen her before?'

'No, she must be a new one. In any case, you must forget her.'

'Because she belongs to the Golden Circle of Abydos?'

Techat frowned. 'Who told you about that?'

'A gardener.'

'It's merely a poetic expression – don't attach any importance to it. And I repeat: forget that young woman. She lives in a world you will never know. If you like dancers, there are more alluring ones who are much more accessible.'

In a remarkably short time, Iker had filed all the archives of the Oryx province, but he had found no trace of the two sailors or their ship. Techat, too, had met with disappointment: none of her informants had been able to provide any reliable information.

She decided she must find him another post so that his mind was kept occupied. His heart must be freed from the idea of vengeance, and he must be persuaded to settle in the region, where he would become a high-ranking scribe.

She was marshalling her arguments as she stood high on her terrace, gazing at the new moon that marked the triumph of Osiris, when a voice made her start.

'May I speak to you, my lady? Don't be afraid: I wish you no harm. But don't on any account turn round. If you try to see me, I shall knock you out.'

'What . . . what do you want?'

'As regards the two sailors and their ship, I may have a lead. It passes through the province of the great priests of Thoth. You must let Iker go there.'

'Who are you to give me orders?' demanded Techat angrily.

'A friend.'

'You're lying. Tell me the truth or I'll have you arrested.'

'If I do, you'll throw me in prison.'

'I propose a bargain: the truth for your freedom.'

'Have I your word?'

'You have.'

'I'm acting on the orders of Pharaoh Senusret. By protecting Iker, you have already helped me a great deal. Now he must be permitted to pursue his quest.'

'Let Iker forget about the past and live happily in peace.'

'If you can convince him to do that, why not? But be honest with him and tell him about this lead.'

'We must discuss your future,' Techat told Iker. 'What would you say to settling here and continuing your scribe's studies?'

'Your offer is generous, but I cannot accept. As you've found no new information, I must go and seek it somewhere else.'

'And what if this wandering leads you nowhere?'

'My life was stolen from me. I want to find it again and understand my destiny, whatever it costs me.

'You might lose that life, once and for all.'

'Doing nothing would kill me even more quickly.'

'Well, since your mind is made up, I'll help you one last time.'

'Are you sending me away?'

'You are to go to the province of the Hare.'

'Does that mean you have a clue?'

'Yes, but it's so faint that I can't give you any details. Go there and find them.'

'Will Lord Khnum-Hotep let me leave?'

'I shall settle that with him. You will carry an official document for Lord Djehuty. I shall say you are an apprentice scribe who wishes to perfect his skills, that we have no place for you here, and that I ask him to look favourably on you. Let us hope he will accept you. If you have that good fortune, be as discreet as possible in carrying out your searches. Djehuty is not an easy man – you must not anger him in any way.'

'How can I ever thank you, my lady?'

'I'd have liked to keep you here, but the province of the Oryx is too small for you. Here is my final gift. It will protect you.'

She handed him an object shaped like a crescent moon.

'This talisman was cut from the canine tooth of a hippopotamus. My father, who was a great sorcerer, engraved a griffin and a hieroglyphic inscription upon it. Can you read it?'

'"I am the spirit who cuts off the heads of male and female enemies."'

'At night, before you go to sleep, lay it on your belly. It will drive away the forces of destruction.'

31

The Herald's sermon had been cheered even more loudly than usual. In the name of his one God, whose orders he passed on, the people of all the towns in Canaan were to unite and set off to attack Egypt, kill the pharaoh, wipe out the oppressors and take power. Then the victors would impose their beliefs upon all lands – by violence, if necessary.

'You have awoken the sleepers,' commented Shab the Twisted. 'They'll soon be a formidable army, which will unleash its force upon the world.'

'I am not sure of that,' said the Herald, dampening his right-hand-man's enthusiasm.

'But these people believe in you – they'll follow you to the death.'

'I don't doubt that, but they have no weapons and they aren't real soldiers.'

'Do you mean they might be . . . defeated?'

'Everything will depend upon the strength of the Egyptian reaction.'

'Up to now, it's been non-existent.'

'Don't be foolish, my friend. If the pharaoh is taking his time, it is probably in order to strike all the harder.'

'But then the population of Sichem will be massacred.'

'That's what happens to bait, isn't it? And bait is what these first faithful few are. They will die with dignity, certain of going to the paradise I've promised them. The important people are the men Crooked-Face is training. They must escape and wait in the shadows, ready to act the moment I give the order.'

The two men went to the training-camp, arriving just as the corpse of a youth with an over-fragile skull was being removed. No holds were barred in Crooked-Face's training, and he put his men through more and more dangerous exercises.

'Are you satisfied?' the Herald asked him.

'Not yet. Most these lads are still too soft. I don't despair of training a few of them, but it will take time.''

'I fear we haven't a great deal left.'

'If we're attacked, we'll see what they can do in the field.'

'No, Crooked-Face. You and your best men are to leave here and take refuge in a safe place, two days' march north-east of Imet, in an uninhabited part of the Delta. You will wait for me there.'

'Why all these secretive goings-on?'

'You sound disappointed in me.'

'Oh no, my lord!' said Crooked-Face hastily.

'Then continue to trust me.'

His lungs on fire from running, a lookout halted at a respectful distance from the Herald. 'My lord, they're coming! Egyptian soldiers – hundreds of them!'

'Calm yourself, my good fellow. I told you they'd come, didn't I? Alert our supporters, and tell them to prepare to defend Sichem. God will be at their side.'

The Herald gathered together the section leaders in the main square and reminded them what they must do: every man must fight to the death. Victorious or vanquished, his faithful would know eternal happiness.

The commanders of the King's Walls forts thanked the gods that they were still alive. Summoned by the pharaoh himself, they had suffered his censure and his cold anger, which was more terrifying than any loud outburst. They had been castigated as incompetent and useless for having neither foreseen nor prevented the Sichem rebellion, and they saw themselves sentenced to forced labour in a work-camp at the very least.

However, Senusret had decided otherwise: to leave them in their posts but to inform them that their next mistake would be their last. That thorn, thrust deep into the flesh of career soldiers who had relied on an illusory security, had proved most effective. Jerked out of their torpor, the officers had undertaken to regain control over the areas they administered, to revitalize their men and to become once again Egypt's bulwark against invasion.

Senusret's firmness and authority had acted like a tonic. The knowledge that they were serving a king of such stature aroused great enthusiasm.

Having rectified the situation along the King's Walls, the king led his army towards Sichem.

'Is there still no news from the town?' he asked General Nesmontu.

'None, Majesty. But we are corresponding normally with the other settlements in the area, which would tend to indicate that the rebellion is limited.'

'The outward appearance of a tumour does not always indicate how serious it is,' said the king. 'Send out ten scouts: they are to observe Sichem from all sides.'

All the reports said that Canaanite lookouts had been posted at the four cardinal points.

'The town has indeed rebelled,' concluded Nesmontu, 'and our little garrison has probably been wiped out. But why haven't the rebels tried to spread their uprising?'

'For one simple reason: they wanted to know first how Pharaoh would react. Before retaking Sichem, you are going to block off all the roads, tracks and paths leading to it. Not one person must escape. When our troops are in place, we shall attack.'

Convinced by the Herald that God's help would enable them to fight off the invaders, the inhabitants of Sichem yelled as, armed only with farming tools, they rushed to attack Senusret's footsoldiers. The king's army was initially taken aback by the enemy's bloodthirstiness, but soon gained the upper hand. Under General Nesmontu's leadership, the Canaanites were soon utterly crushed.

The victory was so quick that Senusret did not need to intervene in person. But the loss of around thirty soldiers showed how fierce the fighting had been. Even many women and children had preferred death to surrender.

Once the town had been retaken, the houses were searched one by one. No trace of a stock of weapons was found.

'Have you arrested their leader?'' the king asked Nesmontu.

'Not yet, Majesty.'

'The survivors must be carefully questioned.'

'Half the population died. All that is left are some old men, the sick, and children and women. The women claim their husbands wanted to free themselves from Egyptian oppression with the aid of the one god.'

'The one god? What do they call him?'

'The god of the Herald. He revealed the truth to the inhabitants of Sichem, and they all followed him.'

'So he's the one who inspired this disaster! Gather as much information as you can about him.'

'Are we to raze the town to the ground?'

'No. I shall put in place the magic number of men needed to avoid a recurrence of these events. A new, larger garrison will ensure the safety of the colonists who will settle here from next month. In addition, General, you are to make a tour of inspection of all the towns of Canaan. I want the people to see our army and know that it will act ruthlessly against the enemies of Egypt.'

In several places, notably near the sacked temple, which was to be rebuilt without delay, Senusret buried fragments of red pottery on which were written texts of execration concerning the dark forces and the Canaanites. If they broke the peace again, they would be cursed.

The king asked himself: was this Herald just a madman greedy for violence, or did he represent a real danger?

Now the Herald knew. Senusret was not one of those soft, indecisive rulers who let themselves be swayed by events without knowing what to do. This pharaoh would not recoil from using force, and they could be sure he would show no cowardice.

The struggle for the final triumph would be all the more exciting. But open battle had proved impossible. Even if they were all gathered together, which was highly improbable in the near future, the Canaanite tribes and the sand-travellers could not provide enough soldiers to take on Senusret's army. The only effective method, therefore, was terror.

By spreading fear through Egyptian society, by setting protestors, rebels and destroyers of all kinds against it, he would eventually poison it and make it fall apart.

Crooked-Face and his raiders had fled south before the enemy set up its blockades. The Herald, Shab the Twisted and three experienced men had chosen a very winding track to the east, which ran between sun-scorched hills.

'Where are we going?' asked Shab, worried at the thought of another march through the desert.

'To convert tribes of sand-travellers. Then we shall rejoin Crooked-Face.'

When night fell, the little group halted at the foot of a

ravine. The Herald climbed to the top of a mound in order to see which direction to take next.

'Don't move,' ordered a gruff voice. 'If you try to escape, you'll be killed.'

From nowhere there appeared twenty desert guards. They were armed with bows and clubs, and were accompanied by their fierce dogs.

Even by using his powers, the Herald could not kill all these hardened professionals, especially the dogs, which had no fear of desert demons.

'Are you alone?' asked the guard.

'Yes, I'm alone,' he said loudly, loudly enough for his companions to hear. 'And as you can see, I'm unarmed. I'm just a sand-traveller in search of my goats, which wandered off.'

'You haven't by any chance come from Sichem?'

'No, I live out here, far from the town, with my flock. I only go there to sell cheese and milk.'

'Fine. Follow us. We'll check all that.'

One of the guards bound the Herald's wrists tightly with a length of rope, and then passed another round his neck to drag him like an unwilling animal.

'Anyone else around?' asked the guards' leader.

'He's the only one we found, sir.'

32

The lady Techat had given Iker the price of the voyage to Khemenu, 'City of the Eight',* capital of the province of the Hare. As he gazed out over the Nile, whose majesty fascinated him, he felt someone's eyes on him.

He turned and saw a tall, rather thin man, whose eyes were full of authority.

'Are you stopping at Khemenu,' he asked in a dry voice, 'or continuing south?'

'Why should I tell you?'

'Because you are on my territory.'

'Are you the governor of this province?'

'I am his right-hand man, General Sepi, and I see that our laws are respected. Strangers who cannot give good reasons for their arrival are expelled immediately. Either you tell me your intentions or you leave.'

'My name is Iker. I have come from the Oryx province with a recommendation from the lady Techat that I be granted permission to continue my scribe's studies here.'

'The lady Techat? Isn't she dead?'

'She's very much alive, I can assure you!'

'Describe her.'

---

*Dwelling-place of the Ogdoad, a community of eight creative divinities divided into four couples.

Iker did so, but General Sepi's expression did not lighten. 'This recommendation – show it to me.'

'It is addressed to Lord Djehuty-Hotep, and no one else may read it.'

'You are very uncooperative, young man! Have you by any chance got a guilty conscience?'

'I've learnt to distrust strangers. How can you prove that you really are a general?'

'Not only uncooperative but mistrustful, eh? Those are good points rather than bad.'

The boat berthed at the landing-stage and some twenty soldiers scrutinized the travellers, who were subject to lengthy questioning.

An officer came over to Sepi and saluted. 'It's good to see you again, General. I don't like to ask if—'

'My mother is dead. I had the good fortune to be with her during her last moments and to direct her funeral rites. She was an upright woman, and I know that Osiris will judge her favourably.'

Iker dared not move away.

'Is this boy with you, General?'

'I'm taking him to the capital. Put your baggage on a donkey, Iker.'

Iker obeyed; the animal was hardly overloaded.

General Sepi strode off at a good pace. 'You say you've come from the Oryx province. Why did you leave?'

'Lord Khnum-Hotep doesn't need any more scribes. Besides, I was born at Madu.'

'At Madu? Really?'

'Really.'

'Why did you leave your family?'

'I'm an orphan. The old scribe who taught me the rudiments of the profession died.'

'And you tried your luck in the Oryx province. Why?'

'Chance.'

'Chance,' repeated the general, sceptically. 'Are you by any *chance* looking for someone?'

'I've come here in the hope of becoming a good scribe.'

'You seem so determined that a very special fire must burn within you. I understand that you aren't willing to tell me the whole truth straight away; but if you wish to make a career in this province, you will have to explain yourself.'

'When can I see Lord Djehuty?'

'I'll speak to him about you, and he'll decide. Can you be patient?'

'If necessary.'

Governor of the prestigious province of the Hare, Djehuty-Hotep, 'Thoth is in Plenitude', preferred not to think about his age. High Priest of the mysteries of Thoth, and priest of Ma'at, he belonged to a very ancient family whose origins went back to the time of the pyramids.

After living through the reigns of the pharaohs Amenemhat II and Senusret II, he must now put up with that of Senusret III, about whom his advisers and informants told him extremely bad things. Why didn't the king stay shut away in his palace at Memphis, surrounded by the endless flattery of his courtiers? If he really was devising a plan to abolish the provincial governors' prerogatives, civil war would be inevitable.

But what criticisms could the king level against administrators as conscientious as Khnum-Hotep or himself? Their provinces were well managed, their flocks large and healthy, their workshops prosperous. True, they had well-equipped armies, but then the pharaoh's own little army was incapable of guaranteeing the provinces' security.

Nothing must be changed, and that was that. And Djehuty had sufficient authority to convince his colleagues.

One of his little pleasures was to use a different travelling-chair each day for his numerous journeys. He had three, each equipped with a sun-shade and all so big and comfortable that he could almost lie down in them. Several teams of eight men worked in shifts, cheerfully singing the ancient song: 'The bearers are happy when the chair is full. When the master is present, death departs; life is renewed by Sokar, regent of the depths, and the dead are brought back to life.'

Djehuty was shaven-headed, and made it a point of honour not to wear a wig, although this did not prevent him from being vain about his appearance. He liked to dress in an elegant, closely woven cape and a long kilt which covered his legs. Taking care of oneself held back old age.

After listening to his tenant farmers' favourable reports, the governor had decided to treat himself to a walk in the country. But just as he was about to get into his travelling-chair, he spotted his lifelong friend General Sepi.

A simple exchange of glances was enough to make him realize that his friend was deeply distressed. He said, 'No one can share your grief – I know that you don't want soothing words from me. If you wish to rest before giving me your report . . . ?'

'Despite my mother's death, I fulfilled my mission. The news is not good, I'm afraid.'

'Has Senusret decided on a trial of strength?'

'I don't know – my contacts at court suddenly went silent.'

'That must mean the pharaoh has taken matters back in hand. A bad sign, a very bad sign. What else?'

'The town of Sichem rebelled and killed the whole Egyptian garrison.'

'How did the king react?'

'Brutally: he ordered General Nesmontu to launch a massive attack. Sichem is back under Egyptian control.'

So the monarch did not hesitate to use force. That was a clear message to the provincial governors who refused to obey him.

Djehuty turned away from his travelling-chair. 'Come, let

us go and drink some wine in my garden. Sichem, you said; we have trading-relations with Sichem, haven't we?'

Sepi nodded.

'Being so warlike, the king will probably accuse me of being the rebels' accomplice. Place our soldiers on alert immediately.'

'Egyptians killing other Egyptians . . . What an appalling prospect.'

'I know, Sepi, but Senusret leaves us no choice. Write and tell Khnum-Hotep and the other governors that war is imminent.'

'They may think you're trying to manoeuvre them into an alliance they don't want at any price.'

'You're right. Forget about writing – it'll be every man for himself.'

A servant brought the wine and poured it. It was excellent, but in his current mood Djehuty thought it was poor.

When the servant had gone, the general said, 'A foreigner would like to see you.'

'Not a Canaanite from Sichem, I hope?'

'No, a young man from the Oryx province. He has a letter of recommendation from the lady Techat.'

'That isn't like her – usually the only person she recommends is herself. Send him away. I'm not seeing anyone today.'

'I shall permit myself to insist.'

Djehuty was curious. 'What's so exceptional about this young man?'

'I'd like you to decide that for yourself.'

Djehuty knew the general was an honest man, who never sought preferential treatment. 'Very well,' he said, 'I'll see him.' He called a servant and told him to bring the visitor out into the garden.

As soon as he saw Iker, Djehuty understood Sepi's interest in him. Despite his apparent modesty, the young man glowed with a fire so hot that the annual flood itself would not be enough to put it out. Moreover, Techat's letter was a hymn of praise.

'In the present circumstances,' said Djehuty, 'I need soldiers, not scribes.'

'But, my lord, I came here to become a scribe. There's no better place to learn than the province of Thoth himself.'

'Why do you want to be a scribe?'

'Because I'm convinced that the secret of life is hidden in the words of knowledge, and only a detailed knowledge and practice of hieroglyphs will give me access to it.'

'Aren't you being rather over-ambitious?'

'I'll work day and night.'

'Prove it by beginning straight away. My steward will take charge of you, and find you lodgings in the apprentice scribes' district. Try not to cause any ructions – I loathe troublemakers. If you don't satisfy your teacher, you'll be expelled from my province.'

Iker bowed and withdrew.

Djehuty turned to his friend. 'Determined, brave, independent – you're right, Sepi, this is no ordinary boy.'

'Like me, you saw that he has more than just a strong character.'

'Do you think he's capable of entering a temple?'

'Let him prove that himself.'

33

Techat had known Khnum-Hotep would be furious, and she waited calmly for the storm to pass.

'Techat,' he fumed, 'why did you give that boy permission to leave?'

'What was so special about him, my lord?'

'We'd turned him into an excellent soldier, and I need good soldiers to defend my independence.'

'I know, but Iker wants to be a scribe.'

'Scribes won't fight against Senusret's soldiers!'

'He couldn't have defeated them by himself.'

Khnum-Hotep folded his arms sulkily. 'I repeat: why did you give him permission to leave?'

'Because he seems particularly gifted for his future profession and because the Oryx province could not give him the best training. The province of Thoth, on the other hand, will give him exactly what he needs. And after all, my lord, you yourself told him you didn't need any more scribes.'

'Well, perhaps I may have done. But I'm the one who makes the decisions in this province – the only one.'

Techat smiled. 'If I didn't deal with minor matters, my lord, you'd be overwhelmed with work. And you know as well as I do that Iker had to go to meet his destiny.'

'And you know that this destiny can by found by way of the province of the Hare?'

'My intuition tells me so.'

Khnum-Hotep shook his head. 'He's a strange boy. He seems so determined that nothing will ever distract him from his goal. I'd have liked to get to know him better.'

'Perhaps we'll see him again.'

After a hearty breakfast, during which Iker sat apart from the others, the apprentice scribes went to their classroom, where they sat down on mats.

When the teacher entered, Iker was at once disappointed and angry: General Sepi! So Governor Djehuty had tricked him by sending him to a place where soldiers were trained.

He stood up. 'Forgive me, General. I have no business to be here.'

'Don't you want to become a scribe?' asked Sepi.

'Yes indeed.'

'Then sit down.'

'But you are a general and—'

'—and in charge of the principal scribes' school in the province of the Hare. Either people obey me unquestioningly or they go and seek their fortune elsewhere. Those who work under my direction must be thorough and disciplined. I require punctuality and an impeccable appearance – you will be expelled at the least sign of carelessness.

'Now, let us begin by paying homage to our divine master, Thoth, and to the ancestor of all scribes, the sage Imhotep.'

Sepi hung a plumbline from the classroom's main roof-beam.

'Look at this attentively, apprentices, for it is the symbol of Thoth, immutable at the heart of the scales. It drives back evil, weighs words, offers peace to him who is knowledge-able and brings back that which was forgotten.'

From a papyrus basket lined with cloth, General took out a scribe's writing-materials: a sycamore palette, a cylindrical case containing styluses and brushes, a bag of papyrus-sheets, another of pigments, a small mallet-shaped tool used for polishing, a smoothing-tool for making corrections on papyrus, several inkpots, cakes of red and black colour, some wooden tablets and a grater.

'What is the name of the palette?' he asked.

'*Maa-sedjem*, "See and Hear",' answered one of the apprentices.

'Correct,' nodded Sepi. 'Never forget that the palette is one of the incarnations of Thoth. He alone will enable you to know the Words of God,* and to enter into their meaning. Thanks to his palette, the duration of the life of Ra, the Divine Light, and the royalty of Horus, protector of Pharaoh, are written down. Using the palette is a grave and sacred act, so it must be preceded by a rite.'

The general set on the ground a statuette of a seated baboon with deep, meditative eyes: the incarnation of Thoth, it inspired the contemplative scribe. Then he filled a pot with water.

'For you, master of the sacred language, I pour out the energy that will give life to the mind and the hand. Here is the water of the inkwell for your *ka*, Imhotep.'

After a long silence, the teacher corrected the posture of several apprentices, which he considered too limp or too stiff. Then he presented them with the finely tooled styluses and brushes, each nearly half a cubit long.†

'Do any of you know the best material for making them?'

'Reeds that have grown in a salt marsh,' replied one pupil.

'Wouldn't hare's-ear be better?' suggested Iker.

'Why?' asked Sepi.

'Because it's resilient and it also repels insects.'

'You won't be writing on papyrus yet,' Sepi went on.

---

*Hieroglyphs is a Greek term meaning 'sacred engravings'. The Egyptian name is *medu neter*, 'Words of God."
†About 25cm.

'You'll use wooden tablets covered with a thin layer of hardened plaster, which will enable you to erase mistakes and clean the surface easily. When this layer is destroyed, you will apply a new one. Your principal enemies are laziness, sloppiness and indiscipline. They will make you stupid and stop you progressing. Be sure to listen to the advice of those who know more than you, and work hard every day. If you are not willing to do so, leave this school immediately.'

Scared by the instructor's sternness, two apprentices left.

'Thoth separated the world's languages,' continued Sepi. 'By distinguishing the spoken words of one land from those of another, he turned upside-down the thoughts of humans who turned away from truth and from the right path. During the golden age the gods lived, speaking the same language; today human beings confront each other, cut off from the Divine and unable to understand each other. But Thoth also passed down to us the words of power that you will learn to decipher and to write on wood, leather, papyrus and stone.

'You must scrupulously obey one fundamental rule: do not put one word in the place of another, do not confuse one thing with another. Here you will be taught the writing of the House of Life, made up of signs that are so many elements of knowledge, symbols charged with magic and mystery. The radiance of the spirit depends upon correct writing. If you believe that hieroglyphs are only drawings and sounds, you will never understand them. In truth they contain the secret nature of beings and things, the most subtle essences. Sacred language is a cosmic force, it is that which created the world. Only Pharaoh, first among scribes, is capable of mastering it. That is why his name, *per-aa*, means "the great temple". Hieroglyphs have no need of men, they act through themselves. So you must be respectful of the texts you discover or pass on, for they are much more important than your small person.'

Iker was spellbound. He had half sensed much of this; but

Sepi expressed it with such precision that several doors opened on to several paths.

'It is not for your own glory that you will become scribes,' stated the teacher, 'but in order to carry on the work of Thoth. He measured the heavens, counted the stars, established time, years, seasons and months. The breath of life dwells in his fist; his cubit is the foundation of all measurement. He who is victim neither of disorder nor of irregularity establishes the plan of the temples.

'The learning of Thoth does not consist of vain speculation, for too much facility and knowledge is harmful. Through his words, you will learn to build, to share out food justly or to measure the area of a field. That which is above is like that which is below; that which is below is like that which is above; and twice-great Thoth will teach you not to dissociate the heavens from the earth.'

'But then, sir,' objected an apprentice, 'all we'll do is copy words that have already been written. Isn't that an admission of weakness?'

'If you wish to be strong,' replied Sepi, 'be a craftsman in words. True power is expression, for well-used words are more effective than any weapon. Some scribes are merely copyists, that's true, but they are no more contemptible for that. A few others – and only a few – enter into the sphere of creation.'

'What are the qualities demanded of them?' asked Iker.

'Listening, understanding and the mastery of the fires. You apprentices are still very far from that! Take up your tablets and your pens. I am going to dictate to you from the *Book of Kemit,* and then we shall correct your errors. Now, what does "*Kemit*" mean?'

'The word is formed on the root "*kem*",' said Iker, 'and means either "the black earth" – that is, the earth of Egypt fertilized by the Nile's silt – or "that which is achieved, complete".'

'Both meanings must be taken into account,' said Sepi.

'This book contains, indeed, a complete teaching for apprentice scribes and its goal is to make their spirits fertile. Prepare your writing-materials.'

Iker filled two shells with water and diluted his cakes of ink.

Then Sepi began to dictate.

The *Book of Kemit* began with wishes for eternal life, unity and blossoming from the Master. Then it dealt with the necessary 'justness of voice' in the face of the gods and the souls of Iunu, the sacred city of Ra. From Montu, the bull-god of the Theban province, it asked for strength and help; from Ptah, joy and a great age.

'May writings make you happy' was the wish that one made for the scribe, on condition that he listened to the Master, respected his elders, was close-mouthed, loved accuracy in all things and read useful texts, those that contained light.

One passage – '*May the good scribe be saved by the perfume of Punt*' – startled Iker so much that he almost lost his place in the dictation.

At the end of two hours of hard work and concentration, the apprentices were tired. Some had cramp, others aching backs.

General Sepi walked slowly along the rows of students, inspecting their tablets.

'Deplorable,' he pronounced. 'Not one of you has succeeded in writing all the words correctly. Your minds wander, and your hands are unsure. Tomorrow morning we shall begin again. Those who have made too many mistakes will be transferred to another school.'

Iker slowly got his things together. When the other apprentices had all gone, he went up to the teacher.

'Sir, may I ask a question?''

'Only one – I'm in a hurry.'

'The book mentions the perfume of Punt. But Punt's an

imaginary land, isn't it?'

'You think so?'

'Why would a good scribe copy out dreams? And why would the perfume of an imaginary land save him?'

'I said just one question, Iker. Go and join the others.'

Their welcome was hardly warm. They were all natives of the province of the Hare, and this foreigner's presence in General Sepi's class, which was so difficult to get into, rankled with more than one of them.

A short, brown-haired lad with bold eyes opened hostilities. 'Where are you from?'

'I'm here – that's the important thing,' replied Iker.

'Who recommended you?'

'What does that matter? It's up to each one of us to prove his abilities. When it comes to the test, we're all alone.'

'Right, as that's how you see it, you'll be even more alone than the others.'

The group moved away from the intruder, throwing resentful looks at him. They would gladly have beaten him to teach him a lesson, but General Sepi would have punished them severely.

Iker ate his midday meal on his own, re-reading his copy of the *Book of Kemit*. The word 'Punt' continued to haunt him. It was because of that mysterious land that he had almost died.

34

'Prepare your materials,' ordered General Sepi dryly.

Iker opened his bag, and disaster met his eyes. Someone had replaced his tablet with one so worn-out that it was almost unusable. His pens and brushes had been broken; his cakes of ink were as hard as stone, and he would get nothing good out of them.

He stood up. 'Mine have been damaged.'

Amused and satisfied, all eyes turned on him.

'Do you know who the culprit is?' asked Sepi.

'Yes, sir.'

Whispers ran round the room.

'Making an accusation is a serious matter,' the general reminded him. 'Are you sure of your facts?'

'I am.'

'Then give me his name.'

'The culprit is myself. I was stupid to think no one would ever do something so contemptible. I now see the full extent of my stupidity, but it's too late.' Head hanging low, feet dragging, he headed for the door, watched in delight by the others.

'Is it ever too late to correct oneself?' asked the general. 'Come back, Iker. Here is a bag containing all the materials needed by a professional scribe. I am entrusting it to you. If you fail just once more in your vigilance, you will not set foot in here again.'

Iker received the priceless gift with veneration. He could not find the words to express his gratitude.

'Go and sit down,' commanded the teacher, 'and get ready quickly.'

Iker forgot his enemies and concentrated on the fine, brand-new things the general had given him. With a steady hand, he produced a superb black ink.

'Write down these words from the Maxims of the sage Ptah-Hotep,' said the teacher, 'beginning with Maxim One. "May *your heart be not vain because of what you know . . . Take counsel from the ignorant as well as the learned, for one does not attain the limits of the art, and there exists no craftsman who has acquired perfection . . . Perfect words are more hidden than green stone, yet they are found among the serving-women who work at the grinding-stone.*"'

Many other passages followed. The text was far from easy, the opportunities for making mistakes numerous, but Iker's hand moved with dexterity. He paid attention to each word, while keeping in his mind the meaning of the full sentence.

When Sepi eventually stopped speaking, Iker didn't feel at all tired. He would willingly have gone on for much longer.

The general examined the tablets. Everyone held their breath.

'Half of you do not deserve to study in my class, and will continue your apprenticeship under different masters. The others still have a good deal of progress to make, and I shall certainly not keep all of them. One single pupil made only two mistakes: Iker. He will therefore be responsible for keeping an inventory of the writing-materials, and for the care and upkeep of this room, which he will clean each day. I am entrusting him with the key.'

The other apprentices were not unhappy about this decision, which they saw as humiliation for the outsider – they'd never lowered themselves to doing domestic tasks. But Iker considered the duty an honour, and he was delighted to be in charge of inventorying the writing-materials, a task to which he devoted himself with his usual zeal.

What happiness to be in contact with these things! He classified the tablets according to material and gave each a number: raw clay tablets requiring a hard point; rectangular tablets made from sycamore and jujube wood, made up of several pieces held together by hooks; limestone tablets with a meticulously smoothed surface.

Not seeing his fellow pupils all day long was a real stroke of luck. He hoped that General Sepi, who was far from Iker's idea of a military man, would continue to give him as much work as possible, so that this situation could continue.

Night had fallen when Iker left the classroom to go to the dining-chamber, where he had a meal of courgettes with soft cheese. The Maxims of Ptah-Hotep had been so deeply engraved in his mind that they haunted his thoughts like bewitching music.

When he reached his bedchamber, he saw a ray of light under the door, though he knew he had not left the lamp lit. Anxiously, he pushed the door slowly open and saw . . .

His mat had been torn up, his kilt lay in shreds, his clothes-chest was in a thousand pieces, his washing-things had been reduced to fragments, his sandals ripped apart, and the walls spattered with paint. Sickened and on the verge of tears, he wondered how he would ever manage to replace even the minimum he needed in order to live.

But he had no choice but to stay, so he did what he could to restore order to the room and then, exhausted, fell asleep.

When he awoke, Iker wondered gloomily if there was any point in continuing in such a climate of hatred: he'd probably have to face more and more bullying and hostility. What would his fellow pupils dream up next to discourage him? Alone against everyone; it was too uncomfortable a position to be held for very long. He decided that he would sweep the classroom before the lesson, then present his resignation to General Sepi.

When he opened his door he saw a parcel lying outside. More trouble, he thought, and he hesitated for a long time before undoing the string.

To his astonishment, the parcel contained two brand-new shirts and kilts, a pair of sandals, washing-things, a good, strong mat – he'd actually gained by the destruction of his possessions! Had one of his enemies regretted what they'd done? Or was he benefiting from the aid of a secret protector? Greatly heartened, he hurried off to begin his daily chores.

A well-dressed Iker greeted his teacher and fellow pupils in a classroom as clean as a virgin sheet of papyrus.

The other apprentices were astounded. Where had he got these new clothes? From his calm face, no one would have dreamt that his things had been damaged.

'You are to write some more of Ptah-Hotep's Maxims,' said General Sepi. 'Soon, this school must produce several papyri containing the complete version of this major work. We shall begin with Maxim Thirty-nine. *"When listening is good, words are good . . . He who listens is the master of what is profitable. . . Listening is profitable to him who listens . . . Listening is better than anything, for (thus) perfect love is born."'*

Suddenly, Iker had the feeling that he was no longer copying, but was actually writing. He was not simply passing on phrases that had already been uttered: he was participating in their significance. Through the form of his glyphs, the specific nature of his drawing, he was giving an as-yet-unknown colour to the sage's thoughts. It was a minute act, certainly; yet for the first time the apprentice felt the power of writing.

At the end of the lesson, Iker swept the classroom again. On his way out, he encountered a group of his students headed by the brown-haired boy with the bold eyes.

'Don't bother thinking up any more vile tricks,' Iker told them calmly. 'Next time I won't take it lying down.'

'You think you can frighten us? There are ten of us and only one of you.'

'I dislike violence, but if you carry on being destructive I'll have to punish you.'

'Just try it!'

The brown-haired boy tried to hit Iker with his clenched fist. Before he knew what was happening, he was flung into the air and fell heavily on his back. Running to the rescue, his closest crony suffered the same fate. And when a third, the strongest of the band, joined them in humiliation, the others backed off.

From the look in Iker's eyes, they all realized that he could have done a great deal worse than he had.

'He must have had military training,' said a scrawny youth. 'That lad's quite capable of breaking our bones. Let's get away from here before he really gets angry.'

Even the brown-haired youth didn't argue.

As the group hurried away, Iker thanked his lucky stars: if they'd thought of attacking together, he'd have had no chance at all. He also thanked Governor Khnum-Hotep, for compelling him to become a passable fighter.

On the way to the dining-chamber, he saw an ibis take flight, and it was so majestic that he stopped to watch it. The bird of Thoth began to fly in wide circles above him, as if wishing to make him understand that it really was addressing him. Then it headed towards the Nile, came back towards him, and flew off again in the direction of the river. He followed it.

Several times, the ibis repeated these patterns of flight. Benefiting from his experience in running, Iker covered the distance to the Nile in record time. The bird was waiting above a papyrus thicket. It perched for a few moments at the top of the parasol-shaped leaves, pecking them with its pointed beak, then soared off into the sky.

Clearly, the messenger of the god of scribes had brought Iker here in order to show him something. However, venturing into this tangle of reeds was not without danger – a crocodile or a snake might be hiding there – so he stamped his feet several times before parting the reeds and thrusting his way into the thicket.

To his amazement, he heard a whimpering. There was a baby in this thicket!

Forgetting the risks, Iker pushed forward as fast as possible and found a donkey foal trapped in the mud. It had an injured hoof, and was crumpled in on itself as though dead.

Slowly and gently, so as not to frighten it, Iker freed it from the mud that imprisoned it. The poor little creature was no more than skin and bone, and its ribs were staring.

'I'm going to pick you up,' Iker told it, 'and I'll take good care of you.'

Its big brown eyes filled with fear: it obviously had bad memories of its first contacts with the human race.

To calm the foal, Iker sat down next to it and made a first attempt at stroking it. It trembled, as if afraid he was going to hit it. But eventually the touch of a gentle, affectionate hand surprised and reassured it, and little by little Iker gained its trust.

'We must leave here and find you some food,' he said, and he carefully picked it up: it weighed alarmingly little. Iker was afraid it might struggle, but in the event it relaxed in his arms, at last feeling safe.

Suddenly, as its rescuer carried it along along the path to the fields, the foal began to wriggle and whimper in fear. The reason was not difficult to guess: a peasant armed with a pitchfork was striding towards them.

'Throw that monster into the marsh,' he shouted, 'and let it be eaten by the crocodiles!'

'What monster? This is nothing but a starving, wounded foal.'

'You haven't looked at it properly.'

'Oh yes I have, and I saw that it has been abominably mistreated. If you're the guilty party, you'll be punished by the courts.'

'Guilty of ridding myself of a bad-luck creature? I won't be punished, I'll be congratulated.'

'Why do you say that?'

'Here, I'll show you.'

'No, don't come any closer,' ordered Iker.

'Look on the back of its neck. Look at the mark.'

Iker looked, and saw a few reddish hairs.

'That foal is a creature of Set – it brings bad luck.'

'It was Thoth's ibis that led me to the place where you abandoned this foal after beating it. Do you really think the god of scribes can't tell evil when he sees it?'

'But the mark . . . Everyone knows that red-haired animals are Set's!'

'Perhaps this one will have Set's strength but be purified by the ibis of Thoth.'

'And who are you?'

'An apprentice scribe from General Sepi's class.'

The peasant's tone changed abruptly. 'Very well, perhaps we can come to an agreement. That foal's my property, but I'll give it to you on condition that you don't lay a complaint against me.'

'You're asking a lot.'

'Look, I thought I was doing the right thing, and a court would certainly find me innocent. How could I tell that Thoth would intervene?'

'Very well, my friend, you have your agreement.'

Relieved to have come out of it so well, the peasant made himself scarce, and at once the foal relaxed again.

A gentle northerly breeze began to blow, and the donkey

sniffed the air with interest. For the first time it registered curiosity about the world around it, and its eyes filled with love for its rescuer. It was awakening to life.

'Well, that settles your name,' said Iker, smiling. 'You shall be called North Wind.'

35

Hidden in the Delta, two days' march north-east of Imet, Crooked-Face and his trainees lived by hunting and fishing. They ate well every day, and their leader used this as a reason to make their training even harsher. In this terrain, it was easy to lay ambushes and think up difficult exercises. Only two more recruits had been killed, which pleased Crooked-Face because it showed that the training was yielding results and that the raiders would soon be ready to act.

Becoming leader of the finest band of looters ever seen on Egyptian soil: that was Crooked-Face's goal. He would inflict so much suffering on his enemies that the mere sound of his name would fill them with terror.

One of his men hurried up to him. 'The lookout reports intruders, sir.'

'Really? Well, we're going to enjoy ourselves. Everyone into position.'

Of course, Crooked-Face had foreseen this possibility, and his men knew how to deal with the inconvenient arrivals.

'How many are there?' he asked.

'Four.'

'That's too easy! Two of us can take care of them.'

It was a lucky day for Shab the Twisted, for Crooked-Face recognized him just in time, and didn't hurl his dagger.

With his recruit, he burst out of the reeds like a wild
animal. 'Greetings, Shab. Did you have a good journey?'

'You scared me, you idiot!'

Crooked-Face looked around. 'Where's our great leader?'

'A patrol of desert guards arrested him – they've probably
taken him to Sichem.'

'Why didn't you kill them?'

'There were too many of them, and anyway the Herald
ordered us to run.'

'That's a sad end to the career of a man like that,' mourned
Crooked-Face.

'What are you saying? We're going to go to Sichem and
free him.'

'You're crazy! Do you really think the Egyptians would
make the mistake of leaving the town unguarded? There'll be
a whole regiment stationed there, and we couldn't possibly be
a match for them.'

'Aren't your recruits well trained?'

'For individual operations, yes, but not for a frontal
assault.'

'We won't attack via the barracks. We'll try the prison.'

'First, it'll be well guarded, and there's no guarantee we
can free the Herald. Second, we'd be too late.'

'Why?'

'Because he'll have been executed. Pharaoh's hardly like
to show mercy to the leader of the rebels.'

Shab grimaced.

'Your Herald's already dead,' said Crooked-Face. 'For us
to go to Sichem would be suicide.'

'Then what do you suggest?'

'That we accept fate and look to our own future. With these
men we'll do better than the sand-travellers.'

'You're probably right, but the Herald—'

'Forget him. He's roasting in the furnaces of hell.'

'But supposing he's been given a chance?'

'What kind of chance?' demanded Crooked-Face, astonished.

'A chance to escape. You know very well that he's no ordinary man. His powers may enable him to escape.'

'But he was arrested.'

'Supposing that's what he wanted?'

'Why on earth would he want that?'

'To prove that no one can imprison him.'

'You seem to think your Herald's a god.'

'He has the power of the desert demons, and he'll know how to use it.'

'That's just talk. We're free, very much alive and ready to rob some Egyptians.'

'Let's stay here until the new moon,' suggested Shab. 'If the Herald hasn't arrived by then, we'll leave.'

'Agreed. And we'll take the opportunity to eat and drink well while we wait. The farms and the nobles' estates must contain big reserves of wine and beer. And when we've got those, we'll take care of the girls.'

In a cell with a beaten-earth floor ten men were confined. They were all prostrate, except the Herald. Hidden in a fold of his tunic, the queen of turquoises kept evil fate at bay. In fact, as soon as he had been thrown into this evil-smelling jail, the future had become clear, for one of the prisoners was so like him that they could have been brothers, though he was lacking in his wits. The simpleton was almost as tall as the Herald, with a similarly thin face, and even the same walk; all that was needed was for his beard to grow for another few days. The Herald was sure he had that much time, because the Egyptian soldiers would finish their detailed interrogation of Sichem's inhabitants before dealing with the shepherds arrested in the countryside around the town.

'You men don't know me,' declared the Herald, 'but I know you.'

Questioning eyes were raised to his face.

'You are brave men, abused by an occupier so cruel that you have given up fighting. I have come to help you.'

'Can you knock down the walls of this prison?' asked a shepherd sarcastically.

'I can, but not in the way you imagine.'

'What will you do?'

'Have you heard tell of the Herald?'

Only one prisoner responded. 'Isn't he a sorcerer allied to the demons of the desert?'

'Indeed he is.'

'Why would he come to free us?'

'He won't come.'

'Then you're talking nonsense.'

'He won't come because he's already here.' The Herald laid his hand on the simpleton's shoulder. 'Here is your saviour.'

'Him? But he can scarcely speak!'

'Up till now, you haven't recognized him, and that is your gravest mistake. In less than a week, he will be ready to strike down the adversary and free us.'

The shepherds all shrugged dismissively and huddled in their corners.

The Herald began training his substitute by making him repeat a few simple phrases which the people of Sichem had heard a thousand times. Happy to be taken in hand and to escape from the heavy prison atmosphere, the simpleton was only too willing to do as he was told.

A week later, the door of the cell slammed open and half a dozen Egyptian guards marched in.

Their officer ordered, 'Out, all of you. Your turn to be questioned.'

'We only obey the Herald,' declared a shepherd who had agreed to play the game.

The officer almost choked. 'Say that again!'

'The Herald is our guide. We take our orders from him, and only from him.'

'And where is he, this famous Herald?'

'Here, among us.'

The prisoners parted to reveal the simpleton, dressed in the Herald's turban and tunic.

The officer set the end of his club against the simpleton's chest. 'Are you really the Herald?'

'I am.'

'And it was really you who caused the Sichem riot?'

'God has elected me to strike down the oppressors of the people, and I shall lead them to victory.'

'We'll see about that! We shall introduce you to General Nesmontu, my lad.'

'No enemy can overcome me, for I am the ally of the demons of the desert.'

'Tie him up,' the officer ordered his men.

The real Herald came forward. 'We're only shepherds,' he whined, 'and we don't understand any of this. Our animals are waiting for us. If we don't see to them very soon, we'll lose everything.'

The guard was a peasant's son, and receptive to this argument. 'Very well, we'll question you first. Then we'll see.'

Following the agreed plan, the shepherds protested their total innocence. One after another, they were freed. The guards were only too happy to have found a succulent titbit to enliven their daily fare.

General Nesmontu regarded the turbaned man with suspicion. 'So you're the rebel who ordered the slaughter of the Sichem garrison?'

'I am the Herald. God has elected me to strike down the oppressors of the people and—'

'—and you will lead them to victory. I know, I know. That's twenty times you've said that. Who's behind you? The Asians, the Libyans, or just the Canaanites?'

'God has chosen me to—'

The general slapped him. 'Sometimes I regret the fact that Pharaoh has forbidden the use of torture. Now, here's a clear question and I want a clear answer: are you acting alone or with other conspirators?'

'God has chosen me—'

'Enough! Take him away and continue the questioning. When he is thirsty enough, perhaps he'll talk.'

Thanks to the Herald's teaching, the simpleton was convinced he was a match for the Egyptians. None of them managed to get anything out of him except the set phrases he'd learnt, which he repeated imperturbably.

'We really have laid our hands on this mad criminal,' said the general's second-in-command.

'I think a last check is necessary. Take him out and lead him through the streets of the town.'

At first, the soldiers guarding the prisoner thought he was a mere impostor, for no one reacted as he walked past.

But suddenly a woman shouted, 'It's him! I recognize him!'

An old man chimed in. 'The Herald's come back!'

In a few seconds a crowd had gathered. The guards freed themselves roughly and led their prisoner back to the barracks.

'No doubt about it, General,' said the guards' leader. 'This madman really is the Herald. If we want to avoid further trouble, we must show the people his dead body as soon as possible.'

'Give him poison,' ordered Nesmontu.

While the general was writing the pharaoh a long report on the affair, the simpleton went to his death with perfect unconcern. After all, the Herald had promised that he would be admitted to a magnificent palace, filled with bold women who would satisfy all his desires while cup-bearers offered him the finest wines.

36

Iker had formed no bonds with any of his fellow pupils and devoted himself exclusively to his work. In the evenings, he was content to dine on lentil, green bean and onion soup, and a crust of bread rubbed with garlic, before going to his room to continue his studies. He worked by the light of a lamp fuelled by castor oil, which was cheap and which could also be used instead of ointment.

Over and over again he copied out the classical texts in order to engrave them in his memory, to school his hand and to develop a writing-style which was both quick and clear. As he drew, he made each thought so alive that he espoused its many contours. The hieroglyphs were much more than a succession of images; in them the gods' creative acts echoed, giving each word its full effectiveness.

Could one prolong life and make it sparkle by writing? As his spirit assimilated the signs, and was transformed into them and by them, Iker was more and more convinced that one could. He was not interested in being a minor scribe restricted to administrative work. He wanted to get to the heart of the mystery of the language – both abstract and concrete – that Egyptian civilization had created.

When intent on his work, he managed not to think of the priestess. But often, at the end of a phrase or passage, her face would reappear and lead him into insane hope. His only hope of seeing her again was if his skills as a scribe opened the doors of Abydos to him. Perhaps there would be other festivals or other rites which she would honour with her presence . . .

No, he would not give up. It was for her as much as for himself that he had set his heart on conquering grammar, vocabulary, the correct layout of the hieroglyphs which, by their arrangement on the wood, papyrus or stone, emitted a harmony which only the masters of writing knew.

Iker often went to see North Wind, now comfortably settled on bedding which was changed every morning. The foal had a hearty appetite, and seemed to grow before his very eyes. The starvation and injury would soon be no more than a bad memory.

On their first walk in the country, the donkey both led the way and then found its way back without hesitation. Iker thought it looked very happy.

'It's good to have a true friend,' he confided. 'I can tell you everything.' And he did: as he returned the foal to its stable, fed it and bedded it down for the night, he told it the whole story, leaving nothing out. North Wind's long ears flickered attentively.

'I'm not worried that this gang of scribblers doesn't like me. In fact, their dislike strengthens me. When I see those imbecile heads so full of their own affairs that they respect neither others nor the sacred signs, all I want is to forge my own path without wasting a thought on their opinions. What characterizes them is their sterility, which makes them envious and jealous. They try to destroy anyone who isn't like them. You and I are truly brothers, North Wind. Together we can do anything.' The donkey licked its rescuer's hand, and in return received many caresses before Iker closed the stable door and went back to his room.

As he did every night, before going to sleep Iker laid on his belly the ivory talisman that Techat had given him, in order to ward off evil spirits. In the morning, as soon as he awoke, he slid it over his amulets to recharge them with energy.

Out of the whole class, Sepi had selected just ten pupils to receive advanced training, and he made them work very hard. So they were more than glad when, at the end of class one afternoon, he told them, 'Tomorrow is a rest day.'

As usual, Iker was the last to leave the classroom. 'General, may I ask a favour?'

'I give you permission not to sweep the classroom on the rest day.'

'No, it isn't that. May I have permission to consult the province's archives?'

'Wouldn't you rather rest and enjoy yourself?'

'Sooner or later, I shall have to cope with those sorts of document. I'd like to begin learning about them as soon as possible.'

'Which section of the archives?'

'Oh, a little of everything. I don't want to confine myself to a particular subject.'

'Very well. I'll write you out a letter of authorization.'

The young man could barely hide his excitement.

Armed with the precious letter, he went to see the scribe in charge of the archives, who checked the general's seal carefully and then asked, 'Which documents do you wish to consult?'

'All those relating to boats, crews and trading expeditions.'

'From what date?'

'Let's say . . . three years ago.'

The scribe led him into a vast, brick-built hall lined with shelves on which papyri and tablets were meticulously arranged.

'I do not permit untidiness or carelessness here. If you show the slightest sign of either, I shall ask your teacher to cancel your permission.'

'I shall respect the rules to the letter,' promised Iker.

Although impatient, he was thoroughly methodical. The long time it would take to scour the documents did not alarm him. On the contrary, he was sure that in this huge store of documents he would find a clue somewhere.

The province of the Hare had many boats, but none called *Swift One*. Having got over this disappointment, Iker hoped that the two sailors might have belonged to other crews in the records. But, search as he might, he could find no trace of either Sharp-Knife or Turtle-Eye. As for the trading expeditions, none had had Punt as its destination. Only the companionship of North Wind, who was fully recovered and growing by the day, and the riches he found in General Sepi's teaching prevented him from giving in to pessimism.

One afternoon, as he was coming out of the classroom, which he had just cleaned from top to bottom, Iker was accosted by three young girls. They were elegantly clad in light dresses, with bracelets at wrist and ankle, pearl necklaces, diadems decorated with cornflowers . . . They looked like princesses, proud of displaying their wealth.

'Are you Iker the scribe?' asked the tallest one in a ravishingly beautiful voice.

'I'm only an apprentice.'

'You seem to work much too hard,' purred the youngest, with a sly and mocking look.

'As far as I'm concerned, my lady, one can never work hard enough. There are so many major texts to study.'

'Isn't that a bit boring, in the long run?'

'Oh no, far from it. The more you practise hieroglyphs, the more marvels you discover.'

'And what do you think of us?'

Iker blushed to the roots of his hair. 'I, er, I . . . How can I judge? Forgive me, but I must go and feed my donkey.'

'Aren't we more interesting than an animal?' asked the third girl.

'Please accept my apologies – I really am in a hurry.' And he turned and fled.

As he fed North Wind, he thought about those three elegant and graceful girls. They were surprisingly alike, and were of much the same age, so that it was hard to tell them apart at first glance. But their beauty was too artificial, their charm too affected; and he formed only one wish: that they wouldn't bother him again.

His wish did not come true.

That very evening, the youngest girl knocked at the door of his room. Her face was over-painted, he thought – too much green kohl round the eyes, too much red ochre on the lips – and was wearing too much perfume.

She smiled seductively and asked, 'Am I disturbing you, Iker?'

'No . . . Well, yes, actually . . . You can't come in, because—'

'Because you've already got a girl in there?'

'No, of course not!'

'Then let me give you something I've prepared specially for you.' She set down two dishes in front of him. 'The first one contains cakes with jujube fruits,' she explained. 'My serving-woman ground the grain to a very fine flour, and I myself added the honey before cooking the cakes in the oven. The second one contains cheese with herbs, prepared with the milk from our most beautiful cow. I don't suppose you ever have the chance to eat delicacies like these, do you? Well, if you're nice to me, you can eat them all the time.'

'I cannot accept them, my lady.'

'Why not?'

'You're obviously someone very important, and I'm only an apprentice scribe.'

'Why don't you become important, too? I can help you, believe me.'

'I prefer to make my own way.'

'Come, come, don't be so stubborn. Dare you say that I don't please you?'

Iker looked her straight in the eyes. 'You don't please me.'

'You like taking risks, Iker. Do you really not know who I am?'

'Whoever you are, I must refuse your generous offer.'

'Have you already given your heart to someone?'

'That concerns no one but me.'

'Forget her. How can she possibly compare with a daughter of Djehuty, governor of the province of the Hare? My sisters and I choose the men with whom we take pleasure. You are one of the lucky few.'

She began to slide one of the straps of her dress down over her shoulder.

'Please leave at once,' said Iker.

'If you refuse me you'll pay dearly for it.'

'Stop this distasteful game and leave me in peace.'

'Is that your last word?'

'You heard me perfectly.'

She readjusted her strap and threw a look of hatred at Iker.

He ignored it and picked up the two dishes. 'Don't forget these – they belong to you.'

'You will not spend many more hours in this province, you insolent little cur!'

The next day, after feeding North Wind, Iker went to the dining-hall for his evening meal. It wasn't until the last spoonful of soup that he noticed that it tasted strange. He drank plenty of water to get rid of the taste, but it didn't work. Indeed, the water itself seemed undrinkable.

He wanted to talk to the cook, but he had disappeared.

Suddenly his head began to spin, so much so that he fell

over and could not get up again. His sight was blurred, but he could make out the faces of Djehuty's three daughters.

The youngest bent over their victim.

'Don't worry,' she said, 'you won't die of poison. We've only given you a sleeping-draught so that you're at our mercy. Now we're going to make you drink date-wine, lots of it – your clothes and your skin will be soaked in it. The servants will find a drink-sodden little scribbler. Amusing, isn't it?'

Iker tried to protest, but his words were incoherent and ran together.

'Sleep well, you impudent boy – this will teach you to reject us! When you awake, we'll have our revenge and you'll have lost everything.'

'You are like a twisted rudder,' General Sepi told Iker, 'a shrine without its god, an empty house. One can teach a monkey to dance, a dog to walk on its hind legs, one can even catch a bird by its wings, but you . . . How can you be taught? Your heart is disordered, your ears are deaf. You, a pupil from my class, got drunk and soiled the kilt of a scribe!'

'I was the victim of a conspiracy,' protested Iker, whose mind was still clouded.

The general's anger seemed to abate a little. 'And who might the conspirators be?'

'People who took advantage of my credulity.'

'Name them!'

'I'm the one responsible – I ought to have been more careful. My food was drugged and I was made to drink date-wine.'

'By whom?'

'If I told you, you wouldn't believe me. And even if you did, you couldn't punish the culprits. They wanted to disgrace me in your eyes. The least a drunken scribe deserves is to be expelled from your school, and even from the province that welcomed him.'

'The facts are the facts, Iker, and your explanations are too mixed-up to be credible. If you want to prove your innocence, you must name the people who did this and arrange to confront them.'

'It wouldn't lead anywhere, General.'

'Then only a sign from the other world can change my decision.'

Sepi called two soldiers and told them to escort Iker to the southern border of the province and see that he left. It was regrettable parting with his best pupil like this, but Iker's offence was too serious to overlook.

'General, look over there!' exclaimed one of the soldiers, taking a step back and pointing.

Sepi saw a white-bellied chameleon just inside the door of the room. It raised its strange eyes towards him, and he hurriedly spoke words of appeasement. After a brief hesitation, the animal withdrew.

'The chameleon is one of the manifestations of Anubis,' he told Iker. 'You seem to benefit from remarkable protection.'

'Do you mean . . . you aren't expelling me?'

'I'd have to be mad to neglect the intervention of Anubis.'

'Do you believe, General, that one day I shall belong to the Golden Circle of Abydos?'

Sepi froze. Iker had the feeling that he was gazing at a statue with questioning eyes.

'Who told you about the Circle?'

'It's more than just a poetical expression, isn't it?'

'Answer my question.'

'A gardener. Our roads crossed, then parted.'

'The poets know how to make us dream, my boy. But you are working to become a scribe and deal with reality.'

37

Standing in front of Djehuty, who was hunched in his high-backed chair, his three daughters were stamping with impatience.

'Can we talk to you now?' demanded the eldest.

'In a moment – I must finish studying this file.' He took his time doing so and rolling up the long papyrus. 'What is it, my sweet ones?'

'Father, we are very upset and we appeal to our supreme judge for justice.'

'You mean Ma'at?'

'No, you! Abominable acts have been committed in your province, and the guilty man has gone unpunished.'

Djehuty looked solemn. 'That is indeed serious. Do you know any more?'

The youngest said vehemently, 'Iker the apprentice scribe stole date-wine and got drunk, which is thoroughly unworthy and unacceptable behaviour. But this morning we saw him going into General Sepi's school as if nothing had happened. You must act immediately, Father, and expel Iker from our province.'

Djehuty regarded his daughters with a gravity tinged with irony. 'Don't worry about it, my sweet ones. I've brought the matter out into the open.'

'What . . . what do you mean?'

'That unfortunate young man was the victim of a malicious trick, but Anubis, in the form of a chameleon, came to protect him, and enabled us to understand that Iker was telling the truth.'

'Has he accused anyone?' asked the eldest daughter uneasily.

'No, and there can be no better proof of his generous nature. Would you and your sisters perhaps have any suspicions?'

'Us? But how . . . No, of course not!'

'I thought not. You should know that I consider Iker a future scribe of great worth and that I shall not ignore it if any more tricks are played on him. Whoever the culprit may be, he will be severely punished. Do we understand each other, my sweet ones?'

The three girls nodded and almost ran out of the audience chamber.

As soon as they had gone, in came a short, thin, frail-looking man, carrying a leather satchel which looked too heavy for him.

'Ah, Doctor Gua!' said Djehuty. 'I've been hoping for quite some time that you'd come.'

'You may be the governor,' retorted the doctor in a pinched tone, 'but I have other people to treat besides you. What with people's rheumatism, earache and ulcers, I don't know where to turn any more. You'd think all the sick people have been passing the word around this morning! My young colleagues ought to be a little more skilful and put more of their hearts into their work. Right, what are you suffering from today?'

'A nasty attack of indigestion, and—'

'I've heard enough. You eat too much, you drink too much, you work too much and you sleep too little. And then there's your advancing age, which you refuse to accept. Medicine can do nothing in the face of such obstinacy, and it's no use hoping you'll change your ways. You are the very worst of all my patients, but I am nevertheless obliged to treat you.'

Each consultation began with the same lecture. Djehuty was careful not to interrupt Gua, whose treatment always proved as good as his diagnosis.

From his satchel, the doctor took a pot shaped like a man, one knee resting on the ground, carrying a vase on his shoulder and supporting it with his left hand. Written in the doctor's hand, the inscription read: '*I am weary of bearing everything.*'

'Here is a laxative made of yeast, castor oil and a few other ingredients you do not need to know. Your stomach will leave you in peace, you will forget about your digestion, and you'll think you're in good health. You'll be quite wrong, of course, but what can I do? I'll see you again the day after tomorrow.'

And Gua scurried off like a tireless ant, to take care of another patient.

The next person to appear was Sepi. He bowed and asked, 'Are you in good health, my lord?'

'It could be worse, but I think the time for regeneration has come.'

'The priests are ready,' said Sepi. 'The water of Abydos is at your disposal.'

'You'll need an assistant scribe: why not Iker?'

The general was doubtful. 'Isn't it a bit too soon?'

'Is it ever too soon to start training someone whose path the gods have mapped out?'

'I'd have liked to have more time to prepare him, to—'

'If he really is what we think he is,' cut in Djehuty, 'experiencing this rite will awaken him to himself. If we're wrong, it will merely make one more braggart who'll break his teeth on his own illusions.'

Sepi would have liked to protect his best pupil, but he could do no more than bow.

The other apprentices still ostracized Iker and were jealous of him – everyone knew that the outsider was the most brilliant pupil in the class, far ahead of the rest. Not only could he discern the meaning of difficult texts with an almost insolent facility, but he succeeded in every exercise as if it held no difficulties at all.

In addition to all that, General Sepi had just entrusted him with drawing up a decree concerning the details of surveying the land after the waters of the annual flood had receded. In other words, Iker had been appointed a scribe of the province of the Hare and would soon leave the school to take up his first post.

After his latest misadventure, he always questioned the cook carefully before each meal. The latter, knowing he'd be held responsible for any mishap, tasted all the dishes.

Not tonight, though. As Iker was about to enter the dining-hall, Sepi stopped him and told him, 'This evening, you will have your meal later. Where are your writing-materials?'

'Here – I keep them with me all the time.'

'Then follow me.'

Iker sensed that he must not ask any questions. The general was as serious as a soldier about to take part in a battle with an uncertain outcome.

On the eastern bank of the Nile, at the top of a hill, the tombs of the lords of the Hare province had been excavated. On one side they overlooked the river, on the other the desert, into which a path wound between two cliffs.

Lit by many torches, guarded by two soldiers, the house of eternity prepared for Djehuty was impressive. The roof of its deep porch was supported by two pillars whose tops were in the form of palm-leaves, and the porch led to a large rectangular chamber with a small shrine at the end.

Iker halted on the threshold.

'I told you to follow me,' Sepi reminded him.

His throat tight and his feet hesitant, the young man entered the tomb.

Djehuty was standing in front of the door to the shrine. Dressed in a simple, old-style kilt, he looked taller and broader than usual. Two priests bearing vases came and stood one on either side of him.

Suddenly, the light dimmed. The only lamp now lit was the small one General Sepi held.

He handed Iker a scroll of papyrus with a superb golden tint. 'Read out these words,' he said. 'Through your voice, they will become reality.'

Iker obeyed: '"*May the water of life purify the Master, may it bring together his energies and may it refresh his heart.*"'

The two priests raised the vases above Djehuty's head.

Iker expected to see water pour out, but instead he was almost blinded – he had to close his eyes – by rays of light which enveloped the old man's body. At first he thought he must be seeing an illusion. He made himself open his eyes again. A gentle brightness now enveloped Djehuty, who seemed to have grown younger by several years.

'You who wished to know the Golden Circle of Abydos,' said General Sepi, 'see it at work.'

38

Iker did not close his eyes all night. The details of the strange ritual were engraved in his memory, and he sought in vain to understand the significance of the general's extraordinary words.

Now, besides tracing the men who who had tried to kill him and discovering why they had, and finding the beautiful priestess, he must also solve the mystery of the Golden Circle of Abydos. That was too much to ask of, and too heavy a burden for, one solitary, penniless young man. For any but Iker! Of course, doubt – even despair – would try a thousand and one times to submerge him. It was up to him to withstand the assaults and to create a path where none yet existed.

The thought of the coming ordeals and difficulties strengthened his determination. If he failed to overcome them, that would be proof that he was unworthy of doing so. Then his life would be pointless.

His musings were interrupted by a voice outside his room: 'Iker the scribe is summoned to Governor Djehuty's palace.'

Iker dressed in haste, gathered up his writing-materials and put them in a satchel for North Wind to carry – he was now strong enough to do so without tiring.

When Iker reached the palace he found Djehuty at the entrance, seated in his most comfortable travelling-chair.

'Proceed,' ordered the governor.

Iker had expected to be one of a whole army of scribes, who would follow their master and write down what he said. But he was the only one, and for a few moments he was seized by panic. How could he, a mere beginner, possibly manage in place of many skilled and experienced men? But he had no choice, so he gritted his teeth and resolved that he would not balk at the task.

Djehuty was carried along beside the main canal that crossed his province. He inspected the green, marshy area set aside for game, then covered part of the agricultural land, where he met peasants, gardeners, vineyard-workers and shepherds. Next, he visited the workshops of the potters, carpenters and weavers, then conversed with bakers and brewers, advising them to pay attention to the quality of their produce, which had declined in recent weeks.

Djehuty's energy was remarkable. He seemed to Iker to know every single one of the people he governed, he always used the right words, and his criticisms were always constructive. Not once during the long day did he show the least sign of fatigue. His scribe managed to equal the governor's diligence, although his wrist hurt from noting down all the conversations.

At last Djehuty returned to his palace, and went out into the garden. The governor called for light beer for himself and Iker, and by the time it arrived he was already studying Iker's notes.

'You didn't do too badly,' he concluded. 'You are to write a summary, which I shall use to check if the measures I ordered have been followed. Discussion is important, but only deeds count.'

'Is a ritual a deed?'

'It is – perhaps even the supreme deed, since it puts into the present what the gods carried out in the beginning.'

'What happened to you last night, my lord, was . . .'

'It was a sort of regeneration, vital for a man of my age

211

who is laden with heavy responsibilities. You had a chance today to take stock of my province's wealth, and see the need for hard work to preserve it. No one here is afraid of hard work, and if anyone tries to cheat I soon know who he is and deal with him. But one man wants to destroy this beautiful harmony: Pharaoh Senusret. He is our enemy, Iker.'

The young scribe was troubled. The governor was not speaking idly. Was this his way of telling Iker the name of the man who wanted him dead?

Djehuty might show satisfaction at the prosperity of his agriculture, but the lack of information from the court in Memphis worried him deeply. Did this silence mean that the king suspected him of complicity in the Sichem rebellion? If so, he would have to take up his staff and unite with the other provincial governors in order to fight off the pharaoh's inevitable attack.

What made him hesitate was the fact that his closest adviser, General Sepi, strongly disagreed. Sepi believed that a hastily formed alliance would lead only to a crushing defeat, devasting for all the allies. He advocated negotiating with Senusret and trying to make him understand Djehuty's point of view.

As he drank his beer, Djehuty yet again brooded over what it would be best to do. This uncertainty, so foreign to his nature, was making him irritable.

A black ibis landed not far from Iker and stared straight at him. Then it took a few steps forward before stopping and impressing the marks of its feet in the ground. With its beak, it drew the top of the triangle thus formed, before flying off.

'What do you think that meant?' asked Djehuty.

'I have learnt that one can confidently drink water that ibis drink, and that they pass on the first light to us by drawing signs. This is one of them, my lord: the triangle, the first expression of creative thought. In other words, create in your turn something great, and your cares will be erased.'

'Sepi has taught you well. That might indeed be the solution.'

An incredible plan had just taken shape in Djehuty's mind. If he succeeded in bringing it to reality, even Senusret would be impressed.

'General Sepi has told me about the Golden Circle of Abydos,' ventured Iker. 'I would like—'

'General Sepi has left on a mission for an indeterminate length of time. And you are going to have a lot of work. From tonight, you will live in the palace, where an office has been set aside for you. You will assemble all the reports concerning the strengths and weaknesses of my province, and identify their essentials. I want to know what we are capable of in the event of war.'

Seated on a chair made from reeds, Crooked-Face was finishing off a haunch of gazelle while Shab the Twisted dejectedly contemplated the papyrus-stalks dancing in the wind.

'We've waited long enough,' said Crooked-Face through a mouthful of meat. 'It's time to leave.'

Shab had run out of arguments. This time, even he knew that the Herald would not be coming back. Without his leader, he faced the prospect of turning back into a petty thief with a bleak future.

'We make a good team,' said Crooked-Face. 'No one can resist us. The rich estates of the Delta are ours. Forget the past, my friend, and let's go and make our fortune.'

A cry of pain filled the humid air of the marsh.

'It's the lookout,' shouted one of the men. 'He's been attacked!'

The fighters seized their weapons and set about trapping the attacker by surrounding him.

The sudden appearance of the Herald stopped them in their tracks.

'Which of my faithful would dare attack me?'

'You did escape!' exclaimed Shab in delight.

'Well,' said Crooked-Face. 'Well . . . Did you knock down the prison walls?'

'Better than that: our enemies think they have executed the Herald. For the Egyptians I no longer exist. That gives us a considerable advantage: we can act in the shadows without anyone knowing where the attacks are coming from.'

Shab drank in his leader's words. 'Shouldn't we continue to spread rebellion in Canaan, my lord?'

'No. Senusret reacted very vigorously, and now has soldiers stationed throughout the region. The new garrison at Sichem is made up of experienced soldiers who would savagely put down any attempt at sedition. But that is not the most serious matter. On my way here I passed through many towns and villages, and I realized how cowardly their inhabitants are. They're sheep, and they'll never rebel against the occupier and give their lives to impose the rule of the true God. To rely on them would be utter folly.'

'That doesn't surprise me,' declared Crooked-Face. 'I've never believed in those people – they're no more than a joke. We don't want cowards.'

'You must have a new plan,' ventured Shab anxiously.

'The Sichem adventure was very useful,' said the Herald.

'Then,' cut in Crooked-Face, 'do we begin with a farm or a noble's estate?'

'Which do you think would be better?'

'An isolated farm with few employees. We need to learn how to do it properly. As regards the loot—'

'You can keep it all, my friend. Meanwhile, Shab, five men and myself will establish ourselves in Memphis.'

Crooked-Face gaped at him. 'In Memphis? But the city's full of soldiers and guards!'

'We shan't commit any crimes. We shall make a place for ourselves as honest traders, so as to acquire as much information as possible. I must know this pharaoh and his entourage much better in order to defeat him. Our objective will be to obtain an ally in the heart of the palace itself.'

'But that's impossible!' said Crooked-Face.

'There is no other way, my friend. Your raids will make you very rich, and you will provide the help I need when I need it. And you won't ever even think of betraying me, will you?'

The Herald's stare was more terrifying than a desert demon's. Crooked-Face knew that the turbaned man would read his mind and could never be deceived. The Herald laid a hand on his shoulder, and he had the feeling that a bird of prey's talons were sinking into his flesh.

'You had a worthless life as a petty thief, and I'm offering you the stature of an assassin who will instil fear into an entire country. Stop acting like a miserable criminal and understand that the exercise of supreme power rests on two plinths: violence and corruption. You will be the first, Shab will be the second. Fortune will reward you, my faithful friend, and you shall buy whatever you desire. But you must be patient, you must strike only when you are asked, and you must progress in planned stages.'

For the first time, Crooked-Face was fully convinced by the Herald's words. This man was a true warrior chief who knew how to devise and implement a plan. To obey him was a strength, not a weakness.

'That suits me,' decided Crooked-Face.

39

Under High Treasurer Senankh's critical eye, scribes were handing out orders to the workers charged with cleaning the canals and strengthening the dykes in preparation for the annual flood. In view of the scale of the task, peasants had been assigned to help bring fallen earth back up to the tops of the embankments, dredge the bottoms of the waterways and pools, and seal the cracks. The blazing June heat made the work arduous, but everyone knew how vital it was. Everything must be done to collect as much water as possible. Between the end of this flood and the beginning of the next, it would be used to irrigate the fields, orchards and gardens.

Other teams were laying down reserves of dried wood for the winter, and yet others were filling jars with dried fruit, a vital food source during the first days of the flood, when the Nile would not be navigable. Many villages would be cut off, and would have to be self-sufficient in food for some time.

To all outward appearances, everything was going well. But Senankh was waiting for vital information from the South. At last it arrived, brought by an army messenger.

Immediately he read it, his well-fed face grew long. Although he had been preparing to eat a hearty breakfast, he no longer had any appetite at all. Much more quickly than usual, he walked to the Office of Pharaoh's Works, where his colleague Sehotep interrupted a meeting to receive him.

Senankh told him the bad news and asked, 'Should we tell His Majesty or is it better to hide the truth from him?'

'You are right to ask that,' said Sehotep. 'If we tell him he won't remain idle and will probably take ill-considered risks. But we are members of his council, and to keep silent would be a serious offence.'

'That's what I think, too.'

The two ministers therefore requested an audience with Senusret.

Senankh spoke first. 'Many observations confirm, Majesty, that the cyclamens are growing longer roots so as to reach the water. There is no room for doubt: the annual flood will be weak. That means that, after three average years, which have not enabled us to rebuild our grain reserves, we run the risk of famine.'

'This disaster does not come by chance,' said Senusret. 'The Tree of Osiris at Abydos is dying, and this is the master of the flood's way of signalling his displeasure. I must go to Elephantine to worship him and re-establish harmony.'

That was exactly the decision the two ministers had feared.

'Majesty,' Senankh reminded him, 'that region is not safe. The governor is a determined opponent of yours, and his army is renowned for its ferocity. Moreover, to reach Elephantine, you will have to cross several other hostile areas. Your boat is sure to be attacked.'

'Do you think I am unaware of the dangers? But there is another danger, and a much more serious one: famine. Whatever the risks, I must try to prevent it.'

'In that case, Majesty,' suggested Sehotep, 'all our troops must be mobilized to accompany you.'

'No. It is essential that we keep a strong military presence in Canaan – only that will maintain the peace we have re-established. I shall take only a flotilla of light vessels. Have it made ready to leave as soon as possible.'

*

General Nesmontu had himself selected the twenty boats and their crews, but this expedition displeased him exceedingly, and he did not refrain from saying so to the king, who listened courteously.

'Let us suppose, Majesty, that your new ally, Wakha, is not a hypocrite and that he really will remain neutral. That is no reason to forget the other five. First, the group of three: Khnum-Hotep, Djehuty-Hotep and Wukh-Hotep. They may each have "*Hotep*", "peace", in their names, but all they think of is increasing the size of their armies – it's fortunate for us that they are so attached to their family privileges that they've never been able to agree to unite.

'If you get past that obstacle, you will come up against Wepwawet, governor of Asyut province. He's a real warrior, and he wouldn't hesitate to launch a murderous attack. And if, by some miracle, we manage to get within sight of Elephantine, there still remains the worst of them all, Sarenput – his armed force is strengthened with Nubians who are fiercer than lions. I hope I have made myself clear, Majesty.'

'You could not have been clearer, General. Is my fleet ready?'

'But, Majesty—'

'In the life of every man, no matter what his rank may be, there comes a moment when he must prove his true worth. For me that moment has come, and everyone senses it. Either I save Egypt from famine or I am not worthy to govern her.'

'But you know that we have no chance and that this expedition will end in disaster.'

'If the north wind favours us and our sailors are skilful, we shall benefit from a not-inconsiderable advantage: speed.'

'I have chosen the best crews in the land – and the fear of death will make them even better.'

Since orders were orders, the old general asked no further

questions. And under his command, no one gave anything but his best.

Medes was suffering from an awkward complaint, caused not by the heat or by tainted food but by his fear of encountering another fleet, a much larger one, carrying armed enemies. At the mere thought of being pierced by an arrow or run through by a sword, his bowels loosened embarrassingly.

The presence of Sobek-Khu did nothing to reassure him. The commander might be highly skilled and experienced, but what could he possibly do if faced with a concerted attack by the provincial governors' armies?

Medes had imagined that his first official participation in a royal voyage would be very different. And, to make matters worse, he had to put on a brave face and utter not a word of criticism of this mad adventure, in which the entire government of Egypt would perish. He looked up resentfully at the sky, where dark clouds were gathering.

'Is something wrong?' asked Sehotep with a malicious smile.

'No, oh no. No, not at all. It's merely that this heavy weather is unsettling my stomach.'

'It looks to me as though the storm will arrive soon.'

'Then we'll have to drop anchor. Our boats simply aren't strong enough to withstand the Nile's anger.'

'You're right about that. In the meantime, drink a little lukewarm beer and eat some stale bread. That will calm your spasms.'

Just as the flotilla was entering the first dangerous area, the storm broke. Flashes of lightning tore the sky open, and the thunder roared with unusual violence.

On board the royal vessel, the sailors prepared to moor.

'We shall continue,' ordered Senusret.

'Majesty,' protested General Nesmontu, 'that would be far too dangerous!'

'It is our best chance of getting through. Beside, you said you'd chosen the best crews in Egypt.'

To his horror, Medes saw that the leading ship was staying out in the middle of the river, preparing to ride out the storm, and that the rest of the fleet were following suit. He felt faint, and took refuge in his cabin so as not to see the ships wrecked.

Savage waves made the vessels' hulls groan; the masts bent almost to the point of breaking; the rails were torn away. Two sailors fell into the water, and no one could rescue them.

Senusret himself took the tiller. Standing very upright, using all his exceptional powers of concentration, he confronted the anger of Set without weakening. At last light began to pierce the thick black clouds, and the Nile began to grow calmer.

The king handed the tiller back to the captain and said, 'In wanting to destroy us, Set has helped us. Let an offering be made to him.'

He lit a brazier, on which he burnt a terracotta figurine of a male oryx pierced by a knife. In the heart of the desert, this astonishing animal could withstand even the fiercest heat. Perhaps it would pass on a little of its endurance to the king.

'We have got through,' declared General Nesmontu. 'That's three provincial governors who can no longer attack.' His optimism did not last long, though. 'Now,' he said, 'there is Asyut and that warmonger Wepwawet. We can expect a fierce fight.'

Night was falling when the flotilla entered the second dangerous region. After several days' uninterrupted sailing, everyone was tired out. No one would normally have risked sailing in the dark, especially in this period when the river's caprices could be as fearsome as hippopotami.

'I propose two rest-days to prepare for the battle,' said Nesmontu.

'We shall continue,' decreed Senusret.

The old general nearly choked. 'But if we light all the of torches we'll need to see our way, the Asyut militia will spot us at once!'

'That is precisely why the torches will not be lit.'

'But Majesty, we—'

'I know, Nesmontu. But forcing destiny's hand is the only way.'

Standing in the prow of the first ship, Senusret gave hand-signals to indicate the required speed and course. The only light was that of the new moon, which made the task particularly difficult. But the pharaoh did not make a single mistake, no god thwarted his actions, and the flotilla slipped forward on calm waters.

Nesmontu was more than a little proud to be serving a man of Senusret's stamp. True, the hardest part had still to be accomplished, but the king's reputation was growing apace among the soldiers and sailors. Commanded by a leader like him, who took an active part in the campaign, what had they to fear?

Even so, the sight that met their eyes made them deeply gloomy.

At the approach to Elephantine, the riverbanks were cracked. Men and animals were suffering badly in over-whelming heat; the sun-scorched fields were crying out for the waters of the annual flood. The donkeys were still at work, carrying sacks of grain from one village to the other while the peasants finished the threshing. But each step, each movement, took an enormous effort.

General Nesmontu pointed out a Nubian perched in the crown of a palm tree and waving to a colleague posted a little further on. Passed from tree to tree like this, news of the arrival of unknown boats would soon reach Governor Sarenput.

'Would it not be wise to heave to and work out the best plan?' the general asked.

'We shall go on,' said Senusret.

The wind had dropped, the oarsmen were labouring at their work, the soldiers' hearts beat faster. Coming up against the large and well-armed local army would not be an easy task. Without a miracle, the battle was lost before it began.

After a period of relative tranquillity, during which his health had recovered, Medes again had painful cramps in his belly. Sarenput's army was renowned for its cruelty. But there might be a way to turn Senusret's inevitable defeat into a victory for Medes. He would have to jump on to the quay at the right moment, surrender to Sarenput's soldiers, swear allegiance to them, reveal the secrets of the Memphis court and propose an alliance.

His nerves on edge, Sobek-Khu was preparing to defend his king – at the cost of his own life, if need be. Before the enemy got near Pharaoh, he resolved, they would suffer such heavy losses that they might withdraw. In any case, that was what he had to believe.

Sehotep seemed as relaxed as a guest invited to a banquet so prestigious that it could not be missed for any reason. To look at him, no one would have imagined that fear was gnawing away at him.

'There they are, Majesty,' announced General Nesmontu, his face grave.

Sarenput had not taken the threat lightly: every one of his boats had been deployed on the Nile.

'I didn't realize he had so many,' said the general.

The king said calmly, 'Sarenput's province is the largest in Upper Egypt, and it's clear that he manages his resources very well. Here is another excellent administrator who has not understood that good management is not enough to maintain the vital link between the heavens and the earth, whose guarantor is Pharaoh.'

'If necessary, Majesty, we shall fight. But is it really necessary to get ourselves massacred?'

40

Senusret watched a boat approaching, with Sarenput standing in the bows. He had a broad face, low forehead, wide-set eyes, prominent cheekbones, a firm mouth, a jutting chin, and the muscles of a man of action, tireless and energetic. On his chest, an amulet in the form of a magic knot hung from a string of beads.

Without hesitation, he climbed aboard the royal vessel.

'Majesty,' he said irritably, 'I deplore the fact that I was not officially informed of your visit. Since you have come here in person, I assume that the reason for this journey is of the utmost importance. I therefore invite you to follow me to my palace, where we can converse away from indiscreet ears.'

The king agreed.

Sarenput returned to his boat, and the two fleets headed towards the main quay at Elephantine.

'Don't go, Majesty,' advised General Nesmontu. 'On land it would be impossible to defend you. This is a trap.'

Senusret remained silent until they had docked. Then, as he descended the gangplank, he ordered, 'No one is to follow me.'

His men watched silently as he was surrounded by Sarenput's soldiers – he was a good head taller than any of them.

The Tree of Life

On the threshold of the palace, Senusret was greeted by Sarenput's favourite dogs, a lean black male with a narrow head and long legs, and a much smaller female, very plump and with prominent teats.

'Her name is Gazelle,' said Sarenput, 'and she has the protection of Good Companion. He watches over her as though she were his mother.'

Good Companion approached the king and licked his hand. Given confidence by this, Gazelle rubbed herself against his legs.

'It is unheard-of for them to be so friendly to a stranger,' said Sarenput in astonishment.

'I am not a stranger. I am Pharaoh of Upper and Lower Egypt.'

For a brief moment, Sarenput met the king's eyes. 'Enter, Majesty.'

Preceded by the two dogs, which showed him the way, Senusret walked through the luxurious palace to the audience chamber, which had two pillars painted with floral designs. Wakha, governor of the Cobra province, was already there.

The old man stood up and bowed.

'The reason I did not destroy your fleet,' explained Sarenput, 'is because my friend Wakha persuaded me not to. He is convinced that you want to prevent a disaster, so he asked me not to oppose your attempt to bring to birth a good flood.'

'That is indeed what I hope to do,' said the king.

'Permit me to be candid, Majesty. That argument is merely a pretext, is it not? In reality, you are here to impose your rule upon my province.'

Senusret smiled. 'With only twenty light boats?'

'It is not much, I agree, but—'

'Let us start with the essential thing: Ma'at, the eternal Rule of life. It is she who creates the order of the world, of the seasons, righteousness and justice, good government, a harmonious life. Thanks to Ma'at, our rites enable the divine powers to remain upon our earth. He who wishes to respect Ma'at must follow the path of righteousness in his thoughts, words and deeds. Are you such a man, Sarenput?'

'How can you doubt it, Majesty?'

'In that case, do you swear upon the life of Pharaoh that you are innocent of the crime committed against the Acacia of Osiris, in Abydos?'

The governor's astonishment looked genuine. 'Why? What has happened?'

'A curse has fallen on this land, and the acacia is dying. So we are in danger of lacking the vital water dispensed by Osiris and the land may be condemned to famine. It is here, at Elephantine, that the secret source of the Nile is born. It is here that one of the forms of Osiris rests. It must be here that his peace was troubled to prevent the flood from spreading its benefits.'

The king's reasoning shook Sarenput, but he refused to accept it. 'That's impossible, Majesty! No one would dare set foot on the sacred island of Biga – no human presence is allowed there. My men guard it well, and no one could have got past them.'

'I believe otherwise, and it is my duty to re-establish the energy flow that has been interrupted. Allow me access to the island.'

'The guardians of the otherworld will strike you dead!'

'I am prepared to take that risk.'

Realizing that this tall, imposing king would not give in, Sarenput agreed to leave with him and Wakha for Biga, and they set out at once.

After travelling along the isle of Sehel, opposite which lay the vast granite quarries, they halted at the foot of the First Cataract, an impassable chaos of rocks and turbulent water at this time of year. A porterage route led off from here, protected by a brick wall. It linked the landing-stages at the northern and southern ends of the cataract.

'Nothing is more effective than this barrier when it comes to controlling goods brought in from Nubia,' declared Sarenput proudly. 'The taxes levied by my officials contribute to the region's wealth.'

But the king was too immersed in his coming task to be interested in material details, and Sarenput, somewhat put out, lapsed into silence.

They boarded a light boat for the brief voyage to the forbidden island.

'Majesty,' said Sarenput earnestly, 'may I advise you one last time against this venture?'

The King looked around and said, 'I cannot see any of your soldiers.'

'They are watching over the porterage route, the trade-posts, the—'

'But not Biga itself.'

'Who would dare set foot on the sacred island of Osiris?'

'Someone certainly attacked the Acacia of Osiris.'

The boat reached the island.

A strange silence surrounded the sacred place. Not a single bird sang, and there was not so much as a breath of wind. The king disembarked into a tangle of undergrowth in which acacias, jujubes and tamarisks grew.

'If Senusret succeeds and brings us the plentiful flood we need,' said Sarenput, 'I shall become his loyal servant.'

'I shall hold you to that promise,' said Wakha.

Sheltered beneath the leaves, three hundred and sixty-five offering-tables, one for each day of the year, were arranged around a rock. Cut into the rock was a cave called 'Shelter of the Master' – in other words of Osiris.

A vase containing milk stood on each offering-table. Every

day, the precious milk, which came from the stars, was regenerated by the creative powers that acted out of human sight. Five of these vases, corresponding to the five last days of the year, notably dedicated to Isis and Osiris, had been broken.

Senusret realized at once why the flood threatened to be so catastrophic. Someone had violated the sacred place, and the energy was no longer circulating.

Seeking a clue to who the criminal might be, he discovered a piece of wool, a material strictly forbidden to Egyptian priests, who wore only linen. Whoever had come here was either unaware of ritual customs or mocked them.

The sound of wings disturbed the quiet of the place. A falcon and a vulture alighted on the top of the rock and stared at the intruder.

'I am your servant,' he said. 'Enlighten me as to the path I must follow.'

The falcon took to the air for a few minutes, but the vulture sat motionless.

'Thanks be to you, Divine Mother. That which must be done will be done.'

Sarenput could not believe his eyes: the pharaoh was still alive!

'Now,' declared Senusret when he rejoined his companions, 'I know the root of the evil.'

'And can you pull up that root, Majesty?'

'Are you daring to suggest that the goddess has abandoned the pharaoh? Look into the distance, Sarenput, and hear her voice.'

At first it was merely a point of light on the horizon, like a mirage. Then it grew and took on the shape of a boat. And the frail vessel moved slowly towards the sacred island.

On board were a tired oarsman and a wondrously exquisite

young woman. Even Sarenput, who had ravishingly beautiful Nubian mistresses, was awed. From what world did she come, this apparition with the perfect curves, the serene face, the gaze so radiant that it lifted the soul?

The young priestess was dressed in a long white gown, held in place by a red belt edged at the top and bottom with yellow, green and red braid. A long wig left her ears uncovered. On her wrists, she wore bracelets of gold and lapis-lazuli. At her throat was a cornelian scarab, set with gold.

'Who is she?' whispered Sarenput.

'A priestess from Abydos, whose help is vital,' said Senusret. 'In a ritual designed to invoke the favour of the flood, she embodied the south wind.'

On the deck of her boat lay a portable four-stringed harp, a rolled and sealed papyrus, and a statuette of Hapy, the spirit of the river.

'Prepare the offerings,' Senusret told Wakha and Sarenput.

Then he and the priestess disappeared into the green labyrinth. They halted opposite the cave. The vulture and the falcon watched them from the rock.

'Isis has rediscovered Osiris,' chanted the pharaoh. 'The last obstacle is raised, the persea fruit have ripened, the canals may be opened and filled with new water. May the Nile sources be generous, may the falcon protect the royal institution and the vulture be the mother who overcomes death.'

The priestess began to play her harp. Between the shell and the casing was a piece of sycamore wood in the shape of the magic knot of Isis. A head of Ma'at adorned the upper part of the instrument, ensuring that this difficult instrument produced music of harmony and peace.

'May Pharaoh eat the bread of Ma'at and drink her dew,' she sang slowly, in a sweet voice.

In the cave, the ground moved.

An enormous green snake appeared, forming a circle and swallowing its own tail.

'The cycle of the past year is over,' chanted the king. 'It gives birth to the new year. By devouring itself, time serves as a support for eternity. May the serpent of the Nile headwaters be the wet-nurse of the Two Lands.'

The falcon and the vulture took flight and flew in wide, protective circles round the king and the priestess. The latter broke the seal on the papyrus she had brought, unrolled it and entered the cave. There, she plunged it into a gold vase. Blank of inscription, the document dissolved in a few moments.

She presented the vase to the king.

'I drink the words of power, written in the secret of the flood, so that they may be embodied in my voice and spread forth their energy.'

In the presence of Sarenput and Wakha, of all the province's leading citizens and of an attentive, reflective crowd, Senusret made the great offering to the nascent flood. Into the river he threw the statuette of Hapy, impregnated with the power of the secret springs, a sealed papyrus, some flowers, fruit, loaves and cakes. High in the sky, the star Sopdet shone. In all the temples of Egypt, lamps had been lit.

There was no room for doubt: it was clear from the turbulent, swiftly rising Nile that there would be floodwater in abundance.

The king chanted, 'Hapy, you whose water is the reflection of the heavens' water, be once again our father and our mother. May only the earth mounds remain above the water, as on the first morning of the world, when you emerged from the *nun*, the ocean of energy, to give life to this land.'

Shouts of joy hailed his final words, and he led everyone in procession towards the temple of Elephantine where, for several days, the words of power designed to strengthen the flood would be spoken.

'He has succeeded,' said Sarenput. 'This king is a true pharaoh.'

'And you must keep your promise,' Wakha reminded him. 'From now on your province is, like mine, in the service of Senusret.'

41

It was a hard life, but the young man did not complain. With the aid of his wife and three peasants, he ran a small farm which brought in enough for them to eat, buy furniture and clothing, and even to consider extending the property. In a year or two, he would take on more workers and build a new house. And if he managed to reclaim the marshy land that bordered his field, he would receive help from the state.

The farmer was hungry: it was time for the midday meal. He went to the reed hut where his wife always left the basket containing his food. It wasn't there. He looked and looked again, but to no avail: there was no basket.

At first annoyed, then worried, he decided to go and ask her what was wrong. As he left the hut he bumped into a bearded monster of a man, who shoved him roughly backward.

'Don't be in such a hurry, peasant. We must talk.'

The farmer tried to grab a pitchfork, but a kick in the ribs knocked him flat and winded him. He tried to get up, but Crooked-Face knocked him down again.

'Keep quiet, friend, or my men will kill one of your workers. To begin with, just to begin with—'

'My wife! Where's my wife?'

'In good hands, believe me. But until I give the order, she won't be touched.'

'What do you want?'

'An understanding between reasonable people,' replied Crooked-Face. 'Your farm's very isolated, and it needs protection. I'll give you that protection. You'll have nothing to fear from raiders, and you can get on with your work in peace. When I say "give", that isn't quite true – every service deserves payment. But I'll only take ten per cent of what you make.'

The farmer was outraged. 'That would be like doubling my taxes – and they're heavy enough as it is!'

'One can't put a price on safety, my friend.'

'I won't do it.'

'As you wish, but you'll be making a bad mistake. Your peasants will have their throats cut, and your wife will be raped and burnt – and you and your children will join her in the fire. After all, I've got a reputation to uphold.'

'Don't do that, I beg you!'

'You know, friend,' said Crooked-Face, lifting him to his feet, 'I can be very nice, but patience isn't my main virtue. Either you do exactly as I say, or I'll tell my men to start work at once.'

Broken, the peasant gave in.

'Good, now you're being reasonable. My men and I are going to stay here for a few days, to see how you work and what results I can expect from our partnership – that way, you won't be tempted to lie to me. After I've left, your farm will be watched. If you were unwise enough to tell the guards, neither you nor your family would live very long. Your deaths, though, would be very, very long, especially your wife's.' Crooked-Face patted the farmer's shoulder. 'Now, to seal our bargain, let's have something to eat and drink.'

Crooked-Face had at first intended to kill his victims and destroy their homes, but this was a much better idea. If he'd left corpses and ruins behind him, he'd soon have attracted the authorities' attention. But by forcing those he 'protected'

233

to pay and to keep quiet about it, he could stay hidden in the shadows while making a lot of money.

The Herald would be proud of him.

Memphis enthralled Shab the Twisted. The port, the market, the shops, the districts where the ordinary people lived, the streets seething with Egyptians and foreigners: everything fascinated him. The days were too short. He'd need months, if not years, to explore the thousand and one attractions of this busy capital, which seemed never to sleep.

However, the Herald was indifferent to the bustle. He slid through the crowds like a ghost, noticed by no one. Thanks to his power to charm people, he had soon found modest lodgings attached to a shop which had been closed for several weeks.

'We're going to be honest traders,' he told his little band, 'and make our neighbours like us. Mix with the people of Memphis, take mistresses, frequent the taverns.'

This order pleased his men greatly, and they cheerfully cleaned the rooms and fitted them out with mats, baskets and shelves, before going out to obey it.

The Herald took Shab to the port to see what information they could learn there.

Suddenly, shouts of joy rose up all over the city, and the streets filled with a noisy crowd loudly singing songs in praise of Senusret.

The Herald spotted an old man who looked a little calmer than his fellow citizens, and asked him, 'What's happening?'

'We were afraid that the flood would be poor, but Pharaoh made peace with the spirit of the Nile. Egypt will have plenty of water, and the spectre of famine has been warded off.' Laughing with happiness, the old fellow rejoined the revellers.

'That's bad news,' said the Herald. 'I didn't think Senusret would dare set foot on Biga or venture as far as the hidden sources of the Nile.'

'You mean you went there yourself?' asked Shab in astonishment.

'Once the five offering-tables of the last days of the year had been desecrated, the circulation of energy was interrupted. But Senusret dared to force his way through the barriers and re-impose order. He is a tough enemy, and won't be easy to defeat. Our victory will be only the sweeter for that.'

Shab the Twisted was afraid. Afraid of this man who, because of his powers, was not entirely a man. He would stop at nothing, not even sacred things.

As if he knew Memphis perfectly, the Herald set off without hesitation down a succession of alleyways behind the port, and eventually knocked four times, at widely spaced intervals, on the door of a dilapidated house.

An answering knock came. The Herald knocked again twice, this time quickly.

The door opened. It was so small that the pair had to bow their heads to get through. They found themselves in a huge room with a beaten-earth floor.

Three bearded men bowed before their master.

'Thanks be to God, my lord,' said one of them, 'that you are safe and sound.'

'No one can stop me accomplishing my mission. Have faith in me, and we shall triumph.'

Everyone sat down, and the Herald began to preach.

His speech was repetitive, and he hammered home the same themes insistently: God spoke to him; he was His only interpreter; unbelievers would be forced into submission, blasphemers executed; women must no longer enjoy the intolerable freedoms that Egypt granted them. The source of all these evils was the pharaoh, and the royal art of making Ma'at live. When that source was at last destroyed, the Herald's doctrine would wipe away borders. The whole world would become one single land, ruled by the true belief.

'Shave off your beards,' the Herald ordered his followers, 'dress in the Memphite style, and immerse yourselves in this city. Other instructions will follow.'

Shab was fascinated by his master's words. As soon as they had left the house, he asked, 'My lord, weren't those men Canaanites from Sichem?'

'Yes, they were.'

'Did you decide to bring them to Memphis?'

'Those, and then many more.'

'So you haven't given up the idea of liberating Canaan.'

'I never give up, but one must adapt to circumstances. We shall eat away at Egyptian society from the inside, without it realizing what is happening. And Memphis the tolerant and the colourful will itself furnish us with the poison destined to kill it. We shall need infinite time and patience, my faithful friend, and we shall also have to use other weapons.'

There were yet more surprises in store for Shab.

In another alleyway they stopped at the porch of a fine, single-storey house. The Herald spoke to the guard in an unknown language. The guard allowed him and Shab to pass.

They were greeted by a warm, talkative fellow whose ample form betrayed his love of good food.

'Here you are at last, my lord! I was beginning to worry.'

'A few minor problems.'

'Let us go into the reception room. My cook has made some cakes which would delight even the most jaded palate.'

Shab did not need to be asked twice, but the Herald did not touch them.

'What stage have we reached?' he demanded, in a voice so stern that the atmosphere immediately became glacial.

'Matters are advancing, my lord.'

'Are you sure, my friend?'

'It isn't easy, you know. But the first expedition will leave soon.'

'I will not tolerate any delay,' said the Herald.

'You can rely on me, my lord.'

'What arrival point have you chosen?'

'The little town of Kahun, which is very important in the pharaoh's eyes. I have good contacts there, and our men will be able to set up without difficulty.'

'I hope you are right.'

'I prefer to take more time than planned, my lord, and not make any mistakes. You will see, Kahun is indeed the right place. This king is a cunning man, careful to surround himself with precautions, and he doesn't trust the Memphis court.'

The Herald smiled strangely. Yes, this track was the right one. His network had worked well.

The tension was dispelled, and his host took advantage of the moment to eat an enormous cake swimming in carob juice. Shab did the same.

'I assume the pharaoh has reduced the number of his advisers,' said the Herald.

'Yes, my lord, unfortunately. According to rumours which I think are accurate, the King's House now comprises only a small inner circle made up of a faithful few.'

'Do you know their names?'

'It's all just rumours – lots of them. It's even said that the king has decided to break the necks of the provincial governors who oppose him, but I don't believe that – it would cause civil war.'

'Haven't you got a contact at the palace?'

'My lord, it's very delicate and—'

'I require one.'

'Very well, very well. I'll take care of it.'

'May I rely upon you, my faithful friend?'

'Oh yes, of course, absolutely.'

'We shall meet again soon.'

Shab the Twisted guzzled one last cake.

Their host's cook was superb, but he didn't care much for the host himself. Once they were a safe distance from the house, he felt obliged to confide his impressions to his master.

'I don't like that man, my lord. Are you sure he isn't lying to you?'

'He's a rich trader from the great Phoenician port of Byblos, and he's a born liar. His profession consists of deceiving his customers, while having his competitors accused of assorted offences, and he wrings as much profit as possible out of even minor transactions. I am the only one to whom he tells the truth. Once – just once – he tried to deceive me, and he still has not only the memory of it but the marks in his flesh. When the falcon's talons sank into his chest to tear out his heart, he repented in the nick of time. The people of Byblos will be very useful to us, my brave friend. Thanks to them, I shall bring many supporters of our cause into Egypt.'

Shab was staggered. So the Herald was using several networks of spies, and knew Memphis like the back of his hand.

Despite the heat, there was not a trace of sweat on the Herald's brow. And when Shab emptied a jar of cool beer, the Herald did not drink a drop, merely murmured words the Twisted One did not understand.

42

Iker folded the leg he was sitting on and raised his other knee in front of him. This was one of the scribe's positions when he wished to consult a papyrus, and the young man had so much work that he rarely left his little office, which was in Djehuty's palace.

Iker wanted to check everything himself. He was not content with summaries prepared by other scribes in order to make his task easier, but returned constantly to the original documents. Almost every time, he was glad he had. Details had been omitted, figures badly copied, factual material cut out. In setting the records straight wherever he could, Iker came to realize something very worrying: several officials had distorted the facts to make Djehuty believe that his province was the richest and most powerful in Egypt.

The reality was considerably less comforting. The army had too many mercenaries, the desert guards too many elderly men, some land was badly farmed, many farms badly managed. In the event of war, Djehuty would probably be short of weapons. So the overall report Iker was planning to write in the next few days would be rather gloomy.

One of his colleagues put his head round the door and said, 'Come and look.'

'I can't – no time.'

'Make time. You can't miss a sight like this.'

Curious, Iker followed him out of the palace. He found that everyone – scribes, guards, cooks, cleaning-women and all the other staff – was running towards the Nile.

On a grassy islet in the middle of the river, about fifty Numidian cranes, with their ash-grey plumage and delicate feet, were gracefully dancing. Twirling together, they pretended to take flight then set down again, sometimes spinning round, sometimes forming a sort of circle with their partners. Like everyone else, Iker marvelled at this unexpected dance, which was hailed with shouts of joy.

'A wonderful omen,' said the man next to Iker, a scribe in charge of land-measuring. 'It means that Pharaoh Senusret has succeeded in bringing us a good annual flood. Don't tell anyone I said so, but it proves he's a great king.'

Iker went off thoughtfully to feed his donkey, which was comfortably settled in the shade of an awning.

'The situation is becoming delicate,' he confided to North Wind. 'If the people take up the pharaoh's cause, Djehuty's position will be untenable. And Senusret's success is so brilliant that it can't be concealed.'

The donkey ate placidly, as if the news did not worry him.

On his way back to the palace, where he was due to go and see Djehuty, Iker saw the face of the young priestess again. Several times a day, and in all his dreams, she imposed herself on him with increasing strength. Instead of blurring, her face was were becoming clearer and clearer, as if she were right beside him.

When would he meet her again? Perhaps at a rite she was participating in, but how would he know in advance? And if she belonged to the Golden Circle of Abydos, wouldn't he have to go to that sacred city, which was inaccessible to an outsider like himself? His love seemed doomed to failure, but he was determined not to give up before speaking to her. She must know the feelings she inspired in him, even if he felt wholly unable to express their intensity.

Despite General Sepi's enigmatic allusion, the Golden Circle of Abydos had lost nothing of its mystery. Had he meant that its action consisted of regenerating old men like Djehuty by inundating them with light? If so, people knew how to handle this energy in exceptional circumstances.

Iker found Governor Djehuty reading the rough draft of his report.

'My lord, those are only a few notes.'

'They seem very clear to me: my government has been flattering me for years, and my army is in no state to engage in war.'

Iker did not hide behind his brush. 'I regret to say it, but that is correct, my lord.'

'Excellent work, my boy. In fact, the dance of the cranes has come at an opportune moment, because it means that everyone knows Senusret will make the land green again and fill it with fruit trees. The Two Lands rejoice, and happy times are in prospect, for he has shown himself to be a true king. Because of him, the flood will come at the right time, making days fertile and the night hours beautiful. The pharaoh is the creative energy; his mouth expresses abundance; he creates what must be, gives life to his people. Hour after hour, without rest, he carries out a mysterious task which weaves together nature and society. He is the sovereign of the breadth of the heart; if he acts righteously, the country is prosperous.'

Iker had listened in growing amazement. 'Does all this mean . . . My lord, are you going to recognize Senusret's authority and swear allegiance to him?'

'I couldn't have put it better myself.'

'So there'll be no war?'

'Indeed not.'

'I'm very glad, my lord, but—'

'But you're surprised by such a rapid decision, aren't you? That's because you don't fully appreciate the supernatural nature of what Senusret has done. How did he succeed in mastering the flood? By taking on the office of Thoth, god of knowledge and patron of scribes, the king proved that he knows everything about the signs of power and that he can procure new water for his people. The nourishing flood is the effusion of Osiris; it springs from his mysterious body; it is his sweat, his lymph, his humours. When the water of the young flood fills the first offering-vase, the king may declare: "Osiris has been found again." But he would have failed without the cooperation of Isis, who appears in the sky as the star Sopdet, after seventy days of invisibility. The primordial couple is formed once again, the first energy makes the Two Lands fertile again. Without it, nothing would grow. Grain is a matrix in which are assembled the elements procured by the world beyond. Know this, Iker: the whole of nature is a revelation of the supernatural. Since Senusret belongs to the line of kings who pass on this mystery, all that remains is for me to bow before him and obey him.

'No, I must do more than that.' Djehuty stood up. 'We must show Senusret what we are capable of. Do you know what the *ka* really is, Iker?'

'The protective spirit that is born with a man and never leaves him, so long as he puts into practice the teachings of the sages.'

'The *ka* is the energy that maintains all forms of life. At his death, a righteous man passes to his *ka*, which he has inherited from his ancestors. All the offerings are destined for the *ka*, never for the man himself. One of the most beautiful symbols of the *ka* is a living statue, ritually brought to life. So we are going to create a gigantic statue of the royal *ka* and present it to the pharaoh. I appoint you to oversee the work.'

'The cubit of God measures the stones,' said the head sculptor. 'It is he who places the cord upon the ground,

242

positions temples correctly, shelters with his shade all sacred constructions where his heart moves according to his desire. And his love gives life to the workshops.'

The song of hammers and chisels rang out in the quarry where the statue would be sculpted, as a support for the *ka*.

The quarrymen had detected the best sections of rock, which they would cut out without wounding it; and the sculptors would work under the leadership of a craftsman initiated into the mysteries. Because the statue was to be so enormous,* the quarry's location posed a serious problem. It would take at least three hours to haul the statue to the Nile, provided the method adopted worked smoothly; a cargo-boat would then carry it across the river; and finally it would be hauled to its destination, the Temple of Thoth. It was a long and difficult journey, which Iker had studied and studied again in order to prevent unpleasant surprises. Choosing another quarry nearer the capital would have made the task easier, but Djehuty had said this rock was the most suitable and he would accept no other.

'This will be the biggest celebration ever held in my province,' he said. 'Wine and beer will flow freely, and my people will rejoice. In thousands of years' time, people will still speak of this statue. My sculptors are creating a true marvel, which marries power with delicacy. When Senusret sees it, he'll be overcome.'

'I don't wish to dampen your spirits, my lord,' said Iker, 'but the problems of transporting it are far from resolved.'

'How many men do you plan to use?'

'We'll need more than four hundred – organizing them into a unified team is an absolute nightmare.'

'Less than half that number will be enough,' declared Djehuty. 'Each of the happy men chosen will have the strength of ten.'

*About 6.5 metres high and weighing 60 tonnes.

'Your soldiers aren't making my task any easier. None of the officers will agree to give up his command to me.'

'Don't choose only soldiers. You must have the youngest and strongest, whoever they are. And don't forget the priests.'

'The priests? But—'

'Transporting the statue is not a task for laymen. Throughout the journey, the priests must recite words of protection. Make all in this little world live together, and you'll become a respected man. But keep one thought in mind: failure is forbidden.'

Iker was grateful that he'd been trained as a runner, for he spent entire days dashing back and forth, in order to select a hundred and seventy-two men from the countless volunteers. If his calculations were correct, that was the ideal number of men for the team that would pull the statue.*

When the giant sculpture was finished, Iker brought the team together and divided it into four sections. One of the outside sections comprised young men from the west of the province, the other from the east. The inside sections were made up of soldiers and priests.

The statue was laid on a sledge and tied securely in place with ropes. The four sections prepared to start hauling, in an atmosphere of celebration. With the specialists, Iker checked that everything was in order, but he was still anxious as he waited to give the word to start.

Officials poured water on to the muddy track, to help the sledge move along more easily.

'Pull!' ordered Iker.

Slowly, the sledge set off. The men were proud to be involved in such an exploit. "The west celebrates,' sang the young men from the west, 'and our hearts are happy when they see their lord's monuments.'

---

*The details of the statue's transport are drawn from the depictions and texts in the tomb of Djehuty-Hotep at el-Bercha.

A good speed, neither too slow nor too fast, had been adopted. Soldiers waved palm-fronds to cool the men pulling the sledge.

The route had been checked a hundred times by Iker, and smoothed as much as possible. There were no unpleasant surprises in store.

Iker's eyes went from each point where the ropes were fixed to each member of the team, then came back to the statue, which was perfectly stable.

But suddenly he felt uneasy. This beautiful harmony seemed on the point of shattering, and he did not know why. Everything looked normal, but he was sure his instinct was right.

Anxiously, he ran about in all directions, searching for the danger. As he raised his head, he saw it: the statue's expression had changed, and its stone eyes held profound displeasure. The statue of the *ka* was demanding the rites due to it.

'Quickly!' he shouted. 'Incense!'

Fortunately, one of the priests accompanying the sledge was carrying an incense-burner. Iker leapt on to the statue's knees and stretched out his hands in a sign of veneration. The priest opened the burner and aromatic smoke rose up, reaching the statue's mouth, ears and eyes. The terebinth resin, the *senter*, 'that which renders divine', surrounded the stone with perfume while Iker remained in an attitude of prayer, facing the path, asking it to open up. They kept the statue wreathed in incense until they reached the Nile.

The river crossing went smoothly, and the final part of the journey took part amid universal rejoicing. Not a single inhabitant of the province wanted to miss the event, especially since, as Djehuty had promised, a tremendous open-air feast would crown its success.

As the statue was set up in front of the temple, the governor congratulated Iker, who was exhausted.

'Well done, young scribe. You have accomplished your

task. But don't forget that each hieroglyph, each sign and each statue, whatever its size, illuminates an aspect of the mystery of creation. Today, the royal *ka* is in the place of honour. And now, my boy, I know you're tired, but you cannot rest until later. First, you must write a detailed report.'

43

The festivities to mark the birth of the statue were combined with those marking the annual flood, and the people were granted two weeks' holiday, during which they feasted, sang, danced and celebrated the gods.

Governor Djehuty, whose popularity had reached new heights, spent several hours every day inspecting the work on his house of eternity. One of the walls was nearly finished, and was then to be devoted to a depiction of the statue being transported. Iker supervised, to ensure that the hieroglyphic texts were accurate.

No one doubted that the young scribe was bound for the highest office, and he was already attracting great jealousy. Experienced, long-serving scribes grumbled about the favour Djehuty showed the outsider, a solitary lad who formed no friendships or other links, just shut himself away and worked.

Nevertheless, no one dared attack him openly, partly because he had Djehuty's protection, and partly because of what he knew about them. In drawing up the balance-sheet of the province's strengths and weaknesses, he had seen exactly who was at fault in which respect. One word from him, and heavy punishment would fall on them.

So it was better to flatter him, but how? Iker went from his office to his bedchamber, from his bedchamber to his office, and never attended parties or receptions. And when he went walking with his donkey, his forbidding air dissuaded anyone from bothering him.

Even during his few moments of relaxation with North Wind, he thought only of his work. The men he led were much older and more experienced than himself, and he knew that any slip on his part would be fatal. However, his demand for perfection was only defensive; it fed him like an inner fire, which lit up his path.

At night, he dreamt of her. Everything he strove to do, he did for her. One day he would see her again, and he must not then be ignorant or incompetent. If destiny had imposed his current ordeal, it must be so that he could face it and demonstrate his abilities by becoming a scribe of the highest rank. Perhaps even that would not be enough in the eyes of the woman he loved . . . He must offer her the best of himself, in order to prove to her that he lived only for her.

There were also the nightmares, full of the faces of murderers, monsters, unanswered questions and the need to avenge himself on those who had wanted to cut the thread of his life. Not knowing, and therefore being unable to do anything, was unbearable.

A mad notion emerged from these bad dreams. A notion so odious that Iker began by rejecting it. But it came back, insistent, and he could not stifle it. It made him sombre and taciturn, isolating him even more.

Fortunately, North Wind was highly sensitive to his changes of mood, and listened to his confidences with tireless patience. When Iker asked a question, North Wind replied 'yes' or 'no' by pricking up his right or left ear. In this faithful companion the young scribe had unreserved trust, and eventually he told him about the idea gnawing at him. North Wind pricked up his right ear.

Doctor Gua was thunderstruck. 'You have spent two weeks feasting, and your liver is more congested than the liver of a force-fed goose. From a doctor's point of view, it is virtual suicide.'

Djehuty shrugged. 'I feel perfectly well.'

'There is no remedy for lack of awareness. If you do not take twenty pills a day to restore your liver functions, I cannot answer for the consequences.' Gua abruptly closed his leather satchel and left the audience chamber.

Immediately there poured in the officials in charge of dykes and irrigation, to make their reports; all were encouraging. They were followed by Iker, whose gravity surprised the courtiers surrounding Djehuty.

'Leave us, all of you,' ordered the governor.

The young scribe stood motionless, gazing fixedly at Djehuty, and said, 'I demand the truth.'

The governor slumped in his chair, laid his hands on his thighs and sighed deeply. 'The truth! Is your heart big enough to receive it? And do you know what a true heart is, the heart that serves as a shrine for the Divine? Everything is created by the heart; the heart gives consciousness, thinks and devises. So it must be broad, large, move freely, but also be gentle. And you, Iker, you are much too stern with others – as you are with yourself. If your heart is troubled, it grows heavy and can no longer welcome Ma'at. The spiritual energy no longer circulates and your consciousness wanders.'

'My lord, my apprenticeship as a scribe taught me not to confuse one thing with another and to try to be clear-headed in all circumstances. I am convinced that your generosity is not freely given. You owe me a debt, don't you?'

'You're imagining things, my boy. I recognized your worth, that's all, and you have succeeded purely by virtue of your merit.'

'I think not, my lord. I am certain you know a good deal about the men who wanted to kill me, and that you're trying to protect me by making me one of the most important scribes in your province. Now I want to know everything. Why I was chosen as a sacrificial victim, who was responsible, whether I am still the plaything of a demon hidden in the shadows, the location of the land of Punt, whose perfume saves the good scribe.'

'You ask far too many questions.'

'No I don't.'

Exasperated, Djehuty gripped the arms of his chair. 'What power in the world could force me to answer?'

'The love of the truth.'

'And what if that truth was more dangerous than ignorance?'

'I almost lost my life, and I want to know why and because of whom.'

'Wouldn't you rather forget those tragic events and enjoy a peaceful life in which you can read and write as much as you want?'

Iker shook his head. 'Living without understanding, living in the darkness – what could be worse than that?'

'That depends on the person, my boy. Most people like being ignorant and have no wish at all to change.'

'I am not like that.'

'No, I didn't think you were. I'll tell you one last time, Iker: don't try to find out things which ought to stay hidden.'

Now Iker knew that his notion was right. His insistent gaze broke down Djehuty's last defences.

'Oh, very well, my boy, but you may regret it. As regards the land of Punt, I can tell you nothing. On the other hand, I have heard of Turtle-Eye and Sharp-Knife.'

Iker started. 'Do you mean you employed them?'

'No, they simply passed through the main port of my province – their ship was moored there for a few days.'

'There's no record of that in the archives.'

'The documents were destroyed.'

'Why, my lord?'

'To prevent . . . fantasies.'

'Fantasies? What fantasies? And am I to understand that you yourself were behind the plot?'

'That's enough, Iker!' thundered Djehuty. 'Can't you see that I'm trying to protect you? I couldn't bear to see you breaking your head against your own destiny.'

'You must tell me everything, my lord.'

'You don't know how dangerous your enemy is.'

'No, but thanks to you I'm going to find out.'

Djehuty gave another exasperated sigh. 'The sailors belonged to a crew which had been granted special privileges. Do you really want to know them?'

'Must I drag the words out of you one by one?'

'At the time, I was not a supporter of Senusret. Now, this boat was under the protection of the royal seal, and the captain asked me to grant him a brief stay for repairs. If I refused I'd cause war, but if I agreed I'd become the vassal of a king whose sovereignty I challenged. So I decided it would be best if the ship and her crew did not exist.

'And then you arrived, with your questions and your strange personality. You aren't like other scribes, Iker. You burn with a fire whose nature you do not understand. That's why I tried to tear you away from your past.'

'Where did the sailors go?'

'To Kahun, a town to which Senusret attaches particular importance. State archives are kept there.'

'I shall go and consult them, and find the answers to my questions.'

'If you go to Kahun, you'll be defying the pharaoh.'

'Why should he want to kill me?'

'I don't know, my boy, but I do know that no one attacks a king without heading for his own ruin.'

'The truth is more important than my life. Help me again by sending me to Kahun. A scribe from the province of Thoth will be welcomed in any town in Egypt.'

Djehuty's face set in lines of sadness. 'You're asking me to send you to your death, Iker.'

'My lord, I owe you unlimited gratitude. But if I stay here, keeping my ears and eyes closed, I'll soon become a bad servant.'

'You are placing a heavy burden of responsibility upon my shoulders.'

'No, my lord. The only person responsible is myself. I persuaded you to lift the veil and let me continue on my way. Thanks to you, I have grown stronger and I feel able to face this new test.'

44

On the isle of Elephantine, at Swenet, Senusret and his inner circle were attending a rite celebrated by Governor Sarenput in honour of Heka-ib, a deeply revered sage of ancient times. A new statue of him had just been erected in the shrine of his tomb; it would enable his *ka* to remain present on earth and to inspire the thoughts of his successors.

Nothing had happened to mar the good understanding that now prevailed between the king's entourage and Sarenput's soldiers. Nevertheless, Sobek-Khu was tense and anxious. Like Sehotep, who was wary and always on the alert, he doubted their host's sincerity and feared that he might be setting a trap for the king. As for General Nesmontu, he would fight to the death to save the life of his sovereign.

In accordance with custom, Medes kept in the background and made himself as discreetly invisible as possible. As he prepared to write down the pharaoh's official declarations, he observed the province's dignitaries and asked them about how it was run. With his friendly, conciliatory attitude, he won himself new friends.

'Majesty,' said Sarenput, 'I should like to show you my house of eternity. Only you – no one else at all.'

Sobek and Nesmontu said nothing, but their every instinct told them to stop the king going, on the grounds of elementary prudence. What they had feared was indeed happening: Sarenput was revealing his true intentions. On the way to the tomb, hired killers would assassinate Senusret.

'I shall follow you,' said the king.

Sobek and Nesmontu wondered what on earth they could do.

'May I act as your oarsman?' offered the elegant Sehotep.

'There's no need,' replied Sarenput. 'I shall row us myself – the exercise keeps me fit.'

To insist would be to humiliate the governor. And he was probably hoping for just such provocation, so that he could give his soldiers the order to attack.

It was clear that Senusret planned to deal with the situation alone. He was a strong man, certainly, but even he would succumb to sheer weight of numbers.

Sarenput rowed vigorously, and the beautiful sycamore-wood boat headed towards the cliff on the western bank, in which the tombs of the chiefs of the Elephantine province had been built since the time of the pyramids. To reach them, one had to climb steep stairs and ramps, bordered by walls.

The boat touched gently against the land, and the two men began the climb slowly, in silence. The powerful southern sun did not hinder either of them.

When they reached the entrance to Sarenput's house of eternity, they turned and looked out over a beautiful landscape: the sparkling blue waters of the Nile, the luminous green of the palm groves, ochre sand and white houses.

'I love this place more than any other,' said Sarenput. 'It is here that I hope to defeat death and spend a life in eternity. One of my ancestors, who bore the same name as myself, engraved these words: "I was filled with joy as I succeeded in reaching the heavens, my head touched the firmament, I brushed against the belly of the stars, being myself a star, and I danced like the planets." What other destiny could one wish for? Come, Majesty. Come and see the most beautiful of my domains.'

Senusret entered a tomb cut into the sandstone, whose floor rose and ceiling descended, to join at an invisible point beyond the shrine at the far end. In the first chamber, which was imposing and austere, there were six pillars. A staircase led to a passageway to the shrine, in which there was a niche containing the statue of Sarenput's *ka*.

As he walked along the passageway, which resembled a ray of light, Senusret admired six statues of Sarenput as Osiris.

'That is my greatest ambition, Majesty: to become the faithful servant of the god of resurrection. There can surely be no more convincing proof of my innocence. Never would I have tried to attack the Tree of Osiris. And what you have accomplished shows that you are the bearer of the wisdom this land needs so much. If I were to oppose that, I would be a criminal. So you may consider me a loyal servant who will never betray you.'

Good Companion walked proudly at the head of the procession. On his right, Gazelle waddled along, hampered by her swollen belly. She had difficulty keeping up, but she would not have missed this great celebration for anything and, head held high, refused to let herself to be left behind.

The two dogs halted before a stele on which Senusret's names were engraved.

'Venerate the pharaoh in the deepest part of yourself,' proclaimed Sehotep. 'Join his radiance to your thoughts, spread forth the respect that must be shown to him. It is he who gives life. He shows generosity to those who follow his path. As Bearer of the Royal Seal, I confirm that this province belongs to the Double Crown.'

Sarenput smiled broadly as he bowed before Senusret.

For the first time in many moons, General Nesmontu relaxed. And Sobek himself, to his great astonishment, had a feeling of security. The king had won a new victory without a drop of blood being spilt.

'I must return to Biga,' the king told Sarenput when the ceremony was over, 'to ensure that the circulation of energy is no longer disrupted. Start preparing the celebrations – during them I shall announce work to improve and enlarge the great temple of Elephantine.'

Waiting outside the cave of the Nile sources, the young priestess saw the king emerge.

'The hour has come for you to go further,' he said. 'Do you consent?'

'I do, Majesty.'

'You will need all the courage and resolution a human being can have. Are you sure this task will not outstrip your strength?'

'I shall do my best.'

The king held out to her a solid gold cobra-headdress encrusted with lapis-lazuli, turquoise and cornelian. This cobra reared up on Pharaoh's brow, to project a flame so powerful that it dispelled the darkness and eliminated the enemies of Ma'at.

'Touch this symbol,' he said, 'fill yourself with its magic and place it in the hand that guides you.'

The cobra was burning hot. She felt its energy passing into her blood and endowing her with new strength.

The king entered the cave, and the young priestess found herself alone again. Deep in contemplation, she savoured the silence of the sacred island and had no fear of what would happen. Since her childhood, she had wished to know the mysteries of the temple, and she knew the journey would be as long as it was difficult. But with each trial she underwent she felt immense joy, which bore her further into an ever-faster landscape. The only thing that had disturbed this journey was the appearance of a certain young scribe, whose name, she had learnt, was Iker. It should have been merely a momentary encounter, but she could not forget him, as though he were someone close to her, almost intimate; yet she would never see him again.

Seven priestesses dressed in long red gowns and holding tambourines formed a circle round her. Then their leader came forward. She wore a wig in the form of a vulture and a *menat*-necklace, the symbol of spiritual birth. The young priestess shivered. Only the Queen of Egypt, the Lady of the Two Lands, she who saw Horus and Set reunited in the being of Pharaoh, could wear this ritual headdress. The hiero-glyphic sign of the vulture meant at once "mother" and "death", for one must pass through initiatory death to find the celestial mother, whose incarnation was the queen.

'May the seven Hathors imprison evil fate,' chanted the queen.

The seven priestesses wound a band of red fabric round the young woman.

'The hour of a new birth is come,' the queen continued. 'You were initiated first into the office of *wabet*, pure priestess, then as *merut*, a musician who spreads love. Today, as you embark upon new mysteries, you become *Ureshut*, an Awakened One. The Venerable Ones of the dwelling of Ptah, the Old Women of the town of Qis and the Hathors of the dwelling of Atum, the creative principle, are your ancestors. They live in the initiates here present and will cause you to hear the music of the heavens, the stars, the sun and the moon.'

A sweet, profound song rose up, to the rhythm of the tambourines and the two sistra the queen held. In turn, the priestesses spoke the seven creative words uttered by the goddess Neith at the birth of light, which itself had sprung forth from the primordial water. Both male and female, existing before any visible manifestation, she had initiated the process of all births by fashioning the gods.

'I am all that has been, all that is and all that will be,' chanted the queen, 'and no mortal has ever lifted my veil, the winding-sheet that protects the body of Osiris. It falls to the initiates to weave it. So you shall be taken into the House of the Acacia, where the souls of Hathor and Osiris shall meet in your heart. On this sacred island of Biga, it takes the form of the cave of Hapy, in which the celestial water joins with the terrestrial water. Traverse this space; may your life be nourished with the cool water of the stars and with the fire of knowledge.'

After being undressed, the young woman entered the cave, where she gazed upon the flame. Then she walked the path of the constellations, passed through the gates of the heavens, bathed in the lake of light and was reborn to the morning with the first rays of the rising sun.

A priestess placed her upon the plinth symbolizing Ma'at and fanned her with an ostrich feather, another expression of the goddess, in order to give her the good wind that would take her to the city of bliss.

Then she was dressed in a red gown, and round her neck was placed a large beaded collar, signifying her rebirth after passing through the region of darkness, where the forces of destruction had failed to hold her.

The queen handed her a scribe's palette and brush to write with, then placed a seven-branched star upon her head.

'You who are now a Hathor, you must also become a Sechat, for a particular office has been assigned to you. You will not be able merely to experience your initiation within yourself and enjoy the peace of the inside of the temple, in company with your sisters. Formidable ordeals await you, and you must know the words of power in order to confront both visible and invisible enemies. We shall help you as much as possible, but you alone can achieve victory.'

45

Iker left before dawn, taking care not to wake anyone in the palace. The previous evening, he had handed back to Djehuty all the documents he had been working on, while turning a deaf ear to the governor's last and most impassioned warnings.

He took the first boat going north. She raised anchor with the rising sun and went with the current, which was as fast as it was deceptive. The captain, an experienced fellow, handled the tiller marvellously well. On board were a dozen travellers, an ox, some geese and North Wind.

'Where are you going, my boy?' asked the captain.

'To Kahun.'

'Let's see: about twenty hours' sailing, a lot of stops, one night's rest if there aren't any hitches . . . How much are you offering?'

'Two pairs of good-quality sandals, a piece of linen and a medium-sized papyrus.'

'You pay well, I must say! Do you come from a wealthy family?'

'No, I am just a scribe from the province of the Hare, in the service of Lord Djehuty.'

The captain nodded approvingly. 'A great and well-respected man. Why are you going to Kahun?'

The questions were beginning to annoy Iker, but he wanted

keep on good terms with the captain, so he said, 'For reasons of work.'

'Something confidential?'

'If you like.'

'Kahun's a strange place. I don't know it myself, but apparently it's well protected and you have to have permission to live there – you can't be just anybody.'

'I'm just a scribe, I told you.' Unable to bear this questioning any longer, Iker lay down on his travelling-mat and pretended to go to sleep.

The captain at once started talking to another passenger. Evidently he was an incorrigible chatterbox.

As the captain had said, there were many stops. People embarked and disembarked, conversations were struck up; people nibbled flatcakes, onions and dried fish and drank sweet beer, and let themselves be carried along to the rhythm of a benevolent river. Iker listened vaguely to family stories, accounts of court cases and domestic disputes.

The next stop particularly interested North Wind, whose ears pricked up. It was not a village but a little palm-grove criss-crossed by irrigation channels. From it emerged two unshaven men with muscular arms like oarsmen's.

Oarsmen . . . They looked like the sailors who had tried to kill Iker. He watched them from the corner of his eye as they settled themselves on the deck.

So the captain had laid a trap for him, and had fooled him by asking questions to which he knew the answers. These two cut-throats were going to finish their work.

Iker went over to the captain, who seemed to be dozing.

'Aren't you watching the river, Captain?' he asked.

'A good sailor sleeps with one eye open.'

'Let me off, quickly.'

'But we're still a long way from Kahun.'

'I've changed my mind.'

'Well, what is it you want? Where do you really want to go?'

'Let me off.'

'I've no stops planned in the near future. If you insist, I'll need an extra fee.'

'I paid you generously, didn't I?'

'Yes, but—'

'Will a brand-new mat be enough?'

'If it really is brand-new.'

Iker gave him one of his two travelling-mats. Satisfied, the captain changed course towards the bank.

As soon as the gangplank was in place, Iker and North Wind set off down it. The young scribe was convinced that the two oarsmen were bound to follow suit.

He was wrong. The boat sailed away with them still aboard.

'We'll have to walk further than we'd planned,' Iker told North Wind, 'but at least no one will follow us.'

The donkey agreed, and Iker felt relieved.

'Those two fellows had a really shady look about them. After everything that's happened, how could I not be suspicious?'

Iker checked that nothing was missing from his scribe's materials, while the donkey feasted on thistles. Then they continued northwards, taking a path which ran alongside the fields.

'There are so many questions in my mind. At Kahun, perhaps I'll find answers. But why do people refuse to talk to me about Punt? Djehuty told me only part of the truth, unless he knows less than I thought. And the one who wants to kill me is Pharaoh himself! What wrong have I done him? I'm nothing, I don't threaten his power in any way. And yet it really is me he fears. If I was sensible, I'd run away and let people forget about me. But I can't give up trying to find the truth, whatever the risks. And I want to see her again. If I want to fight, it's because of her.'

It was North Wind who decided on the rest times and chose the shady spots where they dozed before setting off again. The two companions met only peasants, some disagreeable, others friendly. At one farm, Iker wrote several letters to the government, with which the owner was in dispute. In exchange, he received food.

As they neared the rich and fertile province of Faiyum, the donkey started to bray insistently. Clearly, he scented danger.

At the top of a mound stood a jackal, long-legged, and with a narrow head. It glared at the intruders who dared venture into its territory. Neck stretched upwards, it let out strange cries, which North Wind listened to attentively. Then the jackal loped down from the mound and set off. North Wind headed purposefully after it.

Iker realized that the two animals had spoken to each other. Of course! The jackal was the incarnation of Anubis, who knew all the paths, in this world and the other.

Adopting the rapid pace of their guide, who, however, took care not to lose them, the two companions soon came within sight of Ra-henty, "the Canal's Mouth", a site marked by a large dyke and a lock, which regulated the supply of water to Faiyum from a tributary of the Nile. Thanks to Senusret II, the area of cultivable land had been increased and the irrigation controlled.

Several guards suddenly barred the travellers' way.

'This is a prohibited military area,' said an officer. 'Who are you, and where have you come from?'

'My name is Iker, and I'm a scribe from the city of Thoth.'

The officer smiled unpleasantly. 'We'll soon see about that. Given your age, it's highly unlikely. I'm the commander-in-chief of the king's army, and I have a speciality: detecting liars. Between ourselves, you could have had better luck.'

'It's the truth, and I can show you a document to prove it.'

Iker made to open one of the bags carried by North Wind. Instantly the guards drew their bows and the officer's sword-point dug into his back.

'Not another move!' snapped the officer. 'You were trying to reach for a weapon, eh? No one goes along this road except the security forces. Who pointed it out to you?'

'You won't believe me.'

'Tell me anyway.'

'A jackal.'

'You're right, I don't believe you. You were probably sent by a gang which is planning to commit thefts hereabouts.'

'Look in my travelling-bags. All you'll find is my scribe's writing-materials – handle them with care.'

Suspiciously, the officer searched the bags. He was disappointed to find no weapons. 'You're a cunning one! And what about this famous document?'

'It's a rolled and sealed papyrus, addressed to the mayor of Kahun. The seal is that of Djehuty, governor of the Hare province.'

'If I break it the mayor will dismiss me for tampering with an official letter, but if I leave it intact I'll have to take your word. Another fine trick, my lad! I am willing to bet that document's a decoy. But I'm not one to be tricked. I know your sort like the back of my hand.'

'Why don't you stop this nonsense and take me to the mayor of Kahun?'

'He's got better things to do than receive criminals.'

'You can see perfectly well that I'm a scribe.'

'Where did you steal these things from?'

'They were given to me by General Sepi.'

'Don't know him. Anyway, you could invent any name, so why not a general's?'

'You're wrong. Everything I've told you is true.'

'What I want to know is whether you were planning to act alone or with accomplices.'

Iker was beginning to lose his temper, and the other man sensed it.

'No false moves, my lad, or I'll run you through with my sword, and all my men will testify in my favour.'

There were too many of them for Iker to defeat them by fighting, and he couldn't outrun the archers' arrows.

'Have the mayor of Kahun break the seal and read the letter of recommendation. Then you'll see that you're making a very big mistake.'

'Threats now, eh? You're going to spend a good long time in prison.'

'You have no right to lock me up.'

'You think not? Put the shackles on him.'

Three guards bore down on the young scribe and flattened him to the ground. When they pulled him to his feet, his hands were pinned behind him in wooden shackles.

'What are you going to do with my donkey?'

'It's a fine, strong, healthy animal. I'll find a use for it.'

'And my writing-materials?'

'We'll trade them for clothes.'

'You're nothing but a thief!'

'It's the other way round, boy – you're the thief, and I shall be congratulated for catching you. When you've spent a few months in a stinking jail with criminals like yourself, your back will bend more easily. Then several years of forced labour will restore your taste for hard work and good behaviour. Take him away – get him out of my sight.'

Iker spoke not a word to the guards who took him to the prison, which was outside the town. They threw him into a cell occupied by three poultry-thieves, one young and two old.

'What did you do?' asked the young man.

'Nothing.'

'No, me neither. And how many geese did you steal?'

'None.'

'Don't worry, you can talk freely. We're on your side.'

'How long have you been here?'

'A few weeks. We're waiting for the judge to find time to deal with us. Unfortunately, he's not a lenient man so we're likely to be put away for a good while, seeing as this isn't the first time we've been here. If you confess and pretend to repent he shows a bit more mercy. If you don't know how, we'll teach you.'

'I'm a scribe and I haven't robbed anyone.'

One of the old men opened an eye. 'A scribe in prison? Then you must be a great criminal! Tell us about it.'

Wearily, Iker sat down in a corner of the cell.

'Leave him alone,' said the young man.

Iker had lost everything, but he refused to give in to despair. He couldn't have fallen into yet another trap, because he had been guided by the jackal of Anubis. All this was no more than a misunderstanding. Even if it took time to clear it up, he would succeed.

46

The cell door opened noisily. 'You,' a guard said to Iker, 'get up and follow us.'

'Where are you taking me?'

'You'll see.'

Three guards escorted him out of the prison, but to his great surprise they did not put on the wooden shackles.

'Am I free?'

'Our orders are to take you to the authorities. If you try to run away, we'll kill you.'

The hope of a better fate vanished. The judge would impose a long sentence, probably several years' forced labour in the copper mines or at an oasis in the Western desert.

It was one against three, and that might be manageable. But the guards would have to move a little further away so that Iker could get effective holds on them. Unfortunately, they were good professionals, and gave him no opportunity.

Iker had his first sight of the town of Kahun. It was small – only about 770 cubits by 670 – and was bordered by a curtain wall twelve cubits high and six thick. The main gate was in the north-eastern corner.

There were four soldiers in the guard-post at the gate.

'We've brought you the prisoner,' said one of Iker's guards.

'We'll deal with him,' said an officer, and he beckoned forward two of his men.

The soldiers, who were more solidly built than the guards, were well armed. If they were skilled at using their throwing-spears Iker would not get far, so he resigned himself to following them.

They set off along a wide street, off which branched streets serving the two main districts. Even at first sight, it was clear that the town had been laid out with care and corresponded to a specific plan. The atmosphere was unusually calm for an Egyptian settlement, and Iker felt immediately at ease.

There were few shops, the white-painted houses were attractive, and everything was spotlessly clean. Iker would have liked to explore all the corners of Kahun, but the soldiers compelled him to walk fast.

'Hurry up. The mayor hates being kept waiting.'

The mayor's house was built on a hill overlooking the town. It was enormous – Iker estimated it must have about seventy rooms – but its entrance was narrow. On either side was a manned guard-box.

'Here's the prisoner the mayor wants to see,' announced the officer.

'One moment. I'll inform his steward.'

To the left, a paved pathway led to the kitchens, the stables and the workshops. The steward, the soldiers and Iker followed the path to the right, which ended in an anteroom. Out of it led a corridor which opened on to a large courtyard closed on the south side by a long porch where the master of the house liked to take the air. Leaving the private part of the house, comprising the bedrooms and washrooms, the steward guided the visitors to the two-pillared reception hall.

His head hanging low, the administrator of the Valley Temple of Senusret II was receiving a severe reprimand. Embarrassed, the steward turned to usher the little party away.

'Come here,' ordered the mayor. He was a small man, with a narrow forehead and thick eyebrows.

'Here is the prisoner you—'

'I know,' cut in the mayor curtly. 'Go, all of you, and leave me alone with him.'

'He may be dangerous,' said the officer, 'and—'

'Be quiet and do as I say.'

Iker was left alone with the mayor, whose scowl did not augur well.

'You are called Iker?'

'That is my name.'

'Where were you born?'

'In Madu.'

'And where have you come from?'

'From the city of Thoth.'

'Do you recognize these?' The mayor pointed to Iker's writing-materials, which were laid out on a low table.

'They're mine.'

'Where did you buy them?'

'General Sepi gave them to me. I had the good fortune to be his pupil, then to accede to the dignity of scribe. Governor Djehuty granted me my first post.'

The mayor reread the papyrus the guards had brought him, and whose seal he had broken.

'My town is guarded well,' he said, 'but the men's intelligence is not always of the high quality I'd like in the forces of order. The guards did not realize who you are. A scribe as young as you, who attracts glowing praise from a governor who's usually sparing with compliments, deserves attention. So tell me, why do you wish to work in Kahun?'

'To try to become a member of the scribes' highest rank.'

The mayor's gaze became less hostile. 'My boy, you could not have chosen better. This town was built by mathematicians and priests instructed in the mysteries. They also built a pyramid; then this place became an administrative

268

centre of the first order. I manage lands, quarries, granaries and workshops, carry out censuses, oversee movements of labour in Faiyum, check daily purchases and expenses, ensure that the priests, craftsmen, scribes, gardeners and soldiers do their work properly. All this work is so demanding that it leaves me no time to devote to my first love, writing.

'Of course, everything has already been said, and no one, not even myself, can invent anything new. Oh, if only I could utter surprising words, fashion unexpected expressions! Every year weighs more heavily than the last, justice is not just enough, and the actions of the gods remain mysterious. Even authority is not sufficiently respected. If you want my opinion, everything's going awry. But who notices it? Who takes the necessary counter-measures? Who dares to drive away evil? Who really helps the poor? Who fights hypocrisy and falsehood?'

'Isn't that what Pharaoh should do?' ventured Iker timidly.

The mayor's fervour evaporated. 'Of course, of course. But always remember, my boy, that the essential thing is writing. Writers don't build temples or tombs: their only heirs are their texts, which survive them and ensure their renown, century after century. Your children are your brushes and your tablets. Your pyramid is your book. I'm wasting my talent in never-ending administration.'

'Are you planning to appoint me to a post?'

'I warn you, you'll be working with highly qualified scribes who loathe amateurs. They won't tolerate any mistakes, and they'll demand your dismissal if you don't know enough. I'd like to believe that Governor Djehuty hasn't drawn too flattering a portrait of you. Ah well . . . I need someone in the secretariat that deals with the granaries.'

This was certainly not the job Iker had hoped for, but he hid his disappointment and said, 'I've done a lot of work in archives and—'

'I've got all the scribes I need in the archives and they do the work perfectly well. Didn't General Sepi teach you how to manage a granary?'

'Yes, I learnt that discipline. I should like to thank you, Mayor, for trusting me.'

'Only reality counts, my boy. Either you're competent or you aren't. If you are, Kahun will be a paradise for you. If you aren't, you'll be sent straight back to where you came from.'

'I hope I shan't disappoint you. There's one point, though, on which I must insist.'

'What is it?'

'My donkey. He is my companion, and I want him back.'

'With your pay, you can buy another.'

'You don't understand. North Wind is unique. I saved his life, and he advises me.'

The mayor's jaw dropped. 'A donkey advises you?'

'He knows how to answer my questions. With him, I'll succeed. Without him, I'll fail.'

'Do you know at least where he is?'

'Probably near the prison where I was held.'

The mayor wrote a few lines on a wooden tablet. 'Here is a note which will enable you to recover him legally. My steward will show you to your official lodgings.'

Iker bowed respectfully.

'Did General Sepi talk to you about the great scribes who have penetrated the secret of creation?'

'Listening, understanding and mastery of the fires: he said those are the qualities one must have in order to do so.'

'You had an excellent teacher. But you must also think about equipping yourself properly.'

'Won't my own writing-materials be returned to me?'

'Of course they will. I'm talking about something else: the words needed to pass through the doors, to obtain the boat from the ferryman or to escape from the great net that

270

captures the souls of evil travellers. Without that knowledge, you'll never be more than an ordinary scribe.'

'Where can I acquire it?'

'That's for you to work out, my boy. Schooldays are one thing; your time as a professional is another. Is it not said that the best craftsmen make their own tools?'

Iker was troubled as he left Kahun and went back to the prison. Why had the mayor uttered such enigmatic words? Why had he revealed the existence of inaccessible knowledge? Like Sepi and Djehuty, he was hiding behind a mask. However, the prospect of this new test did not discourage Iker. Quite the opposite: if a hand really was being held out to him, he'd grasp it so as not to drown in the river. And if nothing existed but illusions, he'd dispel them.

On the threshold of the prison, a guard with his arm in a sling was dozing.

Iker tapped him on the shoulder, and he awoke with a start.

'What do you want?'

'I've come to fetch my donkey.'

'Would it by any chance be a big one, with a head harder than granite and a ferocious temper?'

'That sounds right.'

'Well, look what it did to me! And it's injured three other guards by kicking, butting and biting.'

'That's not surprising – he doesn't obey anyone except me. Release him.'

'Too late.'

'What do you mean, "too late"?' asked Iker, his throat tight.

'The commander decided the only thing to do was kill it – took ten men to subdue it.'

'Where did they take him?'

'To the wasteland behind the prison.'

Iker ran as fast as he could. He found North Wind lying on

his side, surrounded by guards; his hooves were held fast by ropes tied to stakes. A priest was raising the sacrificial knife.

'Stop!' shouted Iker.

Everyone turned, and the donkey let out a bray of hope.

'This animal is highly dangerous,' said the priest. 'The dangerous power must be driven out of him.'

'He belongs to me.'

'And I suppose you've got the documents to prove it,' said the guards' officer sarcastically.

'Will this one do? It's signed by the mayor of Kahun.'

The officer had to climb down.

Iker seized the knife from the priest's hand and cut the donkey free. Well aware that his master had saved his life again, North Wind licked his hands.

'Come along, North Wind. I've got a lot to tell you.'

47

Abydos, the spiritual centre of Egypt, was sinking into darkness. The town was isolated from the rest of the country by vigilant guards who checked all visitors, even the temporary priests, with the greatest care. The permanent priests appointed by the pharaoh were unstinting in their efforts, and carried out their duties meticulously. But the territory of Osiris seemed deprived for ever of the gentle light that had formerly brought its sacred buildings to life.

Despite the weight of years and a heart whose voice was becoming ever weaker, the old High Priest, Bearer of the Golden Palette, visited the ailing Tree of Osiris every day. Its deterioration had been arrested, but there was no sign of improvement. Would Osiris live in the tree for much longer? Would it continue to unite the heavens, the earth and the underworld? Would it still plunge its roots into the ocean of primordial energy? The old man had no answers to these questions.

Until this crisis, his life had been the peaceful one of a priest concerned only with celebrating the mysteries and passing them on. Nothing had prepared him for this tragedy, in the face of which he felt powerless and helpless. The only hopeful sign was that, since the beginning of the building work ordered by Senusret, one branch of the tree had grown green again and had not dried out.

Cllinging to this slender hope, the Bearer of the Golden Palette poured water and milk at the foot of the acacia each day. Then, with his increasingly halting step, he went to the site where the craftsmen, all sworn to absolute secrecy, were building Senusret's temple and house of eternity.

Today the walk was even more difficult than usual. A cold wind chilled him to the bone, and the sand stung his eyes.

The master-builder came to meet him and offered him his arm. 'Shouldn't you rest for a while, sir?'

'In these difficult times, one must not think of oneself. Have you received your supplies of meat, fish and vegetables?'

'We have everything we need. Supplies reach us regularly and promptly, and the cooks you provided serve very good food.'

The High Priest looked at him closely. 'Your words are confident, but your tone of voice is not. Have you had difficulties?'

'A whole series of them,' admitted the master-builder. 'Tools that break, a badly cut stone in the quarry, minor injuries, illnesses – anyone would think a malevolent force was trying to slow down the work.'

'How are you countering these problems?'

'With the morning ritual and the team's unity. In a situation like this, each man knows he must rely on the others. It would be unjust to accuse one man or another of subterfuge or incompetence. We must remain united, under the king's protection. Work on this site is ten times harder than expected, but don't worry: we'll stand firm.'

'If you don't, Abydos will be condemned to death – and its death will lead to that of the whole of Egypt.'

'The work will be carried through to its completion.'

The Bearer of the Golden Palette went slowly back to the temple and checked that the priest whose actions remained secret had arranged the god's shrine properly. He also checked that the daily libation had been poured on to the offering-tables, and that the Servant of the *Ka*, who was charged with celebrating the cult of the ancestors – never had their help been needed so much – had carried out his duties.

For a moment he thought his heart had stopped beating, and he had to sit down. When he had got his breath back, he continued his inspection by going to the tomb of Osiris, which was guarded by the priest who watched over the oneness of the divine body.

'Are the seals firmly in place?'

'They are.'

'Show me.'

The High Priest examined them closely and found nothing amiss. 'Has anyone tried to come near the tomb?'

'No, no one.'

'Any incidents, however minor, to report?'

'No.'

The Bearer of the Golden Palette was reassured: the priest was clearly guarding the tomb with utmost care and the interior of the tomb must be untouched. He could not check for himself: strict and conscientious in his performance of his duties, he would not open the door of this most sacred of all places except on the order of the man who directed the ritual of the Mysteries of Abydos.

The old man had still to question the Shaven-headed One, who was consulting the archives of the House of Life. Constantly performing the ancient rituals, he extracted from them words filled with power, which were then integrated into the year's ritual.

The High Priest loved this place, which was imbued with harmonious vibrations engendered by the thoughts of the sages, set down on papyrus. The air was full of an agreeable smell redolent of the past and of happy times.

The Shaven-headed One's temper was not improving with age. 'I suppose,' he grumbled, 'it's no use asking you to reduce your workload.'

'None at all. Tell me, have you had any visitors in the last few days?'

'No, and anyway I wouldn't have let in anyone except you. When I'm working, especially on subjects as difficult as the navigation of the sacred ship, I don't like being disturbed. I think my research may have useful results, because certain obscure points may be clarified.'

Constantly refining and perfecting the rites, which were the main means of perceiving the Invisible, was the eternal preoccupation of the brotherhood of Abydos. It was also the best way to fight curses.

The last place the High Priest inspected was the shrine tended by the seven priestesses charged with charming the divine soul. Through music, song and dance, they perpetuated the harmony linking the celestial powers to their earthly manifestations. Through the celebration of the feminine rites, they kept Osiris outside death. Without them, Abydos would never have existed.

The youngest priestess came to meet him. In her, joy was united with seriousness. Since her return from Elephantine, where she had been raised to the rank of Awakened One by the Queen of Egypt herself, she looked even more beautiful.

'Do you need anything?' asked the High Priest.

'Only some fresh olibanum and another offering-table. Please, won't you take my arm, and come and sit in the shade?'

The old man did not refuse. The heavy tiredness that had oppressed him since he woke up was getting worse.

He asked, 'How do you perceive the ritual you experienced recently?'

'As a door opening on to a new world. A new reality and different colours have appeared. The landscapes were there, very near, but I could not see them before – we humans are obstacles to the Light. I also know now that I must offer up fruitful gifts of far more than ordinary quality. The queen did not hide the difficulty of the ordeals awaiting me on the path of initiation.'

'The gods wished it thus, and God has agreed with their decision. You, child, will never be a priestess like the others. Sometimes you may wish you could be like them, but do not shut yourself away in that illusion.'

'Please will you, if it is permitted, explain a little more?'

Pain suddenly lanced through the old man's chest. His eyes turned up in his head, and he collapsed.

The priestess did not panic, for during her training, she had acquired sufficient knowledge to recognize a heart attack.

She helped him to lie down, and said, 'I'll go and fetch water and a cushion.'

'No,' he said faintly, 'stay with me. These are my last moments, and I want to keep your face in my memory for when I confront the guardians of the otherworld. Your mission . . . your mission is greater and more perilous than you can possibly imagine. I have confidence in you, so much confidence . . .'

The old man clutched her hands, and let out a very long sigh.

The Shaven-headed One dissolved some grains of natron in magnetized water, then knelt before a cut stone, and a priest poured a little of the water over his hands. Purified, the Shaven-headed One in turn purified the Servant of the *Ka*, who offered milk, wine, bread and dates to the statuette of the High Priest.

Mummified and entombed the previous day, the Bearer of the Golden Palette now belonged to the circle of righteous ancestors. The brotherhood knew that he would never abandon them, so long as his memory was celebrated.

The Servant of the *Ka* brought an incense-burner shaped like an arm and raised the lid so that the smoke could rise up to heaven, where the reborn fed on the most subtle of perfumes. Then he raised an alabaster bull's forefoot, which symbolized victorious power. Next, the priestesses chanted the list of foodstuffs engraved on the offering-table and presented bands of fabric to the ancestor. The ceremony ended with the reading of the words of transformation into light, which rendered the soul capable of travelling throughout the universe.

One of the five most senior permanent priests had been unable to concentrate during the ritual. He was thinking not of the late High Priest but of himself and of the promotion of which, this time, he would inevitably be the happy beneficiary. The post of Bearer of the Golden Palette and High Priest could not fall to anyone else. He had performed his part in the ritual perfectly, and no one had noticed that his thoughts were wandering. The old man's death caused him little grief: at last, the post he coveted was vacant.

His colleagues felt such respect for his austere nature and such admiration for his learning that he would be appointed without even a murmur of opposition. Once he was the head of the most illustrious priesthood in Egypt, what would he do? Curiously, he had not yet thought about it. The important thing was to gain that post, with all the many advantages it would bring him.

'The master of the great Mysteries has arrived,' announced the young priestess.

This unexpected visit did not perturb the future High Priest. The king might participate in the celebration of the Mysteries of Osiris, but he did not live in Abydos. He would necessarily defer to the permanent priests in the choice of the new High Priest.

Pharaoh Senusret meditated for a long time beside the dead man's sarcophagus. He read the words of resurrection, taken from the Pyramid Texts, the Sarcophagus Texts and the secret ritual of Abydos. Then he gathered together the five priests and seven priestesses in the temple.

'There is no need,' he said gravely, 'to stress the importance of your role. Even in normal times it is of great significance. In the present circumstances it is absolutely essential. I have many battles to fight, and my strength rests upon the rituals you celebrate here in order to keep Osiris and his sacred tree alive. If you fail, the foundation of the pharaohs will crumble, and the Two Lands with it. Barbarity, corruption, fanaticism and violence will be imposed. The links between the heavens and the earth will be broken, and the gods will leave this land – and perhaps even the world of humans.

'There are very few of you living in secrecy, by secrecy and for secrecy. Your duty consists of preserving it out of the reach of evil, baseness and the corrosive tears of a humanity which weeps over its own mediocrity. We are not certain of emerging victorious from the terrible struggle in which we are engaged, but we shall fight to the end, without any concessions to the enemy. May Ma'at be our Rule. May she guide us and protect us.'

The king's words shook the future High Priest a little, but he was too impatient for the principal decision to be truly interested in them.

Senusret went on, 'The priest whom I appointed to bear the Golden Palette and to lead this brotherhood was an upright man. Before he appears before the divine court, we must give our judgment of him. Mine is favourable. Has anyone an unfavourable opinion of him?'

Silence fell over the assembly.

'Since it is so, the rites shall be celebrated to their end. May this man of just voice on this earth be recognized as such in the heavens and voyage for ever in eternity.'

The would-be High Priest was finding it more and more difficult to contain his impatience.

At last, the king came to the main question. 'The present order of priests and priestesses shall continue its work under

the leadership of the Shaven-headed One, and with the same
thoroughness. As for the Golden Palette, on which are written
the words of knowledge, as Pharaoh I have decided to retain
it.'

The would-be High Priest thought he must have misheard.
Senusret was not asking the brotherhood for their opinion, he
was not appointing anyone – it was a nightmare!

'I intend to be linked permanently to Abydos,' continued
the king. 'The Shaven-headed One will be my representative,
and will rule your community in my absence, but will not
make any changes without my explicit agreement. He will
receive my instructions regularly and will keep me informed
of everything – no matter how insignificant – which happens
here.

'Any fault, however minor, will result in the offender's
expulsion from the brotherhood. We are at war, and the
enemy is far more dangerous than thousands of soldiers.
Error, inattention or any other weakness will amount to
treason and will be punished as such.

'Now, let us arrange a ritual feast to celebrate our brother,
whom the beautiful goddess of the West has just welcomed
into her bosom.'

Despite having knots in his stomach, the disappointed man
ate the consecrated foods and put on a brave face. No one
must detect his anger and resentment, which were aimed at
Senusret, at Abydos, at the priests and the priestesses who
had failed to speak in praise of him.

Vengeance would not be enough. He must also reach his
goal. To do so, one thing was essential: he must get rich. He
would have to buy a lot consciences and make himself the
most important person in the sacred city, while all the time
spinning his web in the shadows. But how could he make his
fortune without giving himself away? The problem seemed
insoluble.

'You look depressed,' commented one of the priestesses.

'How would I not be? Losing such a great High Priest is hard to bear.'

'We shall come though it together. And we shall need your wisdom and experience.'

'You can rely on me.'

48

'I am Gergu, head overseer of granaries, appointed by High Treasurer Senankh. Show me your premises.'

The scribe responsible for the grain-stores in the little village of Hill of the Flowers was most surprised by the visit of such an important person.

'We are very busy, my lord, and—'

'Do as I say – now! – or I shall call the guards.'

'Please, my lord, come this way.'

With Senankh, Gergu had already inspected the granaries of several large towns. He knew how to keep his place, had proved discreet and respectful, and obeyed to the letter the instructions of his superior, who therefore thought most highly of him.

As soon as Senankh was kept back at the palace, Gergu seized on the occasion to be over-zealous, by taking an interest in the small farms. There he gave full rein to the prerogatives of his office.

The scribe took him to the courtyard where the village grain-stores stood, surrounded by a curtain-wall.

'This wall is not high enough,' said Gergu. 'Thieves could get over it easily.'

'We all know each other here, my lord, and none of us is a thief.'

Gergu pushed the courtyard door and it swung open. 'Why is there no lock?'

'We don't need one.'

'The grain reserves must be kept safely. That is not the case here.'

'I can guarantee that—'

'Rules are rules.'

Now very worried, the scribe showed Gergu into the courtyard. A staircase led up to a terrace, on which were the openings to three grain-stores built against the back wall. Almost at ground level were vertical trapdoors, which when open gave access to the grain.

'The staircase does not meet regulations,' declared Gergu. 'There are too few steps, and they are badly built.'

'I did not know about that regulation. my lord.'

'You do now.'

Gergu opened a trapdoor. 'The wood is worn – it should have been replaced a long time ago.'

'But it works perfectly, my lord, I assure you.'

'The names of the owners of the fields should be engraved on the wall.'

'They are, my lord. Look, there.'

'They are almost worn away. Is this an attempt at tax fraud?'

'Of course not, my lord. The agents of government know these farmers very well, and there has never been any problem.'

Gergu climbed the staircase cautiously, as if it were dangerous. 'This terrace is much too narrow. The risk of an accident is high – you clearly pay little heed to the welfare of the farm workers.'

'On the contrary, my lord, they're treated very well here.'

Gergu looked inside the grain store. 'This needs urgent attention. The general state of cleanliness is deplorable.'

'I cleansed and repainted it before it was refilled, and I—'

'This case is particularly serious. I have never seen so many infractions of the law on one site. In my opinion, you should be arrested at once.'

The scribe paled. 'I don't understand, my lord. I—'

'There is an alternative, however. If you pay a large enough fine, I might be able to prevent your going to prison.'

'How large would it have to be?'

'No, that probably isn't the best solution, for I should still have to write a report to my superior.' Gergu paused to let his words sink in. 'There is one other possibility, but I hardly like to mention it.'

'Oh, please do, my lord.'

'I reduce the fine by half, and I don't write a report. In return, you give me what I demand and say nothing about it to anyone.'

The scribe did not need much time for reflection. 'Very well, if that will be the end of the matter.'

'It will. But if you were to breathe a word, it would be my word against yours. I'd accuse you of attempted bribery, you'd go to prison, and you'd lose everything you have.'

'I shan't say a word, my lord.'

'You are an intelligent man. Thanks to me, you have escaped the worst.'

Gergu could never thank Medes enough for procuring him such a rewarding post. Each check of small grain-stores enabled him to get richer without fear of a complaint from the scribes he blackmailed. Moreover, he was zealous in writing detailed reports for Senankh.

Face to face with the High Treasurer, Gergu played the virtuous man, so concerned with serving the general good that he scarcely took the time to take care of himself.

'We are leaving on another journey,' Senankh told him.

'Where to?'

'Abydos.'

'But Abydos is forbidden to outsiders, isn't it?'

'Pharaoh's orders.'

'Does His Majesty suspect fraud or theft there?'

'We must inspect all the major temples without any prior assumptions – this one as well as the others. Be ready to leave tomorrow morning.'

Gergu pondered. Didn't the pharaoh have a detailed inventory of each temple's riches? On reflection, that was unlikely. Several provinces were still independent, so in effect Senusret controlled only the Delta, the Memphis region and the north of Upper Egypt. The purpose of these journeys of inspection must therefore be to ascertain exactly what resources he really had and could use to consolidate his power. For there could be no doubt that Senusret's real goal was to attack the rebel provinces, kill their governors and extend his rule throughout the entire country.

While sheltering behind Senankh, Gergu decided, he would obtain as much useful information as possible, as much for Medes as for himself. That way, if Senusret's intentions were not what he thought, he would soon find out.

Although Senankh had given his name and titles in full, the officer in charge of the landing-stage guards saw that he and Gergu, as well as their possessions, were searched thoroughly. The security orders were extremely strict, and even the most senior officials had to obey them.

'Guards will accompany you. You must never move about alone – if you do, the archers have orders to shoot.'

'I must go to the temple to meet the Shaven-headed One,' said Senankh. 'My assistant, Gergu, will see the steward of the city of Pharaoh Senusret.'

'I shall inform him. Please wait here.'

Senankh and Gergu sat down on stools in the shade of a sycamore tree. A soldier brought them some water.

'This is a rather unwelcoming place,' commented Gergu.

'The treasures and secrets of Abydos really are well protected! What work do the priests do?'

'They study the heavens, medicine, magic and all the branches of learning that Thoth revealed. Their principal duty, at least as regards the summit of the priesthood, is to celebrate the Mysteries of Osiris. If the rites were not performed correctly, disorder would prevail.'

'Isn't the deployment of all these soldiers and security guards rather strange?'

'Not at all,' said Senankh. 'Abydos is the most sacred site in Egypt, and its protection entails special precautions.'

'But surely the gods are more than able to defend themselves? In any case, who would dare profane the domain of Osiris?'

'Human beings are capable of even worse things than that.'

'Well, at all events, I am delighted to be seeing the temple.'

'I'm afraid you won't be able to – you'll have access only to the administrative buildings. You are to ask if the food reserves are satisfactory, listen to any complaints and assure the priests that any necessary action will be taken as quickly as possible.'

'And what about you? Are you are going to see the temple?'

'My mission is secret.'

The Shaven-headed One received High Treasurer Senankh in an annexe of the Temple of Osiris where the priests met to exchange information and to report any daily problems they faced – these must be resolved quickly and in the best way possible, so that nothing might hinder the proper progress of the rites.

Senankh had discovered almost nothing about Abydos, where the atmosphere was heavy, almost painful. And the Shaven-headed One's expression did not lighten the mood.

After the exchange of formal greetings, Senankh said, 'Pharaoh Senusret has entrusted me with a delicate but vital task.'

'Why has he not come himself?'

'Because urgent matters require his presence elsewhere. As a member of the King's House, I am authorized to act in his name.'

'Have you an official letter signed by him?'

'Don't you trust me?'

'Not at all.'

'Here is the letter.'

The Shaven-headed One studied it for a long time, then said, 'This is indeed the royal seal and His Majesty's writing. What do you want?'

'To find out exactly what treasures the temple has.'

'That is a state secret.'

'I am the official representative of the state, and you are therefore obliged to give me this information, which I shall pass on directly to the king – and only to him.'

'Let him come to inspect the treasury himself, then it will not be possible for the information to seep out.'

'You seem to misunderstand. I have been given an order, and I must carry it out. You have no choice: you must obey me.'

'I shall obey no one but His Majesty.'

'I must remind you that it is he who sent me.'

'I require confirmation of that.'

Senankh changed his tone. 'You insult me and you insult the King's House!'

'Better that than incaution. You may be the High Treasurer, but you have no business here. No palace affairs must disturb the peace of this place, and only Pharaoh can clarify the situation. Now, please excuse me. I cannot waste any more time on pointless discussions.'

Left alone, Senankh smiled. Senusret had sent him to

Abydos to put the Shaven-headed One to the test. The pharaoh wanted to know whether he would behave as a loyal servant of the pharaoh, or whether power would go to his head, leading him to believe that he could conduct all the temple's affairs without reference to the king.

Senankh had received a clear answer. The Shaven-headed One would not yield to pressure, from whatever source, and was true to his word: only the king himself could take major decisions. The High Treasurer's mission could not have had a better outcome. He hoped Gergu's would be equally successful.

Gergu had been taken into the administrative building, where a small number of scribes, chosen with care by the king himself, watched over the well-being of the residents of Wah-sut, the 'City of Everlasting Sites', created by the builders of Senusret's temple and house of eternity.

In these austere surroundings where no one so much as raised his voice, Gergu felt ill at ease. It was a far cry from the bustle of Memphis.

The head steward did not look like a man to be trifled with. He asked bluntly, 'What do you want?'

'I am assistant to High Treasurer Senankh.'

'I know.'

'I oversee the grain-stores.'

'Abydos's are well filled.'

'I am glad to hear it. But my mission goes beyond that.'

'Go on.'

'Well, it's very simple but rather delicate: I must make sure that no one here is short of anything.'

'As regards Wah-sut and the brotherhood of the builders, there are no problems at all. If food supplies were delayed, I should alert you at once. As regards the permanent and temporary priests, I cannot give such an undertaking. I shall therefore ask another priest to speak to you.'

Curiously, Gergu was beginning to be affected by the peace of this place. Never yet had he had such strange sensations, as if he was distanced from himself, as if violence and corruption were not necessarily the best solutions in all circumstances. Gergu was surprised to find himself dreaming of a less brutal world, in which some people were not murderers or thieves or ambitious.

Annoyed at being distracted by such thoughts, he shook himself like a wet dog. Powerful sorcerers must have lived here and impregnated the place with their foolish ideas – he must be wary of Abydos in future. All the same, he would not fail to take an interest in its secrets, even though he had little hope of discovering them.

The priest who entered the room was a strange-looking man. He was frankly ugly and his manner was icy. Gergu could tell straight away that this knife-blade was devoid of all sensitivity. But at the same time, and despite the unlikeliness of such a thing, he sensed that they had something in common.

The priest said, 'I am told that your name is Gergu and you have been sent by the High Treasurer to check that we have all we need.'

'My task could not be summed up better. With your help, I will carry it through to fruition.'

When he had first seen this coarse creature, whose fondness of the pleasures of the flesh was only too apparent, the priest's immediate instinct had been to dismiss him curtly and demand to speak with someone else. But now a strange contact had been made.

It was obvious that Gergu had made corruption and baseness his rule of life. Could this meeting, coming when the priest was planning both to avenge the insult to himself and to seek ways of becoming rich, be a sign from providence? He must be cautious and above all not let himself be dangerously carried away. It would take time and several visits before even the beginnings of an alliance could be considered.

He said, 'We do in fact have a few problems. They might hinder the accomplishment of our sacred tasks.'

'I am here to resolve them and ensure your perfect peace of mind,' said Gergu piously.

After a time of reflection, which had changed nothing of his first impression, the Shaven-headed One chose to send Senusret his decision, in accordance with the king's request.

Yes, strength and vigour must be restored to the Golden Circle of Abydos. Yes, High Treasurer Senankh was worthy of belonging to it.

49

Iker rubbed his eyes. 'Am I really to live here?' he asked the mayor's steward.

They were standing outside a superb house in the eastern district of Kahun, where the largest and most luxurious houses had been built.

'It belongs to Heremsaf, your superior in the grain-store secretariat, who has agreed to accommodate you in his own house. Tread carefully: he is not an easygoing man.'

This town was not like any other Iker had seen. The eastern district was separated by a wall of unbaked bricks from the western district, which was much smaller and was crossed by ten parallel streets. A substantial thoroughfare, nine paces wide, crossed the town from north to south. Evidently the plan had been conceived and executed by someone who hated untidiness.

The steward knocked on the door of the house.

The man who opened it did not, indeed, look as if he had much sense of humour. His square face boasted an elegant moustache, trimmed to perfection.

'This is Iker, the scribe assigned to the grain-stores secre—'

'I know what he will have to do and what I have to do. That will be all.'

The steward bowed and left.

Heremsaf pointed a long finger at North Wind. 'What is that?'

'My donkey. He—'

'I can still tell the difference between a donkey and a human being, even if that difference is sometimes extremely small. What is he used for?'

'He carries my writing-materials.'

'Where did you obtain them?'

'They were given to me by General Sepi, my teacher in the province of—'

'I know who General Sepi is, and where he teaches. When and why did he expel you from his class?'

'I was not expelled! As I was his best pupil, Lord Djehuty entrusted me with a difficult task.'

'Even the most careful people can make mistakes. What was this task?'

'Drawing up an inventory of the strengths and weaknesses of the province. I examined the other scribes' reports in detail and presented the governor with a critical appraisal.'

Heremsaf raised his eyebrows. 'You're much too young for him to have assigned you such a delicate task.'

'I assure you that—'

'I know the profession, you do not. The truth is probably that you were given old records to file. You must learn to listen, for "listening is better than anything. When one listens well, one's words are good."'

Iker completed the maxim: '"He whom God loves is he who hears."'

'So you know the Maxims of Ptah-Hotep. Good. However, you will do well to remember this one: "The ignorant man does not listen; he considers knowledge to be ignorance and lives by that which causes death." Now, tell me the truth: why do you want to work in Kahun?'

'Because this is where the best scribes in the kingdom are trained.'

'And you want to become one of them, no doubt. Are you not aware that greed is the worst of faults, an incurable evil, the source of all ills?'

'Is it greed to wish to excel in one's profession?'

'We shall see. Are you certain you have told me everything?'

'For the moment, yes.'

'Fortunately for you, I have room in my stable for your donkey. But I accept only hard-working, highly disciplined animals – and scribes. My cook will prepare your meals, but my serving-woman will not clean your bedchamber or washroom. You will do that yourself, and if you do not do it well I shall send you away: this house must remain a model of cleanliness. If you encounter a problem, I want no misplaced use of your own initiative. You will consult me and you will follow my instructions. Now go and unpack your things quickly, and take your donkey to the stable. We leave in an hour.'

When he saw his new lodgings, Iker forgot his host's acid comments. The room was large, light and airy, and was furnished with two top-quality mats, a low bed with a headboard and cushion, fine linen sheets for the summer, thick ones for winter, several storage-chests and two oil-lamps.

Dazed by such luxury, Iker led North Wind to the stable, which stood behind the house, not far from the open-air kitchen. It lived up to the house. North Wind had a huge space to himself, plenty of fodder and a well-filled water trough.

'I think, my friend, that we shall have to show we deserve this stroke of good fortune.'

The donkey pricked up its right ear.

'Eat and drink your fill, North Wind, but don't take too long. I suspect our host does not like being kept waiting.'

Iker was right. When they got back to the house, Heremsaf was already waiting on the threshold, tapping his foot.

'Can that donkey carry my equipment, too?'

'What do you think, North Wind?' asked Iker.

The donkey pricked up his right ear.

'If I understand aright,' said Heremsaf in astonishment, 'it was the donkey who decided.'

'He is my only friend.'

His lips pursed, Heremsaf packed his palette, writing-tablets and brushes in one of the panniers, then said, 'It is time we were off.'

The atmosphere of the whole town was quiet and studious. Even the street-sweepers who kept the main and side streets clean did not call out to each other.

'Let the situation be quite clear,' said Heremsaf. 'Pharaoh has appointed me steward of the pyramid of Senusret II and the Temple of Anubis. This means I must oversee the deliveries of jars of beer, loaves, meat, grain, fat, perfumes, and also check the accounts, the employees' work, and the distribution of food, not to mention the upkeep of the day-book. This heavy burden of work leaves me no free time to correct other scribes' mistakes, so anyone working for me must prove that he is highly competent – ineptness is not tolerated here.'

Iker was most impressed by the area where the grain-stores stood: their number and size meant that the inhabitants of Kahun need never fear famine. The little town certainly benefited a great deal from the king's favour.

'Well, boy, show me you know what you are doing,' said Heremsaf caustically.

Iker took out his writing-materials. On a tablet, he first noted down the number of grain-stores that stood alone. Then he turned to those arranged in banks, which were between four and sixteen cubits high. Next, he inspected the interiors, checked the quality of the bricks, the strength of the roofs and made sure that they were waterproof, which was essential to prevent the growth of fungus which would make the grain inedible.

When the sun began to sink, Iker rejoined his superior. 'I shall need several days to find out whether there are any defects in the grain-stores,' he said. 'I must put my notes in order, and then investigate more closely.'

Heremsaf did not respond to Iker's words. Instead, he said, 'I am going to the Temple of Anubis. Go back to the house, where you will be given your evening meal. Be here tomorrow, at the first hour of the day.'

The stoppers used to close the loading-hatches at the tops of the grain-stores were in order, but some of the unloading-doors at the front did not slide smoothly in their grooves. Iker made sketches and, in a detailed report, indicated the risks. However, the main problem went far deeper than matters of detail.

Deep in thought, he was wondering how to describe it as accurately as possible when someone tapped him on the shoulder. He turned and saw a tall, flabby scribe of about fifty.

'Are you the new scribe of the grain-stores?' asked the scribe.

'I am only Heremsaf's assistant.'

'Heremsaf is a nuisance. He detests the whole human race and the only thing he enjoys is causing trouble for other scribes.'

'I have no complaints about him.'

'You soon will have! What are you doing?'

'Checking that the grain-stores are in good condition.'

'You're wasting your time. There aren't any problems.'

'How can you be certain of that?'

'Because I checked them all myself last year. There aren't any problems, I tell you.'

'I don't agree.'

'What are you saying, friend? I'm an experienced, well-known scribe. No one calls my word into question.'

'In that case, why did you leave your post?'

'You insolent little puppy! Show me your report.'

'Certainly not. It is addressed to Heremsaf, and no one else may read it.'

'Come, come. Colleagues don't hide things from each other.'

'I'm sorry but I can't let you see it.'

'At least tell me if you've spotted something . . . unusual.'

'Again, that concerns no one but Heremsaf.'

'Let's stop going round in circles. In Kahun we live peacefully and we don't like snoopers. Do you understand me?'

'Yes, I think so.'

'Are you really looking for trouble?'

'All I want to do is work in peace.'

'If you go on like this, you won't be able to. Listen carefully: the grain-stores are in perfect condition, as I reported when I checked them. Is that clear?'

'As day.'

'Well, then! Everything can be settled between professionals of goodwill.'

'The only detail I don't know is your name. But I shall find it out easily and then I shall know who is responsible for the serious defects I've described in my report.'

'You are making a stupid mistake and—'

'No one will prevent me from carrying out my duty.'

Heremsaf rolled up the papyrus, which he had just read a second time. 'These are serious accusations, Iker.'

'They are well founded. Two grain-stores were built of such poor-quality bricks that they will have to be demolished. My predecessor covered up a fraud which might well be very harmful.'

'Are you absolutely sure of that?'

'I have checked and checked again. If I'd had any doubts,

they would have been dispelled by the threats that criminal made – not that I care about them. Is there nowhere on this earth where truth and justice reign, not one single place where one can trust other people?'

'A bad question and a false problem,' said Heremsaf. 'Do you know the secrets of the divine book, the art of the priest, the words that enable the souls of the just to travel through the universe? No, of course not. Then instead of rebelling like an ignorant child, equip yourself.'

'Equip myself . . . The mayor told me to do that, too. But how can I while I have to spend my time seeing to the granaries?'

'All paths lead to the centre if the heart is righteous. Only one question merits being asked: are you an ordinary man, or truly a seeker after the spirit?'

50

Senusret and the King's House listened attentively to Medes's drafts of the proposed decrees. Medes was deeply worried. He had tried to respect the king's thoughts very closely, while avoiding annoying Wakha and Sarenput, who were now declared servants of the pharaoh.

When Medes had finished reading, the king asked, 'Does anyone wish to make any comments or amendments?'

No one asked permission to speak.

'These decrees are therefore adopted. They are to be given out all over the land.'

'In what manner, Majesty?' asked Medes.

'Return to Memphis and use the message service.'

Fear twisted Medes's guts. 'If my boat is intercepted I—'

'You will travel in a trading-boat chartered by Sarenput and you will reach the capital without hindrance. You are to leave immediately.'

During most of the journey, Medes ate nothing but bread and drank only water. He feared an attack at any moment by the hostile governors' soldiers or a thoroughgoing check by their representatives. But all went smoothly, and the boat soon reached Memphis.

As soon as it docked, Medes hurried back to his office, where he called together his main colleagues and ordered them to act promptly – any delay would incur punishment. Being a high-ranking official did not guarantee a job for life. One had constantly to prove oneself worthy of the honour by devotion to one's duties. A hard worker himself, Medes was quick to detect signs of laziness, and always dismissed the offender on the spot.

That evening, as usual, he was the last to leave the secretariat offices, and he took advantage of this to cast an eye over his subordinates' work. He noted that a papyrus had been badly rolled and that there were blots of ink on some new writing-tablets. First thing tomorrow, the culprits would have to find other posts. In a few months, he would have assembled the best team of scribes in Memphis, proving his true worth to Senusret. How could the pharaoh ever be suspicious of such a zealous servant?

Medes did not go home when he had finished his inspection. Instead, checking all the time that he was not being followed, he made for the port area and entered a maze of alleyways where it was easy to spot anyone curious.

Because of his new post and the temple inventory demanded by Senusret, Medes's chances to steal were almost non-existent. With nothing coming in, his secret fortune was no longer growing. His instinct for an opportunity had soon detected another way, but, though it would probably be more lucrative, it was also more risky, since it depended on a cunning and dishonest intermediary. Medes would have to find a way of putting him in his place and keeping him there, without destroying his goodwill.

The man's rich, single-storey house was tucked away in a modest district. A guard stood in the entrance porch.

'I want to see your master immediately.'

'He is not here.'

'For me, he is. Go and show him this.'

Medes handed the guard a small piece of cedar-wood, on which the 'tree' hieroglyph had been carved.

He did not have to wait long. Bowing and scraping, the door-keeper let him in.

The owner, a Phoenician trader, came to meet his guest. Dressed in a long, richly coloured robe, and distressingly over-perfumed, he looked like a heavy wine-jar.

'My very dear friend, what a pleasure it is to welcome you to my modest abode. Please, come in, come in.'

He led Medes into a reception chamber crammed with exotic furniture. Pastries and sweet drinks had been set out on low tables.

'I was about to have a snack before dinner. Would you care to join me?'

'I am in a hurry.'

'Very well. Do you wish to talk about business?'

'Exactly.'

The Phoenician did not much like this hurried approach, but if he was to establish himself in Egypt he must put up with it.

'When will the delivery be made?' asked Medes.

'The boat will arrive next week. I hope all the necessary authorizations have been provided?'

'I'm dealing with them. What is the cargo?'

'Top-quality cedarwood.'

Some trees did not grow in Egypt, and their timber therefore had to be imported – the best fetched very high prices. For a long time, Medes had been studying the field in the hope of making as much profit as possible from it. He had yet to flush out a trader who would both share his point of view and be sufficiently skilful to carry the enterprise through to its conclusion.

'How do you arrange to sell it?'

'In the best possible way, my lord. I have some good contacts in the region, and I offer the wood at half the official cost, payable in advance. As it has never existed and there is no written record of it, neither the seller nor the buyer need worry. Your countrymen like fine materials and are eager to acquire them, even secretly, for use in building their houses or for luxurious furniture.'

'If this first deal is a success, it will be followed by many more.'

'You can be sure of it, my lord. I have the best team of professionals at my disposal, as dedicated as they are discreet.'

'Are you aware that without me success would be impossible?'

'You are the creator of this enterprise, I know that very well. You have all my gratitude and—'

'Three-quarters of the profits for me, and the last quarter for you.'

The Phoenician's heart almost stopped beating. Only long years of experience enabled him to keep a smile on his face instead of strangling this bare-faced thief. 'Usually, my lord, I—'

'This situation is exceptional, and you owe me everything. It is thanks to me that the Egyptian market is now open to you and you will become very rich. As I like you, I am being more than reasonable.'

'I am very grateful to you,' declared the Phoenician.

'But you must never speak of me to anyone. If you make one false move, I will have you arrested for fraud, and your word will count for nothing against mine.'

'You can rely on my absolute silence, my lord.'

'I like dealing with intelligent men. We shall meet again soon, to celebrate our first success.'

Medes did not trust the Phoenician at all, and he himself would have to oversee each phase of the operation, which he would call off at the first sign of trouble. Nevertheless, the trader was so eaten up with the lust for profit that he might prove a useful partner.

*

Gergu was drunk. While waiting for Medes, he had downed cup after cup of strong beer. The cup-bearer disapproved strongly, but was nevertheless obliged to satisfy the demands of this boor, because his master liked him.

When Medes arrived, Gergu got to his feet and tried to stand straight. 'I may have drunk a little, but my mind is clear.'

'Sit down.'

Gergu aimed himself at his chair and managed not to miss it. 'Good news,' he said. 'High Treasurer Senankh is satisfied with me even though, contrary to appearances, he is not an easygoing or trusting man. In fact, I find him remarkably untrusting and am having to take great care not to arouse his suspicions.'

'What about women?'

'I only use prostitutes now. That way, there's no fear of complaints.'

'Continue to do so. I don't want any scandals involving respectable women. Now tell me, what are Senankh's weaknesses?'

'Food – he hates dull food and inferior wines.'

'That isn't enough – we can't bribe him that way. You think too much about yourself and not enough about other people. I need more information. And tell me more about this good news.'

'Senankh took me to Abydos. He dealt with the temple treasury, while I checked the priests' living conditions.'

Medes's interest grew. 'Were you allowed to enter the temple?'

'No, only an administrative building. All the same, I did not waste my time. First of all, I established something very odd: the site is guarded by soldiers.'

'Why?'

'I have no idea. I didn't dare ask questions in case someone became suspicious.'

Medes was enraged. 'You actually entered the sacred territory of Abydos and you learnt nothing of importance? Sometimes, Gergu, I wonder if you are worthy of my friendship.'

'I haven't finished yet. Next, I met a priest with whom I hope to stay in contact. He's an odd fellow – I think he might interest you.'

'In what way?'

'When our eyes met, it was a strange feeling . . . That fellow may be a great scholar, but I had the impression he isn't content with his lot and would like to improve it.'

'Aren't you imagining this?'

'I have a sixth sense for corruptible people.'

'A priest of Abydos? Impossible!'

'We'll see. If I'm summoned to see him again I'll know more.'

For a moment Medes allowed himself to dream: having an ally inside Abydos, the spiritual centre of Egypt, being able to manipulate him, discovering the secrets of the covered temple, using them for his own benefit . . . No, it was a mirage.

He asked, 'Do you know his name and office?'

'Not yet – he simply presented himself as an intermediary ensuring the well-being of his colleagues. Our conversation ought to have been quite ordinary, but I sensed that it was something else.'

'Did he say anything that confirmed that impression?'

'No, but—'

'Your imagination is running away with you, Gergu. Abydos is unlike any other place in Egypt. Don't hope to find ordinary men there.'

'My instinct rarely deceives me, I assure you.'

'This time it has.'

'But supposing I'm right?'

'I repeat: it's impossible.'

51

Very slowly, Sehotep undressed the young woman he had met the previous evening at an official dinner. They had not taken their eyes off each other, and at the end of the meal had promised to see each other alone. As the Bearer of the Royal Seal and the pretty brown-haired lady had exactly the same intentions, they had not wasted time on useless conversation.

True, she was slightly betrothed, but how could he resist the charm of this well-bred lady, whose eyes sparkled with intelligence and desire? Custom did not require girls to be virgins when they married, and it was better to have a little experience in order to please one's future husband.

As for Sehotep, he could not manage without a woman for more than a few days. To live without them – their magic, their perfumes, their sensuality, those movements which belonged only to them – was unbearable. He would never marry, for there were too many enchanting souls to discover and delicious bodies to explore. Despite the reprimands of Sobek the Protector, who was a stern moralist, Sehotep remained a man for all women.

As the atmosphere had noticeably relaxed in Swenet since Sarenput had rallied to Senusret's cause, the Bearer of the Royal Seal was thinking once again of pleasure, both given and received. As overseer of all Pharaoh's works, he had supervised the plan for enlarging the Temple of Khnum on the isle of Elephantine, and first thing tomorrow he would check the health of the flocks belonging to Sarenput, who – as a loyal vassal – would accept this verification without question.

Sehotep had been worried that someone might arrive to spoil his evening, but no official appeared. So he paid attention, with as much delicacy as fervour, to the magnificent landscape waiting to be explored. The hollows, the valleys and the hills of his new conquest would have delighted even the most jaded adventurer.

His secretary had the good taste to wait until he had finished his journey before disturbing him. He brought him a letter written in coded script, which only Sehotep and the pharaoh could decipher.

The contents justified an immediate meeting of the inner council.

'Everything's calm, Majesty,' declared Sobek-Khu, 'but I have not lifted any of the security measures.'

'Without lapsing into blind optimism,' added General Nesmontu, 'I must admit that Sarenput has given me no cause for concern. His soldiers are now under my command, and I have no adverse incidents to report. His declaration of allegiance seems to have been decisive.'

'Unfortunately it is not,' replied Senusret. 'The text of the decrees has reached all the provincial governors, and we now have their responses.'

He gestured to Sehotep, who said, 'Wepwawet, ruler of half the province of the Pomegranate Tree and the Horned Viper, has delivered an aggressive speech in order to reaffirm his independence. Wukh, who rules the other half, has done likewise. Djehuty, governor of the province of the Hare, has announced a great surprise which will astonish His Majesty.'

'Probably a surprise attack,' growled Nesmontu.

'As for Khnum-Hotep, governor of the province of the

Oryx, he proclaims loud and long the power of his family, which will continue to rule his inalienable territory.'

'So these four want war,' said the general. 'Even with Sarenput's and Wakha's men, we have little chance of defeating them.'

'It is too soon for these troops to be engaged in battle,' said Senusret. 'Their allegiance is too recent. But we cannot remain immobile, either.'

Nesmontu feared a new grand gesture which, this time, would be fatal to the king. He said, 'Majesty, I advise you to exercise the greatest caution. The hostile governors have clearly hardened their position. Confronting them with forces weaker than their own would end in disaster.'

'The man responsible for the acacia dying is one of those four,' Sehotep reminded him. 'Whatever method we use, he must be eliminated.'

'By reuniting the provinces,' said Senusret, 'we assemble what was scattered and we take part in the Mysteries of Osiris. When Egypt is divided, Osiris no longer reigns and the process of resurrection is interrupted. Death invades the heavens and the earth. We are therefore going to leave Swenet and head north.'

'With what forces?' asked Nesmontu anxiously.

'With the flotilla that enabled us to conquer Swenet without bloodshed.'

'Majesty, the situation is very different! Sarenput was isolated, but our four adversaries all live in the same region, and their reaction to the decrees indicates that they are united. Wepwawet is known for his aggressive, indomitable nature. He won't hesitate for a moment to launch his army against you.'

'We leave tomorrow morning,' ordered the king.

In the house of the Canaanites from Sichem, the Herald delivered a long sermon preaching rebellion against Pharaoh and the destruction of Egypt. Spellbound, his followers drank in the words they so wanted to hear.

They badly needed their leader's encouragement, for their integration into Egyptian society was not proving as easy as expected. Finding work had not been too difficult, but they were disgusted by their contact with the population, especially the women, whose liberty, open way of speaking and influence they hated: women ought to lock themselves away at home and humbly obey their husbands. In addition, Pharaoh remained very popular. People expected justice and prosperity from him. Now Senusret had brought about an ideal annual flood, which would dispel the fear of famine for a long time, and his new government enjoyed a reputation for honesty and thoroughness.

In view of all this, it would not have been surprising if they had given in to discouragement, a state of mind apparently foreign to the Herald.

'Would it not be better,' suggested one of the Canaanites at the end of the sermon, 'to go back home, make our whole land rise up, and then attack the Delta?'

The Herald spoke to him gently, as though addressing someone weak-minded. 'I myself would have preferred that solution. But achieving a quick and complete military victory is now impossible – the Egyptian army of occupation would nip any attempt at rebellion in the bud. So we must fight from the inside, learning to live here, to know the enemy, his customs and his weak points. It will be long and difficult, but I shall help you and your companions.'

The Phoenician trader's house was not very far from the Canaanites', but the Herald took a tortuous route which led him away from it.

'We must separate,' he told Shab the Twisted. 'Let me go ahead and then hide yourself.'

'Do you think we're being followed? I haven't noticed anything.'

'That's because the man following us is skilful.'

'Shall I kill him?'

'No, just watch him and make sure he's alone.'

Shab was perplexed. Who could have spotted them? There were watertight partitions between the Herald's different networks, which only he knew in their entirety. As for their members, without exception they were fierce opponents of Egypt. No traitor could have slipped in among them.'

The Twisted One sat down under an awning and pretended to be dozing.

From an alleyway, he saw emerge the Canaanite who wanted to go back home, the very one the Herald had comforted. The man ran, retraced his steps, then took the narrowest alleyway. There was no one with him.

Shab fell in behind him.

The Canaanite had clearly lost the Herald's trail. He hesitated, unsure which way to go. Eventually, he bore left.

Shab heard a curious sound, like a falcon swishing through the air as it stooped on its prey. The Herald emerged from nowhere, and laid his hand on the head of the Canaanite, who cried out in pain, as if a bird of prey's talons had entered his flesh.

'Is it me you were looking for?' asked the Herald.

'No, no, my lord – I was just going for a walk.'

'Lying is futile. Why were you following me?'

'I assure you, I—'

'If you refuse to tell me, I shall put out one of your eyes – the pain is unbearable. Then I shall cause you even more appalling agony.'

In terror, the Canaanite confessed. 'I wanted to know where you were going and who you were meeting.'

'On whose orders?'

'No one's, my lord, I swear. I couldn't understand why you

won't form a Canaanite army, and I suspected you of being an Egypt spy who wanted to destroy our rebellion.'

'It's more likely that you're the one in the pharaoh's pay.'

'No, my lord, I swear I'm not!'

'This is your last chance to tell the truth.'

A talon sank into the Canaanite's eye, and he screamed in agony.

'No, not the pharaoh, it was my tribal chief at Sichem – he wanted to get rid of you.'

A last scream, short and intense, froze Shab the Twisted's blood. The Canaanite collapsed on the ground, his eyes and tongue ripped out.

The Phoenician slowly climbed the staircase that led to the terrace of his home, where costly perfumes wafted on the air. He was followed by the Herald and Shab. The latter was suspicious and made sure to check all the rooms.

'I like to sit here at sunset,' said the Phoenician. 'The view is magnificent – one feels like the king of Memphis.'

Indeed it was magnificent. They looked out over the white houses and far beyond, to the temples, those dwellings of the false gods. The Herald would raze them to the ground: not one stone would remain on top of another, and the statues would be smashed and burnt. No priest would escape death. No trace of the ancient spirituality must survive.

'We are not here to admire the enemy's capital,' said the Herald. 'Have you heard any news of Senusret?'

'Only conflicting rumours. Some say he's a prisoner of Governor Sarenput at Swenet, others say he has seized whole the South of Egypt after a terrible battle. But no one knows his plans – assuming he's still alive.'

'He is,' said the Herald. 'Why aren't your informants more reliable?'

The Phoenician ate a cake to soothe his nerves. 'Because I haven't yet had time to build up the networks, especially in the South. It will take a long time, but I promise you that—'

'Take the time you need, but don't let me down.'

Vaguely reassured by the Herald's conciliatory tone, the Phoenician was frank about the difficulties he faced, and explained how he recruited his informants and how he implanted them in the population. The main problem was slowness; sometimes there was no means of easy communication because of the hostility between provincial governors and the pharaoh. It was not uncommon for Khnum-Hotep to blockade the river and requisition boats' cargoes. Moreover – and this was by no means a minor detail – the Phoenician's agents had to familiarize themselves with local customs and speak the language perfectly before contacting the soldiers and officials from whom they hoped to glean useful information.

The Herald listened attentively. 'You work well, my friend. Continue to do so. Patience is a vital weapon.'

'I'm in business with an odd fellow,' went on the Phoenician. 'All I know is that he's an influential senior official who wants to make a lot of money. I must learn more about him and I hope, through his intermediary, to make a high-ranking contact in the royal palace.'

'That will be one of the most difficult slopes to climb,' said the Herald. 'Be extremely careful. What is the name of this . . . businessman?'

'He hasn't told me – and if he had, he'd have lied.'

The Herald closed his eyes and tried to see the face of this strange trader by entering the Phoenician's memory.

'The trail looks interesting,' he concluded. 'Find out who he is, but be very careful. What is your business with him?'

'Smuggling imported timber. He opens up the Memphis market to me, but at a price – and what a price! I shall earn hardly anything.'

'Don't forget that out of that "hardly anything" you're to pay my network its share.'

'Oh no, I shan't forget, my lord.'

'Has the expedition to Kahun been organized?

'That will also take time – a lot of time. To succeed, I'll need a lot of accomplices, and not one link of the chain must give way. However, there is one piece of excellent news: my first agent has arrived in Kahun, has found work there, and is beginning to observe how the guards handle security.'

'Is he skilful?'

'Skilful and undetectable, my lord. One cannot ask the impossible, but it's a good beginning.'

52

Iker was present at the demolition of one of the badly built grain-stores. The man responsible for the crime would not threaten him again, for he had been tried and sentenced to a long period in prison. The construction of the new store would begin the following day, using Iker's plans, which had been approved by the mayor.

In the little world of Kahun, Iker's reputation had just taken a considerable leap forward. At first regarded with scorn by his colleagues, he was fast becoming a dangerous rival, perhaps even a candidate for high office. The outsider's success in unravelling the grain-stores affair so quickly implied a high level of knowledge, and he was living up to the reputation of the city of Thoth, where he had trained. Nevertheless, his rapid rise had alarmed some officials, who feared that the established order in Kahun might be destabilized.

Indifferent to gossip and secret discussions, as in Khemenu Iker forged no bonds with anyone. North Wind's friendship was enough for him and he felt no need to waste his time chatting with his colleagues, particularly since Heremsaf had just entrusted him with a new and difficult task: dealing with a plague of rats and mice which was causing huge problems.

Iker had decided that sweeping measures were needed: houses must be cleansed with purifying smoke, the vermin's holes must be blocked up, and he would use experienced cats

– not forgetting a few pet cobras, which loved to feast on mice.

Iker dealt with every one of Kahun's buildings and homes, from the large houses in the eastern district to the modest ones in the west. The smallest comprised only three rooms and measured only 120 square cubits, but they were pleasant to live in.

As he was finishing his inspection in the city's poorest district, Iker noticed a pretty dark-haired girl using a stone to mill grains of wheat, which were trickling out of a pouch held between her knees. Her movements were as regular as they were efficient.

'You look tired,' she said. 'Would you like some cool beer?'

'I don't want to interrupt your work.'

'I've finished.'

Her small, round breasts were bare, and she wore nothing but a short kilt. Getting gracefully to her feet, she went into her kitchen and brought out a well-filled cup.

'You're very kind,' said Iker.

'My name's Bina. What's yours?'

'I'm Iker the scribe.'

She looked at him admiringly. 'I can't read or write.'

'Why don't you learn?'

'I must work to live. And anyway I wouldn't be admitted to a school, particularly since I don't come from here.'

'Where do you come from?'

'Asia. My mother died there. My father worked in a caravan, but he died last year, not far from here. I was lucky enough to get work as a cook, and as I know how to make bread and beer, and even cakes, I was kept on. It isn't too badly paid, and I get enough to eat.'

She was spontaneous, cheerful, and, thought Iker, knew how to make the most of her charms. He said, 'You're bound to find a good husband and set up home.'

'Oh, I don't care for boys. A lot of them are only interested in . . . Well, you know what I mean. You at least look serious.'

'Even if you stay single, you should be able to read and write.'

'For a girl in my circumstances, that's impossible.'

'Not at all. Would you like to learn?'

'I wouldn't mind, I can tell you.'

'I'll talk to my superior.'

'You're really kind – very kind.' And Bina kissed him on both cheeks.

'Forgive me,' said Iker, 'but I've still got a lot of work to do.'

'We'll meet again soon,' she whispered, giving him a bewitching smile.

'Excellent work,' Heremsaf conceded. 'The people are delighted. To be frank, I didn't think you'd do it so quickly.'

'First and foremost we must thank the cats: they're true professionals.'

'You're too modest. Without a detailed study of the houses and their surroundings, you wouldn't have succeeded.'

'As to that, I noticed something and I'd be grateful if you'd confirm whether it's true. Is the basic unit measure of construction in Kahun eight cubits, one of the sacred numbers of Thoth? The town itself is divided into ten-cubit squares and its plan, like that of the houses, owes nothing to chance.* In fact, it derives from rules of proportion based on a triangle in which the relationship between base and height is eight divided by five.'

Heremsaf regarded the young man with interest. 'It is more or less so, indeed. Who pointed it out to you?

'No one. I simply tried to understand what I saw.'

---

*Kahun was indeed built according to Divine Proportion or the Golden Number.

'Then you really are a spiritual seeker. Your time in the granaries is over. I have something else for you to do: an inventory of the old storehouses. You are to draw up a list of everything in them, and then we shall distribute whatever is still usable before refurbishing the buildings.'

'Am I to work alone?'

'That's how you usually work, isn't it?'

'I'll be as quick as possible, but the buildings are enormous.'

'I want this done by someone meticulous, who knows how to take his time without wasting it. Nothing must escape you. Do you understand me? Nothing.'

'I understand. May I ask a favour?'

A look of suspicion came into Heremsaf's eyes. 'What are you dissatisfied with?'

'It isn't for myself or for North Wind. I met a young woman who—'

Heremsaf raised his arms to the heavens. 'Oh no, not that! You're rising through the scribes' ranks, you're discovering the many facets of the profession and already you want to marry!'

'Oh no, it's nothing like that.'

'Don't tell me you've done something very stupid?'

'I talked to a servant-girl who'd like to learn to read and write.'

Heremsaf frowned. 'What is the problem?'

'She is a foreigner, and rather timid, and she'd need a recommendation.'

'What is her name?'

'Bina.'

Heremsaf exploded. 'Oh no, not her! Beware of that woman. No one really knows her – she's like deep water full of rocks and sandbanks and a thousand other dangers. Whatever you do, don't get involved with her.'

'She works here, she—'

'It was only because he felt sorry for her that the mayor did

315

not send her back to her native Asia. I order you: do not go near her again. The soul is like a bird, the body like a fish.* It rots from the head down, and yours is sick, my boy! Isn't one of your goals to write? Have you forgotten that the only literature worthy of esteem is that which aids one to understand Ma'at, the righteousness of the universe and the uprightness of beings?

'To speak Ma'at, to do Ma'at, means to exclude stupid passions and ill-considered fits of emotion. Your qualities, your inner life, your profession and your behaviour must be in harmony. If you believe that you can be both a good scribe and an ignoble person, you will leave the domain of Ma'at, for unity is the necessary path to knowing. Do not, I warn you, confuse knowing with learning. You can learn for years without ever knowing. For only knowledge is radiant, and its true goal is the practice of the mysteries. But no one can lay claim to do that without initiation.

'Now leave me. I have another ten reports to read.'

Iker could not understand why Heremsaf was angry. What was so threatening about a young girl who wanted to be taught? Being neither rich nor from a good family, being an orphan and a foreigner were handicaps enough. Why make them worse by refusing her any chance of improving her circumstances?

But Heremsaf had, even if he was wrong about Bina, nevertheless spoken vital words.

Iker stretched out on his mat and laid the ivory talisman on his belly, to protect him while he slept.

The pretty face of the Asian girl disappeared, to be replaced by that of the young priestess. Iker forgot his tiredness, forgot Bina, Heremsaf . . . The woman he loved was so beautiful that she wiped away trials and sufferings. Next to her, Bina's charms were nothing.

*The soul, *ba*, is written as a bird, the body, *khet*, as a fish.

316

Iker knew that his lady was happiness, but inaccessible – as inaccessible as the pharaoh's would-be murderers whom he had failed to track down. But here in Kahun, he sensed, a major key was hidden.

Letting himself drift off into sleep, he dreamt that she was holding his hand lovingly and that they were walking through sun-drenched countryside.

For the moment it was impossible to use the archives. Iker would have had to ask special permission from Heremsaf, who would inevitably ask the reasons for his curiosity. He therefore confined himself to his work on the inventories, though without losing sight of his goal. If his enemies hoped time would wear down his determination, they were wrong. Iker wanted hard proof. And when he had it, he would act.

On the way to the old storehouses, he met Bina, carrying a basket of flatcakes on her head.

She smiled and said, 'I think you're the hardest-working scribe in Kahun.'

Iker smiled back. 'I'm simply trying to learn my profession well.'

'Did you talk to your superior about me?'

'Yes, but I'm afraid he was firmly oppposed to my suggestion.'

'He must be a very hard man,' she said with a disappointed pout. 'I suppose now I shall never learn to read and write.'

'Don't say that. Heremsaf won't always be my superior, and anyway perhaps I'll find someone more conciliatory. Give me a little time.'

She put down her basket and walked slowly round him. 'Supposing you taught me, secretly?'

'I've been ordered not to spend time with you. We might be caught and denounced.'

'Let's take the risk.'

'If we were caught, it would be disastrous for you. You'd be expelled from Kahun, perhaps even from Egypt.'

'I'd very much like to see you again. Wouldn't you like to see me?'

'Yes, of course, but—'

'Surely you have the right to walk past the house where I work? I'll find a quiet spot where no one will disturb us, and find a way of telling you. We'll meet again soon, Iker.'

Smiling mischievously, she put the basket of flatcakes back on her head and walked away.

Drawing up a list of the hundred upon hundred of objects stored in the huge abandoned storehouses was no easy task. Iker began by opening the windows so that he at least had enough light: he saw at once that a long cleansing with purifying smoke was needed. Once that was done, armed with his writing-materials, he set to work sorting, taking notes and writing descriptions.

Agricultural tools such as hoes, rakes, shovels and spades, stone-cutters' tools, moulds for bricks, carpenters' saws, dishes, cups and plates of bronze, stone and pottery, knives, chisels, baskets, vases, even wooden toys – a large part of Kahun's daily life was represented here. A good number of items were worth mending and would be usable again.

While he was sorting through the day's last batch of things, Iker found a knife with a broken blade. Deeply engraved in the wooden handle were rough but still legible signs. They formed two words: *'Swift One'*.

For a long moment, he was speechless. Whether or not the knife had belonged to Sharp-Knife, it could only have come from his ship.

53

'Majesty, we are coming within sight of Asyut,' announced General Nesmontu gravely. 'There is still time to retreat.'

The town was the capital of the thirteenth province of Upper Egypt, whose emblem was a pomegranate tree surmounted by a horned viper; the province was under the protection of the jackal that guided travellers through the dangerous expanses of the desert, bordering the cultivated areas. Here the valley narrowed, forming a veritable bottleneck. Whoever wished to rule Egypt must control this strategic position, which was overlooked by the nobles' tombs carved out of the cliff. Asyut was also a trading-centre, at the end of the caravan routes leading from the oases of Dakla and Kharga. By taxing them outrageously, the governor, Wepwawet, could afford to pay his soldiers well.

'Pharaoh's person must be safeguarded,' said Sehotep, 'so I ask his permission to begin the negotiations alone.'

Many boats came out from the shore and surrounded the royal flotilla. Some barred its way, some prevented it from turning back, while others forced it to dock.

At the prow of his vessel stood Senusret, wearing the *names*, the ancient necklace that enabled Pharaoh's thoughts to traverse space. On his chest was a pectoral bearing strange figures.

Sobek-Khu came over to him. 'This looks like an arrest, Majesty.'

'If Wepwawet lays a hand on the king,' promised Nesmontu, 'I'll smash his skull.'

'I shall disembark alone,' said Senusret. 'If I do not come back, and if you are attacked, try to get clear.'

The soldiers stationed on the quayside watched in astonishment as the tall man descended the gangplank. Instinctively, some bowed, and the ranks parted to allow him through. None of the officers who had been ordered to intercept Senusret and take him to the governor's palace dared do so.

Wepwawet had deployed all his forces. The king saw that even a strong and determined army would not have been certain of victory.

Curiously, it was as if Senusret had taken the lead of these well-fed, well-equipped fighters, who followed him in some confusion. The people of the province watched the strange spectacle and could not take their eyes off the unwelcome guest, whose head emerged from a sea of soldiers.

Suddenly, Senusret halted and gestured to an oxherd who was leaning on a gnarled staff. The man was so emaciated that his ribs stuck out. His hair was straggling and matted, his kilt frayed and shabby.

'You over there,' said the king, 'come here.'

The oxherd looked behind him.

A soldier tapped him on the shoulder. 'It's you he's calling, my lad. Off you go.'

Hesitantly, the oxherd went forward.

'Match your step to mine,' the king ordered him.

The oxherd's life in the marshes was so harsh that the request seemed easy. No doubt this huge man was someone very important, but when you didn't have enough to eat and each morning brought more suffering, what did that matter?

On the threshold of the palace stood a long-nosed, ramrod-straight man holding a sceptre in his right hand and a long staff in his left. Behind him, a priest held up a staff bearing an ebony figure of the jackal-god Wepwawet, 'Opener of the Ways', whose name the governor had taken.

'I am not glad to see you,' Wepwawet told Senusret. 'I know those cowards Wakha and Sarenput have submitted, but do not think for a moment that I shall. The god who protects me knows the secrets of the roads of heaven and earth. Thanks to him, my region is powerful and anyone who attacks it will suffer a crushing defeat. Rule the North, but do not meddle on my territory.'

'You are not worthy of governing here,' declared the pharaoh.

'How dare you—'

The king pushed the oxherd forward. 'How dare *you* allow a single person in your province to suffer such poverty? Your warriors live in comfort while your peasants are dying of starvation. You, who claim to be so strong – to the point of defying Pharaoh – you betray Ma'at and you scorn the very people whose prosperity you should ensure. Why should anyone fight and die for such a deplorable leader? Only one solution is left to you: repair the evil you have done, with the agreement of the Lord of the Two Lands.

'May my protective jackal destroy the aggressor!' shouted the governor.

The ebony jackal moved towards Senusret.

Everyone thought they saw the predator's mouth open. The king touched his pectoral, on which was depicted a griffin striking down the forces of chaos and the enemies of Egypt. The creature wore the Double Crown, symbolizing the pharaoh's sovereignty over both the North and the South.

To everyone's amazement, the jackal's head bowed: Wepwawet, the Opener of the Ways, recognized Senusret as his master.

The soldiers dropped their weapons. Realizing that not a single one of his men would obey him, the governor let fall his sceptre and his staff of command.

'It is true that I have used the riches of my province to equip my warriors, but I feared an invasion.'

'How could Pharaoh invade his own land? I am at once unity and multiplicity. The first does not prevent the second, the second could not exist without the first. When this communion is established, no oxherd can sink into poverty.'

'Spare me the shame of a trial, and kill me now.'

'Why should I kill a loyal servant of Egypt?'

Wepwawet knelt before the king, then raised his hands in a sign of veneration.

'Before the people of your province,' declared Senusret, 'you have sworn allegiance to me, and once an oath is given it cannot be taken back. I retain you at the head of this land, which you shall make prosperous, under the guidance of High Treasurer Senankh. As for your soldiers, they shall be placed under the command of General Nesmontu. From now on, your only concern shall be the well-being of your subjects. Arise and take up the symbols of your dignity.'

'Long life to Senusret!' shouted a soldier, and his fellows took up the cry.

Amid cheers and acclamation, Senusret and Wepwawet went into the palace.

'Never, Majesty,' said the governor, 'would I have thought that you could exercise power over the jackal-god.'

'You did not realize that he is one of the powers participating in the Mysteries of Osiris, which the pharaoh celebrates. You, who were placed under his protection without knowing his true nature, are you the criminal who is trying to destroy the great god's acacia tree?'

Wepwawet was so horrified that Senusret did not doubt his sincerity.

'Majesty, anyone who committed such an appalling crime would see his name destroyed. Now, I wish mine to live on in my house of eternity where, thanks to the rites, I shall become an Osiris. I know that his acacia symbolizes the resurrection to which the righteous aspire. On your name and on that of my ancestors, who would curse me if I lied, I swear that I am not guilty.'

At the great feast held to celebrate the return of Wepwawet's province into the fold of Senusret's Egypt, the atmosphere was all the more relaxed because many had feared a bloody battle. One of a number of poor peasants who were invited, the oxherd enjoyed dishes he had never dared even dream of before.

'What are your relations with your neighbour, Governor Wukh?' the pharaoh asked his new ally.

'Terrible, Majesty. We share the province of the Pomegranate Tree and the Horned Viper, but we have never reached an understanding which would enable us to unite our governments and our armed forces. We each watch over our domains jealously, and we have almost come to war many times.'

'Is Wukh capable of understanding what you have understood?'

'I doubt it, Majesty: he's a proud, stubborn man. To be honest, I would not like my soldiers to have to fight his. Many, many men would die.'

'I shall try to prevent that,' said Senusret, 'but I must continue to reunify the country. It is precisely because of our disunity that malevolent forces have been able to attack the Acacia of Osiris. When all the provinces once again live in harmony, our chances of driving back the darkness will increase considerably.'

Wepwawet hung his head. 'No words could ever have convinced me that you are right, Majesty. It is only because you knew the mysterious ways revealed by the jackal-god that you succeeded. Like me, Wukh believes he is the strongest man in the region, and he is very attached to his acquisitions.'

'One of Pharaoh's names is "Man of the Bee", Senusret reminded him. 'He must remember that each individual counts and plays his part in the creation of flower-gold, but also that the hive is more important than the bee. Without it, without *per-aa*, the Great Dwelling, the Great Temple, in which each Egyptian finds his place, neither the spirit nor the body could live.'

General Nesmontu was amazed. Wepwawet's warriors obeyed him as unquestioningly as if he had always been their commander: not a single instance of indiscipline, not a single protest. They were good soldiers, who wished to be led well and to do their job well.

As he joined the meeting of the King's House aboard the royal boat, the old soldier wondered if the king would see his insane plan through to the end.

'Should we not spread the news of Wepwawet's submission?' suggested Sehotep. 'I know that it is really Medes's responsibility, but we can send messengers to him in Memphis, in the hope that at least one of them will reach him safely.'

'It would be of no use,' said Senusret. 'None of the three governors we have still to confront would pay any heed.'

'I agree with His Majesty,' said Nesmontu. 'Wukh is a mere brute, Djehuty is made of granite and Khnum-Hotep is a pretentious man who will not give up any of his prerogatives. It would be impossible to negotiate with any of them.'

'All the same, they have probably been shaken by the king's successes,' objected Sehotep. 'Negotiations are not necessarily doomed to failure.'

'Our next stage is very close,' Senusret reminded him, 'because it concerns the other half of the province of the Pomegranate and the Horned Viper. We must not waste time on useless debate.'

324

'Do you envisage a full-scale attack?' asked Nesmontu.
'We shall continue using my methods,' decided the pharaoh.

54

The young priestess wore a robe patterned like a panther's skin and scattered with five-pointed stars inside a circle. Upon her head was a seven-branched star. She wrote down the words of power uttered by the Queen of Egypt, who had come to preside over the sisterhood of the seven Hathors.

Her writing was fine and precise, and her text was judged worthy of entering the community's treasury. This 'other way of telling', as the ritual expression had it, would be passed down to future generations to enrich their meditations. Thus the secret tradition would remain alive beyond those who had formulated it in a moment of grace.

When the initiates left the temple, following the queen, confused thoughts seethed in the young priestess's mind. Why had the queen predicted to her that she would have to leave this shrine and fight a perilous battle? Why had the late High Priest also spoken of terrifying enemies she would have to confront?

Since adolescence, all she had thought of was the world of the temple: beside the mysteries it housed, the outside world seemed very dull. During her apprenticeship in hieroglyphs, which a learned priestess had taught her, she had immersed herself with wonder in the interplay of the creative forces the mother letters revealed. In writing the names of the gods, she had discovered their secret nature – Hathor's name meant 'the Temple of Horus', the sacred place where the dazzling light of initiation shone. Moreover, the first part of the name, *Hat*, included the notion of the creative and nourishing Word. The seven Hathors indeed nourished the light by the Word in all its forms, from ritual speech to music.

Each stage she had passed through had been a severe ordeal, both physically and spiritually, but she did not fear the effort or the intense work needed to progress along this way. To her they were inexhaustible sources of joy.

But now, for the first time, she was troubled, and the trouble haunted her mind both when she slept and in her daily activities. Every morning and evening, the sisterhood played music in order to sustain the sap of the Acacia of Osiris. Even then, sometimes, she found it difficult to concentrate, because of this unknown feeling she could not stifle.

She was summoned to the site where Senusret's house of eternity was being built, because a stone-cutter had injured himself while using a defective tool. It was only a minor incident, but it made the atmosphere even heavier, for the man was an accomplished craftsman and felt humiliated by the accident.

The priestess cleaned the wound with tincture of calendula, then applied a honey compress, binding it on with a linen bandage.

'We keep having accidents like that,' said the master-builder worriedly. 'I'm taking more and more precautions, but they make no difference. The work has slowed right down, and some of the men claim the site is bewitched. Couldn't you do something to reassure them?'

'I'll speak to the Shaven-headed One about it today.'

She was as good as her word. She had to give him a copy of her text, to be added to the archives of the House of Life, and when she did so she asked for his help.

'The site worries me, too,' he admitted. 'The best solution

is to repeat the rite of the red cloth band, imprisoning the harmful forces.'

'But what if that is not enough?'

'We have other weapons in reserve and we shall fight to the end. Come with me to the acacia.'

He carried the vase of water, she the vase of milk. One after the other, they slowly emptied the vases at the foot of the sick tree. The single branch that had grown green again seemed healthy but, whereas serenity had onced reigned in this place, now a profound sadness emanated from it.

'We must intensify our search,' said the Shaven-headed One. 'First thing tomorrow, join me in the library. By exploring the ancient texts, we may perhaps find some useful indications.'

She was glad to be given this task, which would occupy her mind. But as she returned to the sisterhood's living quarters, her troubled feeling oppressed her again.

'The queen wishes to see you,' one of the sisters informed her.

The queen and the priestess walked along a path bordered by shrines and stelae dedicated to Osiris.

'What is wrong?' asked the queen.

'Nothing is wrong, Majesty. It is only that I'm rather tired and—'

'You cannot hide anything from me. What is the question that troubles you?'

'I ask myself if I am strong enough to continue on this path.'

'Is that not your dearest desire?'

'Indeed, Majesty, but my weaknesses are such that they might become fetters.'

'Those weaknesses are among the obstacles to be overcome and must not, in any circumstances, be used as an excuse.'

'Is there not danger in everything that takes me away from the temple?'

'Our rule does not oblige you to live as a recluse. Most priests and priestesses are married, though some choose celibacy.'

'Would it not be a mistake to marry someone who lived a long way from the temple?'

'There is no rigid rule. It is up to you to choose that which feeds the fire of knowledge and to avoid that which weakens it. Above all, never deceive yourself and do not try to tell yourself lies. If you do, you will lose yourself in an endless desert and the door of the temple will close again.'

When the queen left Abydos, the young priestess thought once again of the boy whom she had met so briefly and whom she would no doubt never see again. Far from her being indifferent to him, he had engendered in her a strange feeling, which was slowly growing stronger. She ought not to think of him, but she could not drive him from her mind. Perhaps, with time, his face would fade.

When he arrived in Abydos, Gergu saw that the security measures there were as strict as ever. Several soldiers boarded his boat, demanded to see his written orders and checked the cargo with extreme care.

'Ointments, pieces of linen, sandals, all destined for the permanent priests,' said Gergu. 'Here is the detailed list bearing the seal of High Treasurer Senankh.'

'We must check that the cargo corresponds to the list,' said an officer curtly.

'Don't you trust the High Treasurer and his official representative?'

'Orders are orders.'

Gergu realized that he would never be able to smuggle anything through this landing-stage, and he couldn't bribe this many soldiers and guards.

He had to wait patiently for the end of the inspection and, as on his first visit, even his person was searched.

'Are you leaving immediately?' asked the officer.

'No, I must see one of the priests again, to give him this list, find out if he is satisfied with it and deal with any new requirements.'

'Wait at the guard-post. Someone will come and fetch you.'

Once again, Gergu was destined not to explore Abydos. Watched by two guards, with whom he did not even attempt to strike up a conversation, he dozed.

If he did not meet the same priest, this journey would have been in vain. Gergu knew nothing of how the brotherhood functioned, and was worried that they might send him a different representative, very different from the first. If that happened, there would be no hope, and the disappointment would be bitter, because a site guarded so closely must house prodigious treasures.

Gergu reproached himself for not having thought of it sooner. After all, Abydos was the spiritual centre of Egypt, the most sacred of all places, from which the pharaoh derived the essential part of his power. Senusret had not demanded such a deployment of forces without good reason. Something important was happening here, and Gergu was determined to discover exactly what, provided fortune continued to favour him.

'Follow us,' ordered another officer, who was accompanied by four archers.

They led Gergu to the same office as on his previous visit. Tensely, he paced up and down. At last, the door opened.

It was the same priest!

'I am glad to see you again,' said Gergu with a smile.

'And I to see you.'

'Here is the list of items you asked for. Are you satisfied with it?'

The priest read it. 'You are a conscientious man, on whom one can rely.'

'My orders are that Abydos must have everything it needs. What will you need in the coming weeks?'

'I have a new list for you.' The priest handed Gergu a tablet. His eyes held the gleam that had so pleased Gergu at their last meeting.

'Can one speak confidentially in this room?' Gergu asked in a low voice.

'You mean unheard by indiscreet ears? I think so. Why do you ask?'

Gergu knew he must take care not to make a slip which would frighten his quarry away. 'Alongside our official relations, there could be . . . others.'

'Of what kind?'

A first victory: the priest seemed interested.

'My work as head overseer of granaries permits me to exceed my legal charges a little and to complement my salary. One must be discreet and careful, of course, but it would be a pity to waste the opportunity. Abydos is not only a spiritual centre; it is also a small town, which must remain prosperous so that the brotherhood can work in complete peace. Why should the notion of profit be excluded? Why should a priest, however dedicated to the cult of Osiris, not have the right to become wealthy?'

A long silence followed these declarations and questions.

The priest regarded Gergu most attentively. 'As regards the temporary priests,' he said at last, 'there are no pro-hibitions. The situation of the permanent priests like myself is different, since we do not leave Abydos.'

'I, on the other hand, can come and go. If we were to become friends, your prospects would be radically altered.'

'What exactly do you propose?'

'I am convinced that Abydos possesses many treasures.'

'Everyone knows that.'

'Yes, but what are they? You know, I'm sure.'

'I am sworn to secrecy.'

'A secret can be bought. And I am also sure that you have a lot to sell.'

'How can you imagine that I would betray my priesthood?'

'Who is talking about betrayal? Abydos interests me to the highest degree, and you are hoping to grow wealthy, so there is a fine meeting of interests. Help me, and I shall help you. What could be simpler?'

'What could be more complicated and dangerous? First of all, for whom and with whom are you working? I doubt that your superior in this is High Treasurer Senankh, one of Pharaoh's most loyal officials.'

'Your doubts are justified.'

'Then who is it?'

'It is a little too soon to tell you that. We must get to know each other, prove ourselves to each other, establish mutual trust. I shall therefore come back to see you officially, and we shall continue the little game of delivering supplies. Think of ways of getting rich without leaving Abydos, and we shall see if our plans are workable.'

55

Iker was cleaning his bedchamber when he had a sudden and blinding vision of the priestess. She was speaking to him, but he could not hear what she was saying. Then she disappeared as suddenly as she had appeared.

The vision left him dazzled for a long time. What could it mean, if not that she remembered he existed and that their thoughts were capable of being joined? But no, it was probably just a waking dream.

Heremsaf's authoritative voice abruptly called Iker back to reality. 'When you have finished your cleaning, join me in my office.'

Iker was always kept his room scrupulously clean and tidy. He had not been reprimanded once since his arrival, so he had assumed that Heremsaf was satisfied.

When he had finished, he went along an immaculate white corridor and knocked on the sycamore-wood door at the end.

'Come in, and close the door behind you.'

The room was spacious, the windows let in enough light to work by, and the shelves were ranged in impeccable order.

Heremsaf's face was as forbidding as usual. 'Prepare to move house, my boy.'

'Have I . . . Do you think I don't clean well enough?'

'On the contrary, I wish others would do it so well. Your maturity and serious attitude never cease to surprise me.'

'In that case—'

'You are being promoted. The mayor is particularly pleased with your work and is granting you a place in the high rank of scribes. That means you will be given an official house and a servant. On the other hand, your responsibilities and workload will increase.'

'What post am I to fill?'

'For the moment, you will finish the inventory you have begun so well. Then you yourself will carry out the redistribution of the usable items. Next, you will take charge of refurbishing the storehouses. A team of workmen will be placed at your disposal and you will organize the work as you wish. The mayor wants it done quickly, of course, but I am nevertheless granting you a rest day.'

Iker and North Wind strolled through Kahun to explore every part of the town. The surrounding wall gave an impression of security, which was reinforced by regular patrols by the town's guards. The streets were efficiently maintained, and both the main and the side streets were spotlessly clean. From the biggest house, the mayor's, down to the humblest of the two hundred houses in the western district, Kahun prided itself on its appearance: no decrepit housefronts, no shutters with peeling paintwork, no damaged doors, and the gardens were well kept and the waterways in perfect repair. Everyone had plenty of water, and the rules of cleanliness were scrupulously observed. The town was proud of its sacred name, 'Senusret is Satisfied'.

The organization of work was no less remarkable. The temple workers were punctilious in carrying out their ritual tasks, bakers and brewers received all the grain needed to make bread and beer, the butchers received enough meat, which was certified pure by the relevant scribes, the travelling barber plied his trade in the open air, the makers of sandals and baskets displayed them in the market, beside the sellers of fruit and vegetables. In Kahun, nobody went short of anything.

Iker stopped by the stall of a man who made wooden toys: bewigged dolls whose limbs moved, hippopotami, crocodiles, monkeys, pigs . . . and all very lifelike. One toy in particular caught his attention, a model ship of wonderful quality. He could have sworn it was a model of the *Swift One*.

'Your toys are superb,' he told the craftsman.

'The parents like them as much as their children do. Are you a father yourself?'

'Not yet, but I would like to give this ship as a gift.'

'It's the only one I didn't make myself, and it's also the most expensive. A little work of art, isn't it?'

'Who made it?'

'A retired carpenter – the best in Kahun, according to his colleagues. He's nicknamed Plane, because he's so gifted with that tool.'

'If he still lives here, I'd like to congratulate him.'

'That'll be easy. He lives in a little house in the western district,' and the toy-maker gave Iker detailed directions.

'How would you like to be paid for the boat, in goods or in hours of work? I'm a scribe and can write any kind of document.'

'That suits me very well, as it happens. I want to write to some relations who live in the Delta. Ten letters, will that suit you?'

'The ship's so lifelike that I shall give you twelve.'

A servant-girl was sweeping the doorstep of the carpenter's house.

'Could I see Plane?' asked Iker.

'He's ill.'

'It's very important.'

'You won't upset him, will you?'

'I'm a scribe and I'd like to congratulate him on his talent as a craftsman.'

The servant shrugged. 'Very well. Take off your sandals, wash your feet, wipe them and don't get anything dirty. I'm not going to clean this place again today.'

Iker obeyed her instructions and went into the house, whose first room was set aside for the cult of the ancestors.

Plane was in the second room, which strongly resembled a workshop, with lengths of wood, tools and a workbench. But the old man was not working. His hair unkempt, his back bowed, his belly swollen, he was sitting on a high-backed chair and holding a cane, on whose handle his chin rested. He was gazing fixedly at a saw and a short-handled adze used for smoothing planks.

'I am Iker the scribe, and I should like to speak with you.'

'It's best to forget the past, my boy. I was the most agile and tireless on the great sites, and now look at me. I dare not even go out any more. Old age is a great misfortune.'

'But you still make models, like this one of a ship.'

Plane glanced at it distractedly. 'A powerless man's pastime. I am almost ashamed of it.'

'You shouldn't be – it's superb.'

'Where did you find it?'

'On the toy-maker's stall.'

'That's what I'm reduced to since I retired. I get enough to eat, but neither my head nor my hands can accept this idleness.'

'Did you once work in a warship yard?'

'Of course I did. It's obligatory for any carpenter worth his salt.'

'Then you must have participated in the construction of many boats.'

'Small ones, big ones, cargo-vessels . . . Whenever a really difficult problem arose, it was me they called for.'

Iker showed him the model. 'Was this inspired by a ship you saw being born?'

Plane ran his hands over it. 'Of course. A superb ship, she was, designed for the sea, not just for the Nile. She was so strongly built that she could withstand even the worst storms.'

'Do you remember her name?'

'*Swift One.*'

The young man found it hard to contain his joy. At last, a real clue!

'*Swift One*,' repeated Plane. 'She was my last important job.'

'Did you ever meet her captain and crew?'

The old man shook his head.

'Do you at least know their names?'

'No, and they wouldn't have interested me. What I was interested in was a hull strong enough to resist anything the sea and wind could throw at it.'

'Do you know what became of her?'

'No.'

'No one spoke to you about her destination, the land of Punt?'

'Punt? It doesn't exist, my boy, except in the imaginations of storytellers. Not even *Swift One* could take anyone there.'

'Who was her owner?'

The old man was astonished. 'Why, the pharaoh, of course. Who else do you think a ship like that would belong to?'

'Turtle-Eye and Sharp-Knife: are those names familiar to you?'

'Never met them. They don't live in or around Kahun. But tell me, my boy, why all these questions?'

'I knew some of *Swift One*'s crew, and I'd like to know what's become of them.'

'All you need do is consult the archives. One detail comes back to me: I didn't finish my last job in the boatyard, I

337

finished it here. It was an acacia-wood box, as beautiful as it was strong. The buyer's instructions were very detailed, and I took care to observe them. I thought a box of that quality must be for a temple, but when the man came to fetch it, he said he needed it for a long voyage. I thought of the *Swift One*, but no doubt I was wrong.'

'Who was this man?'

'A stranger passing through. As he paid in advance, and generously, I didn't ask questions.'

'Would you recognize him?'

'No, because my sight's getting worse every day. He was tall, I think.'

'It might be prudent not to tell anyone about our conversation,' suggested Iker.

'Why not?'

'Just suppose *Swift One* had got mixed up in—'

'I don't want to suppose anything at all and I don't want to hear any more. I thought there was something behind all those questions. I'm old and I want to die in peace. Leave my house and don't come back. If you do, you'll find the door closed to you.'

Iker did not persist, but promised himself to question the carpenter again. The old man had a lot more to tell.

The Phoenician's spy had watched Iker to see if he would try to contact the talkative old craftsman. He'd thought there was little danger of it, for who could set the young scribe on that trail? But he had to face facts: Iker was not paying Plane a mere visit of courtesy.

Although highly improbable, this eventuality had been planned for. So the spy knew what to do.

56

'The Nile is empty of boats!' exclaimed General Nesmontu incredulously.

At the approach to Qis, capital of the fourteenth province of Upper Egypt, Senusret's flotilla had expected a warlike reception. But Governor Wukh's warships remained at their moorings, and the pharaoh and his men disembarked without the slightest opposition. There was not a single soldier on the quayside. The place seemed deserted.

'It must be a trap,' said Sehotep. 'Let me go and scout the area, Majesty.'

'That is an excellent idea,' nodded Sobek the Protector. 'I'll escort him.'

'No one respects a cowardly king. Follow me,' and Senusret took the lead.

Sobek stayed close to him, constantly scanning the surrounding area, trying to work out where the attack would come from.

Until they reached the entrance to the town, they neither saw nor heard anyone. There was not a living soul in the streets, and all doors and shutters were closed.

'What can have happened here?' asked Sehotep.

At last, the king spotted some people, but they were in a state of collapse, their heads on their knees. They seemed overwhelmed with despair, and didn't respond when he spoke to them.

In the approaches to the palace, the ground was scattered with bows, arrows, spears and swords: the soldiers had abandoned their weapons.

An officer was slumped in front of the main guard-post.

'What has happened here?' asked Sobek.

The soldier raised eyes which were red from weeping. 'Our governor has died.'

'Was there a rebellion against him?'

'No, of course not – no one would have dared rebel against Lord Wukh. He died because the province's sacred snake died, because its sacred vase was shattered, because the fields have dried out, because the flocks are ill . . . And all this because our protective symbol no longer fulfils its function.'

Senusret hurried to the temple, which was dedicated to Hathor. Civilians and soldiers were gathered outside, eager for a sign of hope.

'Worship the pharaoh!' shouted Nesmontu. 'He alone can put an end to your misfortune.'

They all turned towards the king.

A priest ran forward and bowed. 'Majesty, our rebellion has been harshly punished. Spare our lives, I beg you.'

'No one has anything to fear.'

One or two of the people showed signs of a smile. If Pharaoh would protect them, the evil would be driven away.

'I must show you the disaster, Majesty.'

Senusret followed the priest into the temple. There, in a shrine, the province's most sacred item was kept, a papyrus from which two feathers emerged, surrounding a solar disc flanked by two uraei.

One look was enough for him to see the extent of the disaster. The papyrus had withered, the disc had lost all its brilliance, the cobras' eyes no longer shone. In this symbol, which bore the name of *wukh*, the same as that of the province's governor, the life-energy was almost extinct.

'We're all going to die,' prophesied the priest. 'This place has been cursed.'

'Calm yourself,' ordered the king.

Only the two feathers still retained some semblance of vigour. The embodiment of the radiant air that circulates around the universe and makes fertile the seeds of life, they offered one last chance of survival.

'A canker is eating away at the acacia tree, and it has spread here, too,' said the king. Concentrate your thoughts on the solar disc, live each of the words I am going to utter, make the power live again by communing with the Word.'

Sehotep, Nesmontu and Sobek united themselves with the royal words to form one consciousness.

Senusret's voice rose up, chanting an incantation to the rising sun.

'Appear in the region of Light, light up the Two Lands with turquoise. Drive away the darkness, be reborn each day, come to the voice of him who speaks your name. Unique one who remains unique, unite yourself with your symbol. It reveals your nature without betraying it. Create that which is below, as you create that which is on high. Flame that dwells within its eye, be the builder, enter your shrine.'

Little by little, the papyrus grew green again. Then the cobras' eyes reddened like burning coals. Lastly, the disc's brilliance returned, lighting up the shrine.

'Go and fetch the priests,' the king told Nesmontu.

When they saw their symbol reborn, the priests bowed before the king and began to sing in praise of him.

'That's enough,' cut in Senusret. 'The rites have not been correctly celebrated, and you almost paid the ultimate price. Instead of feeling sorry for yourselves, perform the dawn, noon and sunset rites meticulously. At the slightest sign of danger, inform me immediately. This province now belongs to the being of Pharaoh.'

341

As soon as he emerged from the temple, the people began to cheer and applaud Senusret.

Suddenly, the celebrations were interrupted and the onlookers parted. About thirty soldiers appeared, with huge dogs on leashes. They were the finest of the late Governor Wukh's men, and their commander did not seem motivated by the best intentions.

'We shall never bow our heads. This province is independent, and it will remain—'

'Stop those stupid declarations,' interrupted Nesmontu. 'His Majesty has just saved it from utter destruction. From now on it will obey him.'

'We don't need an outsider to rule us,' said the commander stubbornly. 'I proclaim myself the new governor and I shall drive all intruders out of my lands.'

'Rebelling against Pharaoh is punishable by death,' Senusret reminded him. 'I am quite willing to forget your fleeting madness, but submit now.'

'If you take one step forward, I shall unleash the dogs.'

'Do not take any risks, Majesty,' said Sehotep. 'There are not enough of us to resist them. Let us go back into the temple.'

Senusret walked forward.

The commander and his men unleashed their dogs, which leapt towards Senusret. Sobek-Khu tried to step between them and the king, but Senusret pushed him aside.

Less than a stride from their prey, the dogs reared up, spun round, bared their fangs, started to bark furiously, and then suddenly quietened. They became a peaceful pack, whose leader came to demand caresses before lying down at the king's feet.

'These animals know who I am. You, commander, are not worthy of giving them orders.'

The frightened officer tried to run, but two of his subordinates clubbed him down, breaking his skull. The people began cheering again.

Even as he acknowledged the cheers, Senusret thought of the events following on from his fight. The fate of all Egypt depended upon that of the acacia, and more disasters must be expected.

One thing was certain: it was not Wukh who had put a curse on the Tree of Osiris. There were only two suspects left: Djehuty, governor of the Hare province, and Khnum-Hotep, governor of the province of the Oryx.

One small room for the cult of the ancestors, a modest reception room, a bedchamber, latrine and washroom, a kitchen, a cellar and a terrace: Iker's official house had nothing of the palace about it and was sparsely furnished, but it had recently been whitewashed and would be a pleasant place to live. As luck would have it, a nearby stable housed only one old she-donkey, with whom North Wind struck up a friendship immediately.

Iker had so few possessions that the move did not take long. As he was putting the last few things in their new places, a man arrived at his door.

He was a pitiful sight, very skinny and with long hair, unshaven face and stooping shoulders. He hung his head and said, 'I'm the servant allocated to you – two hours, twice a week.'

Iker felt like sending him away and managing on his own, but he suddenly realized that he knew this man.

'No, it can't be – is it? Sekari?'

'Er, yes, it's me.'

'Don't you recognize me?'

The miserable fellow dared look at his new master. 'Iker? You're very well dressed!'

'Whatever happened to you?'

'Oh, nothing unusual. But things are a bit better now. Will you employ me?'

'To be frank, it rather embarrasses me.'

'It's the mayor's office that pays. With ten houses to clean, shopping to do and a bit of maintenance work here and there, I don't do too badly out of it.'

'Where do you live?'

'In a garden hut. I look after the garden and and I'm allowed to have some of the vegetables.'

'Come in and have a drink.'

The two former companions talked of their adventures in Sinai, though Iker gave no details of what had happened to him since their separation.

'So here you are, a high-ranking scribe,' said Sekari, 'with a fine career in prospect.'

'Don't judge by appearances.'

'Have you got problems?'

'Well, perhaps we'll talk about that later on. For now, organize your work as you please – this house is yours, too. And now forgive me but I must go to work – I've got a lot to do.'

By working furiously, Iker managed to calm himself. He now had proof that his nightmare had been very real: *Swift One* had been built by a team of craftsmen from Kahun, and she could only belong to Pharaoh Senusret. No one seemed to believe that the mysterious land of Punt really existed, but he knew very well that it had been *Swift One*'s destination.

He decided to go and see Plane again. This time he would make the old man tell him everything.

The door of the house was closed.

The scribe knocked, but no one answered. A neighbour called to him.

'What do you want?'

'I'd like to see Plane.'

'No chance of that, my poor boy – he died last night. Are you a relation?'

'No, but we knew each other, and there's something I wanted to ask him.'

'That old skinflint won't be telling anyone anything ever again, though at the end he was saying all sorts of things.'

'What did he die of?'

'Of old age, of course. He had a bad heart, lungs, back – everything was worn out. He can't complain, he didn't suffer.'

'Did you spend time with him?'

'As little as possible – like his other neighbours. He bored us all with his endless stories of carpentry, and he was losing his mind. And if you didn't listen closely he got angry.'

'Did the guards visit him shortly before his death?'

'The guards? Why? What had he done?'

'Nothing, nothing . . . It was just a question.'

The neighbour gave him a meaning look. 'Ah, I see, the old fellow was mixed up in smuggling. You're not from the guards, are you?'

'No, I was just a friend.'

'A bit young to be a friend of Plane's.'

Iker beat a retreat. He would have liked to search the house, but what would be the use? He didn't believe the old man had died a natural death, and the murderer would of course have got rid of anything incriminating.

The only people who could act with impunity were guards who were obeying orders from above, certain they'd never be investigated. The mayor must know about it. Above the mayor, a minister. Above the minister, the protector of Kahun, King Senusret.

Iker wanted the truth and he wanted justice. The knife-handle proved that *Swift One* had existed, but his main witness had died, and the authorities would tell him that a mere knife-handle was not enough to open an inquiry.

There was nothing for it but to go to the town archives. Only there would he find the documents containing the proof he needed.

At the entrance to the archives building were two of the town's guards.

'Name and office?'

'Iker, scribe.'

'Written authorization to enter the premises?

'I only want to see the head scribe in charge of the archives.'

'One moment.'

The archivist agreed to see Iker, of whose achievements he had heard. He was usually reserved and exacting, but showed the young man his affable side.

He asked, 'What is it that you want?'

'It's rather delicate. It concerns a mission . . . let us say, an extremely discreet mission.'

'I can understand that, but I must have more details.'

'My superior, Haremsaf, has sent me to consult the archives regarding the warship yards. He would very much like to check one detail.'

'Why does he not come himself?'

'Precisely because of discretion. My presence here will not arouse anyone's curiosity, whereas his . . .'

The archivist seemed convinced. This was probably not the first time he had been confronted with a matter in which it was important to leave no trace.

'I understand, I understand . . . But I would prefer to have a note signed by Heremsaf.'

'Perhaps that may not be essential, and—'

'For my personal archives, it is. Come back with the note and I shall see if I can help you.'

'What game are you playing, Iker, and what are you hiding?' demanded Heremsaf with cold anger. 'The head archivist tells me that you dared use my name for an illegal consultation! You – you to whom I gave my absolute trust!'

'Would you have granted me an authorization in good and due form?'

Heremsaf's eyes narrowed. 'Don't you think it is time to tell me the truth at last?'

'I might ask the same question of you.'

'You go too far! It was not I who tried to get access to the archives.'

'It was you who ordered me to sort through the contents of the old storehouses, and who insisted that I should inspect every single item.'

'True, and what of it?'

'Were you not thinking of a knife-handle on which a ship's name is carved?'

Heremsaf looked surprised.

'And isn't the region's principal warship yard under your authority?'

'You're wrong there. It falls under the Master of Works at Faiyum.'

'But I'm not wrong about the knife-handle, am I?'

'What are you seeking exactly?'

'Ma'at, of course.'

'You won't find it by lying to the archivist.'

'If you have nothing to hide, give me permission to consult the archives.'

'It isn't that simple, and I do not have full powers. There are several archive departments, and only the mayor can grant access to all of them. Listen, Iker, you're rising fast, but you have few friends. Your thoroughness and skills plead in your favour, but good work alone isn't enough to guarantee a brilliant career. My support will be vital, and I've given it to you because I believe in your future. I will agree to forget this moment of madness, on condition that it does not happen again. Do we understand each other?'

'No, we do not,' snapped Iker. 'What I want isn't a brilliant career but truth and justice. No matter what it costs me, I shall not give up my quest. I refuse to think that everything in this country is rotten. If it were, that would

mean that Ma'at has left it. And if that were so, there would
be no point in going on living.'

Without asking permission, he turned and stalked out of
the room.

By sending him back to the mayor, who must be an
accomplice of the carpenter's murderer, Heremsaf proved his
own guilt. But why had Heremsaf set him on the trail of the
knife-handle in the first place? By doing that he had helped
Iker, but by refusing him permission to consult the archives
he was preventing him from going forward. How could those
contradictions be explained? Perhaps Heremsaf had in fact
not known about the knife-handle?

Iker knew he would be dismissed from his post and
expelled from Kahun. But he would come back, and would
somehow succeed in getting access to the documents he
needed. Aware that that would be well-nigh impossible, he
walked along aimlessly, trying to think of a solution.

'You look annoyed,' murmured Bina's musical voice.

'There are problems at work.'

'You didn't even notice me! Shouldn't you enjoy yourself
a little?'

'I haven't the heart to enjoy myself.'

'Then let's talk. I've found a quiet place, an empty house
just behind the one where I work. Join me there this evening
after sunset. Talking will do you good.'

57

As the king's flotilla neared Khemenu, capital of the Hare province, the landscape became gentle and charming. Everything here evoked peace, repose and meditation.

Aboard the king's boat, however, no one could think of anything but the coming confrontation with the formidable Djehuty.

Some information Nesmontu had received did not bode well. 'The governor has a small, well-paid and well-trained army of battle-hardened men,' he told the pharaoh. 'In addition, he has a reputation as a good strategist.'

'In that case,' said Sehotep, 'he will be amenable to negotiations. When Djehuty learns that provinces thought to be bitterly opposed to the king have now become allies, he will realize that fighting would be pointless. I therefore put myself forward as envoy to him.'

'We shall continue to apply my method,' decreed Senusret.

Nesmontu, Sehotep and Sobek were all of the same opinion: the king did not fully appreciate the danger. Djehuty was no insignificant opponent, and he would not surrender his weapons without a devastating battle.

However, the pharaoh's calm seemed unshakeable. He was like a brilliant craftsman, able to execute exactly the right move at exactly the right time. They could not help trusting this giant of a man, who since he had ascended the throne of the living had not made a single blunder.

Khemenu, 'City of the Ogdoad', the brotherhood of eight creative powers, was both capital of the Hare province and the city of Thoth. Master of hieroglyphs, 'the Words of God', the god offered initiates the chance to attain knowledge. In revealing himself by the moon's knife, the most visible symbol of death and resurrection, he stressed the necessity for decisive action, not tepid enthusiasm and compromise. The beak of the ibis, the bird of Thoth, did not seek: it found. No one could rule Egypt justly without controlling this province. Today Senusret was ready to get down to work.

'Majesty,' said Sobek the Protector, 'permit me to accompany you.'

'That will not be necessary.'

There was not a single warship on the river, and not a single soldier on the quayside.

'Incredible,' murmured Sehotep. 'Has Djehuty also done us the favour of dying?'

The flotilla docked without interference, as if there was no dispute between the new arrivals and the officials of Khemenu, and the king prepared to disembark.

At the foot of the gangplank stood a thin man with a serious face. He unrolled a papyrus covered with hieroglyphs set out in columns. There was one single figure, but it was rarely depicted: a seated Osiris, wearing his crown of resurrection, holding both the *was*, the Sceptre of Power, and the *ankh*, the Key of Life. His throne bore the symbol of millions of years. Around him were circles of fire, preventing the unworthy from approaching.*

'General Sepi,' said the king, 'I am glad you have returned safe and sound from Asia.'

'My task was not easy, Majesty, but I took advantage of the lamentable disorganization among the tribes.'

*This is the figure depicted on his wooden sarcophagus, which includes the text of the *Book of the Two Paths*.

'It would have been deeply regrettable to lose you just after your entry into the Golden Circle of Abydos.'

'Thanks to my initiation, life and death are so different that one no longer faces ordeals in the same way.'

Watched in amazement by the sailors of the royal flotilla, the pharaoh and his spiritual brother embraced.

'What conclusions did you reach?' asked Senusret.

'Asia is under control. Our troops in Sichem have quelled the Canaanites' desire for rebellion – the people are treated justly and have enough to eat. A few still speak longingly of a strange character called the Herald, but his death seems to have led to the disappearance of those who followed him. However, we must not be foolish or lower our guard; the whole area must remain under close watch. Above all, our military presence must be maintained, or even strengthened. I am concerned about the possible spread of resistance in the towns, which might lead to isolated disturbances.'

'I value your opinion greatly,' said the king. 'Now tell me how matters stand here in the province of the Hare.'

'I did not return until yesterday, so I can tell you only a little. But Djehuty seems greatly changed. He is cheerful, relaxed, happy to be alive.'

'Has he given the order to attack me?'

'Not exactly. He told me he has a surprise in store for you, and asked me to greet you alone, without weapons or soldiers.'

'Have you managed to persuade him to avoid bloodshed?'

'I am not sure, Majesty. Ever since Djehuty took me on, I have quietly but constantly tried to make him see the impossibility of his position. It would be vanity to believe that I have succeeded.'

'Whom do the soldiers obey?'

'Him, not me.'

'Well, let us go and see this surprise.'

On the road to Djehuty's palace, the soldiers and the young

people of the province formed a guard of honour, waving palm-fronds. As surprised as Senusret, Sepi led the king to the audience chamber, where they found not only Djehuty but his daughters awaiting them.

Dressed in beautiful clothes and with their faces skilfully painted, the three princesses wore their most beautiful smiles as they bowed before the pharaoh.

Their father got to his feet with difficulty. 'May Your Majesty forgive me, but I am suffering pains in my joints and am always cold,' and he gestured apologetically at the cloak that wrapped him from neck to ankles. 'But I am still in sufficiently good health to offer my province's homage to the King of Upper and Lower Egypt.'

Three travelling-chairs carried the pharaoh, the governor and General Sepi to the Temple of Thoth. In front of it stood the huge statue.

'This is the incarnation of your *ka*, Majesty,' said Djehuty. 'It is for you to grant it the final light that will make it live for ever.'

Sepi handed Senusret a club from Abydos, which had been consecrated during the celebration of the Mysteries of Osiris. The king raised it and pointed it at the statue's eyes, nose, ears and mouth. With each gesture, a ray of light sprang from the end of the club. Vibrations ran through the stone, and everyone sensed that from now on a part of the royal *ka* would always be present in the city of Thoth.

The feast was lavish: exceptionally fine food, perfect service, musicians worthy of Memphis itself, young dancing-girls who gracefully executed the most acrobatic moves. The prettiest of them exchanged knowing looks with Sehotep, who was very much alive to her charms. The only garment she wore was a beaded belt.

But Djehuty noticed that the pharaoh's face was still full of care.

'I enjoy life very much, Majesty, and I am proud of my

province's prosperity, but that does mean I cannot think clearly. By providing us with an ideal annual flood, you showed that you alone are worthy to rule a reunified Egypt. You have my loyalty; I am your servant. Command, and I shall obey.'

'Are you aware of the disaster we face?'

'No, Majesty.'

A look from General Sepi confirmed that Djehuty was telling the truth.

'The sacred Tree of Osiris is gravely ill,' said the king.

'The Tree of Life?' said Djehuty, thunderstruck.

'The very same.'

The governor pushed away his alabaster plate. His appetite had vanished. 'How has it happened?'

'Through a curse.'

'Do you know how to break it?'

'I am constantly fighting that battle. As we speak, the tree's deterioration has been halted; but for how long? The building of a temple and a house of eternity will produce an appreciable amount of energy, and I am convinced that a reunified Egypt will help us to fight. Can you swear to me that you are innocent and that you have taken no part in any plot to destroy the acacia?'

As if he were dying of cold, Djehuty pulled his cloak more tightly round him. 'If I am guilty, may my name be destroyed, my family wiped out, my tomb demolished, my body burnt. These words are spoken in the presence of Pharaoh, the guarantor of Ma'at.' Djehuty's voice shook with emotion.

'I know that you are not lying,' said Senusret.

'This province belongs to you, as do its wealth and its soldiers. Save Egypt, Majesty, save her people, preserve the mystery of resurrection.'

From the pharaoh's attitude, Djehuty knew that his trust was well placed. If any one man was capable of healing the Tree of Life, it was Senusret.

A guest asked permission to speak.

'I am the priest who aided the young scribe named Iker, who was in charge of transporting the *ka* statue and setting it in position – no easy task! Iker has left the province, but that is no reason to forget his courage, and I suggest we drink to his health. Without him, we would not have been able to bring the statue to the temple.'

Djehuty nodded, and everyone drank a toast to Iker. In the general rejoicing, it was followed by many more.

Senusret had invited Djehuty and Sepi to attend a meeting of his inner council.

'Your presence is not merely ceremonial,' he told them. 'Here, we decide and we act. I have reconquered all but one of the hostile provinces, and without spilling a single drop of blood. Only the Oryx province still holds out, and I must therefore conclude that its governor, Khnum-Hotep, is the criminal who is attacking the Tree of Life.'

Sehotep nodded. 'The Oryx is an animal of Set, the murderer of Osiris,' he said. 'From what we know of Khnum-Hotep, he will stop at nothing to retain his territory.'

'He belongs to a very ancient family,' said Djehuty, 'and is fiercely attached to his independence. He is opposed, as a matter of principle, to negotiation, and his army is by far the best in the country. It is given regular, intensive training, has weapons of the highest quality, and is utterly loyal to its lord, over whom no one has any influence. I must be frank and say that even His Majesty's recent successes are unlikely to impress him. Feeling alone against everyone will more likely strengthen his determination. And as he is a true leader of men, his soldiers will fight for him with utter determination.'

'In that case,' said General Nesmontu, 'I advise an all-out attack.'

'Celebrating unity on mounds of Egyptian corpses is not the ideal solution,' objected Djehuty.

'I fear there is no other way,' insisted Nesmontu. 'The pharaoh cannot allow Khnum-Hotep to sneer at him and compromise the foundations of what he is building.'

With heavy heart, everyone realized that they must prepare for a battle whose ferocity would leave everlasting scars.

'As it is not a question of fighting a foreign power,' Nesmontu went on, 'we need not send Khnum-Hotep a declaration of war. From my point of view, it is a security operation designed to re-establish order on Egyptian territory. It would be therefore logical to launch a surprise attack.'

Neither General Sepi nor the other council members raised any objection.

'Have the necessary arrangements made,' ordered the king. 'Now to other matters. During the feast, a scribe named Iker was mentioned. Was he trained here?'

Sepi nodded. 'He was my pupil; in fact, the best in my class by a long way.'

'That is why I soon entrusted him with big responsibilities,' said Djehuty. 'As you know, he organized the transport of the statue remarkably efficiently, and he would have risen rapidly to the head my government.'

'Why did he leave?' asked Senusret.

Djehuty stood up. 'I am not worthy to be present at this council, Majesty, for I have committed a grave offence against you.'

'Explain what you mean, and allow me to be the judge of what you say.'

The governor sat down again; he suddenly looked much older. 'Iker is a tormented boy, who has been through harsh ordeals which he cannot put from his mind. He constantly asked questions. He was looking for two sailors, Turtle-Eye and Sharp-Knife, who once sojourned briefly in Khemenu. But I had had the episode struck out of my archives, because their ship bore the royal seal, which I refused to recognize. It seemed to me, Majesty, that those men could only belong to your warfleet, and so I told Iker.'

'So because of you,' said Sehotep, 'he believes that Pharaoh is his enemy.'

'That is certain.'

'Is he motivated by a desire for vengeance?'

'That is equally certain. I tried to persuade him to forget the past and remain in my service, but his determination was unshakeable. This boy is as intelligent as he is brave, and he may become an enemy – and a formidable one – because he is now convinced that the pharaoh is responsible for his misfortune.'

'What happened to him?'

'I do not know exactly, but probably an attempt was made on his life.'

'Where was he planning to go?'

'To Kahun, to find clues and evidence which would enable him to bring the truth out into the open.'

'He is also interested in the Golden Circle of Abydos,' said General Sepi, 'and he saw its effectiveness, though without understanding its nature, at a regeneration rite practised on the person of Djehuty.'

'The boy is probably an accomplice of the criminal who is attacking the Acacia of Osiris,' suggested Sobek. 'Did he have links with Khnum-Hotep?'

'He came from his province, and had worked for him there,' said Djehuty.

58

Most of Iker's meagre baggage was packed. After his quarrel with Heremsaf, he was expecting to be dismissed at any moment.

So he was not surprised by the arrival of a long-haired scribe, renowned as a bringer of bad news. He would soon be followed by town guards who would take Iker out of Kahun and forbid him ever to return.

'I am ready,' said Long-Hair.

'So am I. You're alone?'

'Today, yes, because there is so much work at the administrative offices. Tomorrow another colleague will help me.'

'So I am to have a day's grace until tomorrow.'

Long-Hair frowned in puzzlement. 'Even if there were ten of us, we wouldn't finish in a week! They couldn't impose such a short time on you – it must have been a mistake. Bearing in mind the amount of work, it will take us at least a month, working from dawn to dark.'

'What work are you talking about?'

'Well, the work you're doing, of course: the inventory of furniture destined for the storehouses, and the description of each item.'

'You mean you haven't come to expel me?'

'Expel you? What on earth gave you that idea? Oh, I see! I

must confess that Heremsaf's underlings are a little bit – or even a lot – afraid of you. Beware of them, because they can be dangerous. Fortunately, though, you have Heremsaf's support.'

Iker's head was spinning. So neither the mayor nor Heremsaf had decided to expel him. What game were the two of them playing? Or were they playing against each other?

Unable to answer these questions, Iker concentrated on his work. Long-Hair helped to the best of his ability, but he was unused to working so hard and so fast. He stopped several times an hour to drink water, eat a fresh onion, wipe his brow or answer a call of nature. And he never stopped talking.

Iker listened with half an ear to his long and boring family stories. Then it was endless gossip about town employees, derived from vague comments and vaguer rumours.

As the sun was going down, Long-Hair put away his materials. 'There we are, the day's over at last. Here's a piece of good advice, Iker: work a lot less hard, or you'll make all the other scribes angry. Some of them, and not the most minor ones, are already annoyed, even humiliated. Be a bit slower, and you will rise more quickly.'

Iker went home. Sekari was not there, but he had cleaned the house. The young scribe fed North Wind, then went out again to the meeting with Bina. Even if he was not hoping for anything specific, in his present situation he ought not to reject his only ally.

When he reached the street of the empty house, there was no one around. He went silently into the house.

'Bina, are you there?'

'In the back room,' replied her musical voice.

Iker walked across fallen plaster. He made her out in the darkness and sat down beside her.

'So you have problems at work?' she asked.

'Differences of opinion with my superior.'

'I'm sure it's more serious than that.'

'Why do you think that?'

'Because you've changed. Your worry is so deep that even the most insensitive person could see it. A simple problem at work wouldn't have overwhelmed you.'

Iker sighed. 'You're right, Bina.'

'You've been the victim of injustice, too, haven't you? Tyranny spares no one in this country, even those who think they're safe from it.'

'Tyranny? Whom are you accusing?

'I'm only a servant-girl from Asia. I'm despised, I'm not allowed to learn to read and write. You're educated and you already hold an important post. But we're as unfortunate as each other, because both our futures are blocked because of Senusret, who grinds the country under his heel. That king is a bad man. My people wanted a little freedom and justice, and he answered them by sending his army. Men dead and wounded, women raped, children beaten, entire villages reduced to poverty, while Pharaoh's soldiers enjoy themselves and get drunk. Senusret has utter contempt for humanity – all he knows is force and violence. I've heard that he's currently fighting an appalling civil war against the provinces that dared challenge his omnipotence. That brute has no hesitation over spilling the blood of Egyptians.'

Iker thought of Khnum-Hotep and Djehuty, who had both helped him. Civil war and the reconquest of all Egypt by a king who would stop at nothing to impose his supremacy: was that the key to the mystery? But Iker was no obstacle in Senusret's path.

'If the king is your enemy, he is also mine,' he said. 'He ordered my death.'

'Why?'

'I don't know, but I shall find out. I want proof of his guilt and I shall demand justice.'

'You're dreaming, Iker! The only thing to do is to unite all the oppressed people and fight the tyrant.'

'Aren't you forgetting his army and his guards?'

'Certainly not, but there are other ways of fighting besides a frontal attack.'

'What are you thinking of?'

'Of you, Iker.'

'What on earth do you mean?'

'You're a brilliant scribe, and you've won the favour of the mayor of Kahun, the tyrant's favourite town. Stop behaving like a rebellious child in pursuit of a mirage. Make amends, go back to work and rise up the ranks of scribes.'

'A fine career cannot replace the truth.'

'You know that truth already: Senusret wants you dead. He is a destroyer and a murderer who will trample on thousands of lives. The only answer is for you to become a senior scribe so that you will be presented to him.'

'With a view to doing what?'

'To killing him,' whispered Bina.

Shocked, Iker tried to imagine the scene. 'It would be impossible. He'd be closely guarded – I wouldn't have a chance to act.'

'A deed of such magnitude must be prepared down to the most minute detail. It's out of the question for you to take foolish risks and fail. You will have to get rid of the monster's guards so that you can strike with certainty.'

'Do you see us, you and me, united in this insane enterprise?'

'You may be alone, but I have allies.'

'What allies?'

'Oppressed people who, like us, care about freedom and are ready to sacrifice their lives to get rid of the tyrant and give the people back their happiness. There can be no more beautiful destiny, Iker, and you will be its privileged instrument.'

She came closer to him, then, sensing that he was gripped by inner torment, made no further move.

'It's madness, Bina!'

'No doubt, but how do sane people behave? They bow their heads, and close their eyes, mouths and ears in the hope that only their neighbours will be affected. Senusret understands all too well how easy it is to dominate cowards. If you belong to that accursed race, Iker, there is no point in our seeing each other again.'

When he got home, Iker's throat was so dry that he drank three big cups of water. Unable to think calmly, he took up the knife-handle marked with the name *Swift One*. If it had a new blade, a long, sharp one, it would make a formidable weapon.

To take revenge was legitimate; to deliver Egypt from a merciless oppressor was the most noble of ideals. Iker forgot his own destiny and thought of his country's and of the unfortunates who were groaning under Senusret's yoke. If he did succeed in killing the king, a new era would dawn.

All the same, could he find it in himself to cause anyone's death? In becoming a scribe, he had wanted to escape from violence and arbitrary power: killing horrified him. Perhaps the best thing would be to leave Egypt – if he went into exile, he might be able to forget the demons that tormented him. With his knowledge and his skills, he could easily find work as a steward on an agricultural estate and could build himself a new life.

The young man set about packing his last few possessions so that he would be ready to leave at daybreak. As he was slipping his brushes into a case, suddenly she was there before him.

Her face was as stern as it was radiant. In her eyes, Iker read her message: 'Do not run away. Remain in Egypt and fight so that Ma'at may be accomplished.' Then the beautiful priestess faded into the flickering brightness of the oil-lamp.

His nerves stretched to breaking-point, he went to bed. Before lying down, he reached for his ivory talisman so he could lay it on his belly and enjoy a peaceful night's sleep. It was not there. Iker searched the house from the terrace to the cellar, but could not find it. Someone had stolen it.

Tortured by a final nightmare, Iker awoke with a start, not knowing where he was. Little by little he took back possession of his senses, and started another search, but with no more success than the last time.

To his surprise, he heard someone snoring. There, curled up on the doorstep, head pillowed on his arms, was Sekari, sound asleep.

Iker shook him.

'Wha . . . what's the matter? Oh, it's you.'

'Have you been here long?'

'Not very. My evening and my night were very busy, if you know what I mean – a real terror, who wouldn't let me go! As she knows where my hut is, I couldn't take refuge there. My only chance of escaping her was to come here. If you tell me to go away—'

'No, come in. You'll sleep better inside.'

Sekari yawned and stretched. 'I say, you don't look any fresher than I am.'

'I've been robbed.'

'What was stolen?'

'A protective ivory talisman which meant a great deal to me.'

'Lots of people like those things – they sell for high prices.'

'Forgive me, Sekari, I didn't sleep well and I—'

'Are you trying to ask if I stole it? No, I didn't – if I had I'd never have dared show my face again. But you're right not to trust anyone. I think this house ought to be better protected – with a good bolt for a start. And then I'll try to find out if the talisman's been offered for sale. What does it look like?'

Iker gave him a detailed description.

'Do you suspect anyone?'

'No, no one.'

'Let's hope my big ears will pick up some information. Are you absolutely sure nobody's trying to harm you?'

'Shall we have a really big breakfast?'

'Your kitchen's probably empty. I'll go and get what we'll need.'

As Sekari went off, Iker thought of his advice: not to trust anyone.

59

The Phoenician's calm, relaxed manner was deceptive. To maintain it, he ate twice as many cakes as usual. One day, he'd have to think about losing a little weight.

Some good news had arrived from Kahun: as planned in the event of necessity, his agent had killed an old carpenter who had talked too much. On the other hand, the trading-operation that was to give him a key position in Memphis high society was behind schedule, and a good deal behind schedule, because of incompetent go-betweens – he'd replace them at once.

A cargo of superb cedarwood, from Phoenicia had indeed arrived at the port of Memphis. It remained to be seen whether the trade-control officials would pass it through.

The Phoenician perfumed himself for the third time that morning. In a little while, he would know if his Egyptian contact was an ally or an enemy. If it was a trap, his fate was sealed: forced labour for life. The mere thought terrified him. Farewell luxury, beautiful house, fine foods – he would never be able to bear it.

He reassured himself by dwelling on the fact that his instinct had never yet deceived him. The Egyptian was corrupt to the marrow of his bones and thought of nothing but getting rich. But then he started worrying again as he reflected that his efforts to find out who the man was were taking a long time to bear fruit.

His doorkeeper announced a visitor.

The Phoenician swallowed a date-cake dripping with honey, and went down from his terrace.

The man was one of his best spies. Being a water-seller, he moved around constantly in Memphis's best districts. An affable man, he got on with people easily and knew how to make them talk. He was also an expert at reading faces, and – on the Phoenician's orders – had observed the Egyptian who left his house after their discussion.

'Well, my man, have you succeeded in identifying him?'

'I think I have, my lord.'

From the water-seller's expression, the Phoenician feared that something had gone badly wrong.

'He's a big fish, my lord, a very big fish.'

'Are you sure?'

'Absolutely sure. I know a messenger who works for the palace and I often fill his water-flask. Yesterday he was ordered to carry a royal decree to the outer part of the city. While I was filling his flask, three men came out of an official building. "Goodness," he said, "the one in the middle, that's my master. He's the one who writes the decrees and the administrative documents on the king's orders." I recognized the man straight away. He was the one you asked me to follow.'

The Phoenician felt ill. A very big fish indeed – probably too big. He, the fisherman, had fallen into the net of someone close to Senusret. All that remained was for him to flee the city before the guards arrived.

'So you know his name, obviously.'

'He's called Medes. He's said to be hard-working, ambitious, heartless and merciless to his scribes. He's married, with two children. He made his career in finance before being appointed to this post. I shall dig deeper, but with great care. A man of that stature cannot be approached lightly.'

The doorkeeper appeared again. 'Another visitor, my lord. He says it's urgent and important.'

'A guard or an officer?'

'Oh no, my lord, nothing like that. He has a deeply lined face and dishevelled hair, and has difficulty expressing himself.'

The Phoenician was hugely relieved. It could only be the captain of the boat transporting the cedarwood.

'Send him in. And you,' he told the water-seller, 'leave the back way.' Keeping his spies apart from one another was vital for survival.

What he needed was a cup of carob juice, sweet and smooth. In a few moments, he would know.

The captain looked just what he was: an experienced sailor, ill at ease on dry land, and uncomfortable when speaking. 'It's all right,' he said.

'What does that mean, Captain?'

'Er . . . that it's all right.'

'Has the cargo been unloaded or seized by the guards?'

'Er . . . yes and no.'

The Phoenician could have strangled him. 'Yes to what and no to what?'

'No, to the guards – we didn't see any of them. Yes, the cargo has been unloaded and stored in the agreed place.'

Medes handed the doorkeeper a little piece of cedarwood on which the hieroglyph of the tree was engraved. The servant bowed and showed the visitor into the reception chamber, with its excess of exotic furniture. A remarkable display of cakes and wine-jars lay on low tables. A heady perfume floated in the air.

Pink-cheeked and glossy-haired, the Phoenician was full of enthusiasm. 'Dear friend, my very dear friend, I have marvellous news.'

'This was our last planned meeting,' said Medes. 'If the matter is not concluded, we shall not see each other again.'

'But it is, indeed it is.'

'Partly or completely?'

'Completely. You have fulfilled your part of the contract, and I mine. The stock is safely stored.'

'Where?'

'Would you like to taste the works of art created by my cook? And I hardly dare present you with the wines I have the pleasure of offering you: they are the best vintages from the Delta.'

'I am here to talk business.'

'You are wrong, I assure you.'

'Don't make me waste my time. Where is this storehouse?

The Phoenician sat down and poured himself a cup of white Imau wine, which smelt as delicious as it tasted. 'We have long since ceased to be children. The first stage of our collaboration has been completed, and I congratulate myself that we have played the game openly with each other. You hold the list of buyers, I have the location of the storehouse. That is fair, wouldn't you say?'

'You are not in a position of strength. Given a little time, I'll find out.'

'Of course. But without me you will never have access to the chain that leads from Phoenicia to Memphis. So why should we fight instead of continuing a collaboration which has begun so well? Anyway, I have a new proposition to put to you. I am a trader, you are not. I do not know your exact office, but you must be high in the government, since you saw to it that I was spared a trade-control check. Selling this wood, negotiating, obtaining the best prices . . . That chore can hardly thrill you. It might even compromise you. Whereas I am used to that kind of dealing. So why not leave it to me while you remain in the shadows?'

'The idea does not displease me. However, I assume it is not free?'

The Phoenician raised his eyes to the heavens. 'Alas, nothing is free in this base world.'

'You want a larger share of the profits, don't you?'

'Well, yes, I would like that.'

'How much larger?'

'We share half and half. I shall have the cares, you the peace of mind.'

'You are forgetting my work regarding the authorities.'

'Not for a minute. Without you, I don't exist.'

Medes thought quickly. 'Two-thirds for me, one-third for you.'

'Do not forget my expenses. You cannot imagine how many go-betweens I need. In all sincerity, my profit is not enormous. But it pleases me greatly to deal with you, and I am convinced that we shall not leave it at that.'

'You have other plans?'

'That is not impossible.'

From his informants, Medes knew that the Phoenician's operation had gone remarkably smoothly. The smuggling offered him the opportunity to work with a skilled professional, and an opportunity like that was worth paying for.

He said, 'Very well: half and half.'

'You won't be disappointed. A little wine?'

'Let us seal our agreement.' A lover of fine wines, Medes had to admit that his host had not been boasting.

'Do you still wish to remain anonymous?' asked the Phoenician.

'It's better for both of us. How long will you need to sell off the stock?'

'As soon as you give me the list of purchasers, my sellers will set to work.'

'Have you any writing-materials?'

The Phoenician noticed that Medes did not leave behind any documents written in his own hand. Under dictation, the trader took down the names and addresses of fifteen prominent Memphis citizens.

'In about a month,' said the Phoenician, 'we can plan for another delivery.'

'We'll meet again in five weeks, at the full moon. I'll bring you a new list.'

The Phoenician collapsed on to a softly cushioned chair. He had just concluded one of the most profitable deals of his career, and this was only a beginning! He was beginning to enjoy living in the Egyptian style.

'Do not relax,' advised a serious voice.

The Phoenician leapt to his feet.

'You! How did you get in?'

'Do you think that a simple door could stop me?' asked the Herald, whose thin smile had a chilling quality. 'Did you get the results we were hoping for?'

'Better than that, my lord, much better!'

'Do not boast, my friend.'

'The man who has just left is called Medes. He is the one who writes out Pharaoh Senusret's official decrees, so he is one of the most important people at court, and I have him in the palm of my hand! Although he holds this eminent position, it is not enough for him – he wants to be rich as well. And he is my partner in the timber-smuggling trade.'

'Excellent work,' agreed the Herald.

'Medes does not know that I've identified him,' continued the Phoenician. 'Of course, he will have had me investigated, and he must have concluded that my trading-networks are the best. He gave me a first list of customers, whom I have undertaken to satisfy.'

'In the process, no doubt you remembered to increase your remuneration.'

'Well, but that is normal, my lord.'

'I am not blaming you for it. Your contribution to our cause will be all the greater.'

'Oh yes, my lord, you can be sure of that.'

'You must gain the trust of this man Medes,' ordered the Herald. 'To do so implies several good business deals which will satisfy him.'

'You can rely on me – I know my trade. Medes will get very rich very quickly.'

'And what about matters in Kahun?'

'The talkative Plane will talk no more.'

'Did the guards question him?'

'No, my lord. But he was beginning to talk to his neighbours and his visitors. Our agent felt that all this storytelling was becoming dangerous and he obeyed his instructions to maintain security.'

'Good. Continue to build up your network and carry on your trade as normal.'

'Certainly, my lord.'

'And regulate your habits. Eating too much interferes with thought, drinking too much leads to a lack of prudence.'

60

'The inventory is finished,' said Iker.

'In a week? You must have worked day and night!' exclaimed Heremsaf in astonishment. As he examined the papyrus scroll covered with fast but very readable writing, it did not take him long to appreciate the exceptional quality of the work done. 'Long-Hair complains that he has fallen ill because of working too many extra hours,' he commented.

'I'm sorry about that – I told him to keep to his room while I dealt with the final details myself. But the mayor wanted the list quickly, didn't he?'

'Indeed, indeed, but neither of us had said it must be ready this soon.'

'I was led to believe that—'

'Congratulations, my boy. You have done the town a great service. We must now think of something else for you to do. What would you prefer?' Heremsaf knew what the answer would be, of course: the archives.

Very calmly, Iker pretended to be thinking. 'I should like to be posted to the Temple of Anubis.'

'The one whose steward I am?'

'Given your heavy burden of work, I could be useful.'

For a moment, Heremsaf wondered if the young man was mocking him. But his tone was humble, his words were considered and his behaviour respectful.

'Have you at last seen sense, Iker? I tell you again: if you forget the past and its mirages, a brilliant career lies in store for you. For my part, I have no recollection of our recent altercation.'

'I am grateful to you for that.'

Heremsaf was still not wholly convinced of Iker's sincerity, but the lad did seem to be genuine . . . He said, 'The Temple of Anubis? That is not a bad idea, especially as the library is badly in need of reorganization. The librarian died last month, and the apprentice working there at the moment does not have the necessary knowledge to sort and arrange the ancient manuscripts according to their importance.'

'That will satisfy my love of books,' said Iker.

The Temple of Anubis was a modest-sized building in the south of Kahun, near the surrounding wall. Its library was quite different, a venerable institution frequented by the learned men of the town. The trainee was not at all put out by Iker's appointment; on the contrary, relieved to see a senior scribe appointed at last, he got on with the tasks his new superior assigned him.

Iker was filled with wonder at the quality and quantity of the papyri: literary texts, law books, treatises on medicine and mathematics, summaries on animal health. The majority of these writings went back to the time of the pyramids. Multiple copies had been made of all too few of them, and Iker's first decision was to put that right.

The hours spent making the hieroglyphs live again in order to pass them on to future generations gave him true happiness. Quick and accurate, his hand ran over the top-quality papyrus, several rolls of which had been delivered to him. No doubt the mayor and Heremsaf, if they were indeed accomplices, were delighted to see him occupied in this way.

Near the library was a potter's workshop, complete with wheel and kiln. Unlike most of his colleagues, this man was not content to produce ordinary earthenware, but made vases and cups of great beauty.

'For whom do you make them?' Iker asked him.

'For the temples of Kahun and its region.'

'Why have you set up here?'

'Because Anubis is the master of the potter's kiln. He who presides over the *ka*s of all the living possesses true power, embodied in the sceptre of Abydos. At night, he kneads the moon so that the initiate, like it, is constantly renewed. With its silver disc, it lights up the righteous. And it is also Anubis who fashions the sun, that golden stone whose rays make energy circulate. Its secrets are preserved in an acacia-wood box which no outsider may open.'

'Is that in Abydos, too?'

'Abydos is the most sacred of all lands.'

'Have you ever been there?'

'Anubis revealed to me what I had to know. He alone is the guide, and there is no appeal against his decision.'

'So you have seen him!'

'I see the sun and the moon, the work of his hands, and I extend it. That is my function. It is for every man to discover his own.'

The potter turned his back on Iker and got on with cleaning out his kiln before relighting it.

Thoughtfully, the young scribe went home for his midday meal. He found Sekari there, roasting some quail.

'I've strengthened the front door and put on a strong sycamore-wood bolt,' Sekari said. 'In the market, I began asking about your ivory talisman, but heard nothing. The thief's careful – he'll wait some time before selling it.'

'What if he keeps it for himself?'

'He'll eventually boast about having something so precious. Shall we eat?'

Iker only picked at his food.

'Don't you like it?' asked Sekari.

'It's delicious, but I'm not very hungry.'

'Why do you torture yourself like this? From what I've heard here and there, you already have a great reputation. A fine career as a scribe in Kahun can take you a long way.'

'I'm not so sure of that.'

'Everyone has a few scores to settle, but shouldn't you draw a line under the bad days, so as to enjoy the good ones all the more?'

'There is a point of no return, Sekari, and I have passed it.'

'If I can help you—'

'I don't think so.'

'Anyway, I must improve my way of cooking quail – they're a bit dry, because I'm not yet an expert cook. And if you really must face adversity, you'd better be well fed.'

As he walked back to the temple library to copy a treatise on eye medicine, Iker thought of the potter's words. They opened a new door on reality, which many people were content to subject themselves to without searching for the hidden meaning. Deciphering hieroglyphs was not enough; the literal meaning was only a first stage. In these signs, the bearers of power, were hidden the functions of creation. Surely, following this path to its origin implied a journey to Abydos?

And yet the role promised to Iker seemed very different. What use would Abydos be if the country was led by a tyrant? Being aware of that problem, he could not hide his head in the sand and continue to live as a hypocrite.

As he passed the potter's stall he saw a man talking to the potter. At first, Iker looked at the man without seeing him and almost walked straight past. Then memory did its work. Disbelieving, he retraced his steps and, this time, stared at him.

He was right: it was indeed the false guard who had questioned him near Kebet, beaten him, and left him for dead. He said sharply, 'Hey, you! Who are you?'

The man turned. His eyes filled with total disbelief, soon mingled with a panic which set him racing off at top speed. Iker gave chase, relying on his endurance. But the fugitive climbed the front of a house like a cat, and, from the terrace, tried to knock Iker out by throwing bricks down at him. By the time Iker had climbed up, too, the criminal had disappeared.

The house was empty. Sekari was probably spending the night with one of his conquests, but he had left fresh bread, a cucumber salad and some pounded beans.

Still in a state of shock, Iker ate without any appetite.

Did the murderer's presence in Kahun mean that he had been following Iker for months? No, because he had been stunned to see him again – he must have believed him dead. But what was he doing here? The potter might know.

Iker went back to the workshop straight away. As the craftsman had left his workshop, the scribe questioned the neighbours to find out where he lived: in the countryside outside Kahun. Thanks to their directions, Iker found his way easily.

The potter was grilling a side of pork.

'The man you were talking to, and whom I chased, do you know him?'

'It was the first time I'd seen him.'

'What did he ask you?'

'He wanted me to tell him about the town, its customs, the influential people, that sort of thing.'

'What did you say?'

'That around here we don't much like inquisitive people. Then he went off into murky explanations. And then you arrived. Now I should like to eat in peace.'

Iker went back towards the town, along a path beside a canal bordered by willows. The air was sweet, the countryside tranquil.

The attack took Iker completely unawares. The false guard looped a leather thong round his neck and tightened it ferociously – it was impossible for Iker to get his fingers between the thong and his skin. Iker tried to unbalance the killer with a kick, but he dodged aside and, accustomed to hand-to-hand fighting, parried his victim's final hold, an attempt to seize him by the hair.

Unable to breathe, his throat on fire, Iker was dying. His last thought was of the young priestess.

Suddenly, the pain eased. He found he could breathe again, and fell to his knees. Slowly he raised his hands to his swollen throat.

A sound. The splash of a diver or of something heavy being thrown into the water.

His sight still misty, Iker could scarcely believe that he was still alive. It was a long time before he could stand up again and make out his surroundings.

The path . . . Yes, this was the path he had taken. At his feet lay the leather thong.

There was no trace of the false guard, whom Iker's saviour must have killed, then thrown into the canal.

Who could that rescuer be? Had it not been for his intervention, Iker would be dead.

Staggering, he returned home.

Sekari was asleep on the doorstep, with an empty beer jar beside him. Trying to step over him, Iker knocked his shoulder.

'Oh, it's you. You look peculiar. Good grief, your neck . . . It looks like blood! What happened?'

'An accident.'

Iker applied a compress soaked in oil and honey.

'How did this accident happen?'

'Like any other accident. Forgive me, I'm tired.'

*

Iker was in no doubt: the murderer had been sent by the pharaoh to kill him discreetly and with impunity. Informed of the young scribe's presence in Kahun, by either the mayor or Heremsaf, the king had resolved to rid himself once and for all of his accuser, who was determined to prove his infamy.

Sekari brought Iker some fresh milk and a hot flatcake stuffed with beans. 'Before you woke up, I had time to go for a stroll. It seems they've found the body of a stranger in a canal outside town – the fish had started eating it.'

Iker did not react.

'It would be a good idea to hide your injury under a scarf, don't you think? You could pretend you've got a sore throat.'

Iker followed Sekari's advice, and left for the library.

The potter was not working at his wheel, and the kiln was unlit. Iker questioned the neighbours. A baker told him that the potter had returned home to the North, and that a new man would soon take his place.

This new incident confirmed Iker in his convictions.

'Are you sure you weren't followed?'

'I was careful,' said Bina. 'What about you?'

'I know that I must not trust anyone.'

'Even me?'

'You're different: you're my ally.'

The young girl wanted to jump with joy. 'Then you'll help me?'

'The tyrant leaves me no choice. One of his men has just tried to kill me. And it was one of your friends who saved me, wasn't it?'

'Yes, of course,' replied Bina eagerly. 'You see, we are watching over you.' But she was troubled: she knew neither who had attacked Iker nor who had saved him.

'I have made up my mind,' said the young scribe, 'and I have a surprise for you.'

He showed her the knife-handle marked with the name of

61

'I am ready,' announced General Nesmontu. 'As soon as you give the order, we shall attack both from the river and from the desert. Khnun-Hotep's men will be caught in our pincers, and surprise will ensure us a swift victory.'

'Let us not be too optimistic,' advised Sehotep. 'From what we have heard, they will fight like wild beasts. If we show the slightest weakness, they will know how to welcome us! If losses are heavy, we must beat a retreat.'

'That is why we must launch the attack at once,' insisted Nesmontu. 'Each day that passes increases the risks.'

'I am aware of that,' agreed Senusret, 'but I must nevertheless wait until High Treasurer Senankh arrives. The information he is bringing might change the course of events.'

The king stood up, signifying the end of the meeting of the King's House. No one would have had the impertinence to speak again after him, and the old general went back to his quarters, grumbling. At the first opportunity he would try to persuade Senusret to go back on his decision and take action with all speed.

As was his custom, Nesmontu had chosen to live in a room at the barracks, in order to be close to his men. He always kept one ear open, and liked to hear more or less muffled criticisms and protests, so that he could put right any problems. In his view, military life must not suffer from failings liable to damage the troops' morale. A well-fed, well-housed, well-paid soldier, respectful of his superior officers, was a powerful weapon.

Entering the officers' dining-chamber, Nesmontu sensed immediately that the atmosphere was strained.

His assistant explained: 'General, we have no beer and the dried fish has not been delivered.'

'Have you questioned the steward?'

'That's part of the problem. He's disappeared.'

'He was appointed by Governor Djehuty, wasn't he?'

'Yes, sir.'

'Inform Djehuty immediately, and tell him to search for him. Ask him also to send us the missing supplies straight away. Oh, one last order: tell the officers to eat none of the food procured by the steward.'

'Do you think—'

'I think one should distrust a deserter.'

After a meal during which he had sampled a grilled perch, a side of beef, aubergines in olive oil, goats' cheese and a few sweetmeats, all washed down with a red wine dating from Year One of Senusret's reign, Khnum-Hotep went to his magnificent house of eternity, whose every detail he checked.

A talented painter was finishing a multicoloured bird perched in an acacia tree. In the face of this masterpiece, the governor was moved almost to tears. The elegance of the drawing, the glowing warmth of the colours, the joy emanating from this paradise vision, fascinated him. His three dogs were as admiring as he, and sat gazing at the painter's latest marvel.

Khnum-Hotep would gladly have spent the afternoon watching the genius at work; however, after a long hesitation the commander of his army dared to disturb him.

'My lord, I think you should speak to a traveller we've just arrested.'

'Don't bother me. Question him yourself.'

'We have done that, my lord, but what he says concerns you directly.'

Reluctantly, Khnum-Hotep followed the soldier to the guard-post where the suspect was being held.

'Who are you,' he demanded, 'and where have you come from?'

'I was the steward at the main barracks in the Hare province, and I have come to warn you.'

Khnun-Hotep's eyes glittered with anger. 'Do you take me for an idiot?'

'You must believe me, my lord! Pharaoh Senusret has reconquered all the provinces that were hostile to him, with the exception of yours. Even Djehuty has bowed down.'

'Djehuty? This is a joke!'

'I swear it is not, my lord.'

Khnum-Hotep sat down on a stool, which nearly gave way beneath his weight, and stared straight into the steward's eyes. 'Whatever you do, don't tell me a sheaf of nonsense, or I shall crush your head between my hands.'

'I'm not lying, my lord. Senusret is at Khemenu with his inner council, and Djehuty has become his vassal.'

'Who commands his troops?'

'General Nesmontu.'

'That old scoundrel! He's as dangerous as a cobra. And what about Djehuty's soldiers?'

'They obey the general, and so do those of the other provinces that have now submitted. The most important thing is that Senusret has decided to attack you.'

'*What?*'

'It's the truth, I assure you, my lord.'

Khnum-Hotep stood up, seized the stool and broke it into several pieces. The soldiers flattened themselves against the walls, afraid he would take his anger out on them. Foaming at the mouth like a mad bull, the governor stormed back to his palace, declining to use his travelling-chair.

As soon as he entered his office, the lady Techat saw that he was in a towering rage, and decided not to present the administrative files she had ready for him.

'To do that to me! Invade my territory! The king has lost his mind – but I'm going to bring him back to his senses.'

'My lord, it is my belief that Senusret is following a carefully thought out plan, and that his resolve is unshakeable.'

No one but Techat would have dared address Khnum-Hotep in this way. He pretended to ignore her words, and went into a reception chamber where the air was pleasantly cool.

His cup-bearer immediately brought him beer and then silently withdrew. Techat, who had followed him, stood quietly in a corner of the room. Slumped in a chair built to take his dimensions, the governor stroked his two bitches, who sat on his knees while the male lay at his feet and watched over them.

'A plan, you were saying,' said Khnum-Hotep eventually. 'And where is it leading him?'

'To rule the whole of Egypt by getting rid of the last rebel left – who now has no allies at all. Senusret has eliminated his opponents one by one, knowing that they would never agree to unite against him.

'If he thinks I'm going to prostrate myself before him, he is very much mistaken.'

'And yet that would be the best solution,' said Techat. 'The king is in a position of strength.'

'He would have been if he had launched a surprise attack against me. Knowing his plan places me on an equal footing, and my battle is by no means lost before it begins.'

'Have you thought of the numbers who will be killed?'

'This province has belonged to my family for many generations, and I shall never give it up, never! Enough talk, Lady Techat. I shall prepare a fine reception for the invader. There will be many dead, especially on his side. And this pharaoh will do the same as everyone else who's tried to seize my lands: he'll draw back.'

Although he had listened attentively to Nesmontu's arguments, the pharaoh was unbending. Bitterly disappointed, the general nevertheless continued to train his attack troops. When the bad news reached him, he informed Senusret immediately.

'The deserter was spotted when he crossed the border of this province and entered the Oryx province. Obviously, he will have warned Khnum-Hotep, so we can no longer rely on the advantage of surprise. The longer we delay our attack, the more the enemy will strengthen his defences, and the fiercer the battle will be – and the more uncertain its outcome. If we should be defeated, your prestige will be destroyed and the provincial governors will become independent again. Forgive my frankness, Majesty, but the thought of such a disaster is unbearable.'

'What sort of defence is Khnum-Hotep preparing?'

'One which is classic and vicious.'

'Then adapt to it, General, and foil him.'

This mission filled Nesmontu with enthusiasm. Instead of a sudden charge, it would be a tactical battle. In those circumstances, his experience would be decisive.

Senankh was exhausted when he arrived in Khemenu with his escort. He had hardly eaten for several days, but he could not even think of food until he had told the king the outcome of his journey.

From his sombre expression, so rare in this cheerful-faced hard-working man, Senusret realized that the news was very bad indeed.

'I sent the Shaven-headed One the samples of gold from the temple treasuries, Majesty. None healed the acacia.'

Senusret knew already that the gold used during the last and far-off celebration of the Mysteries of Osiris in Abydos had also failed. Demagnetized, emptied of its energy, damaged by the curse, it was merely an inert metal.

The demon attacking the spiritual heart of Egypt had launched the most fearsome of offensives.

The king had begun to hope that Senankh would find the vital gold and that he would be able to tell new vassals that the acacia had recovered. They would then have fought at his side without a second thought, and, faced with such a powerful army, Khnum-Hotep might have given in.

'I should add,' went on Senusret, 'that the gold reserves of our temples are the lowest they have ever been, and some temples have virtually none at all. Because of the conflict with the provincial governors, mining has stopped. It's possible that one of the governors has built up a considerable stock for his own use.'

'Khnum-Hotep?'

'That name arises frequently in the accusations, but I have no proof.'

The pharaoh convened his council, to which Djehuty and General Sepi were once again summoned. Nesmontu was expecting a declaration of war, in the proper form, against the rebel Khnum-Hotep.

The king said, 'Our immediate future rests on the quality of your word, Djehuty.'

'I have only one, Majesty. I have recognized you as King of Upper and Lower Egypt, and have placed the province of the Hare under your authority.'

'War with Khnum-Hotep seems inevitable. But before it begins I have a sacred task to accomplish, and Generals Sepi and Nesmontu must accompany me. I am therefore placing you in command of the troops stationed in Khemenu.'

Nesmontu could barely contain himself. Entrust his men to a former opponent? That was absolute madness!

'What are your orders?' asked Djehuty.

'While awaiting my return, you will deploy the troops on the province's frontier, to repel any attack. I do not believe it likely that there will be one, but if there is be content to drive Khnum-Hotep back.'

'It shall be done according to your will.'

The monarch's gaze rested on the other members of the council. 'We are leaving immediately for Abydos.'

62

The Shaven-headed One and the pharaoh walked towards the acacia.

'Your instructions have been followed to the letter, Majesty.'

'What have your colleagues proposed?'

'They are so at a loss that they are confining themselves to their obligations. We now exchange only a few mundane words; everyone is walled up in silence.'

Reuniting in its mystery the heavens, the earth and the subterranean world, the great tree was continuing to fight against degeneration. Osiris remained present within it, but for how much longer would the acacia succeed in plunging its roots into the primordial ocean in order to draw up the energy necessary for its survival?

'Have you found any remedies in the ancient texts?'

'Unfortunately not, Majesty. But I shall have help in my search today and I have not given up hope.'

A cool wind blew over the sacred tree. Little by little, the door of the world beyond was closing.

Accompanied by Sobek-Khu, Senusret visited the construction site. Despite all the accidents and broken tools, good progress was being made; the intervention of the priestesses of Hathor meant that such incidents were now rarer. The master-builder admitted that there had been difficult days, but his determination and that of his craftsmen was unshaken. They knew they were taking part in a war against dark forces, and to them each stone laid was like a victory.

The pharaoh's presence gave them back their heart for the work. Assured of his unfailing support, the builders swore that they would never yield in the face of adversity.

'Prepare the Golden Circle of Abydos,' Senusret ordered the Shaven-headed One.

In one of the chambers of the Temple of Osiris, four offering-tables had been set out according to the cardinal points. The hieroglyphic sign of the offering-table was read as '*hotep*' and signified 'peace', 'plenitude', 'serenity'. These notions characterized the mission of the Golden Circle of Abydos, though in these anxious times its members were not certain they could fulfil it.

The pharaoh and the queen sat at the eastern point. Facing them, in the west, were the Shaven-headed One and General Sepi. To the north were Sehotep, Bearer of the Royal Seal, and General Nesmontu. To the south sat High Treasurer Senankh.

'Because of the task entrusted to you, one of us is absent,' said the king. 'Of course, he will be informed of our decisions.'

All the members of the Golden Circle had been initiated into the Mysteries of Osiris. Indestructible bonds had been woven between them. Sworn to absolute secrecy, like their predecessors, they dedicated their lives to the greatness and happiness of Egypt, which depended precisely upon passing on the Osirian initiation correctly.

Here, death was confronted head-on. Here, as declared a text engraved in the royal pyramids of the first pharaohs, death was made to die. The Golden Circle of Abydos maintained the supernatural dimension of the Two Lands, where dwelt the People of Knowledge.*

'If the acacia dies,' Senusret reminded them, 'the Mysteries will no longer be celebrated. The sap that circulates in the great body of Egypt will dry up, the marriage between the heavens and the earth will be broken. That is why we must seek unremittingly for the cause of this curse, whose author is probably Governor Khnum-Hotep.'

'Can you still doubt it, Majesty?' asked General Nesmontu. 'The innocence of all the others has been established, so only he is left.'

'I want to hear from his own mouth the reasons why he has committed this horrifying crime. We must give battle and take him alive. In this tragic and dangerous period, the unity of the country is more necessary than ever. Our division has greatly weakened us, and that is one of the reasons why a malevolent force has been able to harm the Tree of Osiris, whose cosmic body is made up of all the celestial and earthly provinces brought together.'

'The words of power spoken at Abydos still receive a favourable echo from the divinities,' stated the Shaven-headed One, 'and the permanent priests carry out their duties with great thoroughness.'

'What if one of the priests is the attacker's accomplice?' suggested Senankh.

'That suggestion cannot be excluded,' said the Shaven-headed One, 'but there is no evidence that it is true.'

'Forgive this question, Majesty,' said Sehotep gravely, 'but it must be asked. If you die during the battle with Khnum-Hotep, who will succeed you?'

'The queen will ensure the regency, and those of this Circle who escape will designate a new pharaoh. The vital

*I owe this expression to one of my readers, Mme Ingrid A. My thanks go to her.

thing is to find the means of healing the acacia. Thus far the quest for the gold has failed, so we must intensify our search.'

'Crossing the desert, reaching the quarries and bringing back the vital gold will take a long time,' said General Sepi. 'Not to mention the dangers of the journey.'

'Each of us will have a near-impossible task to accomplish,' said Senusret. 'We must swear a solemn oath that, whatever the risks, whatever the difficulties, we will not give up.'

Everyone present took the oath.

'The time has come to bring our disciple further along the path of the Mysteries,' said the queen. 'True, she is not yet ready to pass through the final door, and it would be both dangerous and futile to hurry her training. Nevertheless, she must try to pass through a new stage in the direction of the Golden Circle.'

The young priestess bowed before the pharaoh.

'Follow me,' he said.

At the heart of the night, they entered a shrine lit by torches. In the centre was a small relic-holder, consisting of four lions placed back to back. In the little hollow monument a pillar had been placed, its top covered by a mask.

'This is the venerable pillar that appeared at the origins of life,' said the king. 'In it Osiris stands tall again, overcoming nothingness. He, Word and spirit, was attacked, murdered and dismembered. But in passing on initiation to a few people, he enabled them to reassemble the scattered parts of reality and to bring back to life the cosmic being from which, each morning, Egypt is reborn. There is no form of knowledge more important than this, and you must master its many aspects. Will you be capable of seeing what is hidden?'

The priestess contemplated the relic-holder, knowing that she could not remain passive. For a moment she thought of removing the veil to uncover the top of the pillar, but her instinct forbade her to commit such a profane act.

It was the lions she must look at, those four guardians with the fiery eyes.

She confronted them one after another. They opened the doors of space and time to her, and made her journey through vast lands full of shrines, hills, fields of golden wheat, canals and fantastical gardens. Then two paths appeared to her, one of water, the other of earth. At their ends was a circle of fire, in the centre of which stood a sealed vase.

The landscapes faded, and the young woman made out the relic-holder again.

'You saw the secret,' said the king. 'Do you wish to continue on this path?'

'I do, Majesty.'

'If the gods permit you one day to reach the sealed vase and to discover its contents, you shall know a joy which is not of this world. Before then, formidable ordeals lie in wait for you. They will be more demanding and more cruel than those imposed on the initiates who preceded you, for we have never known such danger. There is still time: you can draw back. Be well aware of what your decision will mean. Despite your youth, behave with maturity and do not presume too much on your strength. The way of water destroys the being, the way of earth devours it, and the circle of fire cannot be crossed. If you set out on this adventure, you will be alone at the worst moments, and anguish and doubt will eat away at you.'

'All human happiness is but fleeting, Majesty. You have spoken of a joy which is not of this world. It is that which I seek. If my faults prevent me from experiencing it, I alone shall be responsible.'

'Here is the weapon with which you shall succeed in turning away certain attacks by evil fate.' Senusret handed her a small ivory sceptre. 'It is named "*heka*", the magic born of the Light. In it is written the Word that produces energy. Of itself, it is a dazzling word which you must not use without good reason. This sceptre belonged to a pharaoh of the earliest days, to him whom we call 'the Scorpion'. He rests here, after linking his destiny to Osiris. Since Egypt is the land beloved of the gods, the Golden Circle of Abydos has proved that death is not irreversible. But now the acacia is withering and the door to the world beyond is closing again. If we do not succeed in keeping it open, life itself will abandon us.'

As she laid the sceptre on her heart, the priestess knew that she would not draw back. In a surprising way, her thoughts carried her towards the young scribe who, more and more frequently, haunted her nights. At once she upbraided herself for this weakness, for thinking of him at such a solemn moment. It was a sign showing how perilous her journey would be.

Her imperfections and her inner enemies mattered little: it was better to identify them and then fight unceasingly against them. Strangely, what she felt for Iker seemed neither to weaken her nor to distract her from her goal. But the sages taught that human passions ended in wandering and despair, far from celestial joy.

Too many emotions had overwhelmed the priestess for her to be able to think entirely clearly. Gripping her sceptre like a tiller, she accompanied the pharaoh as he left the shrine.

'I am going to celebrate the dawn rites,' he said, 'and offer Ma'at to Ma'at. May righteousness be your guide.'

Alone on the forecourt of the Temple of Osiris, the young woman watched the birth of the new sun. Once more, the pharaoh had vanquished the darkness. If the acacia died, the day-star would be no more than a disc which dried out and burnt everything in nature. However, she savoured the end of this night, which had seen her life change its dimension, and the glimmers of a dawn from which hope was not absent.

Soon, with the Shaven-headed One, she would pour water and milk at the foot of the Tree of Life, while the sacred land of Abydos was covered with light.